THE GIRL

Gilbert Parrell

TotalRecall Publications, Inc.
1103 Middlecreek
Friendswood, Texas 77546
281-992-3131 TL
www.totalrecallpress.com

Copyright © 2022, by Gilbert Parrell
Book Cover Design: Bruce Moran

ISBN: 978-1-64883-064-8
UPC: 6-43977-40648-4
Library of Congress Control Number: 2022942830

FIRST EDITION
1   2   3   4   5   6   7   8   9   10

To Julie, Dave, Dan and Marie Eve.
Keep moving forward; no matter what happens,
keep moving forward.

About the Author

The author, Gilbert Parrell, is a Canadian Military Veteran who served with the Light Infantry and Special Operations Forces for over thirty years. Gib is currently a fulltime author always looking for a new story. He now resides with his family in Ontario, Canada.

About the Book

This is a tale that tells two stories. It is first a tale about the struggle between two sets of brothers and how their lives intersect. The second is a tale of a girl born with immeasurable magic to fulfill a prophecy that will affect these brothers in a way they never imagined. In a world where magic is real and power absolute, can this young girl make the right choice between evil and good?

Just as Merck reluctantly received the mantle of reign from his father, Oman has found himself to be the leader of the Jogahoh. Their lives are in turmoil as each of their siblings vie for control of their land. In the midst of their conflict, a magical child is born, a girl called Anong. An ancient witch who recognizes her for what she is and makes the decision to have her raised with love and kindness. For that, she needs to bring Anong to Oman.

Oman and his wife, Jossa, raise Anong as one of their own, defying their people and laws meant to keep outsiders from their land. But fate has now intervened; Anong's power is recognized, and she is kidnapped by Merck's brother, Tibalt. Tibalt's sorcerer will take Anong's power and use it not for his king but for himself, as her power is all-encompassing. Will she have the strength to stop him?

CHAPTER 1

The calm shadows of evening crept steadily through the woods and toward the small farm. The animals, seeing the encroaching dusk, slowly made their way to their overnight roosts and stalls. Esma's dark eyes scanned the yard as she walked gracefully to her cabin door, undoing the bow that held back her neatly kept, long dark hair. She turned back into the fading light to take a final look around. Satisfied that all her animals were tucked in for the night, she stepped into the cabin and closed the door.

Inside, Esma finished washing her face and made sure all the lanterns were extinguished before slipping beneath the down quilt on the bed. Her breathing slowed, and the warmth from her quilt cocooned her as she fell into a deep sleep. The dream came quickly. She was standing on the porch, watching as a black shadow crept menacingly toward her from the forest. In its wake, it left sickened and dying plants. For the first time in centuries, she felt a shiver of fear as the shadow crawled closer. Its thick, inky darkness and the foul smell of death were overpowering. Esma panicked and dashed into her cabin, slamming the door firmly behind her. The shadow moved relentlessly and effortlessly slipped through the wooden slats of the door, advancing without a sound. Esma, terrified, found herself pressed against the back wall, with nowhere to escape. She could only watch helplessly as it oozed forward and wrapped itself around her. Its icy cold embrace and stench completely overpowered her senses.

Within its grasp, the shadow pinned her arms tightly to her sides. Once in complete control, it began to siphon the magic and life from her body. Esma fought back, gasping out magical enchantments. They should have broken its grip, but nothing worked. She was at its mercy until, with one final push from the bottom of her belly, she managed a gut-wrenching scream. With a jolt, Esma found herself awake and upright in her bed, her heart pounding wildly. She gripped the twisted bedsheets and gasped deeply, sweat running down her face as she struggled for control. Gradually, Esma looked around the small bedroom, trying to see through the darkness. She could only make out silhouettes in the red glow from the fireplace embers. Esma gestured with her hand to the two lanterns on either side of her bed. The lamps flickered into life, eliminating the darkness, and she searched wildly for something that she knew couldn't be there.

Slipping shakily from beneath the warm quilt, she placed her feet down onto the cold floor. Resolutely, Esma stood and walked to the kitchen, picked up a pail of water and took it over to the table. She poured the liquid into a bronze basin and placed the bucket back onto the floor. The nightmare was a prediction of the future, and she had to find out more about it. Steadying herself, she began to swirl her hand through the water. Its icy cold wetness slipped through her fingers, and Esma stroked it gently for a few moments. She started a soft, rhythmic chant, watching with satisfaction as an image finally appeared within the water's depth. The vision, blurry at first, cleared and revealed the scene of a young woman alone in her hut, giving birth. Esma knew this place. The woman was no more than ten kilometers from where she lived. Confused, she asked, *"Why did you bother me with this? Women have babies all the time."*

She watched closely as the young woman's contractions grew more severe and closer together. Finally, the crown of the baby's head emerged and, along with it, the answer to Esma's question. A brilliant light only she could see shone from the child. The woman bore down and pushed hard one last time, and a girl child appeared between her legs. The light surrounded the baby as the young mother cut the umbilical cord and wrapped the child in a worn blanket.

The light began to retract in on itself, transitioning into a small star-shaped birthmark over her heart. The child moved its head slightly, letting out a simple cry, then burrowed her face into her mother's breast. The baby shifted her head again and turned, looking toward Esma. Her eyes were not the cloudy blue of most newborns but clear and bright. Esma was startled; never had a child so young shown so much ability. Nonetheless, she smiled gently at the babe and whispered softly, "You can see me! Welcome, little one."

Seeing the two were safe, she waved her hand over the basin and closed the scene. *Interesting,* she thought as she walked over to her trunk, opened the lid and took out a timeworn, bulky book. Taking it over to the table, Esma moved the lanterns closer and paged through it quickly, knowing exactly what she was looking for. Scanning the old, yellowed script, Esma slid her finger along the lines of a long-forgotten language, stopping at the bottom of the page. She smiled, reading the last lines aloud. *"A female conduit shall be born to one of human blood and body. The magic she holds will be all-powerful and can be good or evil. Shield and train her carefully, for her body and life will be as fragile as any mortal."*

"The future is not yet set, little one. I will do as the scriptures say and keep you safe until you are ready." She walked back to the basin, dipped her hand in the water and commanded, "Show me more." The image darkened, and, she could see a king's vast army of soldiers and his sorcerer searching for the child. They knew of her presence but did not know where to look. Esma watched as they scoured the country, combing every corner to find each newborn. She could see the evil intent of the king and the lust for power on the sorcerer's face. The sorcerer knew the child was the key to the ultimate power he so longed for. Esma nodded and said softly, "The child will be hidden from all until the time is right. I know who can keep you safe."

CHAPTER 2

The Jogahoh people were a secluded race renowned for their need of privacy and adherence to custom. Short in stature, they were naturally robust in build, possessed a keen sense of smell and had great strength and stamina. Their size, dark olive complexion and long, straight auburn hair made them easily identifiable. They stood no taller than eight inches above an average man's waist. They all belonged to one of ten different tribes, depending on where they lived in their country of Sakewan. Each area has its own leader with one overall chief that led the nation. They lived in the northern section of a wild, untamed range that separated a vast kingdom to the east and west.

Sakewan was mountainous to the north, its snow-capped peaks soaring high. Below, the mountains were blanketed with a thick coniferous forest teeming with wildlife. Raging rivers cut through the land, its waters bitter cold. South of the mountains, the terrain quieted into foothills, and a vast prairie spotted with deep lakes. From late spring to fall, the Jogahoh lived, hunted and farmed above ground. The winter season, however, was perilously dangerous for them. Frigid temperatures brought massive wolf beasts down from the high mountain ranges to hunt them. For decades, the animals had appeared, wiping out entire families and communities. In desperation, the Jogahoh started to build their winter homes deep into the ground, not emerging until spring.

They hadn't always been the prey of these beasts. A choice made by the Jogahoh had led to grave consequences. A wizard was travelling through their country and got caught in a winter storm. The man became hopelessly lost and, on the verge of freezing to death, let out one last desperate cry. The leader of the

Jogahoh, who was out hunting that day, heard the weak noise. He moved cautiously toward it, following a horse's tracks through the deep snow. As he closed in, he could see the horse and, on the ground, a man shaking uncontrollably. The Jogahoh loaded the man onto a travois and pulled him back to his dwelling. He and his wife stripped off the wet clothing, wrapped the stranger in animal skins and set him close to the fire. They could feel the man's body shake uncontrollably, his chance of survival slight at best. Over the next three days, they cared for the injured man as if he were one of their own, feeding him, keeping him warm and tending to his injuries. Deep into the third day, the wizard finally opened his eyes and slowly sat up. He asked them how he had gotten there and how they had found him. They answered his questions as best as possible, reassuring him that he was safe. With a grateful sigh, he closed his eyes and fell back to sleep.

A week passed, and the wizard, now fully recovered from his ordeal, was ready to depart. In gratitude, he turned to the Jogahoh leader and asked if he could do anything for them. The man explained to the wizard that he was apprehensive about the encroaching people along their borders. All the Jogahoh lands, he feared, would be absorbed. The small man asked the wizard to surround the Jogahoh country with a barrier that would allow only Jogahoh and animals through it.

The wizard, startled at first, seriously contemplated the request. He knew the Jogahoh possessed no magical ability, unlike others. He warned them that the wish could easily be granted, but they needed to be aware of the possible reactions and consequences. Nonetheless, the Jogahoh leader insisted their request be honoured. The wizard agreed, and an invisible barrier formed once he was out of the country, immediately stopping all trespassers. As a result, no one else could hunt the wolf beasts. With their rampages now unchallenged, the beasts made their way south in the winter, hunting the Jogahoh. Trade caravans were stopped at the boundaries, forcing the Jogahoh to travel long distances to meet them. Dissent grew about the barrier, but it remained intact. Their underground winter homes were the price they were willing to pay for privacy, and for eighty years, the barrier held firm.

••••••

The land on either side of the Jogahoh was commanded by one king. During his lifetime, he fathered two heirs to the throne, both boys. They were only a year apart in age but were as different as winter is to summer. The oldest, Tibalt, always had to be the centre of attention and cruelly enforced his superiority. Merck, the younger brother, had accepted his ranking quietly and acquiesced to Tibalt's position. As the boys grew, their differences concerned the king. By custom, he was to give the entire kingdom to Tibalt. However, his own voice of reason knew that this decision would not be the right one.

Merck showed significant potential when collaborating with other kingdoms and was able to empathize with his subjects. When Merck started building schools, the people were enthusiastic and did not hesitate when it came time to pay their taxes. Tibalt had sneered at his younger brother, saying, "A subject must pay taxes. There is no need for schools or explanations." The king's dilemma was how to keep his eldest son happy and his people with it. The solution was easy; the mechanics of it would be complicated.

Years later, on his death bed, he gathered his sons around him. He dismissed all but the army's commander, who waited patiently for the king to direct him. The king nodded his head toward the door, and the commander closed and locked it. He unfolded a large map and hung it from a square frame.

After studying the map, Tibalt asked, "What is this?"

The king replied quietly and firmly, "My time is coming to pass from this world into the next. I've watched you grow from infants to men and see the potential in both of you to be great."

He paused to draw a painful breath and continued. "So instead of giving the kingdom to you, Tibalt, I have decided to split it between you and your brother."

The blood drained from Tibalt's face, and his jaw tightened. The king frowned at his son's expression but kept talking. "As you can see, the borders will run alongside the land of the Jogahoh, then meet again at their southern border. From there, they run a straight line to the sea. Merck, you have the land to the west of the border, and Tibalt, you will have the east. This will come into fruition on the day I pass."

The two young men stood stock-still before their father, conflicting emotions running clearly through their faces. Merck broke the silence. "Father, I do hope that day will be far into the future."

The king answered, "I'm afraid it will be upon me sooner than I would like. Until then, only the four of us are to know of this." He reached for a goblet of water and drank from it. "Tibalt, I know you are not happy with this decision. I can see it in your face." Tibalt started to speak, but the king held up his hand, stopping him. "Any words you would say now could only betray what your eyes have already shown." Tibalt stood uneasily, his temper boiling as he looked down at the helpless old man in the bed.

"I need you to work with Merck. This kingdom is too large for one man. Set aside your ego and your lust for power. Work together to make the two kingdoms greater than this one ever was. If one is having difficulty, I expect the other to help." He judged them silently for a moment and then asked, "Do you both understand?" Merck nodded hesitantly while Tibalt remained silent, unable to believe what his father was proposing.

"Look at this as a new day for the two of you." The king coughed deeply, and his face reflected the pain of the effort. "Now, let an old man rest. I'm tired, and we will talk more later."

As the three men left the king's chamber, Merck called the

physician standing outside the door. "Look after him, and bring him whatever he needs. Should anything happen, call for us at once."

The commander now spoke. "I have worked for the king my entire life and have been loyal beyond doubt, so he has entrusted this task to me. I have known the two of you since you were children and have trained you well. I expect both of you to carry out his wishes without complaint. The day your father passes, the army will be broken in half, so neither will be left defenseless." He stared coolly at the two young men and said, "Remember what the king said. This stays between the four of us. If you need my advice, I'll make myself available. There will be much work to do. Good day." With those parting words, he turned abruptly and walked away.

Tibalt spoke in a low tone to his brother, "You sniveller. Was this your idea?"

Shocked, Merck countered, "I knew nothing about any of this, Tibalt. Why would you think I would scheme this up? I have no desire for the kingdom and have spent my whole life thinking you would inherit the throne."

Tibalt reached out, seizing Merck by the shirt collar and pulling him close. His eyes glared at him, and he ground out, "For your sake, I hope you didn't."

Merck broke Tibalt's hold and spat back, "For my sake? Is that a threat? Perhaps you don't know me as well as you think you do. Stay away from me, brother."

Merck turned smoothly and strode down the hallway, hearing Tibalt call out, "The kingdom will be divided as father wishes. After that, when you least expect it, I'm coming after it all."

Six months later, with the king's death, the kingdom was split between the two heirs as their father had commanded. Four years later, King Tibalt kept his promise and prepared his army to march toward the border. King Merck always remembered his brother's threat. Throughout his first years, he did his best to keep the boundaries fortified. Nonetheless, the time had now arrived, and a war was imminent.

Tibalt's eastern army was well-trained and equipped, clashing hard with Merck's and pushing them back deep into the west. They halted only after they unexpectedly ran out of reinforcements, supplies and food. Tibalt was furious when he found out there would be a two-month delay. He had the officer in charge dragged in front of his men and immediately killed him by running a sword through his body. Pulling the bloody blade from the hapless man, Tibalt glowered at his second-in-command. "Instead of two months, you now have one month until we march again. Any questions?"

The shocked man sputtered out, "No."

"I didn't think so." He turned to the assembled group. "Get your troops refitted and rested. We march in one month. After that, there will be no respite until this land is under my rule."

Seeing the size and strength of his brother's army, King Merck immediately sent representatives to adjoining lands, requesting reinforcements. Deals were struck with other countries in gold and silver, but the Jogahoh leader, Ninib, had no need for it. Instead, he asked King Merck that the Jogahoh be granted the gift of magic. The king was shocked, but he knew he needed the support and strength of the Jogahoh. At the same time, he did not want them to become so powerful as to be a threat. They finally agreed that if the Jogahoh helped, they would be granted a limited amount of white magic that could be used from spring until fall. The power could only be used for simple, everyday necessities, not granting wishes or malicious intent.

·······

Ninib stood only four feet tall, but his robust, muscular body was capable of feats of strength a man twice his size could not accomplish. His bright red hair was gathered in a neat pigtail down the centre of his back. His jet-black beard and moustache set him apart from the other Jogahoh and gave him a regal air. He gathered his council together and spoke with them of his bargain with King Merck. They knew the price they paid for the magic would be steep, and many would die. Their lust for magic, however, outweighed the sacrifice they were about to make. Resigned to their mission, they sombrely made their way back to their tribes to prepare for war.

Ninib's youngest son, Oman, met his father soon after the council broke. The older man placed his arm around Oman's shoulders as they walked together toward their home. Ninib said, "Oman, tomorrow we will leave to help King Merck in the west. You need to say goodbye to the elders and your friends."

Oman's stomach tightened, and his breath shortened. The young man had been training since he was a child, like all the Jogahoh. However, he had never been to war and had only been out of the country a few times to trade, so he was apprehensive about leaving.

"I'll do that now," he replied dutifully and made his way to the first person he knew he should advise of his departure. Arriving at the front door of a small, neat cottage, he raised his hand and knocked quickly. The door opened immediately to reveal a young woman, arms crossed at her chest, glaring at him.

Jossa did not allow him to say a word. Instead, she said accusingly, "I've heard already. You're leaving tomorrow with the others. Is that true?"

Oman held her gaze steadily. She was a beautiful young woman, slim, with long flaming red hair and hazel eyes. She had captured his heart years ago while they were still school children. "Yes, we ride at sunrise," he replied. He hesitated, suddenly feeling shy. What he wanted to do was embrace her, kiss her and tell her he would miss her. Instead, Oman only managed to squeak out, "I wanted to see you and say goodbye."

"And how long will you be gone?" Jossa asked guardedly.

"I'm not sure. With luck, only a year."

She sighed deeply, walked to Oman and wrapped her arms around him. "A year is a very long time. I'm going to miss you."

Oman breathed in deeply. Her scent was sweet; the smell of the bread she had been baking clung to her clothes. She had done what he had wanted to do without a second thought. He held her and whispered into her ear, "And I will miss you."

The following day, as the sun rose, the solemn mood of the men hung in the air. Oman approached his father, announcing, "We'll be ready in a few minutes."

His father nodded and replied, "Allow the men to say their farewells. We will say our goodbyes to your mother and brother." Oman and his father broke off and drew toward their family, Ninib leading the way. His wife, Tana, stood before them. Her auburn hair, now showing streaks of grey, was tucked into a neat bun. Her small but sturdy frame was tense with apprehension. Salem stood beside her, a self-assured and confident look on his face. Although both brothers had the same dark auburn hair and brown eyes, they were nothing alike. Oman was fit and strong, whereas Salem had a softer, thicker frame.

Tana tried to maintain a controlled, formal expression on her face, but her eyes never left her husband. Ninib took hold of her hand and said, "Keep me in your heart, my love. I will miss you. If times become dire, Salem will send whatever you need." He took her into his arms and kissed her on the cheek before addressing Salem. "As we've discussed, we need you to move to King Merck's court and act as our ambassador."

Salem struggled to maintain an impassive look on his face. He had dreaded joining his father in battle and thought the role would be beneath him. He was relieved when assigned to such a prestigious position that was more favourable to what he considered to be his strength. Trying to disguise his eagerness, he replied, "I will, but you know I would much rather be joining you and Oman."

"I'd hoped as much," his father replied, "but I need you there.

Your job will be to liaise between King Merck's kingdom and our people, ensuring they do not suffer while we are gone." Salem nodded formally, pleased, but said nothing more.

Oman hugged his mother and exchanged goodbyes. He turned to Salem but did not extend his hand. "Good luck, brother," he said formally.

"And to you," Salem replied stiffly. Their relationship, although cordial, had never been close. They were two different personalities. Salem had always been inclined to intellectual, passive activities and preferred his power to come without physical inconvenience. Oman thrived with physical pursuits and had no desire for power, choosing to stay in the background.

Their small troop of men mounted the horses and rode to the west, gathering others at predetermined points along the way. By the time they reached their border, they were four thousand strong. They met with King Merck's forces at a midway point in the western kingdom. Here, they would train for the next month. The first hurdle was melding all the different countries' fighting styles together. The Jogahoh were accustomed to fighting in small mobile groups, taking advantage of their size to slip in and out. Other countries relied on strict troop movements and tactics.

King Merck first integrated the small Jogahoh by providing them with uniforms and supplies. The different fighting techniques were combined, with the most efficient and deadly skills adapted and fine-tuned. Drilling continued with battle formations, marching in column and abreast over rough ground and getting themselves into top fighting condition. King Merck and his generals were apprehensive at the beginning about the Jogahoh. However, as the weeks progressed, they discovered the Jogahoh possessed natural fighting skills and relentless, unwavering stamina.

Oman learned immediately that the life of a soldier would not be simple. Every bit of his time was accounted for, from sunup to sundown. Nonetheless, he thrived, excelling at the work, and was soon promoted to a junior officer, in charge of forty men. His father stood high on a platform during the second week of training as his executive officers critiqued the maneuvers playing out below them. Ninib was pleased with how far they had come in such a short time. The four thousand men were now acting as one cohesive body. His second-in-command leaned toward him and said, "Oman has taken well to his new position. Watch how he commands his troop and how they follow him."

Ninib, with his years of experience, replied truthfully as he watched the men below them. "Yes, he does well, but there are no arrows in flight, no screams from the wounded or battle horses crashing into their ranks. To them, these maneuvers are just a dance, moving from one position to another. The only thing missing is a woman." Turning to the others, he continued, "Leave everything the way it is now. Once we've seen a few battles, I'm sure changes will have to be made."

Three days later, the orders were given, and the Jogahoh marched toward the eastern lines as part of the army. They marched from dawn till dusk for the next seven days, stopping only for short breaks, food and water. On the eighth day, they woke to the sound of bugles signalling assembly. There, they were given the order to prepare for battle. The eastern army was gathered to their front, already deep into the western territory. King Merck rode up to meet and try to reason with his brother one last time.

CHAPTER 3

Oman was nervous but stood tall on the field, his bronze helmet pulled tight on his head, shield and sword at the ready. He watched impassively from his battle station, a position between his men and the battalion in line to his front. He could see the parlay group ahead and, beyond them, approximately five hundred meters, a vast range of enemy soldiers. Twenty minutes later, King Merck pulled hard at his horse's reins, gave a swift kick to the animal's ribs and returned to their battle lines at a fierce gallop. The flags were raised as the bugles sounded. Commands cried out, loud and intense, and the two armies began to march toward each other. Dust began to rise and fill the air as the men advanced, making it difficult for man and beast to see and breathe.

It was soon impossible to determine where their line ended and the enemies began. To the front of Oman, he caught a glimpse of the sun's rays reflecting off the enemies' shields some three hundred meters away. He could hear his father's bellowing voice from the rear, shouting words of encouragement, telling the men to be steady, stay steady. *This is it*, he thought; they were finally going to meet the enemy head-on. His mouth felt dry and his tongue became thick. His knees weakened as each step brought him closer to the battle. Oman pushed his fear aside and did just as his father had done, shouting words of encouragement back to his men. He paced up and down the line, ensuring it stayed straight and tight, with no gaps. All the while, he looked directly into the faces of his men, watching as their eyes stared intently ahead, their jaws fixed. "Shields," was sounded, and each soldier stopped in place, knelt down and brought their shields up and flat. The maneuver formed a roof over the men's heads as an onslaught of arrows rained down on them, hitting the shields and bouncing harmlessly away. "Shields down," was sounded, and the men stood up, moving back to the attack position and continuing to march forward. Oman peered ahead, trying to catch the reflection of the enemy again, but the dust was too thick. Then he heard it: the battle screams and clashes of a thousand swords and shields smashing together. The two armies had finally collided.

Instinctively, Oman gave the command to slow the pace, keeping the gap between his men and the battle to his front. He watched intently for a break in the line that he could shift his men into and thus exploit the enemy. Adrenaline pumped through his veins as his heart raced. His pupils enlarged, and his body felt energized. The field was sharper to him now, and he took a deep breath. In front of him, an opening appeared, and he gave the command to move forward.

Oman stepped off, leading the way, his sword up, his shield held firmly in front of him. The Jogahoh troops followed, cutting through the thin gap and forcing it apart. They split the eastern army, and the western forces swarmed to envelope them. The enemy who had avoided capture frantically retreated toward their lines. King Merck's calvary, seeing the routed force, broke from their position and rode hard into the retreating mass.

Hours later, the battle was over. Oman reorganized his soldiers and set up a defense, assigning a detail to walk through the carnage scattered across the field. Prisoners were ordered to clear the ground of the dead and dying, friend or foe.

Ninib caught sight of his son walking the field and sighed a deep breath of relief. He rode toward the young man and called out his name. Oman, hearing him, stopped and saluted. His father got down off the horse and hugged him hard. "I heard you were alive, but I couldn't find you."

Oman returned his father's embrace and said solemnly, "I'm fine, but some of my men didn't make it, and others are badly wounded."

"We'll take care of them now," his father replied. "The generals said you did well today."

Oman, puzzled by the comment, stared mutely at his father. The battle had been an unending blur of colours, shouted orders on both sides, screams of dying men and the constant clash of metal. What had only taken hours felt like days. Looking back, Oman realized that he felt in control before they breached the gap. Once in the hurricane of battle, he reacted instinctively and could not remember feeling his body. He was only able to respond to what was in front of him. His lungs had burned, sweat had blurred his vision, and his arms ached with the strain of swinging the sword. His whole being had been overwhelmed with a confusing array of complex emotions. So much happened so quickly that his brain was only remembering snippets. Bewildered, he asked, "I did well? Father, I could only react and was so scared I could scarcely control myself." He held up his hand. "Look, I'm still shaking." With that admission, he brought his hand back down to the hilt of his sword. "I had to kill so many people today. I had to see my men wounded and dying." His voice trailed softly away, and he hung his head as he murmured, "I'm sorry."

His father smiled grimly and replied, "Every soldier has gone through what you went through today. There is no need or time for doubt. The fear will always be there, and you are the only one who can decide how to react to that fear. This day will pass, but there will be more like it, with more challenges to come, and it will not get any easier. For now, that is your future. At this moment, we need to tend to our wounded, send our dead home and get ready for the next fight." Ninib gazed at his son and said, "You and your troops did well, and I am proud of that. If you had not exploited that gap when you did, the fight would have been longer and harder. Now go back, look after your men, and tell them what I have told you."

Oman stood silently, watching his father ride away. His

second-in-command interrupted his thoughts. "Sir, I have our casualty count. We had four killed and ten wounded. All are being attended to. Would you like to see them?"

Oman answered with a curt, "Yes." They proceeded to the casualties and went directly to their dead, lying silently under the shade of a copse of trees. There were over one hundred dead in total, but only four were from Oman's platoon. He stopped at each one, looking closely at their still faces. Only hours ago, these men had been alive. Now they lay there, bloodied and motionless in the grass.

King Merck's wizard, Doro, came up to them and said, "Messages have already been sent. We can send these men back to their homes now." Oman nodded. Thanks to Doro's magic, none of his men would ever lie in death in a place that was not their home. The wizard began a soft chant. With a wave of his hand across the four bodies, a silvery mist appeared and enveloped their forms. The bodies were gone an instant later, and four spirits now stood, gazing wordlessly at Oman.

Oman spoke to them, saying, "Your bodies have all been returned to Sakewan and to your families. I thank you for your sacrifice. Your bravery and courage will never be forgotten." They studied him, but there was no harsh judgement in their eyes, only acceptance of their fate. A moment later, they silently raised their hands in a final farewell, turned and disappeared into the afterlife.

For the next two years, the war raged on. King Merck's army had won back the land it lost early in the campaign and gained a small threshold into the east. For the last three months, they pushed hard at the retreating eastern army. After taking a beating at the beginning of the campaign, the western army could now feel victory in their grasp. Still, the eastern army would not yield.

Oman moved up in rank and was now commanding a battalion of seven hundred Jogahoh. The past two years had changed him. He was no longer a green, untested platoon commander. Physically, his body bore new scars, and his eyes held a hardness to them that had not been there before. Mentally, he had lost his self-doubt and gained an assured, confident leadership style. Oman earned his men's trust, and they followed his lead into battle willingly. That day, he arrived promptly at his father's council. The other commanders were there, studying a ground model of the next day's battlefield.

"Commanders," his father started. "The king is hoping tomorrow will be the day to end all of this." He, too, had changed in the last two years. His face held deepened creases, and his body increasingly protested his demands of it. He eyed the exhausted men, knowing he was asking them again for every last ounce of their strength. Ninib spent the next half hour giving strategic orders. When he was finished, there was only a silent understanding. "I've asked you so many times over these past years for more and more of your strength. I know all of you are tired, but I ask this of you one last time. If everything goes according to plan, we will see victory tomorrow. Now go back to your battalions, and ensure your men get food in their bellies and a good night's sleep." The weight of command was heavy on Ninib as he watched them ride away. He'd asked them again for one more push, one more battle that could result in their death.

Oman stayed behind, studying the model of the battlefield and his battalion tasks. He looked carefully at his father, who walked toward him with heavy steps. Oman brought himself to attention.

His father said, "Relax, son," and enveloped him. "This victory will not be an easy one. The men's minds and bodies are tired, and they want to go home." He paused and took a deep breath before he told his son, "I'm asking you to lead your battalion as you always have but take no unnecessary risks. We've made it this far, and I'm hoping with the gods' help, we'll make it through to victory tomorrow."

"Father," Oman said quietly, placing his hand on the older

man's shoulder, "I will lead my men as planned, and we will fight as hard as ever. We will not take any unnecessary risks, but I need you to promise to stay farther to the rear. In the last few battles, you were too far forward and placed yourself in unnecessary danger." Ninib felt a pang of joy. What started out as a father teaching his son had now come full circle. Oman continued, "Listen to your second-in-command. He will make sure you are in the right position and well out of arrow range."

Ninib smiled ruefully. "All right, I'll try to remember. When did you become the teacher?"

Oman answered with a grin. "About a year and a half ago."

Ninib let out a sharp laugh and said, "I will be well back tomorrow. Now go pass on your orders to your commanders and get some sleep. You'll need it."

The following day, the sun broke across the wide-open plane, warming the land. The sound of morning birds who usually sang at first light had been replaced by shouted commands, bugles and horses' agitated neighs. The two armies stood in formation, each glaring at the other across a seven-hundred-metre gap. Oman's battalion was at the front of the Jogahoh troop line, just fifty meters behind King Merck's front line heavy infantry. Oman walked confidently in front of his formation. Gone now was the uncertainty that had once plagued him, making his legs weak and his voice change pitch. The years of standing in command and making life-or-death decisions had strengthened him and given him confidence. He bent down and took up a handful of dirt, letting it fall slowly through his fingers. As it slipped from his hand, the wind whisked it up and through the air.

"The earth is dry," he said to the men standing behind him. "Once we get moving, this whole field will be one large cloud of dust. Ensure you never lose sight of the infantry to your front." He walked up to one of his company commanders. The two of them watched silently as King Merck urged his horse forward and rode ahead with his entourage for one last attempt at liaison.

All eyes were upon them as they watched King Tibalt do the same from his side. King Merck reined his horse to a stop at the halfway point and waited until his brother arrived.

When the two faced each other, King Merck began. "I have a proposal that will benefit both of us. I know you are defeated, and there is no need for useless bloodshed on either side. If you walk away now and leave your diplomats, I will ensure we draw the borderline here and not where we will end up at the end of the day."

King Tibalt viciously reined in his impatient horse and glared at his brother. He spat on the ground and answered contemptuously, "Give up and bow down to you? I will never yield."

King Merck, frustrated, replied, "I'm not asking for you or any of your people to bow down to me or anyone else. I'm asking you to stop this useless bloodshed so that we can go home in peace."

King Tibalt's general pushed his horse forward, leaned over and whispered into his ear. "Sire, we should consider this offer. We all understand the dire circumstances we are in."

King Tibalt's outrage was immediate. He wheeled around and ordered his deputy, "Arrest this man for treason. You will replace him on the field."

Before he could react to the king's words, the general was dragged off his horse and his arms bound tightly behind him. King Tibalt's army watched in disbelief, shocked murmurs rising as the general was ordered to walk back to his lines.

King Merck watched the drama unfold and said mockingly, "I don't think your army agrees with your decision. I think they may side with your general."

King Tibalt laughed harshly. "They will side with me and me alone. They just need to be taught a lesson." Spinning his horse around, Tibalt raced back toward his lines and past the stumbling man. He bellowed fiercely to his troops, "This is what happens to anyone who commits treason." Drawing his sword, he lifted it above his head and turned the horse back toward the hapless figure. Kicking his animal into a full gallop, he raced back and swung his sword across the general's midsection. The blade hit with a sickening thud, almost severing the man in two, and his body dropped to the ground. King Tibalt re-sheathed his bloody sword and pulled hard on his horse's reins, stopping just short of King Merck. "That is what you can look forward to when I win today." With a frenzied look in his eyes, he wheeled his horse around and galloped back to his lines.

King Merck solemnly turned to his command group. "We tried, and once again, it is time to fight. Tell your men I will need their best today. This battle will determine where the border is to be drawn. Raise your battle flags when you are ready."

The group broke away and rode back to their lines as commands were shouted and flags were raised. Twenty minutes later, thirty-thousand soldiers stepped off, marching toward each other. Oman turned around and looked for his father, finally picking him out through the dust. Ninib had kept his promise and was well back. Oman was relieved; it was one less thing to worry about.

A clash of armour, the ringing of swords and the cries of the men signalled that the two opposing lines had met. Oman maneuvered his troops expertly, and his men reacted instinctively. They poured into gaps when they appeared and took advantage of breaking points in the enemies' line. The two opposing armies held at a stalemate for a few moments, neither side making any ground. The eastern troops stood fast for a short while but could no longer take the onslaught. Years of fighting had decimated their lines, and replacements had been few. Yard by yard, they began to give way, leaving their dead and wounded on the line. Forging relentlessly ahead, the west's heavy infantry broke through. The Jogahoh troops pushed forward through the breaks until the eastern line entirely disintegrated and broke into small pockets, where they were enveloped. The western army rushed ahead, squeezing the enemy even tighter until they realized no other option but to throw down their weapons in defeat.

An hour later, Oman's father, seeing the line was secure, rode to his commanders. Dismounting, Ninib walked with them through the aftermath of the battle as work parties gathered up the dead and wounded. The commanders listened as he spoke. "King Merck wants us to hold and push no farther. The border of the western line will be established here, where we stand." A tired cheer of relief rose from the group. Only Oman stood in silence, watching as the weary men around him picked up the remains of the battle. Soon after, his father joined him, and the two of them stood silently together.

"This all could have been avoided," Oman uttered, gesturing his arm around the field.

"Yes, it could have been. But it's over now, and we can go home once we establish our lines and secure the area."

"The men will be happy to hear that."

His father placed his hand on his son's shoulder and gave it a squeeze. "Good work." Without another word, the two men turned and went their separate ways. Ninib began to walk back to the others, and Oman headed to his line. An unexpected flash of movement to his left caught his eye. An enemy soldier who had feigned death rose up with a bow in his hand and notched an arrow. Oman screamed a warning and began running toward the man. Drawing his sword, Oman grasped it with two hands and flung it toward the bowman. The world slowed as he watched the sword spin round toward its intended target. The man released the bowstring, launching the arrow. Oman's sword struck the man's throat a second too late, the impact burying the blade entirely and dropping him to the ground instantly. Oman shouted helplessly as he watched the arrow arch up, then down, toward a group of commanders. His father, a small figure within the group, turned at the sound of his son's voice. The arrow struck him with a hollow thud through his chest. Ninib's hands reached up, attempting to dislodge it, but his knees collapsed, and he fell back. Oman raced up to him, dropped to his knees and collected the dying man into his arms. His father's eyes were open and filled with pain, searching for something Oman could not see.

Ninib coughed up bloody phlegm and said, "You may have been right. I should have stayed farther back. What's an old man doing at the front, anyway?"

Oman whispered softly to him, "Don't talk. We have a healer on his way."

"It's too late for that," Ninib answered, gesturing weakly for his second-in-command. The man stepped forward, and Oman's father ordered him, "Perform the ceremony."

The second-in-command looked down at Oman. "Stand, sir." Another commander gently brought his father up to a sitting position, and Oman stood up. "Place your right hand over your heart and repeat after me," he ordered.

Oman understood what was about to happen and choked back the emotion that wanted to burst out of his chest. He breathed deeply as he ran his sleeve across the tears in his eyes. He realized his father was dying, and he would be sworn in as the new leader of the Jogahoh. *This shouldn't have been me,* Oman said to himself; *the position was never supposed to be mine.* He'd never wanted it and was happy knowing Salem was next in line. He could hear the second-in-command reciting the oath and found himself repeating it as he helplessly stared down into his father's eyes. The relief Oman had felt at the war's end was long gone and replaced by grief and the dread of leading his people.

Ninib gathered the last of his strength, motioning his son down beside him. "I brought you to fight beside me for a reason. This was your training to become our leader. You are the future. You have the strength and wisdom that our people need; it was never your brother. Rule them wisely."

Oman nodded mutely and watched powerlessly as his father took one last breath and shuttered. Gently, Oman closed his father's eyes, laid his head on the man's chest and said quietly, "I swear."

CHAPTER 4

Salem sat stiffly in the ambassador's seat at the Court of King Merck, silently staring to his front, oblivious to the celebration around him. He could barely contain the rage he felt inside. Salem had been informed of his father's death and Oman being sworn in as the Jogahoh leader. *Let them think I am in mourning,* he thought. Salem knew protocol had been broken. He was the eldest son and rightfully the next in line to take over his father's position. His dreams of leading the Jogahoh had vanished, and he was now second in line to his younger brother. Salem picked up a fork to eat his meal, but the frustration inside him boiled. His hand tightened around the utensil, and he felt it bending. Salem took a breath, composing himself, then tossed the fork to the floor. He reached out, grabbed a glass of wine, and drank it down in one gulp. *It may take some time, but I'll have what's mine.*

• • • • • •

Two weeks had passed since Oman sent his father's body home and taken control over the Jogahoh and its army. Reflecting, he knew there was a good chance of either one of them dying in battle. That was a given and easy to accept. To be sworn in as the Jogahoh leader, however, was never expected. He could almost feel Salem's resentment and anger once he found out.

The deputy interrupted his thoughts. "Sir, it's time for your meeting with the king."

Oman nodded and said, "Let's be on our way." He rose, and the two men walked out of the tent and to their waiting horses.

King Merck stood in the sun, watching the riders as they dismounted and walked toward him. They halted and bowed before he motioned for them to sit with him. "Oman," he stated, "I'm very sorry about your father. Ninib was a brave man and a good leader. The Jogahoh fought exceptionally well under his command."

Oman acknowledged the king's words and said, "They have, Sire, and many of us have wounds that will never heal while others have died and will never have the chance to go home. I would like to know when my men and I will be relieved of our duty to you. However, if that is not your wish, we can continue to march with you."

The king laughed and sat back in his chair, smiling. "Oman, you have always been direct and to the point. You are most definitely not like your diplomatic brother, who would waltz with the room first, then ask the questions. I now understand why your father picked you to lead. I will not continue this war, and it ends here."

"My father once warned me that a problem ignored is still a problem and will not go away. Sire, you should consider marching on and taking the entire country. Your brother will not give up his quest."

"I understand, but the people have suffered enough. As of now, you and your army are released from your duty to me. You may start home tomorrow once you are packed and ready to leave."

Oman nodded gratefully and turned to his deputy. "Go and pass the news on to the commanders and have them turn over our lines to the king's men. Ensure every man has a week's worth of food for the journey." His deputy immediately rose from his chair, bowed to the king and mounted his horse, kicking it into a fast gallop back to their lines.

Oman turned back to the king. "Thank you, Sire."

The king called his sorcerer, Doro, forward. He was a small, robust man with short dark hair, who smiled cheerfully when he came up to them. He had a wise face, gentle eyes and a kind disposition. In his hands, he carried a grey, undecorated vase. Its very simplicity made a person doubt that it possessed any kind of magic. King Merck spoke directly to Oman, saying, "It is not within my power to grant your people the gift of magic. That is something a person is born with. For you and your people, I present this gift for your sacrifice on the battlefield with us."

Doro lifted the vase and continued for the king. "I understand you wish to control the magic." He turned the vase upside down, and a small silver piece fell from it into Doro's hand. "Each piece of silver can grant the user one single magical command. If a tribe is hungry, a single wish can feed them. If a man is sick or injured, it can heal him. If travel is required, it can conjure a portal to wherever you wish to go, but there are limitations to its use. It can only be used from spring until fall. If a village requires food for the winter, it must be requested before that. It can never be used for evil intent. Although it can heal, it cannot bring a person back from the dead."

Oman's first reaction was surprise. "So, I can give each tribe as many of these pieces as I wish, and they can use it as they see fit?"

"No. That is why the vase cannot be used from the first snowfall until the spring thaw. The vase needs time to replenish. It can produce only one hundred and fifty pieces of silver to be used through the year, to be distributed as you see fit."

Oman thought of the implications. Each tribe could be provided with ten pieces of silver a year to use as they needed. The remainder would be distributed by himself and the head council if emergencies occurred. "My thanks to you may not be enough to express our gratitude for your generosity, Sire," he said to the king. "This will allow us peace of mind yet maintain our society and way of life. A gift of limitless power would have corrupted and weakened us. This can only strengthen us."

Doro formally gave the vase to Oman and then bowed to him. "Good luck to you and your people, Oman. The vase will not fail you." With that, Doro turned and walked away.

The king lowered his voice and spoke directly to Oman.

"We're alone now and can talk like two ordinary men, face-to-face. You have done well these past years. I have had the opportunity to watch you grow from an inexperienced young man to a seasoned warrior and leader. But, with the unexpected death of your father and being sworn in as the Jogahoh leader, I fear this is where your real challenge begins."

Oman pulled the vase closer to his side, absorbing what the king was saying. A part of him thought, *surely this can't be true. These past years have been the most difficult of my life, and now he says my challenges have only begun?*

The king continued, his face betraying a small smile. "I see the look in your eyes. It is the same one I had many years ago. You are wondering how it could get any worse than this. Believe me, it will. During this war, our decisions were immediate. Life or death. Every man followed orders and worked together toward one common goal. Take some advice from an old man who was once young like you and was also handed a kingdom. It is easy to lead a country while you are at war. The people will always band together against the common enemy. When that is gone, and with no adversity, the people will have nothing to focus on. They will turn their attention to you and your decisions. Your friends and even your family may turn on you." The king now leaned in close to Oman, his eyes narrowing. "Know who you can truly trust, and keep that person close to you. Speak with them in private on decisions you are about to make and let them answer freely. They may have some wisdom that you have overlooked. They can also tell you how the people really feel and give you an inside sense." The king reflected, "I wish I had been given this advice when I was young. It would have been so much easier and would have made so much more sense." He paused again, leaning back on his chair. "You can take my advice or not, Oman. The choice will always be yours. If I can help you not to make the same mistakes I made, perhaps your reign will be easier."

Oman acknowledged the wisdom of the king's words, his apprehension for the future confirmed by them. "I understand, Sire. Thank you for your advice. I will remember what you've said here today."

The king got up from his chair and walked with Oman back to his horse. Oman tucked the vase carefully into his saddlebag and pulled himself up. King Merck stepped back and said, "Have a safe journey home. The Jogahoh will always be welcome in my kingdom."

Oman bowed his head in respect and said, "Thank you," before turning his horse and returning to his troops.

The Jogahoh army gathered their forces and departed the following day, heading for home. As they passed through their border, they separated and began dispersing to their individual villages. Five days later, Oman found himself entering the familiar surroundings of his home. He wearily dismounted his horse in front of his mother's cottage, scratching the animal fondly on its nose. He said, "Just a few more minutes. I need to see my mother first. Then I'll get you something to eat." He was walking to the door when it suddenly flew open, slamming against the outside wall.

His mother, Tana, flew out and threw her arms around him, hugging him tightly. "I expected you sooner. The others were back days ago." Not allowing him to reply, she stepped back and studied him carefully. There was little remaining of the innocent boy she had known. He had grown into a strong man, and his face showed a new maturity, with a trace of sorrow after years of constant fighting.

"I had a few stops to make along the way, but I'm home now."

"You are," she exclaimed, smiling and embracing him again. "Are you hungry?"

"Always," he replied, a tired smile on his face.

"I'll make you something to eat."

"Thank you. I need to tend to my horse first, so I'll be in the barn. Call me when it's ready."

"Good. That should give me enough time to prepare something." She hugged him warmly once more and reluctantly turned back into the cottage.

Oman untied his horse and led the animal to the barn. He fed and watered it, taking his time in brushing her down. The horse looked curiously around her new surroundings, slowly eating the hay Oman had set out. He rubbed her chest, and she brought her head down, nudging her muzzle and forehead against him. He pulled her head up and murmured gently, "We're home now. No more cold nights in the open, and no more riding into battle." Her head suddenly popped up out of his hands, and she looked up, pointing her ears toward the barn door. Oman looked into the doorway but could only make out a dark shape against the brightness of the light. Thinking it was his mother, he said, "I'm almost done, Mother. I'll be in soon."

"It's been a long time, but I very much resent you saying I look as old as your mother," was the response from the silhouette.

Oman's face broke out into a smile, and he moved around the horse to walk toward the figure. "My apologies, Jossa. I couldn't make out who was there. I thought it was my mother coming to get me for supper." Oman stopped and openly stared at her. Jossa had transformed into a stunningly beautiful young woman.

She lifted her chin stubbornly. "I'll accept that apology. I thought you'd be back sooner, but as always, you're the last to show."

"I had a few stops to see some of the families of the fallen."

She lowered her eyes, embarrassed, and wished she'd picked better words. "I didn't mean to sound callous; I understand."

His horse came up behind him now, nudging him between the shoulder blades and pushing him toward Jossa. They both laughed, relieved to break the awkwardness.

She stepped closer to him and their eyes locked. "I'm sorry about your father."

"Thank you," he said, tongue-tied and at a loss for anything else to say.

She asked, "Can I come by later after you've eaten and rested?"

"May I come to your home instead?"

Jossa stood on her tiptoes and leaned into him, kissing him on the cheek. "I'd like that." She turned and walked out of the barn. Shouting over her shoulder, she said, "You smell a bit ripe. You best take a bath and be at my door by seven."

Oman grinned, shaking his head before turning back to his horse, and said, "For years, I've been ordered around by the army. Now, even at home, I'm being told what to do." The horse merely grunted and scratched her hoof on the barn floor. "More hay? Well, all right then. It appears that even you are ordering me around." He obligingly provided her with more hay, oats and water before turning back to his mother's house.

After a long soaking bath, Oman changed into some of his old clothing. The shirt was tight in the chest and arms, and his trousers were loose around his waist.

Tana frowned slightly at the ill-fitting clothes. "I still have some of your father's clothing. They will be a better fit for you. You can change into them after supper."

"Thank you. I appreciate that." He sat down and looked hungrily at the full table of food in front of him.

"Eat up. There will be more if you need it," his mother said, sitting contentedly across from him. She watched as he began to devour the food and said, "It's good, so good to have you home again. I see you haven't lost your appetite."

"These years on rations make one appreciate a full plate," he answered before shovelling in another mouthful.

Tana frowned and wrinkled her forehead, "Remember your manners. You're not sitting around a fire with a bunch of men. Take your time."

Oman's face reddened as he swallowed his food, "Sorry, I forgot."

Tana continued, "The pot on the stove is full, so have as much as your stomach can handle. Did I hear Jossa outside earlier?"

"Yes," he admitted. "Jossa did drop by. She asked to see me tonight."

His mother lifted an eyebrow. "That sounds like a chore to you. I could tell her that you're no longer interested if you want."

Oman stopped eating momentarily, then swallowed the food before putting his fork down. "No, that's fine, Mother. I suppose I'll drop by. It would be impolite not to show up. I wouldn't want her to be heartbroken."

His mother immediately stopped what she was doing and laughed at him. "Jossa? Heartbroken? Maybe you haven't seen her clearly yet, and your eyes are still clouded from the grime of the field. She's a beautiful young woman, Oman. And if you don't treat her right, there are plenty of others here that will."

"Mother, I do care," he said. "I just don't know how to show it at the moment." He got up to fill his plate again, then sat back down.

"Tell her how you feel. She's been waiting faithfully for you. Show her you're happy to see her."

"I will," Oman said.

His mother got up and pulled some of his father's garments out of a chest. "These should fit nicely," she said, handing the bundle of clothes to him.

"Are you sure, Mother? I could spend the evening with you if you prefer. Losing Father was very hard on all of us."

"Take them and go see Jossa. He would want that. Don't worry. I'll be fine."

The two of them looked silently at each other for a long moment, each remembering the man they had both loved. Finally, he accepted the clothing and prepared for his visit with Jossa. That night and over the next several weeks, Jossa and

Oman were together whenever one of them had a free moment.

Oman woke early, ate some breakfast, tucked the vase securely into his pack and walked down the small streets toward the council house. He wanted to get there before the others and prepare for the meeting. Oman had thought long and hard about the vase and knew not everyone would be content with his distribution of the magic. He climbed the steps to the building and pushed the door open. The door slowly swung inward, and Oman stepped inside, closing it behind him. He paused to let his eyes adjust and immediately saw Calam, his father's senior advisor, coming toward him.

Smiling warmly, Calam reached out and grasped Oman's hand in greeting. "Good morning, sir. I heard the door and wondered who it could be. No one else ever comes in this early."

Oman took his hand and said, "Calam, good to see you. I was hoping to be alone and get my thoughts in order before the meeting."

"If you prefer, I could leave and come back later," Calam answered, a puzzled look on his face.

"No need for that, Calam. Besides, I'm not sure where I'm supposed to go. Could you show me around?"

"Sir, I could do that. Before we start, I have a list of names for you to look at to take my position. They are all very qualified."

Oman asked, "Why? Are you leaving?"

"No, sir. I thought that you would want to bring in your own people to look after affairs."

Oman remembered King Merck's words about knowing who he could truly trust. Calam had had his father's complete faith and confidence and managed exceedingly well during their absence. "Calam, my father always trusted you. I am asking you to stay on with me if that is what you wish."

Calam's eyes brightened, and he said, "Yes, I would like that very much."

"Good, it's settled." The two men walked down the hallway

as Oman continued. "I will need you to guide me through this. I know very little of what my father's role was and never paid much attention to it. I always thought Salem would be the one to take over, so my interests lay elsewhere."

"I can do that." Calam glanced over to Oman and asked carefully, "Have you spoken with your brother since you've returned?"

"I sent several messages but have not received anything in return. Mother saw him briefly at our father's funeral. She was distraught, and he didn't stay to speak with her. Instead, he returned directly to King Merck's court."

"You took the first step and the most crucial one. The next step will be up to Salem. If he does not want to engage directly with you, I could be the go-between. It will not be in your best interest if the two of you become confrontational in front of the other leaders. I ask you not to step down to his level and always take the higher road. I will remind you that as the ambassador, he is not required to attend the council meetings unless you want him there."

"I understand," Oman said. "Thank you for your wise words, Calam. I have always respected your advice. When I was much younger, you would scold me for running in the halls during the council, but you were always firm and fair."

"It seems a long time ago now, doesn't it? So much has changed since then. You were just a child, and a bit of a mischievous one, at that. It appears you have outgrown your impulsiveness."

"Perhaps, but I expect you to let me know if I become reckless." The two of them laughed lightly and continued through the council house.

A short time later, Oman started his first meeting with all the tribal leaders. The talk was of a general nature. Tribes to the south were worried about this year's harvest of wheat and corn because of a dry spell. To the north, people were concerned about the lack of fish and game. They were all anxious that there would not be enough to last through the long cold winter. Oman looked out over the group, listening intently as they spoke.

Finally, he stood. "I understand all of your concerns, but the rains to the south should start soon. I am confident that we will still have enough time to reap the harvest. The herds of elk and caribou will start their migration in two weeks. The salmon will also begin their run. Some needs and concerns can be solved in another way." Oman reached into his backpack and pulled out the vase, turning it upside down. A piece of silver fell into his palm. Looking up at them, he began, "King Merck and my father made a bargain in return for us going to war with him. He has kept this bargain and has granted us magic. Each silver piece you see has the power to grant one magical demand." The council room erupted into chaos. The excited shouts and exclamations from the leaders ran untethered until Calam roared a command for them to cease.

"We are not children here. Remember your place, and allow Oman to speak," Calam insisted. Begrudgingly, the men quieted and turned their eyes to Oman. For the next hour, Oman explained the vase's power, discussed its limitations and how the coins would be distributed. The faces of the men changed when he specified how many pieces each tribe was to receive. Oman began to hear mutterings from them, some positive, others irritated at the limitations.

"The magic is precious and cannot be misused," Oman insisted. "Before we start using it to fill our storage bins, we need to harvest what we can and re-evaluate in the fall. The magic should only be used when you absolutely need it. Make sure your people continue to work. I do not want to hear of the tribes not hunting or farming. I do not want us dependent on the vase."

"Can we use the magic to heal? Last year, my people were decimated by sickness. We sent a request to your father for help but received no reply," shouted one of the leaders.

"I can't recall hearing anything about a sickness," Oman said, puzzled. "This is the first that I have heard about it. But yes, the magic has the power to heal." More excited chatter came from the men.

A few tribal leaders tried to convince Oman to use magic more often to make life easier in their villages. After much discussion, they realized he could not be swayed, and they grudgingly agreed. Finally, Oman glanced in Calam's direction, and the older man nodded his head in approval.

"I have one last point before our next meeting in fall. One year into the war, my father called back to you for more men. Some tribes gave beyond what they should have. Others sent only a bare minimum, and those troops were below standard. My father was disappointed and wanted to replace those who did not want to follow his order. We suggested he not do that, and I took on the burden of training those men within a tight timeframe. Because of their inexperience, I lost many of my best soldiers, and the other tribes lost their brothers and sons. What I am telling you is," Oman leaned forward on the table, studying the sitting leaders. "I remember those days. I remember who followed my father's orders, and I remember who chose not to. If you decided not to obey my father's orders, do not come to this council and ask for more silver pieces. We will have only a small surplus in the event of a crisis. You have not made the sacrifice the other tribes have." There was a low murmur among the elders as Oman straightened back up. "The meeting is now adjourned." Oman picked up the vase, nodded to Calam, who rose from his seat to join him, and the elders stood as the two exited the room.

"How did I do?" Oman asked as they strode briskly down the corridor.

Calam laughed. "If you didn't have their attention before, you certainly have it now."

CHAPTER 5

Oman walked into his father's private working chambers and stood in its centre. He looked around the sparsely furnished room and wondered, *how did he do this for so many years? How did he put up with these people? I've had only one day and am willing to give it all up.* A knock on the door interrupted him. "Come in," he said.

The door opened, and his brother, Salem, sauntered in. "Brother, it's good to see you," he said, smiling, opening his arms and striding over to Oman. "Mother said I would find you here among these hallowed halls." They embraced each other awkwardly before stepping back.

"These hallowed halls would suck the remaining life from a dead fish."

"Better you than me," Salem commented smoothly. "I'm content with where I am now. My wife prefers a formal court life; there is so much more for her to do there." He grinned and added, "It keeps her out of my business, as well."

"So, Minza is doing well?"

"There are challenges. Because the palace was made for larger people, the furniture does not fit us. Still, she rather enjoys the gossip and high fashion."

Oman frowned at Salem's tone and only nodded his head.

"We expected you to be present at father's funeral. People were asking where you were," Salem continued, assessing his brother carefully.

Oman answered truthfully, "I was with him when he died and mourned his loss on the field. There was too much work after the final battle and the threat of one last counterattack. We had a funeral for him there, and I sent him home with my second-in-command."

"Yes, your man passed that on. The elders insisted that you should have been there, but don't worry. I calmed them down."

Oman's face was serious. "I'm not happy with their expectations or their demands. My first meeting with them did not go well. Of the ten, only four were loyal to our father during the war. They were upset when I challenged them about not sending Jogahoh to fill our ranks."

"As the politician between the two of us, I can see both sides. Yes, the army was struggling. We know that, but back here, it wasn't an easy time either—especially in the nations to the north. The beasts tore them to pieces the second winter you were gone. We had a problem in the south during the second year as well. Entire villages fell ill with a serious flu that came and went."

Oman was stoic. "We heard the problem up north was precipitated by the homes not being dug deep enough. That was the fault of the elders. I was just advised of the sickness today; we heard nothing about it, and I understand it was hard. But, without our fight in this war, our country would no longer exist. We would have been swallowed by the eastern kingdom. Because of our sacrifice, King Merck has granted us a solution to our problems here at home." He told Salem about the vase and the magic that would change the lives of the Jogahoh forever. Salem reined in a sudden rush of jealousy. *That magic should be mine.* With difficulty, he forced his face to remain impassive, although he tensed. Oman continued to speak, oblivious to his brother's sudden stiffness. "We are unable to use our magic on the beasts in the winter. The elders now have the power to ensure their winter homes are dug deep and built well enough to withstand the beasts' attack. They will now be able to use magic to combat any disease." Oman sighed heavily and said, "I've had enough for today. Tomorrow I can send them all back to their lands, and I won't have to see them until fall." He asked Salem, "Are you coming home for supper? I'm sure Mother would like to see you."

"The king's sorcerer has provided me with the use of a portal, and I told Minza I'd be back in the kingdom this evening, so I'll join you for supper. Will you be staying with Mother long?"

"I will, for the time being. Keep this to yourself for now. I plan to find a place to the north and build a farm there. Once it's complete, I'll move and come in only when I'm needed. They can send a cardinal as a messenger. Father would only be contacted in that way, and he made it work. I thought perhaps I could, too."

Salem frowned slightly and said, "Yes, he did, but it was hard on the family. Don't you remember?"

"I do, but this will give me time to think about where I want to be and where I want to go." Oman noted Salem's expression and tried to reassure him. "I can make this work." The two walked out of the room and headed down the hall. "Where are you off to now?" Oman asked.

Salem placed his hand on Oman's back and said, "To visit with a few old friends. After that, I'll find the elders in their favourite drinking hole and listen to them complain. Then I'll meet you at Mother's for supper."

"Supper will be at six o'clock," Oman said, walking out of the council house and heading home.

Salem strolled through the town, nodding and stopping to talk with people he knew. Forever the politician, he embraced the ladies and took the time to listen to the older men. Once away from the crowded streets, his strained smile dropped from his face. He well remembered the message about the village's illness he was to have passed on to his father. At the time, it had not seemed serious to him, and he ignored the plea for help. *These things happen. I'm sure it couldn't be helped;* he thought and quickened his pace in agitation. The roads grew narrower, and the homes grew smaller, showing signs of neglect and disarray. Finally, he stopped at a small, weathered door, stepped inside and locked the latch behind him. The smell of an unwashed body and stale whiskey immediately assaulted him. The window on the far wall was open, doing little for the stench, but allowed for enough light to see a fire smoldering in the hearth. Salem managed to make out a rumpled bed in one corner and a table with two chairs in the centre.

On one of the chairs sat a man waiting for Salem. In front of him were two glasses, one empty and the other full to the brim with whiskey. The man picked up the glass, toasted Salem, and said, "Cheers. You're late." He tossed the glass of whiskey down his throat. It was Bargun, an old friend of Salem's. They had known each other for years before Salem's father had taken them away from the village to live on their own. At one time, they had been evenly matched, both clever and talented young men, but Bargun had a problem with the drink. He was twenty-seven years old, slightly under four feet tall, with dirty, long, tangled red hair and a moustache. Always looking for an easy way to make money, Bargun was more than happy to meet with his old friend.

Salem walked over to the table, sat down, picked up Bargun's glass, lifted it to his nose and sniffed it. Crumpling his face in disgust, he said, "Yes, my apologies, but I had a few things that needed to be taken care of first." He looked around the room and said sarcastically, "Does the smell come with the rent, or is it extra?"

"Living the life in Merck's court has made you high and mighty," Bargun shot back, insulted. "Why did you want to meet me? I'm sure it wasn't to reminisce about old times."

"No, it wasn't. I want to hire you, put you on my payroll to help me when I need it."

"To do what?" Bargun asked suspiciously, pouring himself another glass of whiskey.

"I need a few tasks done here while I'm away at court. When I need something, I'll send you a message through a cardinal. Once the job is completed, message me back. Simple as that. Do you want the job or not?"

Bargun sat back in his chair, swilling his glass of whiskey and eying Salem carefully. *There may be an opportunity here for me,* he thought, and asked, "Has this anything to do with your brother?"

"That's not your concern. Do you want the job or not?"

"Since I have no current prospects and nothing on my agenda until we go underground this winter, I'll take it."

Salem grunted, "Good. You're hired. Tell no one who you are working for. Now, clean yourself up and get a better room." He reached into his coat pocket and threw Bargun a small leather pouch filled with coins. "Something with a view, perhaps." He stood and walked to the door before turning one last time to Bargun. "I will remind you that no one is to know you are working for me. If anyone finds out, I'll ship you so far north the beasts will have to travel up to find you."

Bargun lifted his glass to Salem and said, "Now that's the Salem I know. Cheers."

Salem dismissed the comment, slipped back out into the street and headed to the pub to meet with the elders. He had connections to re-establish.

••••••

Oman's mother, Tana, found him sitting on a stump near the back of the yard. "I thought I heard you."

"I've been back for a while. My first meeting was difficult. The leaders want to use magic for everything."

Tana sat down beside him. "Do you think your father's meetings always went well? They didn't. He would come back home, dejected, frustrated and angry."

Oman thought back and said, "I'd forgotten that." He straightened and twirled a stick he'd picked up from the ground.

"He tried to hide it, but it was very evident to all of us. He wouldn't let anyone else know they had gotten under his skin. I wished we could have stayed in the country and have him return for meetings, but he thought you boys needed more." Tana reassured him with a pat on his leg and said, "Negotiations take experience. With time, you'll learn."

Oman confirmed his plan to her. "I was thinking of doing exactly that. Live in the country apart from the others and return only when necessary. I want to leave tomorrow after the elders have left and find a place to make my homestead. I'm not certain where I'll end up, but I'll know it when I find it."

Tana's face was resigned. She had just been reunited with her son but knew that he had to get out on his own. "Everyone must find their own way, and you have to find yours. Today was only your first meeting, and I advise you not to dwell on the right or wrong of your decisions. You did the best you knew how to do. Your father made the right decision choosing you to succeed him. Salem is good at what he does, and I love him, but he lacks your strength. You have proven yourself to be a warrior and leader, and you did that the hard way."

"I wish Father would have given me more time and insight into how to do this job. How to listen and understand our people."

"He did," she said. "He took you with him to learn how to be a leader. You worked your way from foot soldier to battalion commander. I think he did his job."

"You're right. I see it now. I never saw it like that before."

"You've made a sound decision. The magic needs control. It's too enticing, and people become dependent on it." She heard someone approaching and turned to see Salem walking toward them. Tana automatically stood and wrapped her arms around him in greeting.

"Sorry, Mother," Oman said, "I forgot to tell you that Salem was coming for supper."

The three made their way into the house and ate before Salem was to head back. He said his goodbyes to Tana and shook Oman's hand. "I'm glad we had this time together, brother. I'd like to stay longer, but there is work at the court to be done." Salem pulled out a magic pendant, which opened a portal to transport him home. It swirled around him, tendrils of light and air spinning faster and faster until, in a blink of an eye, his body disappeared and reappeared in his bedroom at King Merck's court.

Salem's wife, Minza, was asleep in bed when Salem reappeared and woke her. She sat up, startled, and asked, "Salem? Is that you?"

"Yes. Sorry, I'm late. I had to stay for supper with Oman and Mother." He dropped his clothes and slid into bed beside her.

"You're cold," she exclaimed, pulling the heavy duvet tightly around them. Without hesitation, she demanded, "Tell me. Will Oman concede to you?"

"No," he answered. "I thought you liked the comforts here at court. Would you rather be home?"

She declared, "I would rather be here. There is no need to go underground, and we can use the sorcerer's magic anytime."

"I feel the same way, but Oman has been granted a vase that contains magic for the Jogahoh to use."

Minza's eyes widened, and she said excitedly, "A magical vase? For us?"

"I intend to get that vase," Salem continued, his lips curling at Minza's greedy expression. "My plan could take years. When the time is right, Oman will be ousted."

••••••

The following day, Oman gave the vase to Calam. Calam would have control of the vase and the distribution of the silver pieces. Next, Oman told the elders about his plans to live apart. They agreed without comment as his father and ancestors had done the same. Their leader needed to experience how the people lived. After the meeting, he swung a leg up and, settling into the horse, gave the mare a nudge and set off. He headed directly for Jossa's house, where he found her outside, chopping wood.

She stopped when she saw him approaching and silently studied the fully loaded horse as she wiped her sweaty brow. "Are you going somewhere?"

He got down off his horse and said, "I need some time on my own."

"I heard what happened at the meeting yesterday," she interrupted. "If you give me a few minutes, I can pack and go with you."

"It's too dangerous for you to be out there."

Jossa was mildly insulted. She retorted, "I grew up in these woods and can look after myself."

Oman tried to explain. "I know you can. But I need time to myself."

She scrutinized him carefully and then walked to him, a stubborn look in her eyes. "I'm giving you twenty days from today. After that, if I hear nothing, I'll come looking for you. I've waited for years." She placed her hands on her hips and gave him a challenging look. "Don't keep me waiting any longer."

Oman felt like a runaway child but knew that time in solitude would serve to order his thoughts. "This village is stifling for me. I need to find a new home for us, somewhere we can live in peace and quiet ..."

Jossa cut him off. "I know, I understand. My father was the same when he came back. It's not that you don't love us. You just need time. Take your journey and come back in twenty days." She stepped toward him and kissed him gently on the lips.

He kissed her hard in return. They separated reluctantly, and he got back onto his horse. "Twenty days."

"Go," she replied. "Find a place for us to live and raise our family. Something secluded, with lots of water and trees and an open area for a garden."

"I will," he said with a farewell wave. He urged his horse into a slow canter and headed north.

Nineteen days later, he rode back into the village. Jossa and Oman were married in a quiet ceremony surrounded by family and friends. Two days after the wedding, they rode away as man and wife and, one week later, found themselves riding into a large clearing. Jossa gazed contentedly at the small rushing river running through it, the silvery trees lining its banks and the tall grass surrounding her. There was a slight rise in the land where they would build their home.

"It's just as you said."

"You like it?"

"I love it," she said, slipping off the horse and landing lightly on the ground.

CHAPTER 6

The next five years passed quickly and peacefully for the young couple. They built a small cabin and barn and dug out their underground winter shelter. Oman and Jossa were proud of their new home, and life was good. Their love and bond with each other grew stronger year after year. The one thing missing for them was the sound of a child's laughter. As the years passed, Jossa's heart grew heavier and heavier because she could not carry a child. Oman would comfort her, whispering, "The two of us are enough for me, and when the time is right, the gods will give us what we need." Even as he said the words, however, they both tended to blame themselves. They still prayed to their ancestors and gods that someday, somehow, a child would arrive. During these years, others were invited to live alongside them. Soon a small band, including Jossa's sister and her husband, lived only a kilometre away, with others just beyond that.

The cold arrived early that fall, freezing everything in its path. The animals had barely enough time to grow their thick fur coats, and the Jogahoh had little time to prepare their underground winter homes. The snow had fallen heavily, blanketing the landscape. The winds howled and moved relentlessly over the hills and through the valleys, twisting and turning through the white land.

For the next two long months, the sun came up late and went down early. Every living thing waited, impatient for the day when the sun would once again break winter's icy grip. Jossa glanced at her husband as she busied herself around the house. She tried to ignore the restlessness and boredom that had set in after being confined for so long. "Oman, this winter is colder than the last few. We'll need more wood soon."

Oman was leaning back in his chair, staring at the dirt ceiling, watching the frost creep from one side to the other. It reminded him of an advancing battle line. The frost encircled each hanging divot, then surrounded the entire area, just as a battlefield outpost was taken and overwhelmed by the main force.

"Oman, are you listening?" Jossa asked again, drying her hands on her apron and walking over to the fireplace. "We'll need more wood soon, or we'll freeze to death."

Oman, startled, broke from his thoughts, shook his head and got up slowly. *She's right*, he thought. *I should have used magic to extend the tunnels and joined the others. It would have been warmer, and she could've visited with her sister*. Their small group had been given only three pieces of silver, and he decided not to use it for something he could do. He pushed himself from the chair and made his way over to the door, where his long fur cape hung from a wooden peg. Reaching up, he took it down and draped it over his shoulders. He tied a rope around his middle, winching the cape tight. Picking up his axe, he slid its handle between the rope and the cape. Turning back to Jossa, he flipped the hood over his head and said, "I'm just headed to the woodpile. I'll be back soon."

A look of concern and worry appeared on Jossa's face. "Be careful. You know what's out there," she cautioned.

"I will," he said, leaning over and kissing her on the cheek before walking to the door. He stopped and turned back. "This summer, I'll dig deeper. We'll be warmer, and you can visit with the others."

Jossa smiled and watched as he stepped outside, a blast of cold air bursting into the small room as the door opened. When he closed it, she walked over to the fireplace and hung a kettle of water above the flames. *I'll have a fresh pot of tea ready for him when he comes back*, she thought, shivering and pulling her sweater tightly around her.

Oman trudged up the tunnel and poked at the crust of snow

that had buried the opening. He cleared an exit point large enough for his small frame, stepped back and waited for a few minutes. The cold air rushed through the hole, peaking his alertness, and Oman sniffed at the fresh breeze. *No scent of a beast*, he thought, and slipped his hood back off his head to hear more. He carefully made his way through the entrance and out into the forest. Again, Oman stopped and scanned the entire area until he was satisfied that it was safe to proceed. He studied the tall, silent, snow-covered trees around him. The only thing alive was the north wind that swirled, forming a thick layer of frost on his black beard. He had to get moving. The sun would be down in an hour, and the task would take thirty minutes. After that, he could relax in front of the hot fire with tea and Jossa's biscuits.

The trek to the woodpile was draining; the snow was up to his chest and pulled at his body, gripping his clothing, trying to hold him back. Finally, hot with sweat and breathing heavily, he could see the woodpile. He brushed away the snow from the stacked wood, gathered two armfuls, and followed his path back to the mouth of the tunnel. *Four more to go*, he thought, turning and heading back out along the now-broken track.

Dropping the last load just inside the entrance, he turned and looked back. It was then that he heard it. The sound startled him. He drew his axe, automatically stepping lower into the safety of the tunnel. Standing quietly, he willed himself to calmness, and the silence of the forest filled his ears. Moments later, there it was again, a definite cry. Oman stepped toward the entrance, stopped and listened intently to the wind and the rattle of bare branches in the trees. Once more, the cry came, and he turned his head to the sound. "There's no doubt. That is a child," he whispered to himself.

Oman looked again to the west and watched with dread as the lower edge of the sun touched the horizon. *It will be down in a few minutes.* Hearing the cry once again, he started toward it, trying to home in on its source. Nothing showed itself, and all he could make out in the oncoming twilight was the deep snow and the stark, sleeping trees. The beasts would be moving now, and they would be hungry. He dropped the cape from his shoulders to the ground in one motion and gripped the axe tightly in his fist. He ran, pumping his legs through the deep snow, moving from tree to tree, stopping only to ensure his path was clear. He was quickly losing time.

He finally arrived at an old oak, out of breath and with sweat forming on his brow. Oman realized the sound was coming from the other side of the tree. Clenching his axe above his head, he stepped smoothly around its base. He froze, and his eyes widened at the sight of a deep hole in the snow. Peering down, Oman could see a brown, woollen bundle. Cleaving the axe into the tree to secure it, he reached down with both hands, picking up the wriggling package. Oman pulled back the top of the blanket, revealing a baby girl's small, furious and tear-stained face.

Oman hugged the bundle tightly to his chest, attempting to soothe the young babe, and asked, "What are you doing out here, little one?" He suddenly heard the hungry howls of a not-too-distant beast pack on their nightly hunt. Oman could not waste another moment. He tugged his axe free from the tree and raced back to the entrance with the child hugged tightly to his chest.

He reached the passageway just as the tip of the sun passed out of sight on the horizon. Oman raced down the tunnel and spotted Jossa's panicked face by the doorway, searching for him. He barrelled past her and shouted hoarsely, "Close the door! Now!"

Jossa slammed the door shut and bolted it, then turned to admonish Oman. "I was worried sick! You said you wouldn't take ...." she stopped mid-sentence, stunned into silence by what she saw in his arms. Another angry wail emitted from the bundle. She didn't stop to think. Snatching the child from Oman's arms, she brought the baby close to her chest and walked it toward the fireplace and its warmth. Gently, she bent down and placed the bundle onto the fur skin hide. She knelt beside it and began peeling the old blanket away from the child's face. The baby stopped crying immediately, but her tiny, heart-shaped lips still quivered. Jossa turned back to Oman, staring at him in wonder, and tears began to fill her eyes. "After all these years, our prayers have finally been answered."

"Jossa," Oman whispered, "she's not one of us. She's not Jogahoh. The law forbids us from keeping her."

Jossa protested immediately. "I can see that she's not Jogahoh, but I couldn't care less about that damn law. Someone placed this little girl where only you could find her. Just think. A few more minutes out there, and she wouldn't have made it. She's with us now, and she's staying."

Oman moved over to the fireplace and knelt on one knee, looking at the child. Around her neck was a strange, golden crystal fastened with a leather tie. Just above her heart was a small birthmark in the shape of a five-pointed star. He remarked, "I wonder why she has this crystal. Look," he said, picking it up in his hand. "There is a fire burning in its centre." As he held it, it began to glow with a brilliant, iridescent light, and a searing heat burned the palm of his hand. Dropping the stone immediately, he watched in puzzlement as its light dimmed when returned to the child. Oman held up his hand and could clearly see a burn mark branded into his palm. He looked at Jossa in astonishment as she hurried to retrieve a handful of snow for him to place on the burn. "It appears the stone prefers the child," he muttered. Jossa returned with the snow, and the two of them sat on the floor, gazing at the child. A minute, then two, passed in silence as the girl found her thumb and sucked forcefully on it. Oman finally asked, "What do we do now?" They both understood that it was forbidden for anyone but the Jogahoh to enter their country. There would be severe consequences if they were caught, and they could be exiled from Sakewan.

Oman was also puzzled. The barrier had been designed to prevent anyone but the Jogahoh from crossing through their border. He'd seen animals pass through but never a human. *So, how did the child make it through?* he asked himself. There were many questions here to be answered, and there was powerful magic in play. Whoever brought the child was strong enough to penetrate the barrier and place her, unharmed, for only him to find. Oman watched as Jossa picked up the baby and held her to her chest. He'd never seen that look in her eyes before. It was at that moment he knew not even the threat of exile would deter her from keeping it.

Jossa stood up, handing the baby to Oman. "She needs to be fed. I'll warm up some milk. We can use the lamb's old bottle." Oman accepted the tiny form without comment. He looked deeply into her bright eyes as a small smile appeared on her lips. Her legs kicked out from under the blanket, and she reached for his face, grabbing a handful of beard and tugging at it. "Be careful, you," he said gently, and his fingers enveloped her impossibly tiny, soft hand. Jossa soon returned with a bottle of warm milk, the child reaching for it eagerly.

Watching as Oman held and fed the babe, she whispered, "She likes you."

Early the next morning, Jossa woke, slipped from under the warm quilt and tiptoed out of the room. She entered the kitchen to find the fire already lit and the room warm. There in front of the fireplace, Oman sat in the rocker with the baby in his arms. Jossa smiled as her heart skipped a beat. *Finally*, she thought, *we are complete.* She walked up to her husband, kissing him softly on the top of his head.

Oman glanced up at his wife. "I've thought this through, and someone has given us this child for a reason. Even though it's against our laws, I would like to help her. What do you think?"

"I think you already know how I feel."

"It means we'll have to move away from the others to keep

our secret." He sat silently; the warning unspoken between them.

"We'll leave here at the first sign of spring," Jossa answered resolutely. "I suppose we'll head north."

"North would be best."

"We need to give her a name."

Oman held the child in front of him, mesmerized with her bright, sparkling blue eyes. "How about Anong?"

"Anong?"

"We found her during Anong, the time when the stars are just beginning to appear. It's appropriate."

Jossa brought him a warm bottle of milk. "It also means beautiful."

He cocked his head toward her. "I never knew that."

"It's perfect for her."

•••••

Esma poured water into a large copper bowl and sat down in front of it. Her gaze became unfocused, and she closed her eyes as she began to chant words of power. The vision Esma was searching for was indistinct at first but sharpened after a few moments. In it, the man she had tasked to deliver the child had finally returned to his own home. She watched him as he cared for his horse and completed his chores before walking to the house. He was met at the door by his wife. After only a few seconds, two small children joined them. She felt a sudden twinge of jealousy at the scene. She sometimes yearned for her own family, with little children running around and a man to crawl into bed beside after a long day. She had lived that life before and loved it. The giggle of small ones, the embrace of a husband and the feeling of being a family. The memories were torn to pieces as she watched them grow older, get sick and die. She had loved them all so profoundly. The only blessing was that she had never lost a young child. Instead, she watched from a distance as they grew and had children of their own before they passed. One by one, they all left her, every time.

Her mother warned her of the consequences of falling in love. Esma couldn't help herself the first time. It just happened. He was handsome, and it was everything she wanted it to be. When he passed away, she moved to the other side of the world, promising herself she would never fall in love again. But she did, twice more, before finally realizing what her mother told her was true. *It was just too hard on one's heart.* Hardening herself and pushing away her feelings, she could only watch.

Esma now gave her complete devotion to her animals and any other creatures that came her way. She travelled the world but never found exactly what it was she was looking for. Her travels brought her to King Tibalt's kingdom, where she decided to make the small town of Somoza her home. The townspeople were friendly and had accepted her solitary existence. Esma only came into town if she needed something or felt that someone required help.

Breaking from her trance, she wiped a tear from her face. Living in the past had brought back unwanted memories. "I loved you all so much," she whispered. She would see the man from her vision tomorrow. She waved a casual hand over the room, dousing the candles, before getting into bed and falling into a deep sleep.

Esma woke before dawn, carried out her chores and sat down for a quick breakfast. An hour later, she heard a light tapping on her door. "Come in," she said. The door opened, and the man from the vision stood in the doorway. He squinted his eyes, trying to see into the dark room, then stepped across the sill. Esma said, "Good to see you're back."

The man answered, "It's good to be back." He took off his hat and ran his hands through his hair. "The journey was tough, the snow was deep, and the temperatures were freezing, but the child and I got through."

"That's good," she said, then asked, "Did you place her where I told you?"

"Yes. I stayed hidden as long as I could but had to leave as the sun was almost down, and the beasts were on the move."

Esma watched his face go through a range of emotions and waited until he stopped talking. "I understand. Don't worry. The child is fine. She is safe, as I told you she would be."

The man's face turned from one of concern to relief. From around his neck, he removed a crystal and handed it to her. "I didn't think it would work. I've never seen anyone except Jogahoh cross their border."

Esma took the crystal from him and exchanged it for a pouch filled with coins. He held up his hands, refusing the payment, and said, "You've already paid me."

"I will need you again, and your silence on this matter is crucial."

"I will say nothing of it, just as with the other tasks you've entrusted me with."

"I know you would not do so willingly, but the task was arduous, and I value a job well done," she replied, gazing at the man with her hand still outstretched.

He reached out slowly, finally accepting the bag. He wanted to ask her more about the child but knew he would not get an answer from her.

"I'll contact you again when I need you. Not every man would have taken on the task I asked you to do." The man nodded his head, turned and walked out the door, closing it behind him.

Esma took the crystal and walked it over to a large chest at the foot of her bed. She put her hand on top of it and felt a slight vibration as it unlocked. The heavy lid raised on its own. The stone in her hand started to heat up slightly, and she opened her palm and looked at it. "Don't get that way with me, or I'll send you back to the centre of the earth and get another." The crystal cooled immediately, and she took one last look at it. "I'll need you another time, so sleep tight." She placed it deep into the chest and then closed and locked the lid.

Esma walked outside the cabin and looked up into the sky to the west. "Oman," she said, "the task I have entrusted you and Jossa with will not be an easy one. Bring the child up as your own. Raise her to be strong in heart, body and mind, as you are. Our future will depend on it.

CHAPTER 7

It had been five years since King Tibalt had invaded his brother's kingdom. During that time, he had continually relived his crushing defeat. He was obsessed with the humiliation of having victory so close yet having it all snatched away. A knock on the large wooden door pulled him from his dark thoughts. "Enter," King Tibalt barked. The door opened and revealed his sorcerer, Zakalis. He was a tall, thin man in his early forties, with long, tangled silver hair. The man appeared dishevelled and jittery as he came into the room. The king, alarmed, sat up quickly and motioned to a guard as the man grew closer. The guard stepped in front of the king, placing a physical barrier between the two. Peering around the guard, the king carefully accessed the sorcerer; he had never seen the man in this condition. Even during the war, he always looked composed and self-possessed. "What do you want?" the king demanded.

"Sire, I apologize for interrupting you at this late hour, but I have something urgent to tell you."

"Go on," the king replied as he watched the man fidget, his eyes darting nervously around the room.

The sorcerer finally began his tale. "I was woken from a deep sleep by a feeling of impending doom running through my body. I lay on my back, looking up at the ceiling as a white shadow zig-zagged across it, moving faster and faster. I tried to coax it to me, catch and hold it to determine what it was, but it kept just out of reach. I tried to use my most powerful magic to hem it in, but it was so strong it burst through like it wasn't even there. Then it spoke and said in a child's voice, *"You can never hold me. I hold more power than you will ever know."* His eyes again shifted around the room as if he were watching the shadow move.

The king walked toward Zakalis, with the guard still between them. The sorcerer's eyes fell beyond the man, and the king was worried. Under normal circumstances, he would have no time for Zakalis. Still, this sorcerer held magical powers that the king needed. Hesitantly, he said, "I'm sure it was just the remnants of a bad dream."

"No, it's more than that, Sire," the sorcerer insisted, gathering his thoughts together. "I started going through all of my old texts, rereading them, looking for an answer. I went back and found an ancient script about a child that is born of magic from no magical source."

The king scoffed and walked to the window. "We both know that's impossible; to make magic, you need a magic source, and even then, it is never guaranteed. We have many accounts where two people with magic cannot produce a single offspring with the ability."

"That is true, Sire," the sorcerer said, breathing in deeply as sweat started to drip from his brow. "But the script states that every thousand years, a female child with ultimate power will be born to those without magic. Don't you see?" The sorcerer continued, frustrated. "I believe that is why it came to me. To mock me, to taunt me."

"Do you still see the shadow?"

"That is the puzzling part. The source of the magical power and the shadow itself completely disappeared. I can feel nothing now, yet I know in all certainty that it is still there. Hidden perhaps," the sorcerer insisted.

"We both know if this were real, something so strong could be felt in some semblance by you. Am I right?"

"Yes, Sire, you are. However, I believe it may have been found by another and concealed."

"Let me think on this puzzle for a day or two," the king said. "I thank you for your council and ask that you await my orders." He dismissed Zakalis with a wave of his hand. The man, accustomed to the king's mercurial moods, bowed and slid out without a sound.

As the door closed, the king summoned his archduke. He began speaking the moment the man entered the room, describing the sorcerer's vision. When finished, he calmly ordered him. "I need you to investigate and determine if a child as he described could have been born. It must have happened within the kingdom because of the strength of his vision. If it's true and a female child was born with that kind of power, I can use it to take back what I lost and more."

The archduke bowed and said, "We'll begin our search tomorrow."

••••••

Oman stood in what was once the snowbound tunnel leading out to the forest. The warmer weather had melted the snow and left behind a wet and muddy trail. He looked through the leafless branches of the trees and could just make out the woodpile. There was more than enough to last until they departed. He turned and stepped through the doorway, closed the door and secured it before making his way down the steps. Jossa sat at the table, feeding Anong, and he beamed at them while hanging up his coat. "The weather is getting warmer. It won't be long now."

Jossa replied, "It will be good to get out of here and into the fresh air."

Oman walked over to the fire and poured a cup of hot coffee from the pot. "We'll start our move next week while the others are still underground, so no one will see her."

"I wish we could stay; things would be so much easier. I remember when we were out on our own how hard it was in the beginning."

"I know," Oman agreed and sat down at the table. "It took five years, and I'm just getting used to people again. It would have been easier if the child were accepted, but you know that would never happen."

Jossa agreed, "The outcome would never be in our favour.

And I'm not ready to give Anong up, Jogahoh or not."

"As am I," Oman agreed, sipping his coffee. He reached over, holding the baby's hand as she latched onto his finger. The two watched with delight as Anong grabbed it tightly, tugging back and forth. Without warning, a white light emerged from the little girl's fist.

Jossa smiled, "I think she has a bit of magic."

"I have no doubt of that."

Over the next week, the two packed only the essentials they'd need for the trip and prepared the livestock for their journey. They would need their animals to come with them. On their last evening, Oman laid a hand-drawn map on the table, with a circled area much farther north from where they were. Jossa studied the map carefully. She was concerned about the length of time it would take to get there and the area's remoteness. Nevertheless, the two agreed the site would be the only way for them to stay away from prying eyes.

Early the following day, Oman saddled the horses, sorted the livestock and packed their belongings. He had made a small carrier for Anong that was attached to Jossa's back. Once they were ready, Jossa took a note from her pocket. "Oman, please leave this on the table. It's for my sister."

"I didn't want to leave anything," he objected.

"I have to leave something for her. I just wanted to reassure her that we'll be all right."

Oman relented, taking the note and placing it on the table as she requested. The journey took one long week. They moved steadily along spectacular, jagged mountain ranges and deep valleys. Fast-moving rivers, swollen by melting snow, slowed their progress, but they struggled onward. The thick forest supplied them with fresh food when their own supplies dwindled. Early afternoon on the seventh day, they rode into the location they had agreed upon.

Jossa looked around them and said, "This will do just fine."

Oman stood in his saddle, looking across the open ground and along the wood line. "The land is clear and rises steadily away from the river. We'll have fresh water and an ample wood supply."

They got off their horses and set up for the night. Oman gathered firewood and put up the campsite. Jossa, accompanied by a giggling Anong, placed a fish trap in a quiet part of the river that ran beside the clearing. There would be fresh fish for supper that night.

After their meal was complete, Jossa stood up, studying the clearing carefully. "This area is very nice. It has good water, trees, abundant game and edible plants. So why is there no one living here?" Oman turned his head away from her, not saying a word as he put away the last of the dishes. Jossa turned to him, a wary look in her eyes. "Why have the Jogahoh not settled here before?"

Oman could not quite meet her eyes. "Well," he started.

Jossa stared intently at him and interrupted, "What didn't you tell me?"

"Nothing important. It shouldn't much matter."

She paused, a sudden realization hitting her. "You brought us to the land of the Jibay?"

"It's not that bad, and it will keep Anong safe," Oman reasoned. "No one ever comes here. My father brought me here many times, and nothing bothered us but the mosquitos." He paused and said, hesitantly, "Well, there was one time."

She cut him off and raised her hand at the same time. "I don't want to know." Jossa glared at him and sighed in resignation. "We need to gather as much sage as we can, burn it in the fire and make an offering."

"We have nothing to offer."

"Yes, we do. Your tobacco. Let's get started."

They gathered up as much sage as they could find, and Jossa tied it into three bundles, each bundle representing one of them. She tossed all three bundles into the fire while Oman and Anong watched. Anong laughed and waved her arms and legs happily as the sage burned and threw a pleasant scent into the air. Jossa dug her hand into the tobacco pouch and, pulling out a small amount of tobacco, sprinkled it into the fire. As it burned, she took the remainder of the tobacco over to a large flat rock. Jossa stood back, lifted her head and spoke out into the open space beyond them. "We are sorry if we woke you from your sleep. We came to find a place that is safe to raise our child. If you can accept us and are peaceful, please join us. Take this tobacco as a gift for letting us stay in your land." For a moment, everything stayed still, as if the spirits were considering their request. Then, in the oncoming twilight, the grass around them began to softly rustle. Oman and Jossa felt a light breeze passing by them and looked over at Anong. She lay on her blanket, looking up at nothing they could see, laughing and reaching with her hands toward the sky.

Jossa smiled, "They like her."

"Who likes her?" Oman questioned.

"The good spirits of this place. I'm hoping they'll keep the bad and mischievous ones away."

"Jossa, I don't know if I believe in such things. Anong laughs like that all the time."

"Is your tobacco still there?"

Oman walked to the stone and was stunned to find that there was no trace of the tobacco. "It's gone!"

"Well, it looks like we're not alone," she said and walked back to Anong.

•••••

Jossa's sister, Debbie, and her husband walked over to Oman's old winter quarters, noting how quiet it was. They had heard nothing from the two and were concerned but were relieved to see the outer area intact. Her husband knocked hard on the door. It opened by itself, and he stepped inside cautiously. Sniffing the air deeply, he scanned the room, and his eyes settled on the table, finding the note. Debbie picked it up and read it silently. In stunned disbelief, she turned to her husband and said with a soft, choking sound, "They've gone."

"It does look like that," her husband answered. He exhaled with frustration as his wife began to cry. "We both know Jossa shouldn't have married him. He's been a loner ever since the war, and I'm surprised they didn't leave sooner."

His wife reread the note and placed it in her pocket before she walked through the home, stopping at the bedroom. She sat down on the edge of the bed and lit a lantern. As a glow brightened the room, her eyes searched into the corners of the space. On a bench, she saw something unexpected. She reached over and picked up a pair of baby booties and held them tightly in her hand. She knew Oman and Jossa had tried for years to have children without success. Speaking only to the silence of the room, she asked, "Jossa, what is going on?"

CHAPTER 8

Zakalis sat down on his chair and stared out the window. The opulent palace had its obligatory defensive walls but had been built to highlight its stunning vistas. The silver lake in front of him shimmered like a mirror and reflected the sky above it. The sorcerer was silent and lost in thought. Finally, getting up, he took the washbasin and poured a bit of water into the bottom, then placed it on the table. Staring down into its cool depths, he murmured an incantation and watched with satisfaction as images formed in front of him. He saw the archduke with a party of men searching for a child in the surrounding villages. Zakalis was alternately angry and pleased with the sight. It confirmed that the king believed him but did not trust him enough to lead the search. Without warning, the images began to blur as a force started to pull him forward. He had no control, and the scenes picked up speed until they abruptly stopped at a cabin in the country.

He focused on a woman in a yard tending to her animals, and his mind whispered the name *Esma*. She immediately stopped what she was doing and whirled around. He realized with a start that the woman could see him. Esma glared angrily at him as if reading his mind and made a fist. A blast of energy came from the bowl, throwing him onto the floor. He landed awkwardly on the marble stone, shocked and soaked with water. After a moment, he regained his breath, then stood and scowled back into the basin. A woman with that kind of power had to be a witch. It was as if a curtain had been drawn in front of him; there was nothing to be seen.

Further efforts were useless and exhausting. Finally, after an hour, he gave up and stumbled over to the bed. His last thought before sleep overtook him was the name *Esma*.

Sleep came immediately, and with his mind free, his spirit separated from his body. It stood by the bed as if waiting to be commanded. Again, he heard the name *Esma* whispered. A force gripped the sorcerer's spirit, flung him through the castle wall and across the countryside until he found himself once more in the woman's yard. Freed from the power that had dragged him to her home, he searched, but was unable to find the witch. Zakalis was confused. Something had drawn him to this place and this dangerous woman. He knew she was no ordinary witch but one who had mastered the old ways eons before. *Making her very old and very strong.* Again, his spirit was tugged forward, and he found himself moving into the woman's cabin. His gaze ran through the room, stopping at a large black trunk. He needed to see what was inside. It called to him with an insistent, irresistible urgency, and he realized that whatever it was had drawn his soul to it. For what purpose, however, Zakalis had no idea.

Moving to it, the lid opened on its own, and he spotted two bright stone amulets that burned with power. He reached for one of them, and as he did, the stone told him of a journey it had taken into Jogahoh territory with a child of unimaginable power. A sharp burning sensation emanating from the stone seared through his hand and into his mind, and he cried out in alarm. A voice from behind caught him by surprise.

"You again," Esma said and, using her powers, seized his spirit and turned him helplessly to her. The sorcerer tried to push away and return to his body, but she held him firmly in her grip. She spoke again, "First, I find you spying on me from your sorcerer's bowl, and now you're in my home. Why would you do that? What are you looking for?" She clenched a fist, and her grip on him tightened, the pressure affecting his human form, making it difficult for him to breathe. The sorcerer helplessly began to spin while Esma coolly assessed him, waiting for his reply.

Terrified, he blurted out, "After my vision of you from the bowl, I fell asleep, and a force drew my soul back to this place."

Esma considered his words for only a moment, then looked down at the trunk and spotted the two stones, still burning brightly. "I see now," she said, her jaw tightening. "And what have my stones told you?"

Zakalis was angry and jealous of her power over him. With a start, he realized that the child would be his only chance for greatness. "Nothing. They told me nothing. I don't know why I was drawn here."

Esma laughed scornfully and paced around the now-terrified man as he helplessly spun in lazy circles through the air. "You sorcerers think you know everything, but you know very little of the world. You have no idea of the powers that are in play, and I suggest you stay away from things that are beyond your control or ability." She stood facing him, silently judging. Her black eyes pierced into him as if she knew exactly what he was thinking. After a moment, she said, "Pray you never see my face again." Without warning, she brought her hand up, thrusting it at him. Her power flung his soul back to the palace, and he returned to his body with a start. As he reunited with it, he lurched in the bed and collapsed, falling into an exhausted, dreamless sleep.

Esma turned back to the trunk and the two gleaming stones within it. "Your meddling has no place here. Next time you'll be sent back to where I found you." The stones flashed a remorseful bright blue, but Esma ignored them. Without another word, she closed the lid.

The sorcerer woke the following day with a groan. *Was last night a dream?* He felt pain in his palm and lifted his hand to inspect it. In its centre was a stinging burn, and he realized that everything he had experienced happened. The witch, Esma, was real, the stones were genuine, and they confirmed that the child had been taken to the Jogahoh. He dressed without thought, his mind whirling with possibilities. He would first need to find the child, and that meant finding a way into Jogahoh territory.

••••••

Oman was obliged to make periodic trips back to Alfheim for council meetings but kept his time there short. The family stayed in the land of the Jibay and used a bit of the magic granted to them that summer to build their home and barn. Most spirits came just long enough to see Anong and take Oman's tobacco, which he begrudgingly left for them. Jossa could sense two spirits that would visit them regularly, an older man and a young boy. They never interacted and only stood close to the wood line, watching. She tried many times to entice the two closer, but they stayed their distance. This made Oman happy because his tobacco was always in short supply.

They soon needed to make a trade run to the border for supplies. "This will be our only chance before we settle in for the winter. We don't want to get caught outside once the snow comes," Jossa said as she helped Oman with the horses.

Oman swung his last pack over the horse and tightened it firmly on the animal's back. "With the furs," he said, "and the stoneware you've made, we have more than enough for trade."

"How long will you be?" Jossa asked.

"A week should give me more than enough time. Are you sure you don't want to come? I could stay back and care for Anong behind the border while you trade. You're just as good at bartering, if not better."

"It would be nice to get away for a while, but Anong has grown so much. It makes it hard to take her on the horse. We'll be fine here."

Oman sighed, "I'll miss the two of you." He lifted Anong up and kissed her on the cheek. "You look after your mother, young lady," he said before he returned her to Jossa. "And the two of you look after each other." Oman gave Jossa a quick kiss and said, "See you soon." With that, he climbed onto the horse and, giving it a gentle nudge, began his trip to the border.

It took Oman three long days of travel to reach the trading

post just outside the Jogahoh territory. It was strategically situated beside a sizable river that made the traffic of goods fast and easy. The market bustled with activity and was filled with people from both sides of the border preparing for winter. The loud, insistent cries of the vendors and flurry of bodies around the stalls made him appreciate the tranquility of his home. Oman stopped and let the horses rest, feeding and watering them. He decided to wait until the crowd of people thinned out before he slipped a hood over his head and made his way through them.

Three hours later, his wares were sold, and his supplies were purchased. He was about to leave when he noticed a red cardinal flutter above him. Oman instinctively held out his hand, whistling to the bird and thinking it had a message for him. Instead, it flew past him and landed within a group of Jogahoh some fifty yards away. Oman re-secured his horses and quietly made his way toward the group. Slipping through the crowd, he found the bird perched on the shoulder of a district leader from one of the northern nations. He watched as the man pulled a small message from the canister on the bird's chest. Oman shifted closer and listened as he spoke with his wife. "It looks like we have a meeting in five days."

"That's strange. They usually give you at least a month's notice," she replied.

"They do, but it looks like Salem is holding this meeting, not Oman. That's what's strange."

"Shouldn't you contact Oman?"

"He's probably aware. I wouldn't worry right now."

Oman frowned. If there was a meeting, he would have received a message. He thought that perhaps a cardinal had been sent to Jossa. Slipping out of the crowd, he walked back to the horses and started across the border, setting a fast pace for home.

Jossa heard the horses' hooves as they entered the yard and came out of the cabin with Anong on her hip. She looked at him, surprised, and said, "I didn't expect you so soon."

"Did a message come while I was gone?"

"No," she said, puzzled. "Why do you ask?"

"While I was at the trading post, I saw the leader of the northern nation receive a cardinal's message about a council meeting."

"No, there's nothing here. The cardinal would have gone directly to you if it had been sent."

"Salem called a meeting without my consent," Oman said, agitated. He slipped off his horse and began to unload the supplies.

Jossa set Anong down and helped Oman with the horses. "Why would he do that?"

"I don't know. That's what I have to find out. Salem has the authority to act as an ambassador but not as my representative. He's never indicated any interest before now. In fact, he always said that he preferred to work in the court."

The two unloaded and put away the last supplies before Oman wearily sat down at the table and held out his arms for Anong. She gleefully fell into him and wrapped her chubby hands into his beard. Jossa prepared coffee and sat across from him, stirring sugar into her cup. "So, what is your plan?"

"I'll wait until the day of the meeting and show up once it's in progress. Whatever Salem has up his sleeve, we'll find out then," he said, determined. He stared at his daughter for a moment before a thought occurred to him. "If Salem wanted to be the leader of our country, why can't I just give it to him?"

"How do you give away something that isn't yours to give?" she reasoned. "That title was bestowed on you by your father as his last act before he died. If he wanted Salem to take over, he would have simply said goodbye to you, and his title would have passed to Salem. He wanted you to be our leader. The position and title you want to give away are with you until you die. Only then will it be passed on."

Oman drank his coffee, silently pondering Jossa's words. "I'll be there for the meeting and find out what's going on. I can only hope Salem isn't trying to seize power. I don't want to fight with my only brother."

"Two brothers fighting for power would not be good for our country," she agreed, looking at Anong and changing the subject. "Look how much she has grown. She'll need a new bed soon, and I'm glad we decided to raise the doorways and ceiling."

Oman set his daughter on the floor and watched as she lifted her hands in the air, smiling and gurgling. He asked his wife, "Who is she talking to?"

"I think it may be an older woman who found us a few days after you left. She's missing her grandchildren, I think," Jossa laughed. "Anong loves talking with her. Her magic, I think, is getting a bit stronger."

Oman got up and said, "Well, I wish her magic could brush down the horses and feed them for me. Since it can't, I'll be out in the yard, doing just that. I forgot to tell you that the traders like your stoneware and will take more of it."

"Well, that's good to hear. I'll have something to work on this winter."

CHAPTER 9

Salem strode quickly through the council house and stopped at his dead father's official seat. He clenched his fists and angrily whispered, "You old fool, putting Oman in charge when it was my right. Did you not think I would fight for my position? Did you not think I would do whatever I could to take over? Father, if only you could see what is about to happen and how I will take what is mine. I'll place your golden boy where he should be, in the same place he worked when we were children, the pigsty."

"Salem," Calam called out from the doorway, "tomorrow is the meeting, and we still haven't heard anything from Oman. He's always arrived at least a day before."

Salem was startled at Calam's sudden appearance but recovered smoothly, saying, "The messengers were sent out nearly a week ago, so I'm sure he's on his way."

"But the cardinal never came back, which is highly unusual."

Salem walked over and placed his arm around Calam as he guided them through the hallway. "We can't do any more than what has already been done. He's the one who chose to live God knows where with his wife. If he wants to be the head of the Jogahoh, he must be readily available. He can't live his life so far away from us that his people must wait for him."

Calam scanned Salem's face before speaking deliberately, "Oman's always been here before. Never once has he shirked his responsibility. If he doesn't show up, it will be up to you to conduct the meeting." Calam hesitated slightly and said, "I just hope there is nothing more going on here."

Salem, impatient but careful, forced himself to stay civil before replying. "I know my brother has done a great deal for us, and if he's late, there will be a good reason." He turned and began to walk away.

Calam called out to him, "I've also seen Bargun around. He's an old friend of yours, isn't he?"

"Yes, we knew one another while we were growing up," Salem said cautiously.

"He seems to have changed his ways and is looking well."

"Well, that's good news, isn't it?" Salem's face was a blank canvas, revealing nothing. "I always like to see a happy ending to a sad story." He turned and continued down the hallway, calling back to Calam, "I'll see you tomorrow morning."

The following day, the tribal leaders met outside the great hall as the doors unlocked and swung open. They walked inside, taking their positions behind chairs that were placed around a grand table. The men sat down as one and looked to the head of the table, expecting to see Oman, but his chair was empty.

Calam strode to the front and looked over the gathering. "I'm afraid Oman has not arrived, and we've heard nothing from him. I thought perhaps that the messengers couldn't fly north, but I see those tribes are here. I'm asking you to remain for one more day."

A murmuring could be heard as the chiefs talked among themselves. Salem stood and walked confidently to the head of the table. He had called the meeting to increase the number of silver pieces allotted to each tribe. He knew this had been a topic of much dissent for many years. If he, and not Oman, were heading the decision, he would find approval and support from many tribal leaders. He studied the assembly carefully and then began to speak. "We will have to begin without Oman. We have all taken the time and energy to ensure our presence here. We have left our families, our fields and our work. All of us know the duty we must attend these meetings. All of us, it seems, except our leader. My brother." He paused, waiting for his words to resonate with them. "Are we supposed to wait for him? Is our time not as valuable as his? Are his people no longer his priority?"

A rumble of voices started, and the dissent was apparent. Some of the leaders agreed with Salem; others were willing to wait for Oman. Salem plowed on, disregarding those who objected. "I made my way here, but I must return to my duties as soon as possible, just as you must return to your families. So, I say we start without him. I will act in his stead so you can be back with your people tomorrow morning."

The northern tribe leader stood and asked, "Are you willing to make a decision in our favour to increase the number of silver pieces we receive?"

Salem feigned concern over the matter and then replied, "Of course. This, I believe, is well overdue. I'm sure you'll find my decisions today to be most rational."

Calam stood from across the room, arguing, "I suggest we wait. I sent another cardinal last night, and it should find him soon. Oman could be here by this afternoon."

Salem, his confidence building, laughed and said, "I plan to be done by this afternoon. After that, we can retire to the tavern. Let's get started now."

Arguments immediately broke out among the men, and voices rose as the disagreements escalated. Calam rose once more. "Silence! Keep the order, or this meeting will be cancelled." As soon as the last word left his mouth, the back door opened, and Oman stepped through it.

The room became quiet as they watched him walk confidently toward his brother. When he reached him, Oman stated formally, "Thank you for stepping in for me. You can take your seat now."

Salem's face could not hide the surprise and anger he felt at Oman's arrival. He schooled himself to regain his composure and inclined his head to his brother. "It's good to see you finally made it."

Oman dismissed him and turned his eyes back to the assembled group. "I apologize for being late," he began. "Calam's cardinal found me this morning, and I used the magic to come directly here. I did not call this meeting. Who here called it, and why?" The men sat silently. They all knew the meeting had been ordered by Salem.

Salem stood and said, "I called the meeting, brother. I heard the tribes were having a hard time again this year. A decision had to be made to increase the number of silver pieces each tribe was given. I sent a messenger to you, and I don't know why it didn't arrive. The cardinal must not have found you."

Oman questioned his brother further and said, "We all know that if a cardinal doesn't deliver the message, it returns to its origin. Did my cardinal return?"

"I don't remember seeing it."

Oman remained calm and simply replied, "These things happen, I suppose." He continued. "If a tribe requires more silver, send a message to Calam. He can authorize its use when there is a need and if we have sufficient pieces."

Salem said, "Why don't you go to King Merck and ask him for more magic? Why must the leaders always come here and beg? Do you not trust them to use their own common sense?"

"The bargain was agreed upon and settled. I will not ask for more," Oman said. "It's not that I don't trust any of you or your judgement. With this power comes great responsibility and danger. I would rather shoulder that myself. The tribes that need magic will be granted it as necessary. The magic was never intended to be used as a shortcut. We lose our strength and independence when that happens."

The meeting continued well into the afternoon. Salem had retreated into himself, fully aware that his brother had regained the tribal leaders' confidence. Oman leaned back in his chair with a feeling of satisfaction. He managed to reclaim firm control over the others and re-establish order.

Calam waited until everyone had left the room and said, "I'm sorry. I couldn't hold them back any longer, and Salem took over."

"I know you did your best," Oman replied as he picked his belongings up.

"I sent that cardinal to you late last night. How is it that you got here so quickly?"

"I never received any message. I overheard some talk about the meeting. Why?"

"Be careful dealing with Salem, Oman. He wants to take over."

Oman looked at his father's trusted advisor and agreed with him. "I have the same feelings, Calam. I don't want to believe them, but I know deep inside that something isn't right." He changed the subject and said, "Do you agree with my judgement on the use of magic?"

Calam said, "I do. Your father's decision would have been the same."

"I don't want our people to rely on magic and grow weak because of it. It is a great tool for all of us, but now I see it only as a hindrance. Magic is something that could make our lives so much easier but could destroy us at the same time. We need to stay strong and keep our ways. We'll only be using it when we absolutely must."

"Your thinking is correct, I believe. The leaders now know where you stand on it, and the majority agree with you."

"If they need help, you can decide if the request is valid or not. Just inform me of your decision. I trust you."

"I'll do that," Calam replied. Curiosity urged him to ask a question. "Where are you living now?"

Oman laughed and said, "So you've heard the rumours?"

"Of course."

"We've moved away from the others again. It was too crowded for me, so I'll just say we went north."

"I understand your need, but did Jossa have a say in the matter?" he asked.

"She did."

Calam had no choice but to accept Oman's words; however, he was still concerned about Oman living so far from the others. The two men departed the hall together, words left unspoken between them.

•••••••

Bargun stood just inside the town livery stable door, closely watching who was coming and going. Glancing down the street, he spotted Salem briskly striding toward him. As he approached, Bargun stepped back and slipped into the inky, warm blackness of the room.

Salem stepped through the large door and peered into the darkness. Quietly, he called out, "Bargun."

Bargun answered, "Over here, in the corner."

Salem spotted him and made his way over, asking, "You wanted to see me?"

"Yes," Bargun said. "I thought you'd be interested in this," and pointed to two horses standing in their stalls.

"Tell me why I'm interested in these two old nags."

"I saw Oman riding in on these this morning. He was in a hurry and never unloaded them. I took a quick look to see if I could find anything of interest."

"What did you find?"

"This." Bargun stepped closer to the saddlebags and opened one of them, taking out a leather scroll with a band around it and handing it to Salem.

Salem unwound the scroll, opened it and read the contents. It contained the usual writings from a wife to her husband until the last line, *we'll miss you*. Salem scanned the scroll again but suddenly heard someone entering the stable. He quickly rewound the scroll and handed it back to Bargun. Salem pulled out a pouch from his jacket and tossed it to Bargun. "Take this and get rid of it for me. I don't want anyone to find it." With that, he quickly exited the livery through the back door, hurrying through the streets to create distance between him and the barn.

The last line on the scroll still gnawed at him. His mind was thinking furiously. *We'll miss you? They couldn't have children and were alone. Who else was Jossa talking about?*

Bargun walked from the livery down the street and slipped his hand into his pocket, checking for the pouch Salem had given him. He pulled it out and loosened the top drawstring to examine its contents. At the bottom of the bag was a dead cardinal with a small pack attached to it. The trademark showed it was the official courier to Oman. Bargun reached into the sack and ran his fingers over the limp, lifeless body. He manipulated its neck and could feel where the bones had been broken. "Someone has twisted your neck, messenger boy," he mumbled. He pulled his hand from the bag and closed the drawstring. *Getting caught with this would mean harsh punishment*, Bargun thought, *but to get rid of it would be foolish. You never know when you might need a bargaining chip.* He knew who to see on matters such as this.

Bargun soon found himself back in his old neighbourhood, one he hadn't been in since he started working for Salem. Just ahead, he saw a familiar tavern. Opening the door, Bargun stepped into the dimly lit area and hung his jacket up on a pole. Scanning the room, he quickly found the man he was looking for. Jessup was much older and even smaller than most of the Jogahoh. His dishevelled appearance and stale smell marked him as a beggar, and he sat alone in one of the corners, slowly nursing a beer. Bargun smiled to himself. *I thought I'd find you here. Some things just never change.* A minute later, he placed two mugs of beer on the table. "Jessup! I haven't seen you in a while, old friend," he said, sitting across from the man.

Jessup eyed the mug of beer greedily but watched Bargun with suspicion. He finally said, "Old friend? I don't think we were ever friends, Bargun."

Bargun lifted his eyebrows and replied, "Really? Who lifted you out of that gutter and made sure you didn't drown that night?"

"You did. But all my money was gone when I checked my pants the next day."

"The water must have washed it away. I didn't see any money," Bargun countered smoothly.

Jessup hesitated, then reached for the overflowing mug of beer, taking a long pull from it. He set it down and asked, "What do you want from me?" Bargun reached into his pocket, pulled out the sack and placed it in the middle of the table. Jessup had been an alchemist before losing his family and livelihood to drink.

The old man reached for the bag and opened it, peering inside with distaste. "I assume you need this preserved?" He looked closer at the dead bird, spotted the trademark and tried to conceal his alarm without success. "This belongs to Oman. Did you break its neck?"

"I didn't, but I know who did. I also know the penalty for such a deed." Bargun took a sip of his beer and said calmly, "You're right. I need this preserved. It will do me no good as a bag of bones."

"For eight gold coins, I'll have it ready for you in a week," Jessup began reluctantly. He wanted no part in this, but his need for funds outweighed the risk he was taking.

Bargun paid little heed to the old man's demand. "You'll have it ready in three days, and you'll be paid five gold coins. Only you and I know of this. Don't let me hear anything on the street, or I'll come looking for you." With that, he got up from the table and walked out.

Jessup watched with a combination of loathing and fright as the man left the tavern. He would complete his task, but he was well aware that two men could keep a secret only if one of them were dead. He would have to disappear.

CHAPTER 10

O man continued to travel back and forth to Alfheim for council meetings, staying with his mother while he was there. Salem appeared to have abandoned any further attempts at taking over the Jogahoh leadership. Oman's trips were short; his urge to return to his family was stronger than his need to be a leader. His mother knew instinctively that they were keeping something from her but did not push for an explanation. When he was ready, she knew, he would tell her. On occasion, Jossa would leave Anong with Oman and travel home to visit with her sister. Only once did her sister question her about the shoes she had found in their winter home. Jossa brushed it off as nothing more than a wishful thought. Her sister, although suspicious, reluctantly accepted the explanation and was content knowing that Jossa was happier than she had ever seen her.

Anong grew steadily, and before long, she was almost too big for her Jogahoh parents to pick up or carry around. They placed her on a large fur hide at an early age and encouraged her to move about on her own. Happily, she agreed and would struggle about in the long fur, eventually learning to roll over, then finally sit up. The stone around her neck always remained on her. One day, while Jossa was cooking, she heard Anong begin to gurgle with happiness. When she turned around, she saw the little girl on her back, tossing small balls of light into the air. Giggling with delight, she threw the balls from hand to hand and watched them as they spun above her head. A week later, her interest in the balls of light waned. Spotting rays of sunshine coming in through a window, Anong would place her hand in the prism of colours, separate each colour and move them anywhere she wanted. When she was done, the colours would move back to their proper order within the ray of light. One cloudy day, Anong squirmed over to the large mirror beside the fireplace. She sat up and stared at it intently, a grin lighting up her face. Jossa knelt beside her and said, "That's you, Anong."

Anong pointed to the top of the large mirror and asked, "Who dat?"

Jossa saw nothing but a reflection of the room in the mirror. Anong, however, was seeing something or someone, and whatever it was had amused her. Jossa watched the happy girl clap her hands, smile at the mirror and look back at her mother in wonder. Knowing that her daughter would be safe, she kissed her on the cheek and said, "I've got supper to make. I'll be right behind you if you need me."

The spirits began to come closer to the young child. When Anong finally took her first steps, she would stagger about the cabin, holding on to objects as long as she could, then stepping out into the open with reckless abandonment. Just as she was about to lose her balance, invisible hands would steady her. When playing, she would jabber excitedly, but to whom they never knew. Neither Jossa nor Oman was concerned. Anong was never frightened, and her belly laughter let them know the spirits were friendly.

She had an affinity for all the animals. One morning, as Oman stepped onto the porch, he noticed small birds gathered by the front swing, waiting for Anong. When she came out and sat down, she pulled crumbs from her pocket. The birds flew to her lap and began pecking eagerly. She stroked each one gently, scratching their bellies and heads. Once satisfied, they would tuck themselves into her thick sweater and rest there.

By seven years old, Anong was almost as tall as Jossa and only slightly smaller than Oman. She had her own chores to complete, helping Jossa collect eggs and carry water, but she was free to wander wherever she chose most of the time. Her parents were sometimes worried about her venturing too far but knew the spirits would protect her.

One day while exploring, Anong spotted a small clearing lined with grass cropped short by grazing deer. In its centre was a log, and on that log sat a person with their back to her. She was accustomed to seeing spirits around her, but they had always been grownups, and this person was just a boy. Anong walked up behind him and said, "Hello. I've never seen you here before. My name is Anong. What's yours?" The boy's head never turned, and he remained silent, his eyes staring sadly at the ground. She stepped around the log and now stood in front of him, looking at him with concern. He looked slightly older than she was, with a frail, slim build and long, tangled brown hair. He wore worn leather trousers with braces, and his boots had holes in them. She asked, "Are you okay?"

He lifted his face and looked at her. His eyes were a pale blue, and his face was gaunt. In a quiet, accented voice, he replied, "None of the others will play with me. They say they're too old." His lips hadn't moved, and his voice came to her in her head. She walked to the log and sat beside him. Moving her hand close to his leg, she could see her fingers slide into the shimmer of his body. She knew he would feel as cold as winter, like the others. She repeated her question. "Who are you?"

The boy sat silent for a long moment and then replied, "My name is John."

Anong smiled at him and said, "Hello, John. My name is Anong. I live in the cottage on the high ground by the river. I live there with my mom and dad. We have horses, chickens and cows."

"I know," John answered. "I remember the day you came here, but you were a lot smaller then. The old man and I were standing at the tree line, and your mother gave him tobacco."

"Where do you live?"

"We don't live like you do," he said, shifting his body to face her. "We just stay here. Some stay for a long time, like me. Others only stop briefly, then go away."

"Why do you stay?"

He paused, thinking, and said, "I'm not sure. Something happened to me, and I had to go on my own to this next world. When I got here, the old man said the next part of the journey was hard, with many false paths. I'm afraid I'll get lost, so I stay."

Anong felt sorry for the young boy and said, "If you want, we can be friends."

"That would be nice," he said, a flicker of a smile on his lips. "We can play games if you like."

"That would be fun," Anong said. "Can you show me where the creek leads?"

"Sure, that's easy. Let's go," John said, standing up.

A week later, on a particularly hot day, Jossa could not find Anong. She called for the young girl but got no answer. Fearing the worst, she had just begun to saddle her horse to search for her when Anong walked out from the wood line.

Relieved, Jossa ran to the girl, saying, "I've been calling you. Where were you?"

Anong was puzzled and said quizzically, "You told me to be home before supper. Did I miss supper?"

Jossa sighed and said, "No, you didn't miss supper. I was afraid you were lost."

"I can't get lost. John always finds his way back here."

"Who's John?" Jossa asked, surprised.

Anong pointed to John, who was hovering just behind her. "This is John. He's lived here a long time. He knows a lot, and we'll never get lost."

Jossa looked to where the young girl was pointing. She could feel a presence but was unable to see anything. Finally, she said, "Well, I can't see him, Anong. I was worried about you when you didn't return. You went much farther than you were supposed to go. For the next two days, you'll have to stay beside the house and help me with the gardening. Perhaps you can tell John that he can help as well."

Anong sighed but did not object to her mother's demand. She turned to John for a moment, listened to his reply and then said to her mother, "He said he doesn't want to."

"Well, John," Jossa said, "that's what friends do when one gets the other in trouble. They help one another out. Now get cleaned up for supper, Anong. Your father will be home soon."

"Okay," Anong replied and added, "Mother, John says that Father fishes in the wrong spot on the river. The bigger fish are upstream, in the deep, quiet hole around the bend."

Jossa tried not to show her amusement to her serious daughter. "You can tell your father when he gets home."

That evening, once Oman returned, and supper was finished, Jossa asked Anong to lock the chickens in their pen. Oman joined her, and the two strolled out into the yard. The chickens eagerly gathered around the pen door while Anong counted them. She glanced at the rooster and said, "We're missing one of your ladies. You'll have to go find her." Obediently, the rooster ran off. A minute later, he returned, chasing closely behind the inattentive hen. With the chickens now accounted for and safely in their coop, Anong closed the gate, Oman looking on patiently. As they returned to the house, he asked her about what had happened that day. She admitted that she had ventured out too far but explained that the forest was just so much more fun. "And besides," she continued, "I can't get lost when I'm with John. He always knows how to get home."

As they walked, Oman placed his arm around his daughter and asked, "Do you know what Jibay means?" Anong shook her head no, and Oman continued, "It means the Land of the Dead."

Anong looked at him with curiosity and asked, "The dead?"

"Yes," Oman answered. "As long as we can remember, the spirits that were not able to go to the afterlife chose this land to stay in. They remain here until the time is right for them to move on to the next world. Some stay briefly, while others, like your friend, stay for longer periods."

Anong understood now how the boy knew so much about the area and why he was never lost. He had been there for a very long time, since before she was born.

"I know they're not alive, but John is my friend, and we play games together. None of the others want to play."

"You two can play as much as you like. Only promise me one thing. That you and John will always make sure your mother knows where you are going."

"I promise," she replied with a grin.

"And tell him," Oman said with a smile, "thank you for telling me where the fish are hiding."

By the time Anong was ten years old, she had grown taller than both Jossa and Oman. One day, while helping Oman lift a log for the woodshed he was repairing, she asked him, "Why am I so tall?"

"Jossa and I are Jogahoh," he replied honestly. "You are different from us. We will always remain small while you will keep growing for a few more years."

Anong questioned him further. "But why am I different?"

Oman stopped what he was doing and said, "For this story, we will need your mother. If you fetch her, we'll tell you a fine tale."

Anong spun away and, within minutes, the three of them were sitting on the porch with a fresh pot of tea and warm biscuits. Oman started at the beginning. "I found you on a cold winter day, a small, helpless child abandoned in the snow. We took you in and loved you as our own."

"But it is forbidden for anyone other than a Jogahoh to live in our country," Jossa added. "We have a magical boundary that stops anyone but our kind from entering, so how you came to be here, we may never know. If they were ever to discover you, we would all be exiled."

"After we found you, how could we ever let you go?" Oman continued. "You were an innocent child, and we loved you the moment we set eyes on you. That's why we moved here. I knew no one else would enter this territory, and it would be safe for all of us."

Anong took a bite out of her warm biscuit, contemplating what they had told her. "What will happen to me if they find me?"

"We'll deal with that if it happens. Don't worry, for now, my dearest. Know that we will always love and protect you," Oman said, holding his arms out to his daughter. Anong got up and threw herself into him, almost knocking him over in his chair.

"I love you, too," she said happily. "And it makes no difference to me where we live. I like it here. Can I go now?"

Oman and Jossa laughed at her sudden change of subject. "Put your dishes in the sink and fetch me a fresh pail of water," Jossa said. "Then you can go about your day. Where are you going?"

Anong shrugged and replied, "The two smaller horses want me to walk them around the pasture today. Dad's big brown one always picks on them if I'm not there." With that, she put her dishes in the sink, picked up a pail and walked out the door.

Jossa looked at Oman with a mocking grin and said, "I told you that old battle horse of yours was a bully."

••••••

The years passed quickly. King Tibalt and Zakalis continued to search for the girl but found nothing. After many years of fruitless effort, the king's interest dwindled. Zakalis, however, never gave up and knew that, sooner or later, she would reveal herself.

By fifteen years old, Anong had grown into a vibrant, self-sufficient and beautiful young lady. She kept her long, silver-blonde hair in a tidy, tight pigtail, highlighting strong, high cheekbones, a small straight nose and a generous mouth. Blazing with intelligence, her light blue eyes missed nothing. She now stood five and a half feet tall and towered over both her parents.

Their days were filled with homestead tasks, feeding and caring for the animals, gathering hides and preparing trade goods. Their trips to the trading post were usually taken as a family. One morning late in the spring, they realized meat was needed, and trade goods were in short supply. They decided to split up and accomplish both tasks at the same time. Anong and Jossa prepared for a trading trip to the eastern border while Oman was to stay behind and hunt.

At supper that night, before their expected departure, Oman asked, "Are you sure the two of you will be safe going to the trading post?"

"We should be fine," Jossa said, glancing at Anong for confirmation. "We've done it before. Anong will remain hidden on our side of the border."

Anong scrapped the last remnant of food from her plate and popped it into her mouth. "Father, I'd rather go hunting with you. Mom can handle the trading. Besides, you might need help if you get an elk."

Jossa looked at Oman and raised an eyebrow. "She does have a point, and you're not getting any younger."

Oman laughed and said, "I'm not an old man yet. I can handle anything I bring down. Besides, your mother may need help on the way back with all the purchased goods, and I'd rather there be two of you."

Anong replied only begrudgingly; she would rather be hunting and fishing. "All right. But promise me that I can join you on your next hunt."

Oman answered with a patient nod. "It's a promise."

The next morning, Oman packed their horses and ensured nothing had been forgotten. He gave his wife a kiss and walked over to Anong, looking up at her. "You've grown so much," he said as she bent over and kissed his forehead in a mocking tease about his lack of height. "Stop that!"

She laughed and said, "When we go hunting next, I'll get the biggest stag you've ever seen."

"We'll see," he said, and the two women slowly made their way down the trail. Over the next three days, they were up early and riding. By mid-morning on the fourth day, the two women arrived at the border. They found a place where Anong could conceal herself but still watch the trading post.

Jossa said, "I should be back later this afternoon. We'll have time to ride for a couple of hours before bedding down." She walked her horses across the border and toward the market.

Anong watched as her mother crossed through the barrier and then turned to care for her horse. She loosened the girth strap and tied the halter onto a long lead. She found a large spruce tree with pine needles that would make excellent bedding. The lower branches were so long and heavy that they touched the ground, forming a protective wall around her. She settled herself down and watched with curiosity as all types of people mingled among the traders. She spotted her mother, unloading her wares to the same trader she always used, knowing he didn't give the best deal but bought everything. It saved time for bartering on the items she wanted; material for clothing, food stores *and perhaps,* Anong thought, *something for me.*

As always, her eyes gravitated toward the others. She loved Oman and Jossa dearly, but still, she wondered about her real mother and father. *Why did they leave me here? Why am I living with the Jogahoh? Why do I not live with them?* She always asked herself these same questions. Eventually, the combination of the warm sun and quiet surroundings made her eyes heavy. She lay her head on her hands and fell into a deep sleep.

The familiar dream, one she had dreamt so many times before, started immediately. The house was small and shabby. She was in a tiny cradle, staring into the eyes of a tired young woman, when a knock on the door sounded. The young mother answered the door, and a tall woman with long black hair walked into the room. She went to the cradle and lifted Anong up. The two of them solemnly studied each other's eyes. The child smiled at the lady and laughed, a sweet ringing noise that twittered through the room. The woman was startled but smiled back at her before returning her to the cradle. "This one is special. We must be cautious. They will be looking for her."

The two women walked away from the cradle and spoke at length until the young mother began to cry. The dream always ended with her lifting Anong up, kissing her fiercely, hugging her tightly one last time and then giving her to the tall woman.

Anong jolted herself awake. She tried to go back to the dream, but the sound of laughter from children at the trading post got her attention. She always wished she could play with them. At home, there was only John. The difference was these children were real, and the sound of their voices echoed through her.

Out of nowhere, a feeling of impending danger engulfed her. She lifted her head up but couldn't see anything. Her eyes carefully scanned the people at the post, but everything appeared normal. The hair on the back of her neck rose as she sniffed the now-silent air. A rank smell of dirty fur, rotting meat and sweat permeated everything around her. Anong crept from under the tree, determined the direction of the scent and followed it. She moved stealthily, placing her feet around and over dried twigs and branches, stopping to shield her eyes from the glare of the sun and scan the underbrush. After thirty meters, she caught movement from the corner of her eye and focused in tightly. It was a beast, an older one she determined, likely unable to make the return trip to the mountains with its pack. It stood approximately four feet high, with a length from head to tail of ten feet. His head was massive, and his canines were the length of Anong's hand. His jaws gnashed and drooled at the scent of the easy prey in front of him. Its black, matted fur was streaked with grey from age, and he carried an ugly gash over his front right shoulder. If the beast hadn't moved, she would not have seen it. The huge animal advanced stealthily, belly to the ground, stalking the children and selecting his victim. Anong watched its hindquarters tighten; his eyes locked on a small girl playing with the others. Anong knew she needed to act now. She sprung from the underbrush and sprinted as fast as her legs would move through the barrier and toward the small group. The stone that hung around her neck allowed her to pass through without consequence. An oddly familiar, powerful energy started to build in her as she ran, emanating from the birthmark at the centre of her body. She watched in terror as the animal began its charge, oblivious to her. The power within her built now, surging into her hands and feet as she closed the distance between them.

Anong screamed, "Look out," just as the animal leaped into the air, jaws opened, claws out. Anong stopped mid-stride, and time slowed. She perceived the children's terrified faces with a detached sense of understanding as they caught sight of the horror coming at them. She raised her hand and thrust it at the beast. Never had the magic felt so all-encompassing and focused. Energy burst from the palm of her hand and drove into the animal. It slammed into the creature, a red-hot charge that entered one side and burst out the other, instantly killing it. The force of the blast hit the beast in mid-flight, and it dropped with a dull thud onto the ground. Anong was shocked but exhilarated, her body vibrating with strength. *What was that?* Moments later, the energy slowly began to dissipate, leaving her empty and fatigued. She shook herself into action, came up to the carcass, kicked the limp body to ensure it was dead, and then looked behind her to see the children gawking at her. She gazed at them as curiously as they did her. It was the first time she'd been around other people besides Oman and Jossa. She flushed, embarrassed, and said, "You're safe. It's dead, but you'd best go back to the post."

A boy, just a bit younger than her, asked, "Who are you?" Anong understood the question but didn't know what to say. So instead, she pointed toward the Jogahoh border. The boy glanced at the border, confused, and said, "But you're not Jogahoh."

She heard people rushing toward them, shouting, and knew she could not be a part of what was sure to become an interrogation. Anong quickly said, "I must go now" and turned, running swiftly back across the border.

She slid herself back under the evergreen, far enough to be hidden but close enough to observe the group. Anong was dismayed when she realized that Jossa was among the adults. She couldn't hear their voices but ascertained that they were asking what had happened. The children pointed toward the dead beast and to where she'd run across the barrier. The boy who had spoken to her was trying to describe what she looked like. There was apparent confusion with her height, with the boy insisting she was taller than he was. The adults laughed at the children and pointed back toward Jossa, who stood looking worried. It was clear that they did not believe the boy. After a few minutes, they gathered up the children and returned to the post, dragging the beast's carcass behind them. Jossa stood alone and looked across the border to where she'd left Anong.

······

If Anong had been instructed in her ability and how to use it that morning, the burst of power would have been minimal and just enough to kill the beast. Unfortunately, her fear resulted in an untrained blast of magic that pushed out across the land with the strength of a hurricane. The surge was invisible to an ordinary person, but the chosen ones who knew and studied magic felt its force. It rushed toward them, gaining speed and enveloping everything in its path. It took their breath away, leaving them speechless. They realized immediately that someone new, with exceptional ability, was on the horizon.

Zakalis gasped and clenched his hand to his heart, stopping mid-stride as the power pushed through him, making him stumble. It took him several minutes to finally catch his breath. He had felt this before, many years ago, when an essence had come to tease him. Then, he remembered what the stones had revealed to him. It was the girl, he knew, without a doubt. *The child would be coming of age now.*

······

Esma stopped her gardening and rose from the ground, slowly turning herself to face toward the west. Something was coming. She held out both her arms, greeting and embracing the fierce wave as it slid through her. The rush of power left her feeling rejuvenated and young again. *Finally, child, you've used what has been given to you.*

······

That night, well away from the trading post, Anong and Jossa sat around the fire after supper. Staring into the flames, Anong apologized again, "I'm sorry I put us in danger today. I'm not sure I know what happened."

Jossa replied, "Don't apologize. You did the right thing and saved all those children."

The fire crackled and danced as Anong began to dig into the coals with a stick, saying, "The magic was different than what I've used before. I felt a power start in my chest as soon as I saw the beast begin its charge. It was so strong, Mother. When the animal leaped, I acted automatically."

Jossa held her close and kissed the side of her head, saying, "The magic was different because you used it to protect others. When your father found you, we knew you were special. Your magic has gotten stronger as you've grown."

"While I was waiting for you, I fell asleep and dreamt my birth mother was holding me but then gave me over to another woman."

Jossa put a glove around her hand and picked up the pot from the fire, pouring coffee into her mug. She said, "That could be a memory of where you were born and where you came from. I believe the other woman in your dream knew of the power you possessed and knew you were possibly in danger. She must have brought you to us to keep you hidden and safe." Jossa paused and took a long drink before continuing, "Today has shown me that you are ready for our ritual to take you into adulthood. We'll speak more about this with your father when we get home."

Anong, still watching the fire, answered quietly, "I would like that very much."

The two sat for a while longer, then laid out their bedrolls and slept side-by-side. The next morning, they started their journey home. Three days later, just before sunset, they arrived to see Oman with his kill, an elk, strung up in the trees. "You're finally home! How was your trading trip?"

Jossa got off her horse and embraced him, whispering in his ear, "The short answer is that all went well. The long answer is that we will talk later."

That evening at supper, Oman said, "Now tell me what happened."

Jossa turned to Anong and said, "This is your story. Go ahead."

Anong lifted her head, cleared her throat and looked at her father, saying, "Something happened at the trading post."

Oman put his fork down, dread in his eyes. "Did anyone see you?" he asked, alarmed.

Anong nodded. "Yes, some children."

"But the adults didn't believe them when they described her. They thought she could only be Jogahoh. We're safe, for now," Jossa confirmed.

"Tell me what happened."

With that, Anong began, with Oman listening intently.

Anong finished with, "I was afraid I'd given our secret away. I'm sorry."

Oman reached over and placed his hand on Anong's arm. "That was courageous of you, saving those children. I've known both grown men and Jogahoh that would never have taken on a beast, but you did. You placed others ahead of yourself."

Jossa looked over to Oman and said, "I think it's time she goes through the right of passage."

Oman nodded. "I agree."

Jossa asked, "Tomorrow?"

"Yes, tomorrow."

CHAPTER 11

A knock on King Tibalt's door announced the arrival of his sorcerer. "Enter," the king said impatiently.

The door opened, and Zakalis came into the chamber, bowing before the eastern king. "Sire," he said, "you summoned me?"

"Yes. There are rumours about an incident at a trading post along the Jogahoh border. They said that a young girl came across the barrier and saved a group of children from a beast. They also claim she wasn't armed and used some kind of power to blast a hole through the animal."

"I've heard the rumours as well, but I'm concerned that the only witnesses to this were children."

"It still has to be investigated. I'm sending you and two guards to the trading post to question everyone. I need you to determine what happened."

"Of course, Sire. I'll pack my things now."

"I expect you to be back within the week. Tell no one of your purpose and let the guards ask the questions."

"As you wish, Sire," the sorcerer said, bowing before leaving the room. Zakalis smiled to himself as he hurried back to his quarters. He was anxious to finally meet this child.

······

Salem sat in his office in King Merck's court, just finishing up some work. A flash of colour at the window caught his eye, and a cardinal landed with a message pack strapped across its back. He walked over to the window, let the bird in and withdrew the message from its bag. He unfolded the tiny piece of paper and covered it with a cloth to return the document to its full size. The message was a weekly report from Sakewan to keep him apprised of the situation in the country. Salem, uninterested, skimmed through most of it until he got down to the bottom of the text. It referenced an incident at a northern trading post. It spoke of a child crossing the border from Jogahoh territory, killing a beast and saving some children. He knew the area well and had played there as a child when his father used the same trading post. It was near the land of the Jibay. He shivered. Even the name made a cold chill run up his spine. *Something is happening here,* he thought. *I need to look for myself.* Salem sent word to King Merck that he'd be gone for a few days and asked that the wizard transport him to Sakewan.

Two days later, Salem walked his horses across the border to the trading post. He moved through the small kiosks until he found the man that ran the market. Salem came up to him and said, "Good day, sir. My name is Salem. I am the ambassador from the Jogahoh to King Merck's court. Can I talk with you about the incident a few days ago? People are reporting that a beast was killed and some children saved."

The man stopped what he was doing, agitation evident on his face. He sighed impatiently and said, "I'm busy and don't have time for this. I've told the story so many times I'm starting to believe it myself."

Salem persisted and said, "My brother is the leader of our people. We need to find out more about what happened here."

The man stopped, surprised, and looked down at Salem. "Why don't you ask him? His wife, Jossa, was here when it happened."

Salem stared at the man, stunned and completely taken aback by his words. "I didn't know that."

"You didn't know she was here?"

"We live a great distance apart," he replied defensively. "Who else has been asking?"

"Today? The king's men. They're still here, over in the clearing where the beast was killed," the man replied.

Salem followed the trader's directions and soon came to where a tall, gaunt man in a long coat stood, inspecting the ground.

"Salem, I thought you might be here," the man said calmly, raising an eyebrow. "I take it you're as interested in this as I am?"

Salem slowed and studied the man's features before admitting, "I'm afraid you have me at a disadvantage. Have we met?"

"No," the man admitted, looking down at him. "My name is Zakalis. I am King Tibalt's sorcerer. He sent me here to determine what happened."

"Have you found anything?" Salem watched the sorcerer with distaste. He distrusted anyone with magical gifts but would use them if it benefited him.

Zakalis replied, "Not much, really. The whole area has been trampled over. You can draw your own conclusions." The two strode over to where the beast had been killed. The remnants of blood and fur had attracted insects and already smelled faintly of rotting meat. "There has been no rain, so nothing has been washed away." The sorcerer extended his arms, palms facing out, and began to turn his body around in a circle.

Salem, suspicious, asked, "What are you doing?"

Zakalis spun for a few more moments and then stopped. "Every living thing leaves an impression that lingers for a short time after they depart. The sooner I get to a location, the fresher and more accurate the scene I can detect. I'll show you." With a wave of his palm, a scene opened in front of them. "You see everything as it is at this moment in time. What we are looking for is days old and will not be as precise." Zakalis waved his hand in the air as if he were paging backward through a book, muttering to himself as the scenes changed. "No, no, nothing… aaahhh, there it is."

In front of him, a scene replayed itself. He watched as a blurred figure of a young woman that was most certainly not Jogahoh burst through the trees and ran across the barrier. He could see the children frozen in fear and heard their screams. The scene shuddered and skipped ahead to reveal Jossa and the others running into the area. Salem studied Jossa carefully. While everyone's attention had been on the beast and the children, she was looking back at the border as if she were searching for someone. As quickly as it started, the scene evaporated.

Zakalis noted Salem's reaction and said, "You've seen something."

"The young woman that came across the border wasn't Jogahoh," Salem said carefully.

"I think a man with one eye could make that distinction," the sorcerer stated wryly. "The question is, how did she move through the barrier? The magic will let no one through that isn't Jogahoh. To ensure the boundary was still active, I even had one of my guards try to enter. It rejected him. So how could she get across?"

Salem ran everything through his mind one more time and admitted, "I don't have an answer. I was only able to recognize my brother's wife, Jossa."

The sorcerer said, "The Jogahoh woman?"

"Yes."

"That's what I missed," Zakalis exclaimed, his voice rising with excitement.

"While the others were concerned about the beast, she was looking for someone back toward the border," Salem said. "Oman and Jossa live by themselves somewhere up here, but I'm not sure where. It still doesn't explain the appearance of the girl."

The sorcerer remembered the story the stones had told him and knew beyond a doubt this was the child he had been searching for. He realized he needed a Jogahoh contact to find the girl and set about to convince Salem to work with him. "Many years ago, I was warned that a female child had been born with power, a magic that could not be contained and would be dangerous for the world. I was told she had been taken and hidden away. For years, I thought nothing of it because I would have been able to feel her magic. It makes sense now. I believe she was hidden in your land. The other day when this happened, she passed the boundary. That was when I felt a strange ripple of power. It only lasted for a moment, but it must have been her."

Salem took a few steps from the man, his eyes looking back across the border. Realizing a possible link, he turned and asked, "How long ago was it you were warned about this magic?"

"The first time near the end of winter, some fifteen years ago. If she's coming of age now, she'll be a threat to everyone. She must be detained."

Salem silently counted back the years that Oman and Jossa had ventured out on their own. Hesitantly, he said, "I'm not sure if I have an answer yet, and I need to investigate this further. How can I contact you?"

Zakalis took a knife from his sheath, cut off a lock of his hair and placed it in a pouch. "Take one hair and drop it into a pan of water. My image will appear, and we can talk. But be careful," he said in warning, "the girl is dangerous."

Salem took the pouch and put it in his pocket, saying, "I will be. Have a safe journey back." He turned and began to walk away, but the sorcerer's call stopped him.

"One last thing, Salem. I was there the day your father was killed. I know you were overlooked by him. It should have been you, not Oman, leading the Jogahoh." Zakalis took a long pause, knowing he could use the man's ego to get what he wanted out of him. He allowed his words to sink in and said, "If you assist me, I'll ensure you get what you deserve and are placed where you rightfully belong."

Salem nodded silently, then turned and walked away. He knew that conspiring with this magic man might be dangerous, but his desire for power overrode his fears. Besides, he reasoned, Zakalis had told him the girl was a danger to the Jogahoh. Salem rode his horse across the border and found the area he'd seen the girl come from. He moved through the woods and soon spotted a large spruce tree where a person had rested. Walking toward it, he found footprints heading to and from the border and placed his foot alongside one of them. This was no Jogahoh.

•••••

The sun was rising as Oman left the cabin and walked to the tree line. He cut down a young sapling, skinning off the bark and smoothing down the nubs that protruded from the shaft. Oman held it out in front of him, eyed it to ensure it was straight and checked its balance. Feeling it was still off, he worked on it for a few more minutes and retested it. Finally, he carved a small ring around the circumference of the shaft in its centre. Sliding his hand along the wood, he could feel the ridges of the ring. Now a person could feel where the centre of the shaft was without looking. He stood up, then spun it smoothly above his head and back in front of him. It felt right, and the balance was exact. It was no longer a piece of wood but a fighting cane.

Jossa was up and making breakfast when Oman returned to the cabin. She asked him, "Are you hungry?"

"Yes," Oman answered and thanked her as she placed a plate of eggs and meat in front of him. They sat in comfortable silence as they ate. Finally finished, he pushed his plate away and asked, "Where is Anong?"

"She's already eaten and is upstairs, getting ready."

He called for her and heard her footsteps on the stairs. A moment later, she appeared in the kitchen and said, "Good morning. Are you ready?"

"I am. I hope you are, as well. For the next month, we'll be training. I need you to be up early every day, so when the sun is up, so are we. We'll go to bed only when the day's lessons are done." He brought out a small backpack and placed it in front of her. "You need to keep this packed with warm clothes, something to repel the rain, fire-starting tools and a bit of food and water. Make sure the backpack is always within arm's reach. Always keep your knife on your belt. I've made a cane for you; it's outside on the porch. Any questions?"

"No," she answered eagerly. She'd been waiting for this moment since her parents had first spoken of it. With a wide grin on her face, she hoisted the backpack and hurried upstairs to organize and pack.

When Anong left the room, Jossa admonished Oman, saying fondly, "Go easy on her. She's not one of your men, and it will be her first time with any of this."

"It's important for her to learn," Oman replied solemnly. "I'll go easy on her, just as my father was to me and his father was to him."

"That's what I'm afraid of," she said and took the plates from the table without another word.

Anong finished collecting her clothes and came downstairs to pack food and water for the day. When they were ready, they walked out onto the porch. Oman picked up the cane and handed it to her. "This is the fighting cane I made. What did I say about it and your gear?"

Anong formally accepted the weapon and replied solemnly, "I need to keep this and my gear within arm's reach at all times."

"Good," Oman approved. "Your first lesson was a success." He turned to his wife and, kissing her lightly on the cheek, said, "We'll see you tonight." With that, Oman picked up his cane, and they both walked into the forest.

They hiked at a brisk pace for an hour until they came into an open field. Taking her pack off, Anong watched as Oman began to move around the area. He started a series of coordinated fighting moves with his cane. Her father glided smoothly, circling the cane high above his head, then rotating into a half-circle, as if opponents were approaching from behind. Oman maneuvered the cane like a spear at first. It appeared to take on the life of a sword and, finally, a defensive club. After ten minutes, he stopped and motioned for her to sit on a log. He said, "I want you to sit here, close your eyes and listen." Anong did as she was told, and twenty minutes later, Oman whispered to her,

"What do you hear?"

"I hear the wind and a squirrel rustling in the leaves," she replied.

"Yes. What else?"

"A small mouse just walked by me, and there is a deer to our right, grazing in the grass."

"This is your second lesson. To listen. You have been granted a gift. You can hear the animals even more clearly than most. Ordinary people hear but never really listen. When you listen, you understand what the forest wants to tell you. You can use this to protect yourself and others. When there is sound, and when animals move and speak, you can assume everything is safe. If the forest is quiet, and you hear nothing, there is danger. Before I go to bed at night, I step onto the porch and just listen. If I hear the owl hooting in the tree, the elk walking through the high grass and our animals resting quietly, I know everything is safe, and I can rest easy. If I hear no sound, it may mean something else is out there, and I should take the time for a walk around. Listen like this every chance you get. It may help you someday."

Oman walked her to the centre of the clearing. "This will be your first session with the cane. It can be used as a long stick or a walking pole, but it becomes a spear if I tie a knife to one end. If I have no other means to tie my shelter up off the ground, it becomes a tent pole." Oman positioned Anong into a fighting stance. "Always remember to keep your feet shoulder-width apart, toes pointed in the direction of the threat or where you want to go. The left shoulder leads slightly, and your right shoulder is back. Your cane remains at your side, one end on the ground and the shaft running up your body. This is your rest position. When you bring the cane up, hold on to it with both hands. Your right hand is back, and your left hand is forward, pointing toward the threat. This is the on-guard position. At the same time, take a small step forward with your left foot. From here, you can move to any position but always come back to the on-guard."

Oman moved around the circle, thrusting out with his cane as if he were attacking an enemy. He then went on the defensive as if he were countering an opponent's blows. After demonstrating several different progressions, he finally moved into the rest position. Oman walked over to Anong, leaned on his cane and, with a smile, said, "It can also be used to lean against when you are tired." She laughed, and Oman continued, "When we went to war in the east, we had little training in their type of warfare. Most of us had never seen a sword, much less held one. King Merck talked with my father, your grandfather, about getting us ready for battle and integrating with their forces. We needed to learn their basics of movement and defense. We had to learn to work with their soldiers. Our canes were our strength, and we used them while training. We learned how to work together, use their formations to our advantage and use our size against the enemy. Finally, they made swords and armour to fit, giving us a great advantage, especially in tight quarters. In time, we grew into a cohesive fighting unit."

Anong stepped back, lifted her cane and pressed the end of it onto Oman's chest, giggling. "You wouldn't be able to get near enough to me to do anything. I'm much bigger than you."

His next movement was swift, and the strike was harsh as it slammed into her leg. She let out a surprised scream as Oman swept her feet from under her, and she landed on her back. Oman stood calmly above her, cane to her throat and said, "You were saying?"

Anong got up, ruefully rubbing her leg, and said, "That hurt."

"The pain in your leg or your pride?" he asked. "Now, pick up the cane, and take up the on-guard position." She dutifully got up, a slight hint of resentment on her face. "Do you remember your second lesson today?"

"You taught me the rest position."

"No. Your second lesson was to listen. I suggest you start." Oman moved to the centre of the clearing, and they began to drill. Slowly and methodically, they went over the movements, with Oman demonstrating and Anong following. Her natural abilities quickly established themselves. She had little difficulty learning and repeating the motions in sequence. Sweat began to run in rivulets down both their flushed faces. Still, they trained. Hours later, Oman looked toward the west as the sun made its way down to the horizon. "Enough for today. Pick up your kit, and let's go home," he said before asking, "Can I see your leg?"

Still panting with exertion, Anong pulled up her leather trouser, showing a swollen calf and a large bruise encompassing it. "I'm okay. I can use my magic to heal it."

"No. Not today. It's important for you to learn to work through this," Oman said seriously, looking up at her.

She nodded silently. The two began their walk home, Oman content with the day's progression and Anong tired but exhilarated. She placed her hand onto her father's shoulder and said teasingly, "I could get you in real trouble if I showed this bruise to Mother."

"I know, and I'd rather fight a beast with no weapons than face your mother if she saw that leg of yours."

The two continued for some time before Anong spoke again, saying, "I want to learn more, Father, but I can't seem to think quickly enough."

"Be patient, Anong. There is much to learn. Once you do, your body will react instinctively. Everything has a place and will reveal itself in time," Oman replied.

••••••

Salem searched the area across the border and discovered where two horses had returned from the trading post and joined with the first tracks he had found. For the next day, he slowly followed the trail to the north, stopping where they stopped, sleeping where they'd slept. At each location, he searched carefully for clues to their identity. Nothing had been left behind, and the areas had been meticulously cleaned up. *Perhaps,* he thought, *the clue is in no clues.* He reflected back to when they were children. He would leave bits of scrap around the fire when they were camping, and Oman hated it. He would walk around, making sure every last piece was picked up. He'd always say to Salem, "I don't want anyone to know who was here."

Salem looked around the area again, assessing, and said softly, "Like husband, like wife." He remounted his horse and followed the trail for three hours, stopping just as he reached the land of the Jibay. Sharply pulling up his horse, Salem dismounted and ensured the tracks led into the Jibay Territory and not away from it. Dismayed, he stared ahead of him, remembering when their father would take them there. He'd always hated this place. Hated the whispers, the flickers of movement from the side of his eye and the odd touches on his neck. It never seemed to trouble Oman or his father. They ignored it because of its peace and good fishing. He remembered that his father always brought tobacco and sage to ward anything away and satisfy the spirits. Salem's thoughts were disrupted when his horse pawed the ground and snorted abruptly, tossing its head. He pulled sharply on the horse's reins and said, "Calm down. I don't like the place, either." He mounted and rode back the way he'd come, hoping to create some distance between them and whatever the horse had seen or felt.

CHAPTER 12

King Tibalt stood on the high outer wall of his castle. As far as he could see and beyond, everything fell under his reign. He felt invincible, and the day was a fine one. The castle was impregnable, finely crafted and strong. His army was fully trained and ready for battle. His plans were finally coming into play, and everything in his life was in order. He stepped confidently onto the upper causeway that took him between the towers, passing the guards on duty. They acknowledged him as he strode by and paid their respects before continuing their watch. He was interrupted by a horn that signalled approaching riders. Taking out his glass, he extended it, focusing on them. From the colour of the horsemen's flags, it appeared that Zakalis had returned from the northern trading post. He watched silently as the group stopped in front of the drawbridge and waited for it to be lowered.

Crossing over, they dismounted, where they were met by the Sergeant of the Guard, who recognized them but insisted on reviewing their orders. The protocol must be followed. Satisfied that all was in order, the sergeant nodded to the guardsmen, who lifted the massive iron gate and allowed them access to the inner courtyard.

Tibalt bellowed from above, "Sergeant, let the sorcerer know I want to see him within the hour."

"Will do, Your Majesty," he called back and simply turned his head to Zakalis. In a dismissive tone, he asked, "Magic Man, did you hear the king's order?"

Zakalis was insulted. The man was an uneducated simpleton, in his opinion, and unworthy of his time. He spat back, "You imbecile! How many times do I have to tell you I'm not a mere magic man?"

The sergeant stepped in close to the sorcerer, smacking the

front of his helmet into Zakalis' forehead. The sorcerer reeled back in pain, surprised, and held his head. The man pressed closer again, his rank breath leaching into Zakalis' nostrils. "I don't care what you think you are, or what others call you, Magic Man. If you're not in the king's company within the hour, I will hunt you down and throw you in the dungeon myself." With that, he spun around and ordered, "Lower the gate."

A rushed hour later, Zakalis stood in front of the king. Tibalt did not waste any time.

"So tell me, what did you learn?"

"Everything we heard about the attack by the beast was correct. I saw what remained of the animal and examined the hide. It had an entry and exit wound from a blast of some sort. I proceeded to where the body was recovered and did a memory recall spell. The beast was killed by someone that had come over from the Jogahoh border."

The king, impatient, said, "Go on, man."

"There is more to this story that must be known, Sire. The Jogahoh ambassador to King Merck's court arrived to investigate as well. He is the older brother of Oman, the Jogahoh leader."

The king stood silent as he angrily recalled his final, humiliating battle with Merck. "I remember now. My generals advised me the Jogahoh leader had been mortally wounded. Before he died, he made the younger son his heir. Who is this older brother? Is he upset about not being chosen?"

"His name is Salem. He didn't show it, but there is still deep resentment there. I need to show you what his reaction was as he watched my spell unfold." With a wave of his hand and a short incantation, Zakalis replayed the memory. "Watch his reaction when he sees a human come across the barrier and kill the beast. He also recognized a Jogahoh woman at the scene, whom he identified as Oman's wife. She wasn't looking at the beast; she was looking to the border. She knew this girl and was looking for her. The key is the girl. I believe she is who we have been looking for. Salem will work with us, and if he finds anything, he has agreed to contact me."

"I don't understand how a non-Jogahoh can cross over the border. I've personally witnessed people being blocked by the magic. It's always been impenetrable."

The sorcerer presented Tibalt with the only conclusion he could come up with. "Sire, I can think of only one way. Ancient magic was used to hide her within the Jogahoh territory." Zakalis hesitated to tell the king about Esma, the witch. If he told him about her, the king would want to find and use her.

Moreover, Zakalis was jealous of her ability and, if she was found, his services might be rendered useless. "Years ago, I fell into a deep sleep, and my spirit was pulled from my body. It was drawn to a small cottage. Inside, I was beckoned again by a trunk. Inside were two glowing stones that spoke to me. They told me they were used to take and hide a child with power in the land of the Jogahoh. I didn't believe such a thing could happen and dismissed everything as a dream until the incident at the border."

King Tibalt studied his sorcerer with interest and said, "None of what you say explains how this person can cross through the border."

"I think this person bears another stone that allows them to go through the barrier, just as it did when it came to the Jogahoh many years ago. This must be the child we have been looking for. It is the barrier itself that has kept her hidden. As soon as she came across the barrier and used her power to kill the beast, I was able to feel her." The sorcerer was adamant, and his face flushed with purpose. "We must find this girl to see what powers she possesses. If she is as strong as I think, we can use her to retake what was lost in the war."

King Tibalt looked up at the ceiling, thinking silently before saying, "Set yourself up with this Salem person. If this girl is as powerful as you say, I want her. Do you have anything else, Sorcerer?"

"No, Sire," Zakalis replied, bowing slightly.

"You're dismissed." The sorcerer nodded and slipped excitedly out of the room; his mind already busy with a plan. Tibalt waved over his deputy, who was sitting at the back of the room. The king spoke calmly. "Ever since I was a young boy, I would always know when someone wasn't telling me everything. The sorcerer isn't completely lying to me, but there is something he is keeping back for himself. Keep an eye on him. He'll know you're there, but I want him to know that I'm watching."

· · · · · ·

Anong's training had come a long way in the last month. Her mind, as agile as her body, finally grasped the concepts of fighting and self-defense. In the short time they trained, her muscles had become accustomed to rigorous workouts, and she was getting stronger every day.

Oman stood in front of her in the on-guard position. He moved around the girl with his cane, feigning a strike and then pulling back. Again and again, he attacked from different angles, trying to exploit an opening. She countered his every movement with her own, batting his cane away and counterattacking with open strikes. Anong abruptly swung her cane high above her head, feigning an attack from above. Oman moved to counter the blow, but Anong shifted her weight and spun in the opposite direction. Oman, sensing the fake, forced his arms down and countered the attack. He only made partial contact with her, and the blow came in low, smashing into his ribs.

The strike forced air from his chest, and pain streaked through his body. He fell to his knees with a gasp. Anong came back to the on-guard position but immediately realized the blow had made it through his defenses. She dropped her weapon and knelt beside him. With a dismayed expression on her face, she asked, "Are you hurt?"

He looked up at her, wincing in pain. "I am." The words had

just left his mouth when he drew his cane onto her chest. "But now you're dead, and I will live another day. What have I taught you about finishing the fight? The last strike has to be thrown, and you didn't do that. You never know what your opponent will do."

Anong protested angrily, "How can I finish this? You're my father, not an unknown enemy."

"How you train is how you fight. If you hesitate in training, you will hesitate in battle. You must finish with a final blow. In the midst of battle, in the confusion and chaos, you have no time to think, only to react." Anong said nothing but bent down to help him to his feet. He refused her, using the cane to get his feet up under him, and slowly stood up. "I'm fine," he said. "I can do this on my own."

"Father, you're hurt. Let me look after you."

"I'll live. I've been hurt a lot worse than this."

She bent and lifted his shirt to examine the damage she had inflicted. An angry red welt was beginning to develop across the lower half of his ribcage. "I can fix this," she said, reaching out with her other hand to place it over the injury.

Oman gently pushed her hand away. "I will not make use of your magic. I'll be fine in a few days."

"Why do you not use your own, then?" she asked, puzzled.

The two made their way over to a large boulder, where Oman gingerly sat down. He gestured for Anong to join him and said, "There is no great need for magic, and pain is the perfect teacher. It is a reminder to do better."

"You allow everyone else to use the magic when someone is hurt. Why not use it for yourself?"

"I could, but sometimes you have to feel the pain to understand the full reality of the situation. This pain has taught me that you are better and stronger than you were a month ago. It also reminds me that I have slowed considerably over the last twenty years." He laughed softly. "It can teach so many lessons if you only listen to it, but you have to pay attention." He paused, shifting his weight from his injured side and grimaced.

Anong got to her feet and walked over to the water, filling the ladle and taking a long drink. She refilled it and walked back to Oman, handing it to him. Finally, she asked, "Why did you tell me the last strike must always be thrown?"

"What would you do if you were surrounded by a mass of people, all of them fighting?" Oman pulled out a silver piece and, in a swirl of magic, around them appeared a mirage of figures entwined in battle. Anong walked toward the apparition. She could see the sweat on their faces and the fear in their eyes. She felt their bodies surging hard as they fought. The images clashed repeatedly, and she watched, both horrified and fascinated. Beside her, one man was smashed to the ground. When his opponent turned to fight another, the fallen man stood up and ran his sword through him.

Anong turned to look back at her father, who had an unfathomable, sorrowful look on his face. He admitted, "You're the only person I've ever shown that to. It was our first time in battle, and the man was one of my closest friends." She walked back and sat beside him, taking his hand. Oman could feel her shaking. "I didn't mean to scare you. I only meant to teach you."

Anong, her face strained, stammered, "I could feel everything. The fear, the anger, the pain. I saw what happened when the last blow wasn't thrust. His surprise and then, just before he died, the regret of never going home." She hesitated and said, "I understand now."

"Good," Oman said, pushing himself up. His face twisted, and he staggered slightly as he returned to the centre, held his weapon up, and called out, "On-guard."

For another thirty days, Oman trained Anong hard. He pushed the young girl almost to her breaking point and then eased off. Every challenge became increasingly more complex and forced her to become focused and resourceful. Oman refused to navigate around her feelings and fears. Instead, he challenged her to face them, saying, "I know it hurts. Break out and fight through it. You can do this."

Anong's upbringing had taught her the basics of hunting, camping and caring for herself. She was already conversant in what plants were safe to eat and what could be used for medicine. Oman took those basics into a survival mode existence, showing her how to stay alive if she found herself with nothing.

A day of hiking up the glacier and traversing icy streams left her on the verge of hypothermia. Setting up a makeshift camp that evening, she could hardly carry the wood to the fire pit. Her hands shook as she tried to spark the tinder with her flint. She knew she could have easily used her magic, but she resisted the urge, remembering what her father had said. Finally, a spark flew, and she was able to build it into a small flame. Taking her bundle of sticks, she slowly nursed and coaxed the fire to life. Within minutes, it was stable, and she ran back to the stream for water. With a small pot of tea starting to boil, she stripped off her wet clothes and put on a dry set. When their tea was ready, she sat beside Oman, shaking uncontrollably. He took the hot beverage from her, placed it on the ground and said, "Follow my lead." Anong, shaking violently now, nodded mutely and watched her father as he sat cross-legged.

Oman said, "Breathe in deeply. Hold it for a second. Then push it all out. You need to get every ounce of air out before the next breath." As he inhaled, Oman watched her mimic his actions. Her eyes closed softly as she got into the rhythm and continued to listen to Oman's voice. "Breathe in deeply. Now force it all out. Picture a fire starting to burn in your belly. Look into it. Feel its heat and feel its power as it moves through you, warming everything." Oman studied her, concerned. She began to calm, and a small smile escaped him when the blue in her lips finally subsided. "Slow your breathing into a normal rhythm, keep yourself calm, and keep the fire within you burning." Oman hesitated momentarily and then told her, "Stand up." Anong opened her eyes and got to her feet. She still felt cold, but it was controllable, not like before.

She stepped closer to the fire and said, "What was that we just did?"

"That was your body looking after itself once you let it."

"Why didn't you teach me that before?"

"Because you weren't ready."

"I was ready a month ago," she said. "Well, perhaps not a month, but definitely a week ago."

"You weren't," he chuckled, throwing another log on the fire. "I needed to break you down, get you out of your comfort zone. Then just maybe, you'll be ready for something new. The old you may have curled up by the fire, waiting for the heat to warm you, or you may have used your magic. You must always fight to take that first step. You can never give in or give up. The practise will heat you up but be careful. It burns a lot of energy, so have some food ready." He handed her a piece of dried meat. "The technique can be used when you're scared, lost or tired. It will clear your mind and place you on the right path." With that, Oman patted her leg fondly and said, "You did well, Anong. I'm proud of you."

Her gaze turned to him, and she managed only a tired, "Thanks," as she chewed the piece of meat.

CHAPTER 13

Salem had been back in King Merck's court for the last two months. He could still not fully understand the tracks he'd followed back into the land of the Jibay. It was all straightforward, everything except for the girl. That made no sense. The magic had stopped anyone other than the Jogahoh for as long as he could remember. His head started to ache, so Salem threw on his cloak and walked outside into the fresh air.

He wanted the leadership of the Jogahoh and knew that if he helped Zakalis bring about his brother's downfall, that leadership would be his. Whatever Oman and Jossa knew, it would be their undoing if they were involved in this. He had no proof, yet somehow, he had a feeling they were. If this was the key to regaining his position, so be it. He remembered the look on Jossa's face as she searched the woods near the barrier. She had known the girl was there.

It all makes sense now. The reason they had moved off by themselves, the tracks he'd followed to the land of the Jibay. The idea was obviously to hide something or someone, to keep it away and hidden. Because if the truth were found out, they would be cast out.

For Salem, revealing this would mean betraying his brother, his own flesh and blood. A chill in the air made him shiver, and Salem walked back to his council hall quarters. Across from him was a portrait of his father in full battle dress. The painting had been completed when the leader was still a young man. In the picture, he showed no sign of age, and his hair was still a brilliant red, with no threads of silver streaking through it. The look in his father's eyes seemed to challenge him. It seemed to say, *how dare you even think of betraying your own*? Salem laughed grimly as he got up from the chair and walked over to the portrait. He gripped the sides of the frame and said, "I've wanted to do this for a long time." With that, he pulled down hard on the painting, snapping the cord that secured it to the wall and threw it harshly onto the floor. "You ask how I can betray my own blood? Easily, old man." He spat viciously into his father's face and summoned a guard.

The man entered the room and asked, "Yes, sir?"

"Get me a bowl of water immediately."

A few minutes later, the guard was back with the bowl and placed it on a table. "Is there anything else?"

"That picture. Take it out of here.

"Where would you like me to put it, sir?" the guard asked, confused.

"The burn pit," Salem replied scornfully.

The man picked up the painting and asked, "Are you sure, sir? I could just move it elsewhere if you prefer."

Salem turned his back on the guard, dismissing him with a curt, "I said, take it to the burn pit."

After the man left, Salem locked the door and turned to the bowl of water on the table. He took a pouch from his pocket and pulled out a single strand of silver hair, placing it beside the bowl. Salem knew precisely what he wanted but would need the sorcerer's help. He wanted to rule the Jogahoh by any means necessary, even if it meant getting rid of his brother. Salem picked up the strand and dropped it into the water. A pale white mist rose from the bowl, stopping just above it and slowly moulded itself into the face of the sorcerer.

"I've been waiting for you. What have you found?"

Salem bent forward, speaking in a low tone, "I followed tracks to the land of the Jibay and know that they are in there. Unfortunately, I haven't been able to confirm that the girl has powers and couldn't go any further."

"Couldn't or didn't want to?" Zakalis asked.

Salem was immediately defensive, unable to tell the sorcerer he was terrified to go into the land without protection. "I've been gone from the kingdom for too long and had to return. I'll need your help to get into the Jibay land, in any case."

"Understandable. Go on," the sorcerer agreed.

"If I go there, Oman will know it's me. We're the only family that's been there, and it's too soon for me to show my hand. Can you give me something I can use? Then I can bring her out and hand her to you at the border," Salem bargained.

Zakalis thought for some time. He knew of only one magick that had the power to deal with the Jibay and contain someone with the girl's ability. Finally, he said, "I have something that can help you. We need to meet in person so I can give it to you."

Salem smiled grimly, satisfied. "We'll meet you south of the trading post, where the two rivers join. We'll be on the north side of the fork."

"We? I thought you were coming alone." The sorcerer said, immediately suspicious.

"I'll need someone to assist me if we find the girl. His name is Bargun, and I can use him without worry. Besides, if there is any kind of problem, I can easily get rid of him. No one would miss him."

Zakalis kept his anger to himself because he knew he needed the man to get the job done. "Keep the circle of knowledge small. The less your people know of this, the better off you'll be. I'll need time to prepare. The magick I'll be using is involved and is developed in stages. I can be there in a month."

Salem agreed without hesitation. "One month from today, three hours before sunset." He paused and then began, "Now, for what I want in return..."

The sorcerer cut him off before he could continue. "Salem," he drawled mockingly, "I am certain that I already know what it is you want. I must warn you that power sometimes clouds the good judgement of men. Be careful, my friend. It can be a slippery slope."

"I may not have your talents, but I'm willing to do the dirty work. I expect to be rewarded."

Now tired and bored with the negotiation, the sorcerer uttered, "Salem, I'll meet you one month from today."

Salem was unable to reply. The image had already disappeared back into the bowl.

CHAPTER 14

Oman and Anong returned from their last hike up the glacier face and sat with Jossa at the kitchen table, finishing their meal. Anong was tired but exhilarated. She had felt stronger by the day, with every success and failure building up her confidence.

Jossa looked across at Oman and asked, "Is the training finished now?"

He brought his head up and smiled at his wife. "Yes." Turning to Anong, he announced, "Your quest begins tomorrow. For the next three weeks, you'll be out on your own, just as our people have done for the last thousand years. Before we had magic and hardships were real, death was always around the corner. Now we use the magic to help us through. It makes us forget how just one early frost could doom a whole village. How elk not showing up could mean starvation."

Anong asked, "Isn't it good that the magic keeps us safe?"

"It is," he stated, "I just don't want our people to rely on it and become weak. They need to get out and use their minds and natural abilities, or they'll forget how. Even you will forget how. That's why I tell people not to depend on magic. Suppose I found a village that never planted enough crops to sustain themselves or never hunted because it was hard work. In that case, I'd let their bellies get hungry before I intervened. We all must learn, and sometimes it's the hard way." Oman took a long drink from his mug. "You're ready for your final test. It's time to see how well you cope on your own, without using your magic, to see how much you've learned."

Oman pulled out a hand-drawn map and spread it on the table for all of them to view. "Anong, this is the route I want you to follow. You'll be traversing the perimeter of the Jibay land. The first day, you'll arrive at the top of this mountain, where you'll find a clearing." He indicated a point on the map and continued, "A large tree will be at its centre, where you'll remain for the next four days. There are three skins of water already there that will be your only nourishment. From there, and for the next two weeks, you'll move down the valley, hunting whatever you can find." Oman showed her the route she was to follow. "You must move every day. This map will help you stay on course. Use it as a guide, and it will bring you home." He spent the next few minutes showing Anong the route and significant terrain features along the way.

Anong felt strangely excited about the challenge, yet she was apprehensive about the dangers she might find along the way. She asked, "Is there any shelter?"

"There are caves, but be careful. You don't know what lives in them."

"Can I take food with me?"

"You'll have a meal's worth, only to be eaten on the morning of day five, after the stay on the mountain."

Anong glanced at her mother, seeing the concern in her eyes, and smiled confidently at her. Turning back to Oman, she asked, "When do I start?"

"Tomorrow morning. You have the remainder of the day to prepare."

Early the following day, the three stood outside the cabin as Jossa hugged Anong. She looked up at the young woman and said fiercely, "Remember everything your father taught you. I look and pray for your safe return."

"I'll be fine," Anong replied reassuringly to her mother. She knelt and hugged her, breathing in the scent of the woman she'd grown to love so well. Finally, they broke from their embrace. Anong stood up and walked over to Oman. "I'm ready," she said.

Oman's face held no emotion as he helped her with her backpack. When she was ready, she stood motionless before him, a tall, strong and gifted young woman. *How much she has grown,* he thought. "Remember that you can't use your magic. Good luck, and stick to the route on the map," he said, fighting a twinge of concern. With a wave of her hand, the young woman turned toward the forest and walked away.

Jossa watched her disappear but did not say a word. Oman murmured to his wife, "Don't worry. She'll be fine."

She turned her eyes to her husband and calmly said, "I know she'll be fine because you are going to be out there every day with her."

Oman laughed and said, "That's not how this works."

Jossa placed her hands on her hips and said, "If she is sitting under a tree soaking wet, then you'll be doing the same. You'll stay with her until she comes home safe and sound. And the gods better protect her because if they don't, they won't be able to protect you from me. Do you understand me, Oman?"

Oman sighed and said, "She's no longer a child, Jossa. Let her go."

"Pack up your gear. You leave in an hour," Jossa replied stubbornly, turning away and walking back to the house.

Shortly after she reached the wood line, John joined her. They walked together through the dense forest until they arrived at the base of a steep mountain. "You have to go now, John. The rest of this journey will be mine alone," she said.

"I know. I would like to go with you, but I understand. We will be watching out for you."

"I will miss your company, but I must complete this journey on my own. I'll see you when I return."

John watched wordlessly, his face unhappy as she took a deep breath and hefted up her backpack. Waving a casual goodbye, she turned and began the sharp incline. For four hours, Anong climbed steadily upward, stopping only to rest and determine the best route. She had relied on game trails for the most part; the animals could always pick the most accessible pathways.

Clamouring up one last slope, she broke through a thick mound of brush and came into a clearing. Anong looked up and could see a single large tree at its centre. With a weary sigh, she wiped the sweat from her brow and continued toward it, finding four skins of water at its base. Anong picked up one container and drank from it greedily until she was satisfied. She took a long rope from her backpack, tied the pack to it and threw the loose end over a large branch. She hoisted the bag up, securing the rope to the tree. Now nothing could get at it. She picked up her cane and walked out four paces from the tree.

Placing one end of the weapon on the ground, she walked around the tree, scraping the shape of a circle into the earth. Once completed, Anong took another long drink of water and sat down with her back against the tree, staring at the vast, mountainous vista below her. She watched as the sun started to dip below the horizon, the light fading and cooling the air around her. With it, the shadows of the trees and rocks became darker and more ominous. The girl's imagination wandered, and her eyes flicked from one spot to the next. *That looks like a mountain lion*, she thought, gripping her cane tightly and standing up. She walked out to the edge of the circle, where she could see more clearly. It was only the moonlight, casting a shadow from an old stump. She returned to her place beneath the tree and sat down, her stomach growling loudly and reminding her that it was empty.

Anong managed to close her eyes for an hour in an uncomfortable, fitful nap but woke up freezing and shaking with cold. She stood, stretching her cold muscles and slapping her arms, then began moving around the circle she'd made earlier. Around and around, she jogged, confining herself to the small space. The night had cooled significantly, and the air bit into her skin. She slowed to a walk. *What was I thinking?* she thought. *I could be back home in the cabin, around a friendly fire.* Sitting down, Anong picked up the skin of water and took in a mouthful. The cold water hit her stomach immediately and spread, cooling her at once. The walking and running had been for nothing, and she was freezing again. With a shake of her head, she slowly got back on her feet and started the routine once more.

Oman watched her sympathetically from his vantage point at the wood line. *She'll learn*, he thought.

In its thin, frigid heights, the night spent on the mountaintop was the longest and coldest Anong had ever experienced. She searched the sky in the east and was rewarded when she finally made out the approaching grey streaks of dawn. The stars that had shone like beacons disappeared, giving way to a bright, clear morning. Ultimately, as it had done for an eternity, the sun broke the horizon. Its tip first peaked over the lip of the earth and crept steadily upward. Anong leaned back against the tree, her body opening up and soaking in the sun's warmth. Finally warm, she closed her eyes and fell fast asleep.

What Anong had thought was a dream came hard and fast. She felt her spirit leave her body and fly gracefully into the air. Looking down, she could see her physical form curled up in a ball, her head on a waterskin, sound asleep. Her spirit was being called and guided by the crystal at her throat, pulling her toward the scent of magic and power. She did not resist and flew effortlessly over the landscape until she stopped above a small cottage and slowly descended. The place had a familiar feel to it, but she knew she'd never been there before. She glided around the cabin effortlessly when a door slammed and got her attention. She moved toward the sound and then stopped. A woman appeared at the door. She stood straight and tall, with long black hair and eyes, her fair skin showing no sign of age. Anong watched as the woman picked up a bucket and began to feed her chickens, who, having heard the door, ran eagerly to her.

Esma dipped her hand into the bucket, taking a handful of seed and tenderly tossing it to the birds. She scolded them gently, saying, "Hey, hey, there's no need to fight. There's more than enough for all of you." She hesitated for a second before bringing her head up and smiling, saying, "Anong. What a beautiful name." She looked directly at Anong's spirit form and said, "I was wondering when you'd come to visit me again. It's been too long."

Anong, surprised, said, "You can see me?"

"Oh, yes. I see many things." She threw more seed to the chickens and hung the bucket on the fence post. Next, she grabbed an armful of hay with a smooth, practised move and placed it into the cattle trough.

Anong floated behind Esma as she cared for her animals. Curiously, she asked, "You know me, but I don't know you. Who are you?"

The woman continued feeding her livestock and said, "My name is Esma. You came and visited me a very long time ago when you were a mere infant. Oman and Jossa have looked after you well. You must be on your quest now."

"How do you know my mother and father?"

"I've never met them, but I know of them. They are a good couple, and that's why I chose them to look after you. I knew they could keep you safe."

"Safe from what?"

"There are those that are greedy for the power you possess."

A flurry of questions came to Anong. "Do you know my real parents? Who am I? What am I? Why am I here?" she asked excitedly.

Esma laughed and said, "You ask a lot of questions. You must be patient, my dear. There is still time, and you mustn't trouble yourself with that now." She walked over to the pigsty and began to feed them.

"When?" Anong asked impatiently.

"Not now." Esma stopped what she was doing and faced the young girl with a stern expression. "For now, you need to focus on everything Oman has taught you. Focus your energies on that and nothing else. Your life, and many others, depend on it."

"But how do I do that? There is still so much to learn. I can't remember it all."

"It will come to you when the time draws near. It's time for you to go back now. Be patient." With that, the woman lifted a hand, and Anong felt herself being softly pushed away. Her spirit rose into the air, moving on its own back to the mountain. She returned to the clearing, landed softly and eased herself effortlessly back into her body. She woke hours later, stiff and cold from sleeping on the ground. Among lifted her protesting body up and walked around the tree until she was warm again. She looked to the sun. It had made its way across the sky, and the day was almost done. She had slept much longer than she wanted. Was the dream real? Had she really left her body and flown across the sky? Who was this woman she had met? Was she the person who had delivered her to Oman and Jossa? She had so many questions for Esma, and it was frustrating to know she would have to wait for the answers.

Over the next two nights, Anong tried to stay warm and keep her hunger at bay. The temptation to use her magic was strong. A small part of her rebelled and insisted that no one would know, no one would care. She was alone. Still, she resisted, remembering Oman's insistence that she was strong enough to do this on her own. Anong slept during the day, always trying to leave her body and visit again with Esma. Her frustration at not returning to the woman grew until she recalled Esma's departing words—be patient. Finally, she calmed herself and sat down with a sigh, preparing for her final night on the mountain.

Dark clouds began to gather on the far horizon. She had been lucky until now, but tonight would be different. The sun went down an hour later, and with it, the lightning started, its forks of brilliant light illuminating the night. Cracks of thunder reverberated around her, shaking the ground. The rain followed, coming down in sheets. As rivers of water ran down her back, she curled up tightly into a ball, trying to keep herself warm. Her hand slipped up to the stone that hung around her neck. Images of Esma came back to her, and again she could hear her words. *Focus on everything Oman has taught you.* She concentrated on her breathing first, slowing it down with deep inhales. She imagined a fire within her and felt its heat as it moved throughout her body and warmed her. Anong sighed with relief and looked up into the darkness as the storm around her worsened. A flash of lightning lit up the surrounding area, and she could see the spirit form of a woman outlined in the clearing. As she got closer, Anong realized it was Esma. She pushed up to her feet and walked toward the ghostly figure, ensuring she stayed within the circle. When the woman stopped just outside it, Anong asked, "Esma, what are you doing here?"

"I thought you may need some company tonight." Esma stepped into the circle and walked over to the tree with Anong. "I believe you have many questions that need answers. I'll tell you what I can."

Oman watched from the wood line as he lay under his waterproof hide. Through the lightning flashes, he'd seen Anong get up and walk to the edge of the circle, then stop. She appeared to be speaking with someone, but he could see no one else there. Oman watched as she returned to the tree and sat, still in conversation. He was puzzled but, seeing she was safe, closed his eyes and fell fast asleep. The two women spoke until the clouds drained themselves of water and the birds began their morning song.

CHAPTER 15

Anong woke the next day to feel the sun warm on her face. Its heat flooded through her body and began to dry her wet clothes from the night before. Esma had departed shortly after dawn but not before leaving Anong with a better sense of who she was. Questions were answered, and she was satisfied for now. She understood why she had been hidden with Oman and Jossa. A part of her was unhappy that she had never known her real parents, but she hoped to meet them one day. They spoke at length about how she could safely leave her body and travel in spirit form. Her gift of magic was powerful but would need time to grow. Esma promised she would see her again and help her learn more about her ability. Her stomach growled, reminding her this phase of the quest was over. Grabbing the rope she'd tied around the tree days before; she untied the knot and eased the bag to the ground. Opening the drawstring, she eagerly breathed in the faint aroma of her mother's cooking, then reached in and took out a piece of meat and cheese. She sat back down under the tree and ate it slowly. Although she wanted more, she knew she would need the nourishment later and left the remainder of the food in the pack. Anong looked at her map and studied the route she was to take. Satisfied, she hoisted her backpack, picked up the cane and started her walk down the valley.

It was late afternoon before she finally found a clearing just up from the river to spend the night. The ground was flat, and the trees provided shelter from the icy winds that came down from the higher altitudes. The first task was to make a fire. She gathered up tinder, took the flint from her pack and struck it. A tiny spark soon grew into a flame. She added to the fire until it threw off more and more heat. Its warmth made her want to curl up and sleep, but chores needed to be done. Anong took her fishing gear down to the river and tied one end of her line around a large rock. She attached hooks along its length, baiting them with dragonflies. Small wooden pieces were attached along the line to act as bobbers. She picked up the rock and gently placed it into a quiet part of the river, tying the other end to a tree on the bank. Anong made a few adjustments to her handiwork and went back to the camp to build a shelter.

· · · · · ·

Oman rose late the following day and looked across the open hilltop to the lone tree. He squinted hard, looking for movement, but saw nothing. Glancing at the tree, he could see that Anong's pack was no longer there. He hadn't expected her to be up so early after the storm. He gathered his gear and picked up her tracks in the soft ground. *She shouldn't be too far ahead,* he thought.

· · · · · ·

Anong's fire was well on its way to becoming hot, deep coals for cooking. Her lean-to was situated in front of the fire and on high ground. She would be warm and dry. She had erected a firewall that reflected heat, and smoke from the fire would ward off the mosquitos. Anong placed the last armful of pine boughs down as bedding, then headed to the river to see if she'd caught anything. Pulling on the line, she could feel a heaviness, and in the current, she saw the glittering body of a fish. Anong moved to it quickly, grabbing the gills and taking the hook from the fish's mouth. She looked into its eyes. "Thank you for your life so I can eat," she said, unsheathing her knife.

Over the next few days, she followed the river down through the valley until it broke through into an open plain. She sat on a high spot overlooking the expanse of grass and watched a large elk herd grazing peacefully. With luck, she would take an animal down, smoke the meat and dry the hide. The two long weeks she'd been out had begun to take its toll. She glanced down at her leather moccasins: the soles had nearly worn through and needed repair. Although she managed to find enough food to stay nourished, the long days of travel through treacherous terrain had taxed her. She hurriedly set up camp, cooked the last of her fish and fell, exhausted, into a sound sleep.

· · · · · ·

The sun was just above the last hill in the valley and would be down in a few minutes. Oman lifted his nose into the air and sniffed. She was there. He could smell the fire, and the odour of the fish made his stomach growl. He had been following her but staying well out of sight. Oman was satisfied; her survival skills were good, and she used her head. She always did what she had to do, saving her strength in case she needed it somewhere else.

He dug inside his pack, looking for the dried meat, bread and cheese Jossa had packed for him. He wouldn't go hungry but would have preferred the fish Anong was cooking up. Breaking off a piece of cheese, he threw it into his mouth and casually looked down at the ground. His eyes widened, and his breath tightened. Beside his foot, imprinted in the mud, was a large paw print of a mountain lion. He quickly scanned the area but could see and smell nothing. Bending down to one knee, he placed his fingers into the front pads of the track. The outside rim was dry, and the inner indentation cracked. The print was about a day old. Again, he peered through the bush, this time looking deeper and longer. He followed the tracks and realized the animal was shadowing the elk. Oman ate and later moved closer to where Anong was, in case the cat caught the scent of the fish.

· · · · · ·

That night, Anong's spirit lifted up and out of her body with ease. She had struggled during many attempts before this and was excited when she finally had control. She gazed down at the campsite and could see herself leaning against the shelter. She rose higher into the sky and saw the glittering river winding through the rocks and opening onto the plains. Anong flew toward the elk now, watching them as they bedded down for the night. She found a small enclave not too far from the herd that would be a suitable staging area for her hunt. *This is where I need to be tomorrow.*

CHAPTER 16

Salem stopped the wagon close to his mother's barn and stepped down from it. His wife, Minza, hopped down and brushed the dust from her clothing, saying, "We should have used the king's magic to get us here. Look, I'm filthy."

"Minza, I'm sure my mother will have enough water for a bath so we can both get cleaned up," Salem replied.

She ignored him and continued to complain, saying, "That's not the problem. Privacy is the problem. There is none."

Salem unloaded a trunk and placed it on the ground. "Minza, all those years of living in the king's palace have made you soft. We were raised in one-room houses, with a single fireplace and no curtains between the beds."

Minza had held her tongue for days, but she finally had enough. Irritably, she said, "I loved living in the palace. We had our own quarters and people waiting on us. You're the only one that wanted to come back." She was about to continue when they noticed the front door of the cottage opening.

Salem's mother, Tana, came out the door and said, "You're finally here. I thought I heard a wagon."

Salem smiled widely and said, "It's good to see you again, Mother. We're just unloading now." He turned to Minza and spoke pointedly under his breath. "Put a smile on your face and greet my mother."

Minza, with a sarcastic roll of her eyes, gave him an overly enthusiastic, mocking grin and said, "How's this, dear? Does this meet your standard?" Without waiting for a reply, she turned and walked to the older woman with the fake smile still pasted on her face.

An hour later, they were unpacked and sitting around the table, having a bite to eat. Tana said, "I was surprised to hear that you wanted to move back. I always thought you enjoyed court life."

Minza started to speak, but Salem interrupted. "We were happy there, and life was good. We were treated with respect but felt we were missing something. I also thought I was needed here." His foot gave a slight kick to Minza's shin under the table, and she winced.

"Yes, court life was good," she said hurriedly, giving Salem a quick, accusing look. "But because we're getting older, Salem thought it would be better to be closer to family. We missed the winters of being forced down into a hole in the ground and being hunted by beasts."

Tana's eyes widened slightly at Minza's remarks, and Salem hurriedly interrupted. "What she's saying is we missed the camaraderie and the closeness the winters bring."

Minza idly picked up her coffee mug and scrutinized the chips around the rim, not looking at either of them.

Tana immediately noticed and said, "I'm sorry. I should have brought the other cups down, the ones I use for company. I can get them now." She pushed back from the table and began to rise.

"Mother, please stop. These will do just fine. Sit down," Salem pleaded.

Tana, her cheeks red with embarrassment, paused and brushed her skirt flat. She awkwardly sat back down and picked up her coffee mug, saying, "You can stay here as long as you like. I have plenty of room."

Salem reassured her. "We'll only be here a few days. There's a house just out from the village centre, a little bigger than this one. It has the winter quarters already built in. I can work there and be close to the council hall."

His mother nodded. "I know the one. It's a lovely place, but there's no barn for your horses."

"We'll have to find a place to keep them until we build our own," he answered.

Still uncomfortable, his mother stirred her coffee and did not look at either of them. "So, what exactly are you two planning on doing here?"

Salem enthusiastically began to regale his mother with his plans. "I plan on helping our people. I want us not to have to dig down in the dirt every winter and hide out from the beasts. We should be able to go wherever and do whatever we want in our own land. The magic that we earned should be given to us all the time, just as it is in King Merck's kingdom."

Tana was surprised. "Oman believes too much magic will make us weak, and a lot of us agree. We can't always rely on magic to do our work. The Jogahoh must stay strong, and if we weaken, our land could be taken from us. It would be nice to be aboveground in the winter, but it's so cold and having joined underground homes allows us to help each other."

"Mother," Salem interrupted, "Oman has poisoned more than a few minds here with his stories about the magic weakening us. I've been to other kingdoms where it's used all the time, and they live well."

Tana shook her head in denial and said, "The kingdom to the east that started the war your father was killed in was one of those kingdoms. It didn't turn out well for them."

Minza cut in. "Well, I hate to interrupt, but I'm tired and need a bath. The travel and all this talk about magic and the new house have worn me out. I'd like to get cleaned up and have a rest before supper. Where can I do that, Tana?"

Tana pointed to an old tub that Salem knew well. It had sat in the same corner of the room since he could remember. There was only a short wall divider for privacy off to the side. "Salem can fetch the water from the well, and you're welcome to heat it up on the stove if you like."

Minza had not had to heat up her own water for over a decade. Glowering, and with her mouth set in a firm line, she began to heat it, stocking the stove with wood. She shot Salem angry glances as he fetched the water and filled the reservoir. Salem ignored her completely, laughing to himself as he next tended to the horses. Once finished, he sat down on a bale of hay and wrote a message to Oman, asking him for an audience, just the two of them. When he was finished, Salem walked over to the cage of cardinals, took one from its roost and slipped the note into its carrier. Holding the bird up, he ordered, "Find Oman and deliver this message to him." Releasing the bird, he watched it climb high into the sky and fly in a circle above the yard. It abruptly turned north and flew out of sight. *North*, he thought. *The same direction I'd come from after investigating the beast incident.*

CHAPTER 17

Anong woke early, ate her leftovers from the previous day and then tore down the camp. Soon after setting out, she found the game trail that led to the enclave and estimated it would take her most of the morning to arrive at the great plains. Anong had been walking steadily for about an hour when, from the corner of her eye, she caught sight of a bright red cardinal as it flew by. She could clearly see the small message bag the bird carried. *No one else is here,* she thought. *What could that cardinal be doing?* She'd seen the birds many times before, at home delivering messages to Oman and Jossa. They always took the most direct route. A sudden realization came to her, and she scanned her surroundings with interest. She couldn't see him but knew that her father was following her. She also understood this was likely to be her mother's doing. Jossa was, and always would be, protective of her. She whispered to herself, "Mom, I can do this on my own. You don't have to worry." A grin came to her face. Although a part of her felt reassured because of Oman's presence, she was determined to evade him the next day.

••••••

When the bird found him, Oman took the note from the small bag and placed a cloth over it, revealing the message. He was surprised to discover Salem had returned to the Jogahoh and even more surprised to learn that he wanted an audience with Oman. Regardless, Salem's answer would have to wait, and he'd reply to the message later when he had more time. The bird would stay with him until then. Before long, Oman found Anong setting up her camp. He moved into the underbrush and began to write his reply to Salem. He would see him in a few weeks, but it would have to be in Alfheim. Oman called softly for the bird and tucked the message into its bag. Realizing Anong might see the cardinal, he told it to fly back along the valley and then south, back to Salem.

He continued to watch Anong until the sun disappeared, then crawled under his hide and went to sleep. The next morning, he woke and glanced at the smoke of her smoldering campfire. Moving closer, he could see Anong, fast asleep under her blanket. The sun moved higher and higher, and he continued to watch, but nothing moved. Suspicious, he edged closer to the campsite and scrutinized the shape under the lean-to. It had done its job, fooling him from a distance, but up close, he could tell that no one was there. Oman walked into the clearing, laughing to himself. *I taught her too well.* He knew she had discovered he was following her and probably seen the cardinal. He walked around the camp, trying to find any sign of the direction she was travelling, but found nothing. Resigned, he gathered his gear up and placed his pack over his shoulders. *You listened and learned well, Anong. You're on your own until I find you again.*

•••••

Anong had made a good distance from where she was the night before. She laughed as she imagined her father's face when he realized she was gone. She continued to walk for only a minute before a sharp odour of blood and meat caught her attention. Cautiously, Anong brought her cane up and followed the scent through the bush and thick underbrush. A bull elk had been killed and dragged into a small clearing. Wary, she stayed where she was, scanning the area carefully for its killer. Finally, convinced that all was clear, she pulled out her knife and stepped out. Her eyes moved around the dead animal. The fresh paw prints of a mountain lion encircled the elk. It had torn open the hide and begun feeding. Kneeling, she pressed her hand into one of the paw prints. Her hand fit easily into its outline. *A lone male,* she thought, as she nervously glanced again around the circle of trees. She quickly skinned the animal, slicing deeply into its hindquarters, taking a large cut of meat. Anong wrapped the meat and placed it into her backpack before returning along the path she'd walked in on. She moved quickly, hoping to put some distance between her and the cat.

Hours later, soaked in sweat, she stopped beside a small stream, set up her camp and got a fire going. She prepared the meat by cutting it into fine strips and placed it all on a rack she'd made. The trick now was to put the frame at precisely the correct height from the fire. Too high and the smoke wouldn't cure it; too low, and it would be cooked or burned to a crisp. She found the proper distance by stacking rocks and adding the firewood piece by piece. The smoke engulfed the meat, drying it slowly.

Anong picked up the hide and laid it out flat, shaving the remaining meat from the skin. She cut off enough to patch her moccasins and placed that portion in boiling water for an hour. The remainder was stretched and left to dry on a willow branch she had fashioned into a circle. When the boiled leather was ready, she squeezed the water from it and patched the holes on her moccasins. She held up her handiwork, looking closely at it, and smiled. *I think even Mother would be happy with this.*

Her last chore was to fasten her spearhead to the end of her cane. She needed to be ready if the mountain lion decided to sniff her out and make her his next meal. She knew that her magic could easily protect her, and a weapon wasn't needed, but she had vowed not to use it during this quest. Most importantly, Anong was also unsure where or when her magic would come to her. She knew that its power was linked to her feelings, but she had no control over it for now. The incident with the beast at the trading post made that clear. Esma had promised that in time she would gain command of her powers. She hoped that time would come soon.

Her chores finally completed, Anong curled up under her lean-to and wrapped herself in her blanket. *Five more days. I'll be home in five more days*, she thought, before drifting off to sleep.

. . . . . .

Salem and Minza were walking through their new home when Minza said, "This will do, but can I get some house help?"

"You know most people do it themselves."

"I don't care what most people do. I have no intention of doing that."

"Well, then you'll have to ask around town to see if anyone is interested."

She bristled and turned away, ignoring him, before replying. "First, I'll need a cook and someone to do the cleanup, and of course, we need a gardener."

"Whatever you want, dear," Salem sighed in resignation. He knew an argument with Minza would never go in his favour. A knock on the back door got his attention. Minza started to walk toward it, but Salem said, "I think that's probably for me. Why don't you go out and see if you can hire someone?" She leaned in and kissed him, a satisfied smile on her face, waved her hand in farewell and left through the front door.

As soon as his wife departed, Salem headed to the back door and opened it for Bargun. "Come in, quickly," Salem said quietly. "Did anyone see you come around the back?"

"I don't think so," Bargun replied, slipping through the door and glancing through the vast room. He immediately felt a stab of jealousy as he compared his tiny living quarters to his childhood friend's opulent lifestyle. *What did he do to deserve this?*

"Good. If anyone asks, you applied for the gardener's job." Salem wasted no time in getting directly to his point. "I have a job for us at the end of the month. You'll be coming with me on a little trip."

Bargun arched an eyebrow, interested. "Where, and for how long?"

"I can't tell you right now. We'll need horses, camping gear and enough food for a week. That's all you need to know. Can you be ready?"

Bargun calculated the equipment he needed and added a hefty commission to pay for his time and effort. "No problem, but I'll need money upfront for supplies. Maybe fifty coins?"

Salem was agitated and knew Bargun needed far less. Despite that, he tossed him a pouch and said, "There's enough in there for everything you need, plus a bit extra. Don't disappoint me."

"I've never let you down," Bargun countered. He turned to walk out, but Salem stopped him.

"I'll find a place for us to meet outside the village in a few days. We can't leave together."

Bargun nodded and said, "Let me know," before tucking the pouch into his waistline and leaving as quietly as he had come.

CHAPTER 18

O man crossed the river and scanned the bank for any sign of Anong. Finding nothing, he decided to walk back up the river. His eyes stopped at the twisted and broken bark of a branch, and he stepped closer to inspect it. The bark had been stripped away as if someone had used it to pull themselves up from the riverbank. Looking around, he saw slight indentations in the vegetation but nothing that confirmed a footprint. Oman looked ahead and into the forest, imagining Anong's direct line of travel using the natural line of drift, the easiest path any animal would have taken. He started walking, and about 100 meters in, he found it—the first sign of her since leaving camp days before.

Anong had taken the time to conceal everything along the river, but once she had some distance between them, she thought she was in the clear. She would have been had it not been for the one broken branch she'd left behind. Oman knelt to ensure the moccasin footprints were hers. He could see that she had patched one of them, and it left a distinct mark in the mud. He was suddenly aware that another footprint was directly over hers. It was the print of a mountain lion, and it was tracking her.

He looked up at the sky and realized that the sun would soon be down. He would be unable to follow tracks without light and had to set up camp if he wanted to start out early. Oman was worried that his directive forbidding her to use magic was too severe, especially with the lion nearby. That night, he sent a prayer to his gods to watch over his daughter. The prayer reached up and out, moving through the grass and trees like a soft breeze, then soared high into the heavens. Over the hills, it moved with purpose at lightning speed. Finally, it reached Esma's tiny cottage, its energy pushing through her and waking her with a gasp.

Her heart was beating wildly in her chest. Someone needed her. Esma listened carefully to the prayer and realized it was from Oman. She also saw the tracks of a lion and knew Anong was alone. Without hesitation, she sent her spirit out and off into the night, heading directly to Anong.

Landing softly, she walked to the sleeping girl and touched her hand lightly. Through the gentle contact, she could read Anong's thoughts and fears. Surprisingly, Esma could not find any fear in the young woman. Anong, she realized, had discovered the animal's tracks and knew it was following her but wasn't concerned about it. Instead, the girl looked forward to the contact. She had every intention of killing the lion and using the hide as a coat. Moving her hand away from Anong, Esma stepped back and watched the young woman as she slept. "I was worried about you, but now I realize there is no need. Oman and Jossa did the job I knew they would." She turned and lifted back into the sky, heading for home.

Anong woke the next day, picked up her cane and stepped out of the lean-to. She walked around the perimeter of her camp, looking for signs, listening and smelling the wind. Satisfied that everything was in order, she began her tear-down. Only when every trace of her being there had been erased did she head out.

She stopped for a bite to eat and drink at midday, pulling out the map Oman had drawn for her. She looked at it closely, aligning the hills and rivers around her with the ones he'd drawn in. One more valley and Anong could head back home. She rolled the map up and started on her way. An hour later, she found the mouth of the valley. It had a small creek that wandered down its middle, where she stopped to fill her waterskin.

She had filled it to the halfway point when she felt the hairs on the back of her neck stand up. The rush of water from the stream had masked the sounds around her. She grasped her weapon and turned smoothly, pulling her waterskin up from the creek. She stayed in a crouched position, with the cane tucked tightly under her armpit, spear pointed forward. Her peripheral vision caught sight of a tan body coming swiftly toward her, and she automatically flung the waterskin at it. The cat effortlessly jumped back out of the way, snarling at her.

Anong carefully moved away from the stream, stepping around the animal. Her heart picked up speed, and her vision narrowed as she watched the cat approach. Adrenaline began to push into her system. Too soon for that, she knew, and forced herself to control its flow. Her system slowed, and her vision opened again, the adrenaline now held at bay until she needed it. The animal locked eyes with her, its hair standing on the back of its neck, its fangs dripping saliva. A low guttural snarl came from its belly. Crouching low to the ground, it tensed its muscles and feigned a pounce before backing away.

Anong reacted automatically, stepping to the side and bringing the spear point toward the animal's head. She watched its eyes as it moved quickly from side to side, trying to find an opening in which to slash and bring her down. Anong stayed in motion, always facing the animal and keeping her stance wide. Knowing she would have only one chance, she left her right side open to attack. The large cat, seeing the opportunity, lunged toward her. At that moment, Anong allowed the adrenaline to flush her system with all its power, and she nimbly side-stepped the animal. As it brushed past her, its left flank was vulnerable, and the razor-sharp spearhead pierced deep into its body. The encounter happened so quickly that the animal didn't feel the thrust. Its front leg collapsed, and the cat stumbled, falling to one side. Anong, entirely in control, moved swiftly on the wounded beast and pulled out the spear for another strike. To Anong, the hunter had now become the hunted. She felt a thrill as she realized she held power over life and death. She drove the spear deep into its chest cavity and pinned it, looking for a clean, quick kill. Despite the spear lodged deeply in its chest, the animal snarled wildly in pain and tried to stand.

Anong moved in closer and looked into the cat's eyes. Gone now was the fierce look of a predator. Instead, she saw what looked like a hurt child, looking for its mother. She said, "You would have shown me no mercy. I will pay you the same."

The animal locked his mind with hers, and she could hear its reply. "Your words are true. You owe me nothing."

"Why can I hear you?" she asked out loud, stepping back and regarding the animal carefully.

"We are the same, you and I." The cat lay on its side now, its breathing laboured, blood flowing freely from its body.

"We would never be the same. You're a ruthless hunter."

"A hunter, yes. But ruthless, no. We all maintain a balance. We cull the weak, the old and the wounded, and you are none of those things. For that mistake, I have lost my life. So, woman, prove to me you are not a beast. Give me the gift of a quick death and ease my pain. Take my hide, cleanse it, and wear it with pride. It will keep you warm in the cold and dry in the rain, as it has for me for so many years."

The animal snarled in agony as Anong jerked the spear from his chest and immediately plunged it deep into his heart. She pulled the weapon free after a minute and stood back, watching the spirit of the cat rise above its body. It looked back at her calmly, no longer in pain, then drifted off like smoke before disappearing into the sky.

••••••

Minza let the cardinal go from her bedroom window, watching it until it disappeared. The bird would have a long journey today. First, it followed the main river, then changed course, going overland. All day, the tiny bird flew past valleys and hills and over sparkling lakes and streams. It was early evening before it finally arrived at the land of the Jibay.

Jossa was chopping wood when the bird fluttered down and landed next to her. She held out her hand, and it immediately flew into her palm. "Oh, don't you look handsome," she said, stroking the small animal and taking it to the cabin. The creature nuzzled its head against her thumb, loving the attention after the long journey. She placed the bird on the windowsill and provided it with food and water. As the bird busied itself with its meal, Jossa undid the small sack, took out the message and enlarged it. The message read:

Jossa,
Salem and I have moved from Court to Alfheim and now live in the big house beside the town fountain. The place will do for now, but I wish we had more people to help with chores. We did stay the first few days with Tana, but it was dreadful. The place was too small, with no privacy, as you know. The smell from the barn alone almost drove me back to the west.

It's been too long since Salem and I have had a chance to visit with you. I know the challenges between the two brothers, and I wish Salem could just accept Oman as the leader. Please answer as soon as you can and let us know where you live so we can meet.
Looking forward to seeing you and take care.
Friends forever, Minza

Jossa's forehead crinkled up on the last line. The two had been good friends throughout their time in school and while living in Alfheim, but that was a long time ago. When Minza moved with Salem to the king's court, she completely ignored everyone from home and thought herself above them. *Now she wants to get together?* Jossa thought. *How strange. I wonder what she wants.* Oman and Anong would be home in a few days. She wrote a quick note letting Oman know of Minza's request and placed it in the small pack. She waited until the cardinal had replenished his energy and then held the bird up at eye level. "I need you to find Oman and deliver this message, please. Wait for a reply, and then come back to me."

The bird sang a quick trill, flew into the air, completed two circles to get its bearings and headed northeast. Jossa returned to her woodpile to find it neatly stacked. She held up her hand, shaded her eyes and peered toward the wood line. She caught a faint shimmer of light within the trees. Jossa pulled out her tobacco pouch and placed an offering on a large boulder. "Thank you," she said to the spirits. Picking up the axe, she brought the head of it down hard, splitting a log cleanly in half. *There is more to Minza's message, I'm sure.*

CHAPTER 19

Oman followed Anong's tracks to a meadow where a stream flowed down from the hills. He was alarmed when he spotted the clear signs of a battle and a large bloodstain in the grass. His heart stopped for an instant. "Let her be safe," he whispered, looking about for signs of the animal. A minute later, he found the skinned corpse of a mountain lion and sighed with relief and pride.

The trill of a cardinal attracted his attention, and he automatically held out his arm for the bird to land. Taking out the message, he read Jossa's note before murmuring, "Salem, what are you up to now?" He answered the letter, asking Jossa not to reply and letting her know he would be home in a few days.

Oman tucked the note back into the bird's pouch as it sat quietly and waited for a handful of seeds. "Sorry, I have nothing for you," he said apologetically. The bird cocked its head and stared at him as if what he said was utterly outrageous. It fluttered up to his shoulder, latched onto his beard and pulled. "Ouch!" Oman exclaimed. "That hurt! But I suppose I deserved it."

The bird flew off his shoulder, looking at Oman accusingly before returning to Jossa.

Oman laughed softly as he rubbed the side of his face and watched the bird disappear. He would have to remember to always carry seed with him from now on. Picking up Anong's tracks again, he determined she was still a fair distance from him and set out to catch up to her.

Two days later, Oman caught the scent of a fire and fish cooking. He moved to a high point where he could look down on Anong's camp and saw her beside her lean-to. Oman sat back and closed his eyes for a moment. The last few days had been tiring, and he could feel his body drift off. Little flicks along the side of his face, and then his eyebrows, roused him slowly from his nap. At first, he thought it was the cardinal back to torment him, and he kept his eyes firmly shut. He waved his hand in front of his face and said drowsily, "Go back and find Jossa." The flickering continued, and with a start, he remembered where he was. His hand quickly went for his weapon, but he grasped only air. Panicked, he opened his eyes to see Anong squatting in front of him, waving a long piece of straw in his face.

"Are you looking for this?" she asked, pointing to his cane, which she had pulled away from him.

"I was until a moment ago," he smiled.

"Why have you been following me all this time? I thought I was supposed to do this on my own?"

"I wasn't following you. I was just on a bit of a walk-about. I was looking for new game trails before winter. So, it was by pure accident I ran into you today."

"Oh, really? A pure accident!" she said sarcastically.

"Yes. Pure accident," he repeated, a sheepish grin on his face.

Anong stood up and said, "I don't believe you, but I have more fish than I can eat. Would you like to join me?"

"Hmmm. Did you add salt?"

"A little," she replied with a shake of her head and offered him her hand.

Oman heaved himself up from the ground, and the two began to walk back to her camp. "I suppose I'll join you."

The two ate their meal in silence until Anong finally asked, "Did you not trust me to be able to handle this on my own?"

He looked up from his meal and said, "Anong, your mother and I trust you with every bone in our body."

"You certainly weren't looking for game trails."

Oman got up and sat down beside her. "The day I found you was the best day of my life. I will always remember hearing your angry cries through that cold forest. You were so tiny but so strong, despite the frozen tears on your face. I picked you up, ran for the tunnel and handed you to your mother. I had never seen her that happy before." His eyes drifted up as he thought back. "It's as if the gods had given you to us and made us complete. Your mother would never forgive me if something happened to you."

He stood up and kissed her on the forehead. "You're the best daughter anyone could ever want." He sat down and reached for another piece of fish. "Blame your mother. It was her idea for me to follow you."

"So, this is all Mother's doing?"

"Absolutely. I had no say in the matter."

•••••

Salem sat alone in the house, sipping a glass of wine. Minza had left earlier that day to purchase supplies. Restless, he got up and looked out the window, then walked back and drank the last of his wine. As he returned the glass to the table, he spotted his reflection in the mirror. Long gone was the smooth skin of his youth. It had been replaced with wrinkled brows and crow's feet. If the eyes were supposed to be the windows to his soul, his eyes were disturbing. He saw nothing but deep pits of emptiness. *Nothing*, he thought. *I see nothing. Is that what the gods see in me as I try to take my rightful place?*

Salem walked up the stairs to the bedroom, where he kept the pouch with the sorcerer's hair. Taking a strand, he poured some water into a washbowl and dropped the hair into it. A white mist rose from the water, and from within, appeared the sorcerer's face.

"Salem. Such a pleasure to see you again."

Salem nodded a greeting to Zakalis and got directly down to business. "Oman has not yet replied to my request to see him. He has made a home somewhere within the land of the Jibay, but I haven't been able to find out exactly where."

"That will not be of importance. When will you see Oman again?"

"I don't know where or when. I don't think he will allow me to come to him."

"That will not be a problem. Whenever you meet Oman, slip a strand of my hair into his belongings. My potion will track him using the hair strand and will also sense the girl. Just bring the potion to the Jibay land, and it will do the rest. Once you have her, you need only bring her back to me."

The sorcerer continued. "When I am ready, I must advise King Tibalt and then I will contact you. Be prepared to move." He sensed Salem's misgivings and said smoothly, "Salem, never be concerned about what you think you see in the mirror. The mirror can only reflect light and does not show the true you. You are going to take your people to greatness. Remember that."

Salem blinked in surprise. He did not realize Zakalis had been able to read his doubts and fears so clearly and was flattered by the sorcerer's words. *Surely,* he thought, *I am the true leader of my people.*

Zakalis interrupted and said, "I think you have a visitor," and his face evaporated.

The door opened, and Minza stepped in, looking around the room with a puzzled eye. "Who were you talking to?"

Salem turned to her and said, "I didn't expect you home so soon. Did you get what you needed?"

"Yes, I did. Now, who were you talking to?"

"No one, my dear. I was just practising a speech," he replied hastily. He gave her a quick hug and said, "I have chores to complete." With that, he swept out of the room, leaving a puzzled Minza behind.

She wanted to follow him but spotted the basin and peered into it. From the water, she pulled out a long strand of silver hair and inspected it. It obviously did not belong to Salem or herself. *I wonder what that man has gotten himself involved with now,* she thought suspiciously. She tucked the strand carefully into a handkerchief and placed it into the bedside drawer. She knew he was speaking to someone. The question was, who?

•••••

Oman and Anong walked together for the last day of her journey. Just beyond the final turn to home, he stopped and said, "You go ahead. This journey is yours to complete."

"Thank you," she replied and knelt to give him a quick embrace. "See you at home."

Oman waited a full hour before he started the last leg. Walking up to the door, he could hear laughter from the two most important women in his life and smiled. The happy sounds coming from inside the cabin filled him with gratitude. Instead of going in, he pulled his backpack off and sat down on the porch. Stretching out, he took off his moccasins and rubbed his feet, enjoying the warm sun on his back. The door behind him opened, and Jossa stuck her head out.

"You can come in now."

"I don't know. The sun feels good out here."

"I've got your favourite muffins ready for you. They're just fresh from the oven," she said, a patient look on her face.

Oman grinned, picked up his belongings and headed through the door, kissing her on the cheek as he brushed past her.

That night as they lay in bed, Jossa whispered to him, "How did she do?"

Oman, almost asleep, opened his eyes and said drowsily, "I don't like to admit it, but she did better than I did." He paused. "Jossa, you heard what she said. She slew a mountain lion and took its hide as a trophy. There is no way I could have done that at her age."

She moved closer to him and whispered in his ear. "You've taught her well. It's because of your guidance that she can do what she does."

"Throughout her life, I was only there as her guide. She is

more than both of us know. When I look at her now, I no longer see a child. I see a woman who could be a great leader. Why did it take me so long, and why didn't I see it before?"

"You've been busy running this country and looking after your family. I would remind you that you have been her role model, Oman. You've provided her with all the tools needed for her path in life."

"I've missed you, Jossa. It's good to be home," Oman said.

Jossa kissed him tenderly and said, "It's good to have you home, too."

The next day, Oman came into the kitchen, poured a coffee and sat down at the table. Jossa was already there, and she asked him, "Did you sleep well?"

"Yes. It was good to sleep in a real bed again. How about you?"

"Fine, even with your snoring."

"I don't snore!" he said in mock horror and looked at a paper on the table. "What do you have there?"

"The message from Minza. We'll need to reply soon."

He breathed out heavily and said, "I received one from Salem as well. He wants to meet, but I'm not ready. We both know it's not a good idea for them to come." He thought for a second and said, "It's time for a local council meeting. We should go to Alfheim instead. Do you mind leaving Anong here alone? We won't be gone for long."

"She's just come home and has been by herself all that time. I don't know if I want to do that...."

Anong came into the room just as Jossa finished speaking. "What's this about leaving me? What are you two up to now?"

Oman poured her a cup of coffee and replied, "Minza wants to visit with your mother now that she's back in Alfheim, and I need to call a local council meeting. As you know, Minza can't come here. It would be safer for you if we went to Alfheim and left you here."

Anong sipped her coffee and dipped her bread into it before biting off a piece. "Go," she said, unconcerned. "I'll be fine. I'll be busy stretching and tanning the lion's hide. Besides, I'm never without company here. The spirits are always with me."

Jossa said, "We'll use magic to transport us there and will be gone for about four days. Are you sure you'll be all right?"

"Mother, I'll be fine. Go ahead."

Oman joined the conversation and said, "We could be home sooner. We'll leave tomorrow."

Jossa sat down and wrote a reply to Minza. A cardinal was waiting for her and flew to her hand as she came up to it. Jossa scratched it lightly on its head as Oman watched and said, "These birds are for official use. They're not pets, my dear."

"I know, but they love the attention, and they're ever so soft." Jossa laughed, pulling out a small handful of seeds for the bird. She placed the message inside its pack and watched with satisfaction as the tiny animal finished its meal. "You know where to go, pretty boy. Back to Minza, please."

Oman rolled his eyes at his wife, and she laughed as the bird gave a happy twitter and flew off.

CHAPTER 20

When the cardinal returned to Alfheim, it flew directly into its cage and fell asleep, exhausted after the long journey. Minza woke the next day to hear chirping coming from the cage and realized the cardinal was back. Happy to have finally received a reply from Jossa, she reached in and eagerly pulled out the message to read it. A few minutes later, she turned to her cook and said, "I'll take up the tea for Salem myself." Surprised, the cook obliged her by preparing a tray and handing it to her. Minza carried the tray into the bedroom and said, "Good morning, dear. Here's your tea." With a proud flourish, she placed it beside the bed.

Salem rolled over and looked at his wife in astonishment. "Thank you. What's going on? Why are you bringing me my tea?"

She glanced at her husband only briefly before walking out the door. "Oman and Jossa will be here sometime today. There's a lot I have to get done before they arrive."

Salem was startled and asked, "What did you say?"

"Your brother and Jossa will be here today," she repeated as she hit the last step on the staircase.

Salem was agitated. He had wanted to go to Oman, and now he would need to devise a new plan. He tried to call back to his wife, shouting, "How long are they staying?" But there was no answer to be heard. He walked to the head of the stairs and called out again, "Minza, how long are they staying?"

She appeared by the foot of the stairs and calmly looked up at him. "I'm not sure. The message didn't say, but I expect a few days."

Salem dressed quickly, ate breakfast and then took a strand of the sorcerer's hair, placing it in a small pouch for keeping coins.

He tucked it into his pocket and told Minza he would be going to the council house.

She kissed his cheek and said, "I'm inviting Oman and Jossa for supper, so don't be late."

"I would expect only Jossa. Oman will probably be much too busy with council."

"I'll put the offer to both of them. If only one shows up, then so be it."

Salem nodded absently; his mind still occupied with how he could slip the pouch into Oman's belongings. "I'll see you soon," he replied.

As Salem entered the council building, he heard his name and lifted his head up to see the deputy coming toward him.

Calam stopped and said, "Oman arrived today and will be leaving the day after tomorrow. He's requested that we have a meeting with the local council and would like you to be there."

"I'll be there. When? Any idea as to why he's holding the meeting?"

"It scheduled to take place at midday, and he'll be dealing with a few local needs. Our fall meeting is still scheduled as per normal. He understands everyone is much too busy now."

"I'll try to see him before that."

"You're his brother," Calam said formally. "I'm sure he'll be happy to see you."

······

A knock on the back door interrupted the housekeeper's chores, and she immediately went to answer it. She recognized Jossa and let her in. "Good morning, Jossa. Are you here to see Minza?"

"I am. Is she in?"

"Yes, ma'am. Please have a seat, and I'll let her know you're here." The housekeeper disappeared through another door and walked up the staircase. Jossa heard footsteps swiftly descending the stairs a few minutes later, and the kitchen door swung open.

Jossa stood up when Minza walked in, and the two women hugged. She said, "I thought I'd surprise you."

"Surprises are good," Minza answered and asked the housekeeper to bring them coffee and biscuits. "When did you arrive?"

"A few hours ago. We're staying with Oman's mother. He's already at the council house."

"You should have stayed here," she sniffed. "We have lots of room, and there's much more privacy."

"That's a wonderful offer, but we love to visit with his mother," Jossa replied as she followed Minza into the dining room and looked around. "This is a beautiful house." The two women sat down as the housekeeper brought in the tray.

"It will suffice for now. Of course, it's nothing like what we had at the king's court. I found it almost impossible to find good help here, as well." Minza pursed her lips in agitation. The housekeeper only glanced at Jossa and rolled her eyes before leaving the room. Minza continued, blissfully unaware of the woman's insult. "I really wish Salem had reconsidered this move. To be honest, I would have preferred to stay at court, but he feels he's obliged to serve the Jogahoh here, in person."

Jossa was not caught completely off-guard by Minza's comments. She was very aware that Minza craved the limelight and attention, much like Salam. Inwardly, she tensed but forced her features into a sympathetic face and decided to test her. "I'm sure that you will both adjust. If you don't like the conditions here, you could always move out on your own, like we did. Live off the land, hunt your own food, cut your own wood."

Minza looked insulted by Jossa's words. "Why would we do that? Salem's position is much too important."

"Oman and I are doing just fine, and he's our leader." Jossa left the statement hanging and busied herself with her cup of coffee and biscuits. "My, these biscuits are wonderful. Did you make them yourself?"

"I'll get you the recipe," Minza replied, her eyes unable to conceal her horror at the idea of having to fend for themselves. She considered herself above that and decided to change the subject to her real reason for asking Jossa to visit. "Years ago, I spoke with your sister, and she said you two had moved away from the group. I asked her where, but no one knew. They said you left only a note." She reached over to catch Jossa's hand and looked at her sympathetically. "Is everything all right? You can confide in me."

"Minza, don't worry about us; everything is fine," Jossa replied patiently. "Our reasons for living alone are simple. We prefer it. Oman is the best man a woman could hope for, and I love living a quiet life with him. The hard work challenges us and makes us stronger."

"I'm relieved to hear that, but I would have thought that as our leader, Oman would have wanted a more comfortable life," Minza said reluctantly. She had expected more information and would have been even happier with gossip. "So, where do you live now?"

Jossa's head tilted, and she said evasively, "We live up north, not far from here. For this trip, we used magic to travel and save time."

"Well, you're going to have to give us directions so we can visit someday."

"Of course, but the cabin is small, and there really is no privacy. You may not be happy with that," Jossa replied evenly, reminding Minza of her comments about Tana's home. She finished her coffee and announced, "I must be going. I did tell Tana I'd help with supper tonight." She got up from the table, and the two women walked to the door.

Minza was frustrated but managed to keep her composure and said, "Oh, that's too bad. I wanted you and Oman to have supper here, but since you have plans, perhaps another time."

"Oman will be busy for the next two days, but why don't you

drop by Tana's tomorrow so we can talk more?"

"I'd rather we meet at one of the cafes," Minza replied stubbornly. Jossa smiled inwardly to herself. It appeared that living in the king's court had made the woman soft.

••••••

Salem walked across town to his mother's home, hoping she and Jossa would be out. He entered the yard from the far side, where the trees were abundant and hung low. It was the same path he'd used when he was younger, coming home late after a night with his friends. He walked up to the back door, knocked lightly on it and called out to his mother, but there was no answer. Checking behind him one last time, he entered the house. He silently moved to where Oman and Jossa would be sleeping. Salem quickly found what he was looking for, a small tack bag. He undid the flap and reached into his pocket, pulling out the pouch that contained the sorcerer's hair. With a start, he became aware of the muffled sound of two women approaching the house. His heart rate quickened as he hurriedly tucked the small pouch deep into the pack and closed it up again. The front door opened, and he heard Jossa say, "I'll be back in a second." Salem had already begun to move toward the window. He slipped through the shutter opening, landed on his feet and walked away as if nothing were out of place.

Jossa walked in and went directly to the small table beside the bed. She picked up a book that was sitting on it, thumbing through it quickly. "Yes," she said, "this is what I'm looking for." She had just turned when she heard a creak from the window and was surprised to see the shutters had been left open. Knowing she had closed them that morning, she looked out the window but saw nothing unusual. With a shrug, she re-latched it.

Tana's voice came from behind her. "What's keeping you so long?"

"The shutters were unlatched. I thought maybe someone was in here."

"That happens from time to time. It was probably just the wind." A knock on the front door interrupted them.

Before either woman could get to it, the door opened, and Salem stepped inside. "Good morning, ladies! It's so good to see both of you again! I've just stopped by for a short visit. Do you have coffee or tea ready?"

Tana, surprised to see her son up and about, replied, "Salem! Yes, the coffee is always on. You know where the mugs are. What brings you here so early? "

Salem sauntered over to the counter, pulled out a mug and filled it before sitting down at the table. The two women looked wordlessly at each other and then joined him. "I was hoping to catch Oman before the council meeting," Salem announced. "I suppose that now I'll have to wait."

"He mentioned to me that he wished to speak with you," Jossa replied, unwilling to discuss Oman without his being there.

"How long did you plan on staying?" Salem asked.

"We plan to stay for two more days before we return."

"This will be a quick visit, then." Salem changed his tone slightly before continuing, "And where exactly is home now?"

"Minza asked me the same question this morning when I visited her. We're living up north." Not wanting Salem to continue his line of questioning, she abruptly changed the subject. "By the way, your home is grand. Minza seems very happy with it."

"We've been trying to get Mother to stay with us, but she doesn't want to move."

Tana shook her head at her son and frowned. "I have no problem staying here, and I have no need for more room."

· · · · · ·

Oman walked out of the meeting and onto the front steps of the building. They were taking a short break, and he needed the fresh air to clear his mind. He knew he would never be able to do this every day. *How did my father do it year after year?* A familiar voice broke his train of thought.

"Oman, there you are. We'll be ready to begin again in just a few minutes." It was his deputy, Calam, who had been looking for him.

"Thank you. I'll be right there," Oman replied.

Calam placed a hand on Oman's shoulder. "I know this has been a long day for you. Unfortunately, there is only so much I can do without your input."

"Of course," Oman acknowledged. "It's fine. We'll keep things the way they are for now."

"Good," Calam said. "Have you seen your brother today? He dropped by this morning."

"No, I haven't. I expected him at the council meeting. I'm sure he'll find me soon enough. We'll be here well into the night. Can you ensure we have a few lanterns filled and ready for use?"

"I'll do that. It's time to return," the deputy answered.

Oman and Calam were just about to enter the meeting when they saw Salem approaching them. They met, and Oman turned to his deputy, saying, "I'll be there in a minute." With a silent nod, Calam excused himself.

"Brother," Oman said, "I expected you at the meeting."

"I was caught up in some private business matters. My apologies, Oman. I know you're busy, but can we speak alone for a moment?"

"Tell me what's on your mind," Oman said, irritated that his brother appeared disinterested in any council affairs.

"I was thinking of giving up my position as the ambassador, but now I think I'll hang onto it for a bit longer. I've just spoken with King Merck, and he has no problems with my proposal. I can do the job by proxy, just as you are doing here, and will drop into court once a month."

"I understand. If that is acceptable to King Merck, it is, of course, acceptable to me. Is that all? I have to return, and you're welcome to join me."

"Unfortunately, I still have personal business to attend to." Salem hesitated and looked earnestly into his brother's eyes. He added, "Oman, we're both getting older, and time is passing much too quickly. It's time for us to try and make things better between us."

"I agree, Salem," Oman said and held out his hand.

Salem gripped Oman's hand tightly in return and said, "To the future."

Oman repeated Salem's words and watched as his brother walked away. He felt an uneasiness: something just wasn't right. *Only time will tell.*

CHAPTER 21

Once their business was concluded, Oman and Jossa prepared to return home. When they were finally packed and ready to leave, Oman gave his mother a quick hug and said, "Thank you for letting us stay. We'll return before winter."

"You know," she said, raising an eyebrow, "if you two ever decide to return, you can build a house just over there." She pointed to an open area just in front of them.

Oman shook his head sadly. "Mother, you know that will never happen."

"An old woman can hope," she said stubbornly and sighed. "Never mind. I know you're happy where you are."

Jossa hugged her, and as she did, Tana whispered into her ear, "I've packed something in the bag for you. Open it once you get home."

"I will. Thank you," Jossa said. Oman summoned the magic, and an orb of soft light appeared in front of them. When it reached its peak, the two gave a final wave to Tana and disappeared into it.

It had been two weeks since Oman's visit to Alfheim. Salem had contacted Zakalis and let him know that the strand of hair was in place. The sorcerer, now able to locate Oman and his formula ready, sent Salem a message commanding him to meet at the agreed location.

Minza stood in front of their home, upset and anxious. "Why must you go?"

Salem turned impatiently from adjusting his horse's harness. "Minza, it will only be a week or so, and I'll be back. I've told you before. There's a possibility we can open stronger trade with the east. I have to be there to ensure the negotiations go smoothly."

"The roads aren't safe when you travel alone," she insisted.

"I'll be fine. Don't worry about me." He gave her a hurried embrace, and Minza watched with a worried look on her face as he got onto his horse and rode away.

He met with Bargun later that afternoon. It took the men three full days of riding to reach their destination, a small campsite set at a fork in the river just outside the Jogahoh border. They approached the camp carefully and came within yards of the site when they were suddenly surrounded by guards with drawn swords.

From behind the guards came Zakalis, his dark robes fluttering behind him. "I expected you sooner," he said, a deep frown on his face. His eyes fixed on Bargun. "I assume this is your helper?"

"Yes. The one I told you about."

"Can you trust him?"

"You worry about your side of the bargain, and I'll worry about mine."

Bargun interrupted, gripping his sword and blurting out, "I've told no one about this trip."

Zakalis delved into Bargun's mind and read his thoughts. "Bargun. You will not turn him in immediately after you get back. But as time goes by, you will see him gain wealth and riches while you squander all that was given to you. That is when you will try to get a better deal."

Salem said, "If that happens, that will be my worry, not yours."

Zakalis allowed a small smile to pass over his features and said mockingly, "Of course." He turned away from the two men and said, "Settle yourselves into the camp."

"We need to go back and get our horses," Salem replied.

"No need. They've already been looked after."

After supper, Salem was summoned to the sorcerer's tent. He stepped out of the cold night air and into an opulent tent filled with luxurious furniture. A richly coloured carpet covered the floor, and a brightly burning fireplace added warmth and light.

The sorcerer sat on a plush back armchair, sipping a glass of whiskey.

Zakalis waved him in and asked, "What would you like to drink?"

"What do you have?"

"Anything you want."

He hesitated for a moment, but before he could say anything, a mug of beer appeared on the table to his front. "I assume that's what you wanted?" Zakalis asked.

"Yes. Thank you." Surprised and nervous, Salem picked up the mug and looked around for a chair.

"My apologies," Zakalis said. "Let me get a smaller chair for you. You'll feel more comfortable." With a wave of the man's hand, the chair and table next to Salem shrunk down to accommodate his size.

He sat down, took a large gulp of his beer and placed the mug on the table. Not wanting to waste time, he got right to the point. "Why would Bargun betray me? We've known each other since we were children. He's always been loyal to me."

"Salem, you're about to commit an act of treason. You're better off keeping your circle small and trusting only yourself. I see a dead cardinal that has been preserved, and I can see the old man that preserved it. Your circle has gotten wider, even without your knowledge."

Salem was speechless. He never would have suspected Bargun to have betrayed him in such a manner. Before he could reply, Zakalis pulled out a small vial from his cloak and handed it to him. "Here's something you can use. Give it to him once the job is complete. Bargun will not remember any of your interactions. He may remember that he was near the border but will not remember who he was with or any of your dealings."

Salem accepted the vial without a word. He knew Zakalis was speaking the truth. He was livid at Bargun for his betrayal and angry at himself for letting down his guard. Steeling himself, he simply said, "What is the plan for tomorrow? Where are we headed?" The sorcerer got up and walked over to a large table, with Salem following. He rolled out a map showing where they were and where they needed to go.

"You cannot enter the Jibay land. If you do, the spirits will sense it and try to stop you." Zakalis held up a small bronze urn that was sealed tightly with wax. "Once you have arrived at its border, open this urn. Inside is the magic that will seek out the girl and bring her to you. It is a mist that will have the power to put her into a deep sleep, then lift her up and out of the Jibay, but no farther. From there, the two of you must bring her back here."

Salem glanced over the map and placed the urn carefully into his pack. His hand automatically went to the vial that held the potion for Bargun. Although he was listening to Zakalis' words, a wave of anger was still burning in him. The brew was an easy way out. A part of Salem wanted Bargun to suffer, to feel the same betrayal he felt. Unfortunately, Salem could not know what other evidence Bargun may have left behind. He would have to depend on the potion; the man wouldn't remember anything, and Salem's part in this would remain unknown. Returning to the moment, he asked the sorcerer, "Once this is done, when do I get my due?"

"Let's get the girl first. We can discuss our agreement later."

"I'll get her."

Early the following day, the two Jogahoh departed the camp. Three days later, they arrived at a stream that marked the boundary to the land of the Jibay. Salem stopped his horse, dismounted and said, "We'll set up here."

Bargun brought his horse up to Salem and said, "I'll tend to the animals. Do you know where we are?"

"Yes," Salem replied and pulled out his map, gesturing to it.

Bargun looked at the map for an instant and immediately shrunk back, exclaiming, "You've brought us to the Land of the Dead?"

"No," Salem replied calmly, a thin smile on his face. "The Land of the Dead is just over there." He pointed to a tree on the other side of the stream.

"This place is cursed! I won't go beyond the stream."

"We stay where we are. There is no need for us to travel into it. Hopefully, we will be out of here before the sun is up."

Bargun breathed in deeply and grudgingly agreed, muttering, "No longer."

"No longer," Salem replied, and they set about making their camp and waited for the sun to go down. An hour later, the sky darkened, and stars slowly started to litter the black canvas. A chill fell upon the two as the air cooled, and their horses began to stir, whinnying uneasily. The men tried to calm them, but they were sensing something neither man could see.

After another uneasy hour, Salem said, "It's time," and walked over to his pack, taking out the urn. He stripped off the wax that sealed it and took the top off before placing it on the ground. An emerald green mist began to drift out of the urn, twisting and turning in a grotesque dance, slender tendrils of green shooting out in all directions as if searching for something.

Bargun, alarmed, stepped back and exclaimed, "What is this?"

"This is what is going to do our job for us. All we must do is sit back and wait."

The mist pulled itself entirely out of the urn and surrounded the two men. Bargun stood frozen in fear, unable to utter a single cry. Salem, oddly pleased at Bargun's terror, waited patiently and watched the mist in fascination. He could feel its tendrils caressing his face and wrapping themselves around his waist. After a moment, satisfied that the men were of no consequence, it moved away and began searching for the girl. Bargun, terrified, collapsed onto the ground, still unable to speak.

The mist moved slowly at first as it searched for the scent. It soon found what it was looking for, picking up speed and heading directly to Oman's cottage. As it approached, the animals sensed its presence and began to get restless. Tendrils of power shot out from the mist, surrounding each animal and placing them all into a deep sleep. From the forest came the spirits of the old man and boy. Realizing that something was terribly wrong, they moved toward the cabin to warn Anong. Just before they reached it, the mist seized them and, with a violent blast, threw them to the far side of their land. They would return, but by then, it would be too late. The green mist's attention turned back to the cottage, its tendrils lifting the door latch soundlessly. It crept slowly along the floor, infiltrating the entire room. The mist first engulfed Jossa and Oman, placing both into a deep sleep. Finally finding Anong, it hovered over her excitedly, its colours shifting from green to brilliant red. It enveloped her, placed her into a deep trance and lifted her gently from the bed. Bearing Anong weightlessly above the ground, it brought her back to Salem.

Salem woke with a start. He looked at the sky and placement of the moon and determined it would still be a few hours before sunrise. Hearing a nervous whinny from his horse, he slipped from his sleeping sack and walked over to the agitated animal. Suddenly, the night sounds ceased, and the horse turned its head to stare across the stream. Salem followed its gaze and could see the mist slipping through the forest toward them. Immediately, he hurried over to Bargun and gave him a nudge with his boot. "Wake up. It's time to get moving."

Bargun jolted upright and said, "What's going on?"

"It's back," Salem exclaimed tersely, "and we need to saddle the horses." Quickly, the two men hurried about the makeshift camp, packing everything in sight. The mist stopped in front of them just as they finished, the silent form of the girl hovering within it.

"She's not a Jogahoh! How is that possible?" Bargun said in surprise.

"I'm not sure," Salem answered. His eyes were locked on the girl, and he walked through the mist to her. As he approached, he caught sight of a glowing stone around her neck and reached for it. The moment his hand wrapped around the gem a searing heat burned him. He cried out in pain and dropped the stone immediately. Salem and Bargun both looked in astonishment at the blistering wound in his palm. "Perhaps the stone has something to do with her being here," Salem muttered as he pulled out the urn and opened its stopper. The mist immediately lowered the girl to the ground, moved to the urn and slipped in silently. "The sorcerer says she'll stay in her trance till we get back to him," Salem said as he replaced the stopper. "We'll have the mist surround her again when we stop each evening to ensure she stays asleep. For now, wrap her tightly in these blankets. You'll be carrying her on your horse until we reach the border. Now let's get moving."

The two of them struggled to get the tall, unconscious girl wrapped and slung onto the back of Bargun's saddle. Finally settled, they got on their horses and rode toward the eastern border.

······

Oman struggled to wake that morning. His eyes seemed to resist opening, and his body was sluggish and heavy. He knew the sun had risen; he could feel its rays warming the room, but still, he lay in bed, unable to move. Finally, he forced his eyes open and looked up at the ceiling. With a soft groan, he rolled over and was surprised to see Jossa still tucked deep under the covers. *This never happens. She's usually the first up in the morning.* Awake now, he listened for the animals' usual sounds: the roosters' crow, the cows' low groans or the nickering from the horses. Nothing. He gently slid from beneath the covers and walked out of the room. Anong's door was partially opened, and he immediately saw that she was missing. Remembering that Jossa said she was going fishing early in the morning, he dismissed it, walked groggily down the stairs and started the fire in the stove. He warmed up a kettle of water and went outside to feed the animals. The chicken pen was silent as he entered it. They began to flutter only when he placed a hand under them in a search for eggs, but to his surprise, there were none. He returned to the house empty-handed and saw Jossa taking the kettle off the stove. "Good morning," he said with a smile, "or should I say good afternoon?"

"I don't know what's wrong with me," Jossa murmured. "I never sleep this late." She glanced at him and asked, "Would you like a coffee?"

"Yes, please. How did you sleep?"

"It was a deep sleep. I had the oddest dreams. I dreamt the farm was in danger, and we were both unable to move."

"Strange. I didn't dream of anything, or at least I don't think I was dreaming," he replied. "I take it Anong went fishing? I didn't even hear her get up. Come to think of it, her bed cover was stripped off, but I didn't see it hanging outside on the line."

"She may have taken it with her," Jossa said, unconcerned. "It's chilly in the morning."

•••••

Salem and Bargun made it back across the Jogahoh border and to the sorcerer's camp three days later. The journey back had been quick and uneventful, with the girl remaining in her deep trance. They rode up to see that the sorcerer was waiting for them. He waved them over to a wagon, and they transferred Anong into it. Zakalis asked, "Do you have the urn?"

Salem passed Zakalis the urn from his pack, and the sorcerer took off the seal, released the mist and ordered it into the wagon to surround the girl once more. As he locked the wagon doors, he glanced back at Salem and asked, "Were you seen by anyone?"

"None that I know of," Salem said, "but you never know what's watching you in the land of the Jibay."

"I'm not worried about spirits, just people. They can make a good thing difficult. We need to be on our way. I take it you'll be coming with me?"

"I need to get back to Alfheim. I told the wife I'd only be a week on a trade mission, and I'll be well past that now."

"King Tibalt has a proposal for you. He wishes to discuss the terms as soon as possible."

Salem felt a rush of excitement flow through him and replied immediately. "I'll return as soon as I can."

The sorcerer only nodded and began preparations for his departure. As he did, Salem edged closer to him and said quietly, "I need to keep my plan moving forward. I'll contact you soon. Do you have any beer left so we can have a pint around the fire tonight?"

Zakalis knew immediately what Salem was about to do. "Of course. I've already had my guard pack it for you."

CHAPTER 22

Late that morning, Oman began chopping wood, throwing the split pieces into a pile. They already had enough to last them for the winter, but as always, he wanted to make sure. Jossa walked out to see him and said, "I'm going out to where Anong is fishing. If she's caught anything, I can bring it home and get it ready for tonight."

"I'll be done here in a minute if you'd like me to go."

"No, I'll enjoy the ride." She leaned forward, gave him a kiss and rode to the west. A short time later, Jossa arrived at the spot where Anong said she'd be. She called out for her, but there was no answer, just the rushing sound of the stream. Jossa walked the horse slowly along the bank, looking for footprints. There were animal tracks, but she could see nothing belonging to Anong. She walked farther upstream into thick bushes that hampered her progress. Still, she found no sign. Jossa stopped and brought her hand to her chest. Within her, she had an overwhelming feeling of dread, the emotion all-consuming and almost unbearable. She called out Anong's name over and over again. Finally, knowing with certainty that Anong had never been there, she rode back hard to the farm. Oman raised his head in alarm at the sound of galloping hooves. Jossa rode up and hauled up fiercely on the animal's reins, stopping beside Oman. "She's gone. I think she's gone," Jossa gasped.

"Gone?" Oman was confused. "Gone where? You said she was going fishing."

Jossa's eyes lifted and turned to the wood line. "Maybe they know what happened," she said, vaulting herself off the saddle and stumbling forward.

Oman ran after her and called out, "Where are you going? What are you talking about?" His gaze fell on the shimmering shapes of an old man and a boy. Shocked, Oman came up to his wife. "Are you seeing what I'm seeing?" he whispered into her ear.

"Oman," Jossa replied impatiently, "Anong's been telling us about the spirits for years. You've never wanted to believe." The spectre of the old man looked closely at Jossa and then silently outstretched a thin arm to her. Jossa did not hesitate. She placed her hand in his. The moment her fingers touched his, she was flooded with images of what had occurred the night before. She could actually see the eery green mist as it crept toward their home and watched as it attacked the two spirits. The old man showed her the force and intent he had perceived when he encountered the mist, and Jossa knew instantly that it had come for Anong.

The old man's sad eyes drooped even further as he dropped his hand. Jossa collapsed in front of him in tears. For a moment, the two spectres wavered there, watching her. The young boy took the old man's hand, and the two faded from view. Oman knelt beside his weeping wife and asked, "What did they tell you?"

She described everything she had felt and told him what the spirit had conveyed to her. Jossa turned and pointed to where they had first seen the fog. "I think the mist came in from the east. It would have taken her back the same way."

Oman looked to the east, and a feeling of dread descended on him. Filled with anger, he said harshly, "Jossa, I'll bring her back. I'm getting my sword and chainmail."

······

Salem and Bargun had ridden non-stop since turning the girl over that morning. They were now deep in Jogahoh territory, and it would be dark soon. Salem said, "I think it's time we stop for the night."

"Good. I'm dog-tired, and the horses will need to rest," Bargun answered. The two men unpacked their belongings and split the tasks of setting up camp and caring for their animals. Within an hour, they had a pot of stew warming over a crackling campfire. Bargun dug into it and scooped out a large helping for both of them. Sitting down on a log beside Salem, he passed him his bowl and began to eat. The two ate in silence until Bargun finally asked, "Who was that girl, Salem, and why is the sorcerer so interested in her?"

"I really don't know," he replied, lying smoothly as he stared into the fire and stirred his stew. "If I did, I'd tell you," he said. "I just know they wanted her."

"Why did Oman and Jossa allow that girl to stay with them? They know the law."

"I don't know. Maybe that's why they've stayed to themselves all of these years."

"Makes sense, I guess, but how did she get through the border? She's clearly not Jogahoh."

"I have no idea. I will have to report this to the council, of course. Oman should have known better." Salem dished more of the stew out of the pot and tore off a piece of bread for himself.

Bargun was almost finished his meal when a possibility came to him. "Isn't the area we were in the same place a beast was killed? Rumour has it a person crossed over from Jogahoh territory and killed it with some sort of powerful magic. Salem, that's got to be the same girl. She must have power, and they want it."

Salem finished his plate and calmly placed it down in front of him. "Could be you're right, but it's none of our concern."

"Salem, if she possesses magic, we should have kept her for ourselves. We'd never have to work again."

Salem stood up and stretched out, ignoring Bargun. He knew that the man was dangerously close to finding out the truth. It was time for him to put the sorcerer's potion to work. Finally, he said, "The fire's getting low. Why don't you go and fetch some more wood? We can discuss this over a drink."

Bargun went on a hunt for wood, and Salem swiftly unpacked the keg and poured the potion from his pocket into Bargun's mug. He had just tucked away the tiny vial when the man returned.

"I think this will do for the night," Bargun said, throwing the wood down beside the fire. "I could use that beer now."

"Right here, my friend," Salem said and handed him the potion-laced drink. "A toast to friendship." They clicked the mugs together and downed the brew.

······

Oman finished the last of his packing and gave Jossa a final farewell kiss. "I'll be back with Anong, I promise."

Jossa's tears streaked down her cheeks. "Be careful. I don't want to lose you, too."

He hugged her and said, "Don't worry. I'll be fine. I'll send you a cardinal when I can."

She nodded silently and could only watch as he got onto the horse and headed off in the direction the fog had come from. Oman assumed that his daughter had been rendered unconscious and carried away; otherwise, she would have defended herself. *What had they done to her?* Hours later, he arrived at the stream that marked the Jibay boundary. He thought the mist must have been designed to travel unchallenged, or the spirits would have defended their territory. That meant it had to be guided by someone. He crossed over the stream and started to look for any kind of sign. Finding nothing, he cut north and then back south. This time, he went in deeper and repeated the pattern over again but found nothing. He was frustrated and angry at not being able to protect his family. Oman's guilt weighed him down and pushed him harder and harder.

Taking his time, he moved slowly back to his start-point. Oman stood up in the saddle and scanned the area. His eyes spotted the remains of a campfire. Whoever it was had not made any attempt to conceal it. Riding closer, he immediately realized that the hitching point for the horses was low to the ground. He was right. They were Jogahoh. "I have you now, you bastards," he muttered. Getting off his horse, he scrutinized the two sets of footprints carefully. One set was obviously Jogahoh moccasins. To his surprise, the other set were clearly boots, a highly unusual choice for any Jogahoh. He wanted to push on, but it was getting dark, and there was no use trying to follow them. Looking at the tracks leading his daughter away, he prayed. "To you, the one that looks over us, safeguard my daughter until I find her."

· · · · · ·

Salem woke and poked his head out from under his sleeping blanket. The campfire was now only a smouldering pile of ash, and his body was telling him he needed to relieve itself. He got up, threw a cloak over his shoulders and walked out into the woods. On his return, he picked up some wood and placed it over the dying coals. Kneeling, he blew gently on them, coaxing the fire back to life. Finally catching the air, it awoke with a crackle. Salem added additional sticks, stoking it until he was satisfied with the heat emanating from it.

Bargun, who was sleeping just a few feet away, slowly started to move. Rolling over, he stared blankly into the fire, confusion covering his face. "Where am I?"

Salem raised his eyebrows and said sarcastically, "Bargun, you drank a lot yesterday."

"Drinking? We were drinking?" He looked at Salem, bewildered, and exclaimed, "Salem! I haven't seen you in years! When did you get back from court?"

"We met three days ago at the trade mission, Bargun, don't you remember? You must remember that."

Bargun looked at Salem with bleary eyes. "Trade mission? What trade mission? For the life of me, I can't remember how I got here."

"Afterwards, we celebrated our reunion at the pub. I didn't

realize you had drunk as much as you did. I thought I warned you about the potent drinks they serve. You were quite the mess by the time I realized what shape you were in. I couldn't just leave you there by yourself. I had to load everything up and get you here. I couldn't wake you."

Bargun sat up, embarrassed and bewildered. Although he had freely indulged in drinking many times before this, he would always have some recollection of his actions. "I'm sorry, Salem. I'm not usually like that." He paused, still trying to recall what had happened. Struggling to get up, he lifted his hand to his face and rubbed it over his beard before slowly making his way over to where Salem sat.

Salem waited until the kettle was boiling and then poured hot water into two cups containing tea leaves. He handed one to Bargun and asked, "You really can't recall anything? Even before yesterday afternoon?"

The man's face blushed a ruddy red with humiliation. "No, not a damn thing."

"Ah well, you'll just have to listen to me when I tell you the drinks are too much for you. It's time for us to get packed up and go home. Drink up. Your head will feel better soon." They drank their tea in silence. After they finished, Salem poured the remaining water from the kettle into the fire, dousing it. Getting up and turning from Bargun, he walked to the horses, relief on his face.

•••••

Oman woke just before sunrise, packed his gear and was on his way within the hour. The only stop was at a small brook to fill his canteen and let his horses drink. He rode hard, following the tracks for the next day and a half until he crossed the border into the eastern kingdom. It was then that he spotted a long blue strand of ribbon lying in the tall grass. Tana had given it to Jossa on their last trip to Alfheim, and Jossa had given it to Anong. Knowing he was on the right path, he pushed on until the tracks joined with others. The much smaller feet of the Jogahoh were intermixed with larger sets of human boots and the clear impression of wagon wheels. From there, they split off. The tracks he followed headed back toward Alfheim, and the human prints went deep into the eastern kingdom. He knew the tracks could run in any direction after that, and he was torn with indecision. A sudden realization hit him. His brother Salem wore boots. He was following his brother, and his brother had been the one who had taken his daughter from him. Filled with rage, he determined that he first had to confront Salem and find out the truth of what had happened to Anong. Oman's heart sank. To be hated by his brother was tolerable, but to be betrayed by flesh and blood was unbearable. *So, Salem, it has come to this. Your treachery I cannot forgive. I should have settled this long ago. It's time to finish it.*

Oman knew that what he was about to do would not take long. He still needed to go after Anong. Securing his two horses on a long lead, he raised his arms into the air and looked up into the darkening sky. Pulling out a silver piece, he summoned its magic and called out, "Take me now to my brother Salem who has betrayed me." The leaves began to rustle, and a wind began to whirl fiercely around him. An instant later, Oman vanished. A moment later, he reappeared, standing on a road just outside Alfheim. In the fading light, he could make out the outlines of two riders approaching him. Knowing one of them would be Salem, he stepped off the dirt road and hid in the shrubbery. The outlines became sharper as they drew closer, and the two were now easily recognizable. It was Salem and Bargun. They talked loudly, paying no attention to their surroundings as they made their way toward Oman. When they reached him, Oman stepped out onto the road and grabbed for the rein on Salem's horse.

Startled at Oman's sudden appearance, Salem kicked his horse's side, trying to pull away, but Oman's grip forced the animal to stay where it was. Bargun stopped just ahead of them, turned back and looked for Salem.

"Are you crazy?" Salem screamed. "What are you doing? What's wrong with you?"

Oman let loose the horse's rein, stepped back and placed his hand on the hilt of his sword. Without looking at Bargun, he ordered, "Bargun, you can leave. I have no quarrel with you at this time."

Salem, startled and furious, immediately recognized his attacker. He had not expected his brother to discover his connection to the girl's disappearance. He changed the expression on his face to one of confusion as he asked, "What do you want? Why did you come at us like that?"

Bargun called out, "Salem, do you want me to stay?"

Salem did not take his eyes from his brother and murmured, "Go home, Bargun. I'll talk with you tomorrow." With one last unsure look at the two brothers, Bargun reluctantly turned his horse and set off for Alfheim at a gallop.

Oman waited for only a heartbeat before he reached for Salem's leg and dragged him from his horse. Salem landed with a dull thud; his wind knocked from him, and he gasped for breath as he lay on his back in the dirt. Oman came and stood above him, demanding, "Where have you taken her?"

Salem sat up painfully and tried to regain control of the situation. He slowly got onto his feet and brushed off his tunic before asking, "Who are you talking about?"

"My daughter. You camped outside the land of the Jibay and sent some type of magic to kidnap her. You brought her east and handed her to someone. Who was it, and where did they take her?"

"I have no idea what you're talking about. I don't understand. You and Jossa have no children. I was just now returning from a trade mission to —"

"You're lying," Oman interrupted and drew his sword, resting it at his side. "Tell me. Where is she?"

Salem always assumed that, as the elder brother, he held control over every situation. From their childhood, he had pushed and bullied his way with Oman. He thought this time was no different and drew his weapon, holding it out to his front. "This has gone on far too long." He lunged forward with his blade, aiming for Oman's heart. Oman brought his own weapon up quickly and warded off the blow. They moved around each other; Salem using the techniques he'd been taught at court, and Oman using the hard-earned skills he had perfected on the battlefield. "I should have done this a long time ago," Salem scoffed, raising his sword for an overhead strike.

Oman easily side-stepped the movement. "You show your intentions like a court jester. Did you think I learned nothing while fighting beside our father?" He brought his sword up and swung down hard, broadsiding it squarely across his brother's thigh. Salem, stung by the blow, reeled back with a curse. "Where is she?" Oman asked calmly. "Tell me now, and I'll let you live."

"You betrayed the Jogahoh," Salem shot back scornfully. "She's not your daughter; she's not even one of us. How could you be so stupid? Once word of your betrayal is known, you and that wife of yours will be banished forever. Your name will never be spoken again, and you will be forgotten." With that, Salem stepped in with a side-parry, trying to strike a blow to Oman's hip. Oman effortlessly blocked the swing and came in relentlessly, his strikes a never-ending deluge. Salem was forced backward and lost his balance, his sword clattering to the ground as he landed with a thud on his back. Not taking his eyes off his brother, Oman walked over to the weapon, picked it up and tossed it at Salem's feet.

"Take it up."

Salem felt a chill of fear run down his back. He reached over reluctantly and took hold of the sword's hilt, realizing that he was no match for Oman. The years of court life could not compare to that of a trained, experienced warrior. He immediately fell back to what he knew how to do—negotiate. "Let's stop this and try to work something out."

"No, Salem. You were correct when you said it's gone too far. I'll end this now and be done with it. I'll find my daughter on my own."

"You won't be able to. It would take a lifetime to figure it out."

"Then a lifetime is what it will take. Prepare yourself, Salem. Bring your weapon up." Salem had only just raised his sword when Oman's blade crashed down on it. The strikes became relentless, with Salem barely able to block each blow. A quick flick of Oman's wrist with the sword produced a stinging cut across Salem's forearm. The man pulled back, shocked at the sight of his own blood.

"Oh," Oman said mockingly, "they say those really hurt." Again, he began a barrage of blows, playing with him and pressing Salem harder and harder. A final assault knocked the blade from Salem's grip once more, and he fell to the ground. Oman stood over him and raised his sword, its tip ready to be thrust into Salem's skull.

Salem, exhausted and filled with terror, looked into his brother's eyes and could see nothing but death. Panting for breath, he brought his arms up, cowering, and cried out, "She's been taken to the eastern king's palace."

"By who?" Oman demanded.

Salem hesitated, and Oman screamed again, "By who?"

Salem's face whitened, and he stuttered out, "The king's sorcerer."

"Why?"

"I don't know. It was something about her having powers."

Oman's rage engulfed him, and he was ready to drive the sword home. He gripped his sword tightly, but as he did, he heard his father's voice. "Oman, let it be. He deserves what you want to do, but you are better than that." Oman froze, silent as a stone before a deep, frustrated scream rose from him. Without warning, he brought the weapon down as hard as he could on the side of Salem's head.

Salem clenched his eyes as he saw the tip of the sword coming down at his face. He suddenly felt the cold steel sliding past it, and then, piercing pain. His mind reeled, and he lost consciousness.

Oman pulled his sword up and looked dispassionately at the sliced ear lying on the ground in a puddle of spreading blood. "The eastern king's palace. It will be a long ride."

CHAPTER 23

Zakalis did not bring the girl directly to King Tibalt. He needed to test Anong's abilities and see precisely what she could do before speaking with the king. He took her to a stone cottage, a small, secluded building two kilometers from the palace. It consisted of one residence and a guardhouse, both made from stone and ringed by a deep trench. The cottage was deep enough in the forest to remain secluded but close enough for the king to use. In the early days, it had been a refuge. Now it was used to house political prisoners.

Zakalis told the guards to bring the wagon around to the back. Opening the wagon doors and peering inside, he saw with satisfaction that the mist still engulfed the sleeping girl. A wave of his hand ordered it to pick her up and follow him. He watched as it slithered into the room and lowered her gently onto a bed.

Walking to her, he reached through the mist, picked up her hand and held it tightly. Closing his eyes, he hoped to feel some sort of energy, some glimpse of her magic, but nothing happened. He could feel only the warmth of her hand and an erratic heartbeat. Worry swept through him. He imagined seeing the king's henchmen coming for him, dragging him to the dungeon and hanging him from chains. *I'm right. I know I'm right,* he insisted to himself. His concerns were soon replaced with frustration and anger. Still holding her hand, he pulled his dagger from his side and pressed it firmly into one of her limp fingers, drawing a bright red bead of blood.

Anong was in a deep sleep, locked into a dream of endless darkness. She felt a pressing weight on her chest that made it difficult to breathe. She was fighting to wake, but she could not pull away from the oppressive force keeping her tied down, no matter how hard she tried. Suddenly, she felt a sharp, piercing pain in her hand. Anger and outrage immediately engulfed her. From deep within her rose a guttural cry, and a blast of energy erupted from her.

Zakalis was shocked to see the strange birthmark on her chest glow a brilliant red. Without warning, an explosion of energy blasted him, the force of it throwing him off his feet and across the room. He slammed violently into the wall, landing in a heap, his breath completely taken away from him. He felt a flow of energy running through him, filling his mind. He looked around with amazement. Never had he seen the world in such colour and detail. Never had he recognized all the possibilities. Never had he felt so powerful, so alive. *Magic,* he thought excitedly. *The mist has transferred her magic to me.* Intoxicated with the rush of power, greed filled him. *I need more.*

• • • • • •

Esma was startled from her sleep and shot upright in her bed. She waved her hand, and candles flickered to life, banishing the darkness within the room. Her eyes darted to every corner, but there was nothing there. Worried, she threw her blankets off, slipped on a robe and stepped outside, looking around the yard and into the night sky. An oddly familiar force had woken her, but now it was gone. *Something is about to begin,* she thought. Esma shivered and re-wrapped her robe tightly against the chill of the night. With one last worried glance, she turned and walked back to her bed.

• • • • • •

Oman used the magic once more to return and set up camp in the spot where he had left his horses. Brushing them down, he made sure they had enough to eat and talked quietly to both of them. "Get ready for a long ride tomorrow. I can't use the silver pieces. I only have two remaining. I don't know how I'll find her or get into the castle yet, but we're leaving in the morning." He patted both horses one last time, then curled up beside the warm fire. *I'll have to send a cardinal to Jossa tomorrow.*

Early the next morning, Oman woke. The morning's dew had combined with the damp earth, and his body felt stiff and cold. Stoking the remaining coals from his fire, he placed a water tin over the flames and tended to the horses. When they were finally packed, he wrote a quick note to Jossa, telling her about his fight with Salem and warning her that his brother knew about Anong. He called for a cardinal, placed the message in its pouch and let the bird go, watching as it circled once before heading west. Oman finished his coffee and was about to rise when he noticed a boot print on the ground. It was his brother's. He swiped at the mark with his moccasin. "I could have killed you last night but didn't. Just the same, you are dead to me."

A few hours later, he was back to where the wagon and Salem had parted ways. Following the tracks along the road was no problem for the first few hours. The wagon wheels had dug deep into the earth, and they were easy enough to follow. The small road converged with another, and then a third, erasing all identifiable tracks, but still headed east. By midday, he needed to stop again to feed and water the horses. Cresting a small hill, he could see an inn at the bottom of the draw. He rode up to it and tied the horses to a hitching post. The place was unexpectedly large and was a converging point for the many roads that led to it. At the back was a barn big enough to accommodate several horses and carriages. A man walked out from the front door and looked at the horses. Seeing no one, he turned to walk back into the inn.

Oman called out, "Over here."

The man turned in his direction, and his eyes widened. He opened the door to the store and called out, "Mary, come here, quick." From inside, Oman heard a flurry of noise as a woman came through the front door.

"For God's sake, Thomas, what couldn't wait a few more minutes?" She spotted the two horses and asked, "Who owns these?"

"A Jogahoh," the man said in surprise and pointed to Oman.

The woman turned to Oman and looked back at Thomas in annoyance. "Don't you have work to do?" She stepped down the stairs and came up to Oman with her hand outstretched. "I'm sorry. You'll have to forgive my help. What can I do for you, sir?"

In return, Oman grasped her hand, introduced himself and said, "I need to get my horses fed and watered. After that, I'll be on my way."

"We can do that," she said and whistled shrilly. Thomas reappeared from around the corner with a question in his eyes. "Take Mr. Oman's horses, brush them down, then feed and water them." Mary invited Oman in and poured him a cup of coffee. She asked, "Are you hungry? The stew is fresh, and so is the bread."

"Thank you. I would appreciate a bowl," he replied.

Mary returned to the kitchen and came back with a heaping bowl of stew and a plate with two generous slices of warm bread and butter. She asked, "Are you sure you want to leave once your horses are ready?"

"That's my plan," he said, relishing the taste of the thick, savoury stew.

"I only ask because it's getting late, and the road isn't safe at night. There are too many highwaymen in this area. Alone with two fine horses, you are a prime target, even though you seem sufficiently armed."

"Thank you for your concern, but I'm sure I'll be fine."

Thomas walked into the room and took off his cap. "Mr. Oman, the horses will be ready soon, but one of them may need some extra time. He looks truly worn."

Oman pushed back from the table and followed Thomas to the barn. The large doors were open, and his horses stood in its centre with their heads down and eyes closed. He ran his hands over their legs and along their backsides. "You're right. They'll need the night to rest up. They're not used to walking on hard roads. I can't have one of them go lame."

Thomas said, "I can put some ointment on their legs. It should help."

"Thank you."

Oman started to walk away, and Thomas called back to him, "Sir, I'm sorry for what I said earlier."

Oman glanced at him and said, "No offence was taken. Thanks again for caring for my animals." With that, he walked back to the inn and finished his meal.

Mary came up to him a few minutes later and asked, "How bad are the horses?"

"They're tired. I've been pushing them hard, but they should be good come morning."

"How much farther do you have to go?"

"I don't really know," he admitted, wiping the plate with his bread. "The tracks I've been following blended in with the others as the roads merged."

Mary looked at Oman with a puzzled expression. She asked, "So how do you know where you're going?"

Oman had no intention of telling the woman anything more. He only said, "I don't. I can only follow the road."

"All the roads converge here. That's why the inn was set up. It's a good business. What are you looking for?"

"I'm looking for a wagon pulled by two horses. They had at least four outriders, two in the front and two in the back. They would have come through here two days ago."

Mary hesitated, a look of fear on her face. Finally, she said, "I've had several wagons come through the last few days going east. Only one had any outriders. Those were the king's men. Why would you be following them?"

Oman recognized her anxiety but needed to get as much information from her as he could. "Did they have a magic man accompanying them?"

She looked around before she spoke to ensure no one else

would hear her words. Speaking softly, she said, "That would have been the king's sorcerer. They came through here two days ago and stopped just long enough for food and water. There was a guard posted on the wagon the whole time; no one was allowed near it." She searched his face for a moment and asked, "Who are you looking for?"

"My daughter. They have my daughter."

••••••

Jossa had just finished collecting the eggs when she saw the cardinal land at the feeder. She picked it up gently and removed the pack from its back. Sitting down at the kitchen table, she read its contents, a troubled look on her small features. Oman told her what happened with Salem and warned her to be prepared to move on and not to trust his brother or brother's wife. If they dared to show their faces or threaten her with exile, he urged her to move deeper into the Jibay land.

Jossa was furious with Salem. Oman's own flesh and blood had betrayed them, and she could never forgive him. She put the message down and quickly replied to it. Calling to the cardinal, she held it close to her face and, stroking it tenderly, said, "I know you're tired, and you've come a long way. I need this message delivered tomorrow. Eat well, get some sleep, and then find Oman."

That night, she dug through the old trunk her mother had given her when they were first married. Finally finding what she was looking for, she pulled out an old, red leather-bound book and laid it on the table. The book had been a gift from whom she did not know and had been a part of her family for generations. Since then, the book had been placed aside and forgotten. When she was a young girl, her mother used the book to read her tales filled with magic. At the time, it seemed to be alive, its pictures jumping off the pages. Fantastic adventures had fuelled her imagination, and the entire book had come to life. Jossa opened it and paged through the contents. It contained not only children's tales but also remedies and recipes. Its pages were curled, the pictures only faded reminders of what they had once held. Dismayed at its condition, she placed her hands on the book and sighed with regret. At her touch, each page began to brighten, and the pictures flooded with colour. Jossa cried out in relief and began to search.

She had almost reached the last page before finding what she was looking for: the names and locations of persons with power, people who could help in time of need. The words on the page swirled at her touch, and finally, a map showing the location and name of only one person appeared. *Esma.* Jossa smiled. She would not sit idly by while her daughter and Oman were in danger.

CHAPTER 24

Oman stayed the night at the inn and was awake early the next day. He packed his gear, hoisted it over his shoulder and made his way to the barn. Thomas was already up and doing his chores as Oman entered the building.

"Mr. Oman," he said, "good morning to you."

"A good morning to you, as well," Oman replied, walking up to his stalled horses.

"If I'd known you were leaving this early, I'd have had them ready for you."

"No, it's fine," he said, bending over to check the animals' legs and hooves. "The ointment has done its job. They both look fine." Oman saddled his riding horse, then tightened his belongings onto the other. He brought the animals out and tied them to the hitching post before returning to the barn. Pulling out a handful of coins, he said, "I don't have much, but here you go. Thank you."

Thomas was brushing down another horse and glanced over to Oman. "Mr. Oman, Mary pays me. There's no need for that. Safe travels to you, wherever you are heading."

"You've taken extra time and care with them, and that is worth the coin," Oman insisted, pressing the coins firmly into the man's hand. "Thank you." With that, he walked out of the barn and to his horses.

Mary was sweeping the front porch and, at his approach, said, "I thought I'd missed you."

"I'm just about ready to leave now. Thank you for your help and hospitality. I've left payment in my room."

She walked down the steps to Oman and sat down on the porch. "I thought about your missing daughter last night and the king's sorcerer. You're going to need some help."

"I'll be fine," Oman replied, tying the lead line from the packhorse to his.

Mary pulled out a piece of parchment from her apron and gave it to him. Softly, she whispered, "I drew a map for you to a woman who can help. She's a good woman who lives only a day's ride from here. They say she is powerful, and if there is magic involved, she can help. Her name is Esma."

With surprised gratitude, Oman took the map and placed it into his pocket before asking, "Why do you want to help me?"

"During the war with the west, my husband was a general. He was killed on the last day of the final battle by our king. The king had accused him of treason. My husband was not a treasonous man. My family's life was put in danger, and I had to flee the city. That's why I stay here. The sorcerer you are looking for is very close to the king. If you're looking for him, I know the king is involved. They are both dangerous men, Oman. Be careful."

Oman regarded the woman solemnly. "I was there on the day your husband was murdered. He was no traitor." With that, he hoisted himself onto his horse, ready to depart.

Mary's eyes filled with unshed tears as she came up to him and placed a hand on his horse's shoulder. "Perhaps you will be my revenge. Take care, Oman."

Oman acknowledged her words with a simple, "Thank you again." With that, he nudged his horse and started his journey deep into the kingdom of the east.

······

King Tibalt strode purposefully to his sorcerer's quarters in the castle. One didn't have to know where the man lived; all you had to do was follow your nose. The stench was unmistakable. With a grimace of disgust, he opened the door to the man's room and walked in. His first sight of the sorcerer surprised him. The man looked different today; he seemed taller, brighter somehow. Instead of remarking on it, he said, "The stench in here is beyond the hallway."

"My apologies, Sire. My new potion has an unpleasant side effect. It will dissipate soon."

The king wandered around the open room, peering into cages and jars containing dead animals suspended in a clear fluid. He walked over to a window and opened the shutters, pronouncing, "Fresh air is what you need. Tell me, was your little mission a success?"

"It was, Sire."

"And the girl. Is she who you expected?"

"I think she is more than what I expected," the sorcerer answered, recalling being thrown across the room and the power still flooding his system.

King Tibalt's primary concern was no longer the girl. Instead, his priority would be the power his sorcerer was able to drain from her. "Keep her away from the castle. Take everything from her. We will need it. And the little man who was to help you — his name escapes me at the moment. Did he return with you?"

"Sire, his name is Salem. I expect him to be here within days. He wants the leadership of the Jogahoh."

"I will promise him whatever he wants. They are only words, and it will all be mine soon enough. I still remember the Jogahoh fought with the west. Their land and their people in slavery will be my payback."

••••••

When Oman received Jossa's message, he couldn't help but feel she was up to something. What it was, he didn't know, and he could only tuck the note into his pack and continue on his way. Riding up to a crossroad, Oman pulled out the map Mary had drawn up for him. He knew that he needed time and a plan to find out exactly where Anong had been taken and how to rescue her. *If Mary is correct, then this Esma can help me,* he thought. Oman nudged his horse and followed the road that led to her. Late in the day, he arrived at a small farm and rode into the yard. He tied his horses up, and walked about, looking for the woman. He was impressed with the neat, well-kept surroundings. The animals within were well-fed and looked after. The house and outbuildings had been built with precision and care. Oman was about to knock on the door when a woman's voice came from behind him.

"And how can I help a man of the Jogahoh today?" Oman turned his head to look behind him but saw nothing. Confused, he turned back to the door and brought his hand up to knock again.

Once more, the voice spoke. "What is it you want?"

This time, he spun around. In front of him was a tall and slender woman with long black hair braided neatly behind her. Her black eyes regarded him with patience.

She asked again, "Well, what do you want?"

Oman could feel his face redden. The woman was stunningly beautiful, her features timeless, and he felt himself fumble for his words. "I have a problem," he stuttered, "and I was told you may be able to help me."

"Oman, where is Anong?"

Oman gaped at her. "How do you know my name? How do you know about Anong?"

"We can speak about all of this in a moment," she said, turning and walking toward his horses. "There is a lot for us to discuss. In the meanwhile, your animals need care." She ran her hands along their sides and remarked, "They say you pushed them too hard the last few days. This one is almost lame." Without waiting for Oman, she unhitched the horses and, with a tilt of her head, had them follow her obediently to the barn. Once inside, she undid all their gear and placed everything over the stall railing to dry. "They say you left in a hurry."

Oman tried to help her, but she moved so quickly he felt he was only getting in the way. "I had to get moving. There was very little time before the trail got cold."

"What trail?" Esma asked, frowning.

"Someone has taken my daughter," Oman answered. "They already have a head start on me. By the time I found the trail, they were gone."

"Anong is gone? Kidnapped?"

Oman ignored her and demanded, "How do you know us?"

Esma finished with the horses and quickly laid out feed for them. Shutting the stall doors, she said, "Come with me." She strode to her cottage so quickly that Oman was almost running beside her. Opening the door, she motioned for him to sit down at the table. Walking over to an old trunk, she placed her hand on top of it, and the locks snapped open. She pulled a stone from it and brought it to Oman, asking, "Was Anong still wearing a stone like this?"

"Yes," Oman replied quizzically. "She's worn a stone exactly like that ever since I found her as a baby. She's never taken it off. It burned my hand the first time I tried to touch it, but it's never harmed her."

"If she still has this on, she is not missing, and I can find her. I would have known if someone had taken this from her. I would've sensed it. Are you sure she isn't still in the Jibay land?" Oman shook his head and lapsed into silence; his eyes fixed on the bright stone in front of him. Esma noted his fatigue and, without his asking, quietly brought him a glass of cold milk and some leftover roast. "Tell me everything you know."

Oman knew without question that he could trust this strange, beautiful woman. There was something eerily familiar about her, and he was sure she knew something of how Anong had first come to them. He told her everything that had happened and added, "Two of the Jibay, an old man and a boy, said they saw a green mist come into our yard. When they tried to approach it, the mist threw them miles away."

Esma stiffened and pulled out an old book of magic, going through it page by page, trying to find what she was looking for.

She stopped, and Oman watched with alarm as she became agitated and slammed the book shut. Getting up, she began pacing around the small cabin and then remembered the rush of power she had felt the previous night. She cursed and said, "I didn't think that bag of bones could figure this out. I completely underestimated him." Her eyes fell on Oman, and she said worryingly, "I think we may have a problem."

••••••

Zakalis sat back in his room at the castle, feeling drained and exhausted. The channelling he had used to direct her power had worked, but the magic drained from him within two days. When he was filled with her energy, his brain was running on overload. He could see the answers to all his problems and felt invincible. What he was feeling now was the difference between a rich man and a beggar. Yesterday he was wealthy; today, he had nothing. Her power was a drug to him, and he felt addicted to it. His king would get what he wanted, and Zakalis would help, but that would be the end of it. He would find a way to permanently transfer her power to him. After that, he would be through with the king and everyone else.

••••••

Jossa prepared herself for her journey by packing a small sack and used a silver piece to take her to Esma. The magic surrounded her in a tight ball and pulled her through the air out of the Jibay land. She flew past the Jogahoh boundary and then to the east toward Esma's small cottage. She could feel herself start to slow down, hovering for a moment over a small farm before coming gently down to the ground.

Esma was with Oman in the cottage when she stopped what she was doing and tilted her head as if she were listening to something. "We have company," she said, turning for the door.

Oman followed her out and into the yard, curious as to who the visitor might be. He stopped mid-stride, his mouth agape. "Jossa? Why are you here?"

"Oman? You're here, too? I'm here to find Anong, of course. It appears that the gods have pointed us in the same direction." They embraced each other fiercely before Jossa lifted her eyes up to the tall woman and asked, "Are you Esma?"

"I am," Esma replied, an amused look on her face. "How did you find me?"

"My mother passed down a family heirloom, a book of ancient knowledge. I finally had need of it and found your name and location in it."

Esma was surprised and said, "I thought all of those books were gone, lost to time."

"My family has always considered knowledge to be a treasure worth keeping," Jossa answered.

"Let's move back into the house. We can speak there," Esma said. The three of them returned to the cottage and sat at the kitchen table.

"Have you found Anong yet?" Jossa asked Oman.

"I've been following her trail. I think she's been taken to the king's court, but I'm not sure," Oman replied.

"If we can find the sorcerer, we'll find Anong," Esma stated. "It would be easy to do if I had something personal of his." She grew pensive for a moment before a realization hit her. "The spell he used to kidnap Anong...how did he know where your cottage was?" She got up and began talking to herself. "Only one way," she finally concluded. "The mist will always track to its keeper. The mist was following something that belonged to Zakalis," Esma surmised. "Do either of you have anything that doesn't belong to you?"

"I don't understand. Like what?" Oman asked, puzzled. "How big does it have to be?"

"Size makes no difference. It would probably be something small that can be hidden away. Oman, bring me all your gear," Esma ordered.

"All my gear?"

"We'll start with your pack. Everything you carry with you on your journeys."

Oman obediently collected his pack, emptied it out and laid everything on the table. Esma touched every piece, looking and feeling for Zakalis' presence, something that didn't belong. After some time, they still had found nothing, and Oman was discouraged. "There's nothing here. What now?"

Jossa spoke out. "Where is your tack?"

"My tack? Of course, it goes with me wherever I go," Oman replied, a glimmer of hope on his face. "It's hanging in the stall." The three hurried outside and entered the barn, where Oman laid out his saddle and saddlebags.

Esma began a methodical search of his belongings, her hands gently hovering over every piece of equipment. After a few moments, she stopped above a bag, picked it up and emptied it. An assortment of eating utensils spilled from it, along with a small leather pouch. "Does this belong to you?"

Oman looked carefully at every item and said with suspicion, "Everything but the pouch. I've never seen it before."

Esma gingerly opened it and found a long, silver strand of hair. She pulled it out and held it in her hand for only an instant before her face changed. Clenching the strand tightly, she closed her eyes and said softly, "Tell me, who do you belong to?"

An image appeared in her mind, indistinct at first. As it sharpened, Esma could see a tall, slim man walking through the castle. She opened her eyes and said, "It belongs to Zakalis. He's at the castle now, and Anong, I believe, will be nearby." Esma retrieved the box of stones, dropped the strand into it and locked it. "We'll keep this. Now let's find Anong."

CHAPTER 25

The sorcerer made his way to the cottage, unlocked the front door padlock and entered the room. Anong was lying on a bed in the centre of the space. The fog still surrounded her, and she slept quietly. He walked through the green mist and came up to her, whispering an incantation. As he did so, the mist obediently retreated, and she opened her eyes, startled and confused. She struggled to sit up, then looked around, stopping immediately at the sight of the stranger in front of her.

She studied him, and asked, "Where am I and who are you?"

"I've rescued you from your captors. You're safe now."

"My family are not my captors," she replied angrily before asking again, "who are you?"

"My name is Zakalis. I am King Tibalt's sorcerer. You were only an infant when we first met," he replied, remembering that she had come to him years before.

"Where am I and what is this mist?" she demanded.

"The mist is here to protect us both. For now, I would only say that you are home," he replied vaguely.

"I don't need protection," she retorted. "And this isn't home. You are not a Jogahoh."

Zakalis marveled in the tendrils of power he felt seeping into him from Anong and immediately wanted more. He knew, however, that he had to receive it in small amounts, or he would be overwhelmed. "And neither are you," he replied coolly, walking around her bed, his hands behind his back. Zakalis' eyes never left her, as he wondered how to get more power from her. "What you have is nothing that I've ever seen before. I think even that old witch Esma was impressed." Anong was startled at the mention of Esma's name, and Zakalis smiled inwardly. His comment had stirred something in her. He could see it in the way she reacted to the name.

"Where are my mother and father?" Anong asked impatiently. The way he looked at her made her skin crawl. She felt an instant dislike for the man. It was in how he held himself and talked, with self-made importance and a condescending attitude.

"Which ones? Your parents here in the east or the Jogahoh that stole you from them?" Zakalis continued to pace around her bed, the clipping of his heels against the wooden floor beginning to grind into Anong's head. He watched with silent glee as her face changed and even more power surged into him. "I have no intention of tormenting you any longer. Your real parents both died of heartache years ago," he lied. "The two Jogahoh who stole you were executed the night I rescued you."

Anong tried to move her legs and stand, but the mist held her firmly in place. Shock and rage began to boil in her veins; her heart rate quickened, and her eyes narrowed. She allowed herself to be flooded with feelings of revenge and hatred for this evil man. When the magic became a torrent and was ready to burst, she assaulted him with a massive blast of power.

The green mist immediately absorbed Anong's charge and channeled it to Zakalis. The sorcerer fell to his knees and arched his back as the magic surged into his system. The mist had made the transfer tolerable, but it was still overwhelming to him. He could feel it filling every cell membrane in his body, rejuvenating and energizing him. Zakalis felt invincible. *This is it,* he marveled. *All I need to do is get her angry. Her emotions compound the power I already have.* After a minute, the sorcerer got back to his feet, his body vibrating with magic. With a sneer, said to Anong, "I'll see you in a few days."

Anong was stunned and confused. Something was happening here, something she didn't understand. The power she had directed was like nothing she'd used before and should have destroyed him. She watched helplessly as Zakalis strode out of the room, and, once more, she was enveloped by the green mist. She would sleep until she was needed.

•••••

King Tibalt moved away from the window and glanced at the clock. "I'm late," he said to no one in particular. It made no difference, he knew. No one would move until he was ready. Taking his time, he strolled through the great hall with its paintings of past kings and queens staring down at him. He entered the room where all his generals were assembled, waiting for him. The men rose to attention as he made his way to the head of the table. Arriving at his central dais, Tibalt gazed at them wordlessly for a moment and then announced, "Good day, gentlemen. In two weeks, we will be attacking the west and taking back what is mine."

Murmurs of surprise and shock erupted among the men. He let the uproar continue for a few minutes before he held up his arms. The noise subsided immediately. "I know you will have questions on how we can take on such an undertaking in this short amount of time. I'll show you now." He motioned to the rear of the room, and the doors opened. Zakalis walked in and joined the king at the dais. Angry murmurs broke out among the generals; they had had numerous dealings with the sorcerer before, and they all hated him. At the same time, many of the generals were shocked at his appearance. Gone was the stringy, dirty hair, gone the slovenly slouch and shuffling walk. Instead, Zakalis appeared stronger and taller somehow. His face gave off an unearthly flush of colour, and his dark eyes burned with ferocious energy.

One of the generals, unfazed by the change he saw, stood up and said, "Sire, with all due respect, what is this man going to do for us? In the last war, he did nothing but eat and sleep, which was good because his mouth was busy, and he stopped complaining. When we asked him for something as simple as foot ointment to stop blistering, he had nothing."

The sorcerer acknowledged the general with a cool nod. To himself, he marked the man. *I'll remember you when the time comes.* "Yes, sir, you're correct, but that was years ago. We were all much younger and lacked experience. Now stand up and gather around. What I am about to show you will explain it all in more detail." Twenty generals got to their feet and walked reluctantly to the front of the room. The sorcerer began a soft chant and waved an arm toward the group. In an instant, everyone disappeared and reappeared in the countryside, six kilometers from the western border. Gasps of surprise rose from the men; they had not known Zakalis was capable of such magic.

The king stood in front of the crowd, a boastful, proud expression on his face. "This will be our front line, manned by our army of the dead," he announced. "Behind them, we will assemble another five thousand of our troops over the hill and to the east. We will push from here together, toward the western border with ten thousand soldiers as a fighting force."

The generals looked at the king as if he had lost his mind. One of the generals whispered, "What is he talking about? What army of the dead?"

An uneasy buzz grew throughout the crowd. Another general finally spoke up. "Sire, our standing army is no larger than five thousand troops. Where can we find another five thousand soldiers? You speak of an army of the dead. What is this?"

The king turned to his sorcerer and commanded him. "Zakalis, it's time."

"This way," Zakalis ordered and turned to move to higher ground. The generals followed reluctantly but were curious as to what the man would show them. They arrived at the rise of a hill to see the whole valley in front of them. Closing his eyes and holding out his arms to the sky, Zakalis began to weave his spell. His body became surrounded by an orb of dark red light, and ominous black clouds formed, blocking out the sun. Thunder blasted the men's ears, and they began to cower. Lightning strikes rained down on the valley floor, and the earth beneath them shuddered. The flashes of brilliant light seemed to never end, and they could feel the electricity crackling around them. Violently, the valley floor began to quiver and heave upward. To the generals' astonishment, hands and arms started to appear, crawling awkwardly up from the earth. Horrified, the men watched as fully armoured demons in the shape of soldiers began to appear. Finally, the figures stood in ranks so deep that the entire valley was filled with their dark, evil presence. The demon beings stood there, deathly still, as if awaiting their next command. The sorcerer was pale and exhausted now but had a jubilant look of satisfaction on his face. He turned back to the crowd without a word as if he were challenging them.

The king watched with amazement as Zakalis wove his magic. *With this army, I will not fail again,* he thought with vicious jubilation. He led his generals down the hill and through the ranks to inspect Zakalis' creation. Some of them were convinced that the army was an illusion until they looked into the soldiers' blank, unblinking eyes. The demons' skin was greyish in colour and stone cold. They were all dressed in ancient armour that had not been seen for hundreds of years. The men were alarmed to recognize that the soldiers were clones of each other. They stood almost six feet tall, with bulky, muscled arms and chests caked in mud and earth. Each carried a sword and axe, with knives and other weapons strapped to their waist belt.

One of the generals placed his fingers under a nose to feel a breath; he felt nothing. Another touched one, but it produced a chill, and he felt as if his life were being sucked from him. He pulled away from the figure in terror.

A man asked, "What are they?"

"They are the undead. Demons that will fight at my command," Zakalis gloated. "Let me give you a demonstration." Without warning, the sergeant who had challenged Zakalis on his arrival at the castle appeared before them. The hapless man looked around him in confusion.

"You again, Magic Man. What am I doing here?" he asked angrily when he spotted the sorcerer.

"Prepare to defend yourself," Zakalis replied smoothly. Turning to the king, he said, "A short exhibition of their abilities, Sire."

A soldier from the undead ranks stepped forward and halted as if awaiting further orders. "Attack," Zakalis commanded.

The demon hoisted his sword high and advanced toward the terrified man. In complete panic, the sergeant stumbled backward and fumbled for the hilt of his weapon. Shakily, he drew it up, trying in vain to defend himself. The demon came onto the overwhelmed man without remorse or hesitation, using wide, powerful slashes. The first strike cleaved the man's sword in half. The second sliced through the hapless soldier from sternum to waist. He stood for only a second before falling face-first into the ground. The battle was over, and the bloodied monster returned soundlessly to his ranks.

Zakalis turned back to the group, a satisfied expression on his face, but said nothing. The generals, overwhelmed and shocked by what they had just seen, were mute. The king proclaimed loudly, "With this army, we will prevail. You have two weeks to prepare your troops. Zakalis, take us home."

Zakalis woke in his room the next day, exhausted. He'd fallen asleep the instant he had returned but still felt worn out and beaten down. His energy felt drained; he had used the last drop of his stolen magic to bring everyone back into the council hall. *This is what real magic is about,* he thought, *using and conserving energy.* He would need to pull more magic from the girl immediately. Zakalis took his cloak from the rack, had his horse saddled and rode to the stone cottage with the next shift of guards.

· · · · · ·

For two days, Esma tried to find Anong. She placed herself into a meditative state and travelled to where Salem and Bargun stopped just outside the Jibay land. Using a residual memory spell, she saw Salem open an urn and release a mist. The scene in front of her disintegrated into a grey, shapeless landscape, and she could see nothing. A few moments passed before she found herself once again with Salem and Bargun. They were loading an unconscious Anong onto the back of a horse, and Esma realized she was once again aware of Anong. At that moment, she knew with certainty that the mist was responsible for blocking her ability to see the girl. The mist was the key. *But if we can find Zakalis, we will find the girl.*

Oman entered the house, placed a basket of eggs on the table and sat down beside Jossa. "Is Esma still searching?"

Jossa lifted her head from one of Esma's books and said, "Yes, she is. I'm hoping she'll be back soon."

"It's unnatural for a person to be sitting that still for so long. She looks rather strange."

"Have you ever seen yourself when you're asleep, dear?" Jossa asked Oman affectionately.

Oman laughed. "I see your point."

Jossa shook her head in amusement and continued reading. Half an hour later, Esma started to move slightly, tilting her head to relieve the tension. A few seconds later, her eyes opened, and she stretched out her arms and legs in relief. Oman came up to her with a glass of water, and she drank it down thirstily. He asked quietly, "Did you find her?"

"No, I couldn't find her, but I know who has her. The mist you spoke of can mask her essence. Zakalis must be holding her somewhere close by, but I'm unable to see exactly where she is."

"Why would Zakalis take her? What does he want?" Jossa asked in frustration.

"Zakalis has always been a greedy, jealous man," Esma said. "I think he's going to try to take her power."

"Why would he do that? She's only a baby," Jossa asked angrily.

"Anong is no longer a child, Jossa." Esma reflected for a moment and decided it was time for them to know the truth about their daughter. "Once every thousand years, a female child with immense power is born. Anong is that person. This power she holds can be used for good or evil, but that is for her to decide. When she was born, I had a dream, a prediction of a future where she had not been shielded. The eastern king and his sorcerer used her power to destroy this world. I could not let this happen, and she had to be hidden from them. I chose the two of you to care for her and raise her as your own. She has been shielded for all these years and knows the difference between good and evil. Unfortunately, they have now found her. Make no mistake," she said as she watched their faces, "Anong is human and as fragile as you are. That is why she had to be protected."

Esma thought back to her first dream and the evil presence that had almost overtaken her. She shivered and said, "I have tried to protect her, yet the dream is still coming true. Now I see it. There have been rumblings for years that the king wanted to renew his war with the west. Anong's power, directed by Zakalis, will be devastating to this world."

Oman thought back to the tiny infant he had first laid eyes on and the helplessness he had felt coming from her. Finally, he looked up at Esma and simply asked, "So what do we do now?"

"I think it's time for you to visit the castle," Esma said.

He frowned and replied, "There are no Jogahoh in the castle. I'll be very conspicuous."

"You'll appear no different than anyone else."

Esma had Jossa assist her in gathering the required herbs and other ingredients. They put a pot of water into the stone fireplace just above the red-hot coals and waited until it came to a slow, rolling boil. Esma dropped each ingredient into the water separately, chanting under her breath and mixing it thoroughly before adding the next. Once all the ingredients were in, she removed it from the heat and set it to cool.

Oman walked over to the pot and sniffed at it suspiciously. "I hope it tastes better than it smells."

Esma glanced at him, laughing. He and Jossa had a resilience to them, a strength that would be needed if they were to save their daughter. She said, "It's a potion, not your supper. We'll let it sit overnight. Tomorrow morning at dawn, you'll drink it. Then I'll transport you to the castle."

"Are you sure this will work? Is it safe?" Jossa asked.

"What I've prepared is a glamour. Your physical body will remain unchanged. To everyone else, you will look like a human soldier."

Oman nodded in agreement. "I can say I came down from the north for my mother's funeral. That will make any questions easy to answer. Soldiers like to talk with other soldiers."

"What if they ask you a question about the north? What if they know a man from there and ask about him?" Jossa wondered.

"I can work around any of that. There are lots of garrisons up there. If I don't know a person, I'll just tell them he must be somewhere else," Oman replied confidently.

"Your rank will be that of a sergeant. That will give you enough authority to ask questions yet be left to your own devices," Esma said.

Jossa was unsure about having Oman enter the castle. She said, "Esma, could you not send your spirit there? Why must Oman go?"

"The sorcerer is smarter than I initially thought, and he would be able to sense my presence. If he realized I was looking for Anong, he would only make it more difficult to find her."

"That's settled then. Tomorrow will be a long day," Oman said.

· · · · · ·

Minza was horrified when Salem returned to Alfheim with blood still flowing freely down the side of his face. She called for a physician immediately, and he spent the next day being fussed over by his worried wife. Unable to admit what had happened, he claimed to have been attacked by unknown thieves and barely escaped with his life.

Salem knew that King Tibalt wished an audience with him, so he downplayed his injury and contacted Zakalis as soon as he was able. Lying smoothly to his wife, he told her he needed to attend to business in the western kingdom and leave the following day. She objected, of course, but to no avail. He left as the sun broke the horizon through a travel portal provided by Zakalis and reappeared in the sorcerer's chambers.

"What happened?" Zakalis asked bluntly when he saw the bandages covering Salem's head.

"It's nothing," Salem muttered, ignoring the throbbing wound. "I'll be fine."

King Tibalt, he learned, would meet with him personally, as was custom and in keeping with what Salem thought was his due. He was, after all, the ambassador and in a senior position within his brother's court.

Zakalis remained silent as he escorted Salem through the halls and to the king's chambers. "Will you be joining us?" Salem asked.

"Political discussions are not my concern." With that, Zakalis turned and left Salem without another word. Salem knocked confidently on the king's door and waited to be called inside. A few minutes later, the door swung inward. A guard looked at him without expression and said, "You may enter."

Salem walked into the opulent room where King Tibalt sat on an oversized, leather-bound chair trimmed with gold, awaiting him. He bowed slightly to the king and said, "Sire, I am Salem, son of Ninib of the Jogahoh nation. I've been told that you wished to speak with me."

King Tibalt studied the small, self-important man standing in front of him in silence for a moment. *This would be an almost too easy effort on his part.* He knew that flattery would bring him the results he wanted. "Salem, it is good to finally meet you."

"The same, Sire," Salem acknowledged.

"Please sit," the king said, and as Salem did so, a servant poured them a glass of wine. Tibalt raised his glass and announced, "To your health." Both men drank deeply and then placed their glasses down on the table.

Salem commented, "That's a fine vintage. It tastes like it's from the south. It must be at least ten years old."

"Ahh, a connoisseur. Tell me, is that deep underground wine cellar still in my brother's castle?"

"Yes, Sire, it is and, when I left, still stocked full."

Tibalt laughed lightly and said, "I understand you helped my sorcerer immensely in finding the girl. For that, I am grateful. He's also said that what you wish in return is the leadership of the Jogahoh. I assumed that would be granted to you automatically once it's known your brother hid an outsider all these years."

Salem sipped his wine and placed the glass back on the table. "Yes, Sire, it would be; however, I want more."

Tibalt smiled thinly and replied, "I thought for all your hard work and dedication, I could make a bit better of a deal. I understand my brother gave you some magic that can only be used in the spring and summer. Is that correct?"

"Yes, it is," Salem said, then added, "It's a deal I would not have made, Sire, but that was my father."

"I would not have been content with that, either. I'll get right to the point. What I am asking you for is a Jogahoh alliance between us. If I need you in the future, you will come to my aid."

Now was Salem's moment, but the king had set this up, and Salem was falling into the trap. "Sire," he said confidently, "I'm in the process of taking over any time now. I will honour your request, but once all is done, I want magic to use whenever and wherever I want to use it. The power must be given directly to me so that I can distribute it as needed."

Tibalt's face reflected a wide grin. "I am giving you a great gift. I would ask for one more thing: that the barrier be taken down between us. It will allow us once again to have free, easy trade and movement between our countries. We have been kept apart for too long."

Salem considered the implications of having the barrier brought down and could see nothing but positive outcomes. The beasts that had driven them underground could now be hunted and forced even farther north, and commerce would thrive in both countries. Without hesitation, he replied, "We have a deal."

"I will have the sorcerer seal our deal within the next month, my friend. My advice is not to be too generous with this power and hold back enough for yourself in case of a general uprising."

Salem smirked and said, "My thoughts exactly."

Tibalt refilled the glasses. "To a long and lasting friendship," he toasted.

CHAPTER 26

Oman woke before sunrise and quietly walked out of the bedroom. He stoked the fire to take away the night chill and filled a kettle with water to hang over the hearth. The bedroom door opened, and Jossa came out, a tired yawn on her face. "Tea will be ready soon," he said, motioning to the fire.

"Thank you," she replied, pulling three mugs from the cupboard and placing them on the table. "I want you to be careful today."

"I'll do my best, but I don't think it will be an easy task." He took the kettle from the fire and added the tea bags. When he was finished, he walked to Jossa and wrapped his arms around her. "I don't want you to worry. We'll find her, and I'll be careful." Jossa could only nod silently; she was still worried about Oman leaving her behind. She turned and began to prepare them something to eat.

Esma came in through the front door and placed a bucket of fresh goat's milk on the counter. "Good morning. The tea is ready? That's perfect. Thank you," she said, joining them at the table.

"Breakfast will be ready in just a minute," Jossa replied.

A short while later, they finished their quick meal of porridge and bread smothered in butter. The three drank their tea, and Esma began giving Oman his instructions. "I cannot maintain the glamour for more than a day. You will have from the time you drink the potion until sunset tonight. I'll create a portal that you can use to travel to and from the castle. Just remember to mark the spot for your return. It will be linked to only you and Anong, should you happen to find her."

"I understand. I'm ready," Oman answered.

Esma took a full cup of the potion from the pot and placed it in front of him. "You'll have to drink it all," she said, handing it to him. He accepted the cup, took a breath and drank the mixture down. Even before placing the cup back on the table, he began to feel an electrical charge running up and over him.

"The glamour will affect you physically and might take some getting used to. You are no longer Jogahoh, so you will have to adjust how you see and react."

Jossa was staring in astonishment at him. "You're so tall!"

A minute ago, everything in the room had seemed too large for Oman. Now it was just the right height. He wobbled uneasily for a moment, adjusting his Jogahoh size to his new, taller self. He walked over to a mirror and gazed at it. In front of him stood a soldier, almost six feet tall, with long brown hair, tied neatly back in a pigtail. He was young, perhaps thirty years old, with sharp features and a neatly trimmed beard. He was wearing a uniform bearing the stripes of a sergeant. "This may take some getting used to," he muttered.

"In case Zakalis senses this glamour, it will be best for you to stay a distance from him," Esma warned.

Oman took one last glance in the mirror. He wondered if this ruse would work but knew that this was their only chance.

Esma stood and announced, "It's time."

The three of them walked out the door, and Oman turned to kiss Jossa goodbye. She leaned back as he came to her, hesitant at his appearance and only reluctantly kissed him on his cheek. He was surprised to discover that the glamour allowed him the physical freedom to move within his new size. He left Jossa's side and walked to his horse, feeling his height and the length of his stride. Placing his foot quickly into the stirrup, he swung his leg up and over the horse with surprising ease.

"I'll see you tonight," he said gently to Jossa, who had not taken her eyes off him.

"I'll be waiting," she replied.

Esma began a call, her head and arms thrown back, her voice

growing in power and urgency. In front of them appeared a small, swirling circle of wind and brightly coloured light. It grew steadily until it was just large enough for Oman and the horse to travel through. The portal stabilized, and Jossa could see a secluded copse of trees on the other side of it. "Go now," Esma commanded. "Remember. You have only until sunset."

Oman urged his horse forward and walked into the glowing light. As he entered it, the portal gave a final flash of brilliant colour and disappeared.

The two women watched him vanish, and Jossa said, "I hope he'll be all right. I know he's been through a lot worse, but sometimes fate has a funny way of twisting things, just to show you who's in charge."

"Fate does, Jossa, but I feel he'll be fine. I'm so glad I chose the two of you to raise Anong, but I feel the burden I've placed on you was too great. Having to stay hidden all those years from your family under the threat of banishment must have been terrible."

"Esma, we took Anong in as our own with no questions asked. From the moment I held her in my arms, she made us a family. Oman and I couldn't care less about what the others think, and banishment never threatened us."

Esma understood that the woman's love for Anong was indeed a mother's love. She said, "When Oman took her out on the quest, I brought her here to visit me. The aura around her was so strong, and her body and mind were so kind. I was very proud of her, but I was also jealous of the two of you being able to raise her. Yet, I had no choice. When she was born, I had a terrifying premonition of what they would do to her if she were not protected. I couldn't let that happen."

"I'm glad you didn't," Jossa replied.

• • • • • •

One moment, he was at Esma's farm, and the next, Oman was heading toward a copse of trees. He could see the castle in the distance, some two kilometers from him. He turned the horse and gazed back at the portal and its surroundings. He could see it still shimmering in the early morning dew and referenced a large tree directly beside it. It would be used as a marker on his return. He gently nudged the horse with his heels, and they made their way to the castle.

Oman travelled through a secluded wood and then toward a well-used road. As he came nearer, the road started to fill with more people. It was Market Day, and the main gate would be open, giving him access in and out of the area. He arrived at the entrance, got off his horse and walked through the throng of people, making his way over to a group of soldiers standing guard. As he drew closer, they recognized his rank and stood to attention. "I've just come in from the north," Oman said. "Can one of you tell me where I can feed and water my horse?"

"I can, Sergeant," one of the men answered. "I'm about done my shift here."

The two men walked through the tight streets, Oman following closely behind. "I haven't seen you here before," the young soldier said. "Where did you say you were from?"

Oman replied, "I'm from up north. Our unit is tight along the border. Cold as hell in the winter."

"Down here isn't too bad, as long as you don't get posted toward the Jogahoh border. The beasts there sometimes pose a problem. So, what are you doing down here?"

Oman had a grudging respect for the man. Although he was respectfully courteous, he was also doing his job, and Oman was being led through a subtle interrogation. "I'm originally from the south. My mother died some time ago. I always promised her I'd make it to her grave, and that's what I've done. She liked the Edelweiss from up north, so it's what I planted on her grave."

They arrived at the public stable and the soldier, his curiosity satisfied, said, "Here we are, Sergeant." He pointed to an older man sitting by himself on a stool and working on a harness. "This man will take your animal and care for it. Meals are served in the mess hall to your left at twelve and six o'clock."

"Thank you," Oman said. The soldier acknowledged him with a nod, turned and strode away. Oman walked over to the older man, who was still working on the harness. He could tell by his slow, painful movements that the man's life had been a hard one, and he greeted him with respect. "Good morning, sir. I was wondering if you could care for my horse today. He'll need food, water and a good grooming."

The man raised an eyebrow in surprise. "Sir! I haven't been called that in a long time. Your accent isn't from around here, is it?"

"I'm from up north," Oman said.

The older man got up slowly from the stool. "Things must've really changed since I lived up there, but as always, nothing stays the same. What's your name, Sergeant?"

"My family name is Ackerman."

"I've never known that name in the north. I believe it's from the south, isn't it?" he said, a curious eye on Oman.

"Aye," Oman answered. "The south is where I was born and raised, but the north is where I've pledged my military service."

"Ah, well then, you must be glad to see your kin again. I was told the northern army wouldn't start showing up until next week. Are you here early?"

"No, I'm not here for anything official. What's happening?"

"I don't really know. I've just been told to prepare for an influx of troops."

Oman needed more information. "I wasn't briefed on anything before I left, but that was weeks ago. Any rumours about what's happening?"

"They just called it a push. You hear a lot when you tend to horses and keep your mouth shut. When do you want your horse ready?"

"Around four o'clock, if it's good for you."

"He'll be ready." With that, the old man took the horse from Oman and led him slowly into the barn.

A push? Is this an invasion? Oman thought with some alarm. The only direction the king would be going, he knew with certainty, was toward the west. The timing of Anong's abduction and a call to arms by the eastern king could not be a coincidence. He needed to find Anong now. He began his hunt by walking through the streets. By noon, he'd completed a search of the walled city and made his way to the main ramparts and inner wall. He looked at the two guards on either side of the door as he walked through to the other side. These walls were the inner courtyard to the palace, and common people were not allowed. A corporal in charge of the gate guard eyed him and said, "Sergeant, can I help you?"

"Yes, I'm here from one of our northern posts and just in for the day. Do you mind if I walk the grounds?"

"You can. Just stay away from the front." The corporal pointed to a large building. "You can enter the main hall if you'd like, but go no farther, or you'll find yourself in the dungeon."

"I wouldn't want that." Oman nodded and carried on his way. He walked through the main doors of the palace and into the meeting room just beyond them. Once in the meeting room, and seeing no one, he slipped into a hallway on his left. Finding a large staircase leading to the upper and lower floors, he began a search. He had almost checked the entire lower floor before he ran into two maids.

They stopped, and one of them asked suspiciously, "Can we help you?"

"Sorry, I'm new here and seem to have taken a wrong turn. Can you show me the way out?"

"Follow us," the older of the two said. "We're done for the day, and it's time to go home."

"What were you looking for?" asked the younger girl as they walked down the hall.

Oman answered honestly. "I was told there was a young woman of around sixteen years of age here. I was supposed to gather her up and take her to her new quarters."

The younger woman thought and replied, "We've just finished cleaning all the rooms. We've seen no sign of a young girl here, I'm sorry to say."

"I must be mistaken then. My apologies, ladies." He bowed graciously to them. Flustered by his attention, the young girl giggled and tried to keep him engaged in a conversation.

"Now we do have a Jogahoh fella that's just arrived. He's an unusual man. I'd say he's barely as tall as my eight-year-old nephew. He hardly reaches three feet high."

"I heard of the Jogahoh but have never seen one," Oman answered. "What does he look like?"

They had just reached the door leading out to the yard. "No need to describe him. He's coming past us right now," the older woman said as she looked ahead of them. "Don't gawk now, girl," she scolded the young maid, who was staring unabashedly at the Jogahoh coming toward them.

"Did you notice? He only has one ear. I wonder what happened," the maid whispered, unable to take her eyes off him.

Oman stepped back from the two women and made way for the small man to pass. The three watched without speaking as Salem walked past them and into the yard. The Jogahoh's eyes glanced only briefly and without recognition into his brother's face. Oman's eyes hardened as he watched him pass. His brother was more involved than he had ever expected. *Why is he here, and what is he into now?*

Oman thanked the two women for their assistance but kept an eye on Salem. After the women departed, he strode after him, keeping a safe distance between them. He could just make out the top of Salem's head as the small man walked through the inner gate and turned left. Oman stepped out, determined not to lose him. He turned the corner and was relieved to see the crowds in the streets starting to thin. Market Day was ending, and people had either sold everything they had come to sell or bought enough of what they needed. He could see Salem fifty feet ahead of him, stepping in and around people, then almost being knocked over by a large cart trying to make its way through the narrow streets. Oman tucked into a wall opening as the wagon squeezed through and slowly moved on. Once it passed, he stepped back into the street and looked for his brother, but the shorter man had disappeared. Oman hurried up the road to where it merged with a path along the outer wall; still no Salem. The man had only been a few feet in front of him, and he couldn't have gotten that far. Quickly, he moved back down the street, searching each store along the way. After twenty minutes, he was ready to give up when his eyes spotted a placard announcing the Hole in the Wall Tavern. *Of course*, he thought and walked in through the door.

The tavern was tight, with one large window in the front that shed only a bit of light to the inside. Oman stepped across the threshold of the doorway and was stopped immediately by the crowd. Turning sideways, he slid through the throng of people and over to the bar. The clientele had the look and smell of the lower working class, who did all the menial labour to keep a kingdom functioning.

Finding a vantage point at the end of the counter, he ordered a drink and scanned the crowd. There in the corner, at a table by himself, was Salem. He looked small in the oversized chair, and an unwanted pang of pity washed over Oman. No one else would sit with him; Jogahoh were unusual in this kingdom. He looked desperate and uneasy in this environment, his cockiness and swagger gone. He was in a land he did not belong to and was surrounded by strangers.

Oman felt a tug on the back of his coat. "We don't see many soldiers here. They usually drink at the tavern across town. Buy a girl a drink?"

Oman turned toward the woman. She was older but still pretty in the waning light, with her long blonde hair, trim figure and ample bosom. "I'd love to, darling. What are you having?"

She leaned in closer to him and said, "I'll have a gin if that's all right with you. Are you here alone?"

The smell of alcohol on her breath almost made him reel back. The bartender overheard her order and obligingly produced a glass of gin for her before Oman could answer. "I'm alone and just passing through. Quite the crowd today."

"It's always like this on a Market Day. Passing through to where?"

Oman grinned at her as she fluttered unsteadily beside him. "I'm from one of the northern posts and will be leaving shortly."

"That's really too bad. Wouldn't you want some company before you go on your way? The trip, I'm sure, will be a long one. I could make your stay enjoyable."

"I'm sure you could, but not tonight, dear. Maybe you could persuade that lonely Jogahoh over there. He looks in need of company."

The woman strained her eyes drunkenly toward Salem and recognized him immediately. She shook her head slowly and said, "I had no luck with that one. He came in last night with the king's sorcerer, who I won't go near. They spent the evening discussing something about payment for a job. He wouldn't even look at me. Are you sure you don't want my company?"

"My wife wouldn't be happy with me."

"Honey, that's too bad, I suppose. Thanks for the drink." She raised her glass to him, took another sip and tottered off to find another customer.

Oman watched her leave and then returned his gaze to Salem. He knew he had only a few hours left and could do nothing more regarding his brother. He took a final sip of his beer, then turned and went out the door. As he was walking, he could hear the clock strike four. His time was running out. He approached the stable, and Oman spotted seven mounted soldiers in front of it. He hung back to wait until they departed. His luck had been good to this point, and he saw no sense in pressing it. Five minutes later, a tall, slim man with long silver hair approached the group. He wasn't wearing a uniform; in fact, he was dressed in a black robe, yet he appeared to be giving the soldiers orders. Oman watched as the man mounted his horse and began to head to the front gate. Abruptly, he pulled up his horse and turned quickly around, searching the area with a puzzled look. He twisted in his saddle, his eyes probing. Because Esma had warned Oman that Zakalis might be able to sense her magic, Oman instinctively stepped out of view. He heard the horses mull around and, to his relief, heard them depart a moment later. He peered around a wall and watched as the last of them rode out of sight. A sigh of relief escaped him, and Oman realized he had been holding his breath.

He made his way to the stable and saw the old man, still seated in the same spot. Oman asked, "Is my horse ready?"

The old man looked up and replied, "Yes, sir. She's been fed, watered and saddled up, waiting for you in the back."

"Thank you," Oman replied and walked to the back of the barn, where he untied the horse and led it back to the front door. "What do I owe you?"

"Nothing. I'll put your tab on the king's account."

"Who was that group of men?"

"The king's guards. They head out about the same time every afternoon, and the off-duty crew comes back in. The king's sorcerer joins them on occasion." The man lifted his hand and placed it on the horse's neck, soothing the animal. "You ask a lot of questions for a visitor."

"I just like to know what's going on."

"The two maids you saw today," said the old man, still gently petting the horse. "The younger one is my daughter. She comes by every day with a small surprise for me from the palace. Today it was a piece of rock candy. She mentioned a stranger who asked about a young girl."

Oman observed the old man calmly but said nothing, waiting for him to continue.

"I don't know anything about a young girl," the old man remarked, "but if I were looking for my daughter, I'd go out and follow that group."

Oman nodded his understanding and said, "Thank you," before reaching into his pocket and taking out a gold piece to hand to the man.

The old man quietly accepted the coin and said, "Good luck."

Oman rode down the road leading away from the castle walls. The pathway was well-worn and searching for the tracks of the sorcerer and his guards would be futile. He sighed, stood high in the saddle and looked in all directions. A small dust cloud just entering the forest toward the northeast caught his attention. He urged his horse into a steady trot and rode to the edge of the wood line. Oman stopped and spotted the hoof prints of eight riders entering a path leading into the forest. He heard the muffled sounds of men and horses coming toward him. Oman quickly pulled his horse into a thicket of trees and counted the men as they passed by. He counted only six; there were two missing. He listened in carefully as the men were talking.

"Corporal," a man from the rear called out, "I owe you a beer for not making me wait for that magic man."

"I'll take that tonight at the mess," the corporal replied with a short laugh.

Another man said, "I'm getting tired of coming out here every day."

"It's better than staying in garrison," another replied.

"As long as the king is paying us, you'll do as you're told," the corporal said sternly.

Oman watched wordlessly as the group disappeared. He knew his search for Anong was coming to an end. Time was running out, and his glamour would soon be fading. Discouraged, Oman turned his horse and headed toward the portal, returning to Esma's farm.

The sun was just touching the horizon when Esma and Jossa heard hooves coming closer. Walking out of the cabin, they saw Oman sliding off his mount. His glamour had now disappeared, and he was back to looking like himself.

Jossa ran and enveloped Oman into a hug just as his feet hit the ground. Esma called out to him, "Well, how did it go?"

Oman pulled himself away from Jossa only reluctantly and said, "It went well. I never found Anong, but I did find Zakalis, and I'm sure I know where she is. I also discovered that my brother, Salem, is there. He's been working with the eastern kingdom all this time."

"Salem?" Jossa said, a shocked expression on her face. "He was there?"

"He's there," Oman repeated, a flash of anger on his face. "I'm not sure why yet, but I'll find out. In the meantime, Esma, I've narrowed our search for Anong to a cottage not far from the palace."

CHAPTER 27

Zakalis needed an influx of magic that would allow him to control the undead army for more than one day. To obtain it, he would have to pull additional power from Anong. With the green mist as sentry, he set about a slow-waking process, with the mist continuing to have firm control of what she could and could not do.

Anong woke slowly from her slumber, feeling stiff, weak and hungry. She turned her head and saw the green mist still surrounding her and, beyond it, a smirking Zakalis.

"Hello, Anong. I hope you're feeling well."

"What have you done to me?"

"Nothing to hurt you. I've only used a bit of your energy. I'm giving you some time to walk around, inspect this fine home and eat a good meal. You can do whatever you want while you're here, but you will remain under my control. I'll allow you freedom if you cooperate with me."

Anong sat up cautiously and moved her feet to the floor. The mist followed, moving as she moved, always surrounding her. Tentatively, she touched the cold stone floor. She stood up slowly and shuffled carefully to a table that had been set up with bread and meat for her. She did not want to accept anything from him but had no choice. Anong needed to keep up her strength if she had any hope of escape. She reached for the meat and tore into it hungrily. "How long do you think you can hold me like this?"

Zakalis barked out a harsh laugh and replied, "A few weeks, maybe more. Until I'm done with you."

Anong got up from the table, a piece of bread still in her hand, and raced toward him. Before he could react, she seized his arm and released her power into him with a deafening roar of anger. The sorcerer felt a surge of energy searing into him, filling his very being. The sheer thrill of it engulfed him, and he let out a scream of ecstasy and pain. Anong's first thought was that she had gained control of the man. A moment later, she felt a pulling, a drawing of her very life force. Frantically, Anong tried to break free, but the mist gripped her tightly, channelling her energy into Zakalis. From that point on, she could feel and sense nothing. A cry broke from her lips, and she fell helplessly to the floor.

Zakalis stood, gasping with pleasure at the life he felt flooding his system. Her conscious power was all-consuming, and if he were to allow her to remain awake and eating, he could keep her indefinitely. With a short, cruel laugh, he turned and said to the mist that hovered around her, "Look after her. I'll need her again soon." With that, he walked out without a second glance at the unconscious girl lying on the floor behind him.

Days passed, and Anong sat alone in the stone house, the green mist always surrounding her. She had everything she needed, food, water, clothing and heat. Everything except her freedom. She could not use her power in any way. She had tried in vain to open the doors and windows, but they would not move. Anong attempted to attract the guards' attention, but they paid her no heed. It was as if they could not see or hear her. On the days that the sorcerer came to her, he would only upset her. She knew he was lying and would always try to lash out with her magic, but instead of stopping him, it seemed to have the opposite effect. After that, she could only watch as he absorbed her raw power.

Frustrated, Anong walked back to the table and sat down. Pouring herself a mug of water, she took a long drink and placed it back on the table. *Why does he always come here only to upset me?* She stood and began pacing around the room, trying to think of a solution. A few minutes later, she was back at the table. She picked up the mug of water and drained it. Anong placed the mug down and looked into it. She picked up the pitcher and started to refill it, stopping at the halfway point. Anong stared at the mug and then continued to fill it before taking another thirsty drink. A thread of knowledge began to form within her. Once more, she picked up the pitcher and filled the mug to its brim. With a jolt of insight, she stopped. *He comes here to fill himself with my power. He's found a way to take what I have and transfer it to himself.*

· · · · · ·

Esma went into her bedroom and lay down, falling into a deep sleep. Moments later, her spirit lifted from her body and flew toward the castle walls. The night was clear, and the moon lit up the grand structure. She started her search from the main gate and followed the route Oman had given her. Gliding down the road, she discovered a small path that cut toward the tree line. It was the spot Oman had told her he'd seen the guards. Just above the trees, she tried to gain some altitude away from the thick forest but could see nothing. Shooting herself up high into the night sky, she stopped and gazed down at the dark woods. Turning in every direction, she scanned the canopy looking for a sign of life but saw nothing. She knew she would have to follow the path where it entered the forest. Gliding down, Esma kept on for half a kilometer before she began to see the faint flicker of a light ahead. Slowing down, she saw the outline of a building. When she arrived, the horses, sensing her presence, became agitated and started snorting and shuffling nervously. A voice called out, "Check to see what's bothering the horses."

Esma moved over to the guardhouse and drew closer to the men. She listened carefully as they spoke, trying to find out what they were doing there and if they knew what was in the building. The only information she could glean was that it was an ordinary shift, and no one knew what was in the house.

She drew closer to the cottage and tried to walk through its walls but was immediately stopped. The main door also resisted her entrance. Moving to a window, she tried to look inside but could see only blackness. She attempted to send her senses into the building but was again completely blocked. It was as if the cottage were a black hole, a vast, empty, unreachable blot in her world. She flew up and settled herself on the roof, frustrated by the magic she knew was impeding her vision. Looking down into the grass, Esma saw a little mouse make its way over to the stone wall. An idea immediately came to her, and she drifted down to the tiny animal. She asked it, "Can you tell me if a young woman is in the cottage?"

The mouse stopped its search for food and looked up into Esma's face, unafraid and curious. It gave a sharp squeak and moved toward a small hole in the wall before slipping into the cottage. Esma waited patiently and, ten minutes later, watched the tiny mouse return to her. She gently probed the animal's mind and could see what it had seen. Anong was inside, and a green mist surrounded her, blocking her magic and presence from the world. It acted like a jail cell, not made of iron bars and bolts but accomplishing the same aim. She sensed that Anong had ample food and water but was profoundly sad.

Esma thanked the creature and once again moved into the night sky, searching for something that could help her. Spotting two guards, she dropped down to listen to their conversation. They whispered so as not to wake the others. She followed their words for the next hour about their wives and families, but the mundane of everyday life was not what she wanted to hear. Her patience was finally rewarded when the subject changed. The two began to speak about the army advancing to the west. Their mood became fearful and dark when they spoke of a rumour about soldiers that had appeared from the ground. They described the creatures as having grey skin and eyes as lifeless and cold as ice. Esma listened with alarm to the men's words and realized that Zakalis had turned to the blackest magic she had ever known. Her heart raced with fear as she recalled her dream so many years before. She could almost smell and taste the foul stench of death that this darkness would bring. Esma had everything she needed to know. Zakalis was somehow using

Anong's magic. Alarmed and knowing that the sun would soon be coming up, she willed her form back through the night sky and returned to her sleeping body.

She woke early the next morning to find Jossa and Oman already up and finishing the daily chores. She walked out to the front porch, where they were both sitting and speaking quietly.

"You had a restless sleep," Oman remarked. "We could hear you tossing and turning. Was your journey successful?"

"It was," Esma replied gravely.

Jossa interrupted, "Did you find her?"

"I know where she is, but I was unable to contact her directly. A mist is surrounding her, hiding her presence and keeping her from her magic."

Oman and Jossa were relieved but concerned. Jossa asked, "Is she all right? When can we go get her?"

"Physically, I believe she is fine, but I don't know that we can rescue her immediately," Esma said softly. "The sorcerer is somehow using Anong's power. He's found a way to channel everything Anong has from her into him. He has gained so much strength that I'm not sure how to defeat him."

"Can't we just break into the house and take her?" Oman asked.

Esma shook her head and said, "No, the mist has placed a boundary around the cottage. No one can get in, and she can't get out."

The three of them sat silently, Jossa and Oman's first enthusiastic reaction to finding Anong dampened when they realized they could not help her. Esma finally said, "We need to wait for the right time. Anong is a strong, smart woman. When she finds her strength, she can fight him on her own. I know this." She turned to Oman and asked, "Did you hear anything about a push to the west with the army?"

"I only heard about people converging there. Why?"

"Because the guards mentioned it. They also spoke of what

they described as an army of the dead fighting with them."

"He's called up the dead?" Jossa repeated in alarm.

"He has used his blackest magic and Anong's power to invoke them. They are demons and will fight tirelessly for him as long as he holds them in his thrall," she replied darkly. She began to speak again, almost to herself. "But his powers are dependent on Anong's. Holding power over an army of the dead takes a tremendous toll on a person's strength. He will have to replenish his magic often. If his strength falters, I will know it. That will be our only chance to defeat him. If not, his army of death will take over everything that we know."

Oman asked, "How can we stop an army fuelled by black sorcery? How can we defeat an army of the dead?"

"You first need to warn the western army that they are to be invaded. The only way they can stop the undead is through fire. Ultimately, we must stop Zakalis. He is the primary source of this evil," Esma answered.

Oman stood up and said, "I'll go to King Merck now to warn him."

Esma nodded briskly and said, "We'll stay here, and if there is a chance for us to rescue Anong, we'll bring her here. Oman, you must return as soon as you can."

Esma rose and went back to the cottage, Oman and Jossa following closely behind her. He asked Esma again, "So, the only way to kill those things is to burn them?"

"Yes. And to defeat Zakalis, we must deplete his powers. If we cause his forces to take his energy and magic from him, it will weaken him. Only then can we strike. This will be an ugly, vicious battle, Oman, and the early goings will be hard."

"What if Anong doesn't figure out that he's using her? What do we do then?" Jossa asked.

Esma looked steadily at them before solemnly saying, "Pray."

Oman was transported to King Merck's court through a portal that Esma conjured. He hurried to meet with the king's deputy and knocked on the door of his quarters. Oman heard a voice from inside call out, "Enter." Oman opened the door and walked in.

The man had aged since their last meeting, but his defining features, a full, grey beard, black eyes and a head devoid of even a single strand of hair, were still there. Looking up from his chair, he saw Oman and greeted him fondly, "My old friend! You are the last person I expected to see here today." He got up and walked to greet Oman.

Oman answered, "It's good to see you, sir. I hope you are well."

"I am," the deputy answered. "What brings you to the kingdom?"

"I need to warn the king about an army gathering on the eastern border."

The deputy's face turned cold and solemn. "Come with me."

The two men stood with King Merck over a large map hung on the wall an hour later. Oman began by saying, "They say he's gathering his forces along the valleys that lay parallel to the eastern border. The guards were overheard talking about an army of the dead. The regular troops will be arriving in a week and will gather to the rear."

The king and deputy glanced at one another and looked back to Oman. "This doesn't make sense, Oman," King Merck said with a frown. "Look how close this is to our border. If there were an army there, my outposts would have spotted signs of life. They would have given their position away with simple things, like cooking fires and supply trains."

"This is no ordinary army, Sire. It was conjured through black magic and does not live. Although they are dead, they will fight for as long as their maker has the strength to push them forward. I suggest your sorcerer to join us."

The sorcerer, Doro, arrived ten minutes later. He listened with growing skepticism when Oman told him of the dead army. He turned to the king, doubt in his eyes, and said, "Sire, there is no possibility that Zakalis has the power to do this. He can conjure portals, make potions and construct easy spells. He has never had the omnipotent power that would be required to raise an army of demons. Such a power could only come from an ancient, powerful being."

Oman interrupted. "My wife and I were given a daughter, sent to us sixteen years ago by Esma."

Doro was startled by the mention of Esma's name. "Esma? How do you know of her?"

Oman told them how Esma had sent the child to them, how she had been raised and how she had been taken from them. He finished with, "Esma told us that Anong is the woman born of prophecy once every thousand years. Zakalis has found a way to channel her energy into him."

King Merck turned his troubled eyes to his sorcerer. "What does all this mean?"

Doro's face had changed from skeptical to shocked. "It means," he said finally, "that King Tibalt now has the power to take over not only this kingdom but possibly the world."

King Merck grimly asked Oman, "Is there any way we can take her from them?"

"Zakalis has surrounded her with a powerful mist whose boundary we cannot penetrate."

The king turned to his deputy and said, "You'll have to go to the eastern border and gather as much information as you can. Doro will set up your portals for travel. We'll meet back here tomorrow morning. I'll pass the word to our commanders that the army is now on standby. If your news is grim, we march in two days."

A flurry of activity ensued within the court from that moment on. The king had rallied his commanders and set the wheels in motion to move his vast military machine into action. The next day, King Merck, Doro and Oman met with the deputy, who had just returned from his journey. The man looked haunted, his eyes bleak. The king asked him, "What have you seen?"

"Sire, it's just as Oman said. There are thousands of creatures standing in three ranks, ready to march this way. They appear to be men, but they stand motionless, waiting for a command. Their eyes are open and black and have no life in them. Their skin is grey and caked with mud and sludge. I was able to approach them without their reacting to my presence. I even ran one through with my sword. There was no response, and my sword came out blackened and smelling of rotting meat." He turned to the map on the wall and pointed to the border. "They are situated in the valley and seemed to be aligned with the pass. I moved farther to the east, well out of sight from our border outposts, and found they are setting up a rear line for their regular troops."

The king stared down at the map, his face set in resolve, and said, "Deputy, pass on to all the outposts that we move tomorrow morning at sunrise." He pointed to two places along the border. "First Brigade will be to the north, the Second to the south. The Third will remain in reserve to the centre rear." The deputy saluted and briskly walked out the door. The king turned to Doro and Oman. "My first question to the two of you is how do we stop these things?"

Doro stood silently while Oman told the king what Esma had said. When he finished, he remarked, "Sire, I wish I could have come with better news."

Doro finally spoke, confirming Oman's words. "He speaks truly, Sire. The ancient books all say that the undead can only be stopped in such a manner. As long as the sorcerer has enough strength, if they are not burned, they will continue to rise."

"I'll pass this on to the deputy. It will make our battle a difficult one. Oman, thank you for warning us. We can now take a stand, and once this is finished, we will spare the manpower to help rescue your daughter. I'm sorry we can't do that now."

"I understand," Oman replied, "but while you fight, you'll be drawing power from the sorcerer, and that will weaken him. That will be our chance to rescue her."

The king pondered Oman's words and said, "Twenty years ago, you offered to keep marching and take over the entire country. I fear I should have accepted that choice."

"And Sire, twenty years ago, you were correct when you told me to watch the ones closest to me."

CHAPTER 28

Dismayed and frustrated, Anong sat on her bed, looking out across the room. She had walked across it more than a dozen times in the last hour. As always, the mist surrounded her, curling around her body as she moved. She tried to understand its makeup and even attempted to communicate with it, but it would not respond to her. She felt it must be a living entity, playing with her, doing its job and keeping her caged.

Lying down on the bed, she stared at the ceiling, thinking about what her father had taught her. He always told her to look for the reason behind why things happen. So why had this man taken her? What was he using her for, and what could she do to free herself?

The fog could stop her body, and she could not move in spirit form, but her mind was free to travel. Closing her eyes, she let her thoughts drift to a happy memory of sitting on the front porch with her parents and laughing. She could not believe what the sorcerer had told her; she knew he lied with his every word. Her parents could not be dead, and within her, she held an assurance, a certainty, that their spirits were still in this world. She remembered her father telling her to believe in herself and always do the right thing. He always said she should try to relax and let the thoughts run freely through her to find an answer. It was important not to overthink the problem. She should let the thoughts run like a stream, twisting and turning around the rocks and under the ledges. There would always be obstacles in the way, but the stream would move forward, just as the answer would come to her.

She could now see a river of thoughts dart in and out of her mind. With certainty, she knew that Oman and Jossa would never stop looking for her. They loved her. The lies that the sorcerer told her were designed to make her upset and angry. Somehow, the mist was transferring her anger and magic from her to him. She knew she had to keep calm, no matter what he said or did. Zakalis always came to her when he was weak and depleted. It would only be when he was this fragile that she could make her escape.

The door to the room slammed shut, startling her. Anong sat up and watched as Zakalis walked in and sat at the table. He laughed at her surprised expression and said cruelly, "I can see by your face that you've been making escape plans. I don't know why you're bothering." He got up and began gesturing around the room as if he were talking to an audience. "You have nothing to go back to. If you cooperate with me, you could be living in luxury. If you don't want to do that, I can put you back into a permanent sleep and will only wake you when I need you." It was clear to Anong that he was trying to barter with her.

She could feel her anger rising, despite knowing that it was precisely what Zakalis wanted, and blurted out, "You're lying. My parents are alive."

"Which ones? Your real parents or the derelict little people that raised you in the wilds? They're all lying in the dirt now, rotting," he laughed.

Anong could feel her power begin to drain from her. She forced herself to calm down and stopped the flow of magic in mid-stride. Zakalis was startled when he felt the flow wane and thought quickly before saying, "We had a Jogahoh in the castle. A little drunkard, to be certain. He's served his purpose and gone back now. Without him, I wouldn't have you. He said he was your uncle."

Anong had heard her parents speak about Salem and knew he had been incensed after his father passed him over as leader. She could not understand how someone could be so vindictive, especially toward family. Despite herself, she could not help asking, "You had Salem helping you?" Before he could answer, she could feel the rage of betrayal overwhelming her. In a blinding light, it burst from her and into Zakalis.

Instead of throwing him back, he simply held open both arms and allowed it to enter him. "Just what I needed." He walked to the door and looked back at her with a half-smile on his face. "I may not be around for a while, but that will all depend on what I might need. And this I did not lie about. Salem did betray his brother and stole you from him on my orders." He laughed at Anong's expression, then opened the door and closed it tightly behind him.

Anong was furious at herself. She had forgotten everything she had been taught. Self-control. Discipline. She picked up a chair and hurled it at the door. It flew through the air, but a tendril of green mist caught it just before it connected. The fog curled itself around the chair, turned it upright and placed it neatly in its proper place at the table. The sight brought her blood to a boil. In a rage, she gripped the table and tried to flip it over, but it stood fast, not moving an inch. Anong took a deep breath and tried to force out a scream of exasperation. The mist only muffled the noise, and her scream turned into a sob. She had played right into the sorcerer's hand and done precisely what he wanted her to do. As a result, once again, he had taken her power. She knew she had to stop him, but the question was how. *Next time I'll have to test him and find his limits.*

••••••

Oman stayed an extra day with King Merck, helping to devise a plan to stop the invasion. He then made his way back home to Alfheim. He needed to warn them about what was happening. Doro conjured a magic portal at his request, and Oman soon found himself back home outside the council house.

Approaching the main building, he was surprised to see the seconds-in-command of all the tribes milling about. Climbing the steps up to the main hall, he passed a group of men who fell silent at his approach. They stood motionless and only watched as he walked by. Oman paid them no heed, walking through the centre of the group toward his deputy. "Good morning," he said, nodding to him. Calam greeted him, but his face looked dire, and he took Oman by the arm without a word and led him away. Oman stopped him halfway down the corridor. "Deputy, the council hall is the other way."

"Oman, Salem is in there," the man said, embarrassed.

"That's fine," he answered, turning back. "Are you coming? You'll want to hear what I have to say." The deputy started to protest, but Oman ignored him. Striding purposefully, he reached the great door and walked in. Inside, on Oman's chair, sat Salem. The tribe's leaders sat with him around the table. As he entered, they turned, stopped talking and stared at him. Oman looked calmly at each man before he approached Salem and said, "You're sitting in my chair."

Salem stood, panicked at first, before regaining his composure. He had expected to see his brother but not this soon. He knew he would have to cut to the meat of the matter immediately if he wanted to take control. "Oman, it has been brought to our attention that you and your wife have been harbouring a non-Jogahoh. We know you've had the child these past sixteen years." Salem's face reflected his pleasure at the situation Oman had put himself in, and inwardly, he gloated. He gained even more confidence as he continued. "You know the punishment for this act is immediate banishment for you and your family. The leadership of our people has now been handed to me."

Oman ignored Salem's words and addressed the crowd. "I don't deny any of this; it's all true. An infant from outside was placed in our care. We raised her in the land of the Jibay to keep her safe from your judgement of us. We could never have abandoned her. We hoped at first that someone would come back for her, but they didn't. Could any of you abandon an innocent child to our icy cold winters? To the beasts?" The men's uneasy faces told Oman that his words were being heeded. He continued, "By springtime, Jossa and I determined that we would bring her up as our own. We made sure she knew and understood our customs and teachings. Her bravery saved children at the border trading post. We even sent her on a quest, just as our young ones are sent. During that quest, she killed a lion and gave her mother the hide to keep her warm. Soon after, someone came like a thief in the night," his eyes now focused stonily on Salem, "and kidnapped her. So, we went after her and found her."

Oman let the men think about what he'd said for a second. Salem started to speak, but before he could say a word, Oman leaned into Salam's remaining ear and whispered, "I saw you in King Tibalt's castle, Salem." Salem's face blanched, and Oman turned his attention back to the group. "The floor is still mine. One last thing—there is a war brewing in the east. King Merck has been warned and is sending his army toward the eastern border as we speak. The first wave of the eastern army contains thousands of soldiers brought from the underworld. King Merck does not know if he can contain them or even kill them. I suggest we mobilize what we can and move to our borders along the eastern front. We can only hope that they will not be able to penetrate our shield. That cannot be known at this time. Our boundaries were designed against living men, not the dead."

Salem protested. "I received a message from King Tibalt informing me of this action. We all know of the long feud between the two brothers, and he has assured me they have no interest in our country. His only fight is with his brother; therefore, I suggest we sit tight and go about our business."

The tribal leader from the north stood up and said, "Oman's daughter got through our border. Perhaps others can, too."

Another man shouted from across the room, "Why should we get involved with their war?"

A third man stood and said, "I agree with Oman. These

soldiers are from the underworld. The boundary shield was not designed to keep them out."

The room erupted with shouts of arguing men. Among the mayhem, Salem waved his arms and shouted, trying in vain to calm the crowd. One of the leaders, shocked to see Oman now heading toward the door, called to him, "Oman! Where are you going?" The room went silent at the words, and all eyes turned to Oman.

He stopped and turned toward the gathering. "I am no longer your leader. I would remind you that we fought with King Merck's army. King Tibalt knows us as an enemy, not an ally. There is no time to stand and bicker. If I must die, I'd rather do it with a sword in my hand, not as a slave to another man. I'm going to fight with King Merck and when the time is right, I will rescue my daughter. It is for you to decide whether or not you will join me."

Oman pulled the door open and was met by his deputy. Calam said, "I am coming with you. If your words do not get them to stand by you, nothing will."

"I thank you for your steadfast loyalty all these years, Calam, but you must remain here. It is your guidance and skill that our people will need in these coming days, not Salem's," Oman replied. "We can only hope they will make the right decision."

Calam pursed his mouth tightly, knowing Oman's words were true. He nodded silently, and Oman knew that Calam had accepted the task. "May the gods be with you, Calam," Oman said and walked out the door.

•••••

Esma took spirit flights every night, trying to find a way to contact Anong, but the mist continued to block her every attempt. From there, she would move to the western border, where she grimly watched the eastern army gathering. She followed their campfires as they converged and led to an assembly point. Esma flew farther across the western border to discover King Merck's forces gathering in preparation as well. That was a good sign, she knew. It meant that they believed Oman's words and were preparing for the worst. She was, however, dismayed at their small numbers, especially when she discovered the long outline of Zakalis' undead army, spread out as far as she could see.

One night, maneuvering down to them, she walked through the eerily silent ranks. They stood stone-still and lifeless and would stay that way until called forward by Zakalis. She had never seen anything like them in her lifetime. By sheer force of habit, she extended her hand and reached out to touch one of them, trying to find a light within him. Immediately, she was overwhelmed with pain. She could see the harsh, ugly life that the man had led, the torture he had endured and the atrocities he had committed. The cold was unshakable, and she was shocked to discover that its chill was not only seeping into her but trying to suck the warmth and life from her spirit. She screamed out in pain. Back in the cottage, Esma's physical body uttered the same guttural cry, causing Jossa to run to her side. She pulled away from the grey soldier with a final wrench and held her hand to her chest, panting. Esma staggered back to give a last glare at the malevolent beings and then departed up and along the valley slope. She knew with certainty that the west would be defenseless against them. *But,* she thought, *this dead army will take a lot of power to bring to life.* She hoped that Anong could withstand Zakalis' magical drain on her until they could find a way to get her back.

• • • • • •

Oman contacted Jossa and Esma and told them he would fight with King Merck's army. He would try to keep in contact with them until the battle was at its fiercest and Zakalis' energy had waned. That moment would allow Esma to free Anong.

Oman made his way through a column of marching men and finally found the king's wagons set up just ahead of him. He nudged his tired horse toward them. The wagons sat in the middle of a defensive perimeter, with the headquarters in its centre. A company of soldiers took up positions around the entire encampment, ensuring only people close to the king were admitted. Stopping at the front guard station, Oman identified himself and waited for the deputy to meet him. Ten minutes later, he spotted the man walking with another soldier toward him. He came up to Oman and bluntly said, "I didn't expect to see you."

Oman answered, "The Jogahoh tribes have been warned, and I can only hope they will prepare. I will not let my friends face this enemy alone and will fight beside you until Zakalis' power begins to weaken. Only then will I leave you to rescue my daughter and put an end to this war."

"Our thanks, Oman. Follow me to the operations tent, and I'll show you what we have in store for the east."

The men walked into the tent, where a large map showing how the western army was advancing hung on a wall. The deputy explained that they wanted to move forward while the east was still deploying. They were to send three companies of cavalry ahead of their front. Each company would consist of five hundred men. They would move directly to the border, then hold up and wait. When the eastern army arrived, they would commence a fighting withdrawal. The deputy pointed to a tight pass through the mountains and said they could draw the enemy into a kill zone. "This is where we will make a stand. The ambush is planned here." He pointed to the one valley in the range of mountains that allowed travel. "We'll try to get them all into the floor of the valley and block them in. I know a conventional sword won't kill these bastards, so we'll drop barrels of burning oil down onto them."

Oman listened intently to the deputy's words and said, "I'd like to go to the front with one of the companies."

The following day, Oman headed out with the group he'd been assigned to. Its commander rode up to him and greeted him by saying, "I don't expect you to remember me, Oman. It's been a long time, and we're both so much older. We fought together on the same field twenty years ago during the war. We always admired the bravery of the Jogahoh."

Oman looked hard at the man, but his features, like his own, had grown older. He had no memory of the face that looked at him. A spark of recollection flooded him, and he replied, "Our faces have aged much over the years, but the eyes never change, Toka. When I saw them, I knew you. Not as you are now, but as a young man. Those were difficult times."

"You're right," the commander replied. "Although we never knew if we would see the next sunrise, at times, I wish those days were back, if only for a few moments. We were so young and so full of life."

"I understand. The times were simpler. I had only to keep my sword sharp, listen to my commanders and do what was expected of me."

They turned their horses and began to ride to the front. Toka said, "Speaking of that, have you been briefed on where we're heading?"

Oman nodded. "Yes, the deputy briefed me yesterday."

Toka gave Oman a quick rundown of what was about to happen. "The plan is to make our skirmish line as long as possible. All three companies, depending on the ground, will be spread out to about one kilometre. We expect the enemy to come at us with a frontal assault. At that time, or as best we can, the two outside companies will shrink in behind us. It'll be a tough move, as we will all be moving at the same time. Once they are behind us, we'll leapfrog back through them. Hopefully, we can keep this manoeuvre up back to the ambush site."

Oman thought about the commander's plans as he rocked back and forth to the gentle sway of his horse. He finally said, "It's an ambitious plan. I would like to add more but have nothing. I've never fought against a foe like this before."

"Neither have we," the commander said flatly. "The king

expects that as the sorcerer grows weary, so will they."

"I hope so," answered Oman. Needing to return to his duties, the commander excused himself. Oman was left to reflect on what Esma had said about the sorcerer drawing his power from Anong. He hoped she would find a way to stop Zakalis before it was too late. He knew that Anong's life and the lives of thousands of men in this battle would be in jeopardy.

The going was slow as Toka's company pushed deeper toward the border. Their size made it impossible to travel on anything but the main road. They knew they risked detection but had no choice. By mid-morning the next day, they were in position and had set up hasty defenses. The commander sent small patrols to their front to act as an early warning because the area was heavily wooded. Their job was simple: to sit as quietly as possible and look for any sign of the enemy. When they were spotted, the patrols would slip back and give warning. By nightfall, all fires were extinguished, and movement was kept at a minimum. The men tucked themselves behind their embankments and rested until their sentry shift. Through the forest, the owls stirred and began to voice low, echoing hoots through the trees. Creatures of the night began to stir, and the men could hear their soft rustles through the underbrush. The men's fears were set aside momentarily at the ordinary night sounds. It was only when the animals detected danger that all movement and sound ceased.

· · · · · ·

The sun had not yet risen, but King Tibalt stood ready with his command group, just behind the eerily silent line of soldiers. Frustrated, he spun around and shouted impatiently, "Where is the sorcerer? He knows I want to step off before sunrise."

Zakalis heard the king's angry shouts from where he was standing with his undead army. He was neither intimidated nor concerned: his body was overflowing with power, swirls of magic surrounding him. He bided his time, revelling in keeping the man waiting. He walked calmly back to where the king stood and called out, "Sire, I'm here. You did say three hours before sunrise, did you not?"

The king snarled at him, knowing he was being baited. "Just get on with it, man."

"Of course," the sorcerer answered calmly. He turned back to the silent line and stood ramrod still, gathering his power. Zakalis closed his eyes, and from deep within him, words came unbidden to recite a spell not heard for centuries, in a tongue long forgotten. The words themselves, guttural and cavernous, began to pound an ugly rhythm that jarred the minds of the command group. The air around them filled with electricity, and the men shuffled nervously, their hands reaching automatically to their weapons.

Zakalis opened his eyes and bellowed, "Wake and face your creator." In unison, the lines of soldiers shuttered and took in one deep breath. Then, as they exhaled, they turned toward the group, raised their right arm up in unison and brought it back down. The moment the undead turned to them, the stench of rotting meat permeated the air. In horror, the command group involuntarily took a step back, but King Tibalt stood fast.

The sorcerer glanced back at the king and said, "Sire, the troops are at your command. Are you ready?"

The king was repulsed by the sight of the grey, rotting troops but was determined not to show any fear. "Yes," he said grimly. "Set them loose. I want to be just beyond the border by sunup."

Zakalis uttered a sharp command, his voice echoing over the valley. The soldiers responded with a deafening cry and lifted their swords up and into the sky. As one, they brought their swords down, turned about and began their march toward the western lines. The army to the rear, waiting patiently for the call to arms, lifted their heads in shock as the eerie roar echoed around them. The entourage watched in fascinated dread as the undead army began their trek up the valley hill, then over the crest before disappearing. "They will move forward, killing everything in their path, until I command them to stop."

King Tibalt, eyes fixed on the horrifying sight in front of him, said tersely, "You will stay near me until the battle is won."

"Yes, Sire, that's understood," Zakalis said, smiling to himself with satisfaction. They mounted their horses, and King Tibalt gave the rest of the army the order to fall in.

••••••

That morning, Oman woke just as the sun broke the horizon, warming the night's chill from the air. He'd slept well, using his heavy beast hide coat as a mattress, and it had kept the cold from seeping into his bones. A thick blanket over him kept the morning dew away from his body. Oman rolled everything up tightly, saddled his horse and packed his kit securely onto the animal. "These next few days will be hard for you, old friend," he said, scratching the horse's neck fondly. The horse nudged her head gently into Oman's hand, happy for the attention. Her ears then pricked forward, and she jerked her head up, eyes searching, body tense. Oman turned in the direction the horse was studying. He heard crashing coming from the woods and reflexively placed his hand on his sword hilt. A lone man on foot burst through the bush, staggering toward headquarters. Halfway there, he swayed drunkenly and collapsed heavily onto the ground. He had been part of a seven-man sentry sent out as early warning the day before. Oman ran over to where the man was lying. A group of soldiers joined him and gathered around. His clothes were torn to shreds, and his weapons were nowhere to be seen. One of the men lifted him into a sitting position and urged him to drink some water. The man's eyes, wide-open in terror, reached eagerly for the skin of water and drank from it until his thirst was quenched and his throat cleared.

"I need to speak with the commander," he finally said. "Now!"

The men helped him to his feet and began to lead him toward

headquarters. Toka heard the commotion and met them halfway through the clearing. "Report, Sergeant. What's happened?"

The man's words poured from him, his face pale. "Sir, I was on the last shift before sunrise when I told my corporal I had to relieve myself. When I returned, I saw him being lifted into the air with one hand by a tall, grey figure. My man drew his sword and ran the figure through, all the way to its hilt. It never flinched and swung at my corporal's head with his sword, cutting it off with one blow. I rushed the creature and slashed its hamstrings completely through. It fell but got back up. His wounds didn't bleed and closed immediately. I turned and ran to warn the others, only to find they'd met their fate at the hands of other creatures. There was nothing more I could do, so I ran back to warn you."

The commander looked grim as he took in his sergeant's report and gave the word to prepare for battle. At his direction, the men sprang into action. Bugles were sounded, and orders were barked as a flurry of activity started. All around him, Oman saw horses being mounted and men forming themselves into their sections. Carrier pigeons were sent out with messages to the other companies and back to the king's headquarters. Birds from the other outlying groups brought news that they had also encountered the deadly army. Oman mounted his horse and moved to the commander's side. The battle had begun, and the enemy had struck first.

CHAPTER 29

On that same day, well before dawn, Anong found herself once more pacing about her small prison, her only companion the mist that surrounded her. Her night had been restless, and, unable to sleep, she finally gave up trying to stay in bed. She sensed a change in the mist, a feeling of uneasiness mixed with excitement that intrigued her. She knew the feelings were coming from the sorcerer because Zakalis controlled everything about the mist. She began to feel a tugging within her, not a physical pull, but an insistent wrenching on her mind. She abruptly realized that whatever this was desperately wanted her energy. "Something has happened," she said out loud, spinning around and bringing her hands up to her head to calm herself. Unbalanced, and with the pressure in her mind increasing, she collapsed against a stone wall and slid heavily onto the floor. The pull continued, always demanding more, and then, as suddenly as it started, it stopped. She knew without a doubt that he had been unable to pull more magic from her but wondered why he had needed it. She leaned her head back against the wall with a sigh of relief and realized, with a start, that she could feel the wall. Anong stretched her hand to the stone and ran her fingertips all the way down one side and back the other. She excitedly stood up and ran to the door, reaching for the handle. Her fingers could grasp it, but thin tendrils of the mist prevented her from turning it. Frantically, she tried to brush the mist away but to no avail. It was no use. She was still trapped. Spinning around in frustration, she strode to the table, picked up a mug and hurled it at the door. Instead of the mist stopping the mug this time, it crashed and broke into small pieces. *Think,* she thought to herself. *What is happening? What has changed?* She remembered the pull and the pressure she had felt. *What was it?*

The sorcerer had always come to her in search of power. This time, he had attempted to do it from a distance and failed. She knew that whatever Zakalis was doing, he was being drained and was trying to pull more magic from her.

Looking at the broken pieces of the mug, she sighed and walked to the door to pick it up. As she bent over, she was amused to see a tiny mouse running up to her. It stopped at her feet and, showing no fear, stood on its hind legs and looked up at her. Anong held out her hand and was surprised to see the animal hop onto it. She picked it up and walked over to the table, where it scampered off and waited for her. Taking a crust of bread and bits of cheese, she gave them to the mouse. It promptly picked up the food in its tiny paws, brought it to its mouth and began eating. Anong slowly reached her finger out and gently stroked the animal's back. "It's been a long time since I've had company," she said.

The mouse stopped what it was doing, and its dark eyes lifted to her. "You were not alone. The magic man comes, and there are men outside."

"But they are not my friends. I think you could be a good friend," she said, still stroking the soft fur of the mouse.

"And the lady who came," the mouse continued, speaking with his mouth full of crumbs, "she seems like she could be a good friend." He promptly rolled onto his back, urging her to continue her scratches on his belly.

Anong was surprised and said, "I saw no lady. No one has come here."

"She was here. She asked me to come in and see what I could see. So, I did."

Anong stopped her scratches and looked down at the mouse. "What did she look like?"

The mouse was about to reply when a green tendril of the mist drifted toward him. "Magic is bad," he proclaimed, cringing away from it and scampering back to her hand. "Green magic does not like me to eat." Anong shielded the mouse with her other hand and listened as the animal continued. "She was floating, and the men could not see her. She was very pretty, and she had magic because we spoke."

Eyes widening, Anong asked, "Was her name Esma?"

"Names have power. We never give names."

"Can you get a message to her for me?"

The mouse cocked its head at her. "I am a mouse," it said and stood on its two hind legs, pointing to its body. "I cannot travel far. I do not know where she lives, and there are many enemies of mice in the forest."

"I'm sorry. I never even thought of that," Anong answered, chagrined but thinking quickly. "Can you let me know if she comes back again?"

The little mouse said, "I will. I must leave now." He picked up a large chunk of bread in his paws and, before putting it in his mouth, said, "I have a family." Anong took the mouse up to the door and placed it by the same crack it had come in. It poked its head through the hole, sniffed the air and, once sure the area was clear, stepped through it and was gone. Anong walked back from the door with a glimmer of hope forming. They knew where she was, and she was no longer alone. They just needed an opening to help her, and she needed to give them that chance.

••••••

The morning had gone well for the eastern army; they had moved deeper through the border than anticipated and were still marching. The line of undead soldiers stretched out one kilometre on either side of the centre. They strode as one, two meters apart, with just enough room to swing their swords without hitting the other. With Zakalis providing the energy, they needed no rest, no sleep, no food. Because of this, their swift pace never faltered, and it was hard for the humans behind them to keep up. King Tibalt and his generals remained close to the leading edge of the front line, observing the battle carefully. He

wanted to catch the west unaware and was surprised when they
had come across advance reconnaissance parties. King Tibalt
knew the main western army would be close behind. Though the
skirmish lines formed by the west appeared to be quick and
haphazard, they had somehow still been warned. *How*, he
thought angrily, *I do not know.*

It enraged Tibalt that someone had warned Merck of the
invasion. He could tell they hadn't had a lot of time to prepare,
but they still had enough to get out to the border and make a
stand. He saw no real defenses, just running skirmishes. As he
sat atop his horse, watching his army cut through the advance
lines, he wondered if perhaps the Jogahoh, Salem, had cut a deal.
He would not concern himself with that now, but he would look
for the traitor later. King Tibalt shouted at Zakalis, "Do you see
that pass in the distance, Sorcerer?"

Zakalis looked ahead and could see a line of large mountains
to his front. There was a break between them, approximately five
hundred meters wide, he guessed. "Sire, the break directly ahead
of us?"

"Yes. I want your forces centred on that. It's the pass we're
going to use."

"I understand," the sorcerer replied and began his chanting
once again.

The king watched as Zakalis' words filled the air with a visible
swirl of magic. He was surprised to hear the sorcerer falter and
begin his chant again. It appeared to him that the man was tiring.
He would have to watch him carefully, he knew, but the undead
army was responding for now. They had shifted and aligned
themselves directly toward the pass.

Watching the grisly force cut down everything in its path
reminded Tibalt of when he was a boy watching the farmers
during harvest. Once the wheat was ready, the farmer would pull
out his sickle and begin to swing, cutting down every stalk to the
ground as he went. His brother's army would be annihilated in

the same way.

The undead soldiers took their blows head-on. It appeared to have no lasting effect on them. When one fell, others would relentlessly come forward. Minutes later, the fallen man would be up and fighting again. Tibalt watched King Merck's army with grudging respect. The men fought fearlessly but, he knew, without hope.

"Sire, we will need to break before nightfall. Our men need rest," his second-in-command reminded him.

King Tibalt would have preferred to push forward but knew his second-in-command was correct. He nodded curtly and said, "Two more hours." He reined back his horse to speak directly to Zakalis. The sorcerer looked drained, his head bobbing wearily in rhythm with his horse. Tibalt was blunt. "You look spent. Will you be able to maintain this?"

The sorcerer rallied his strength at the king's words. He was still awash with power, although it had drained from him far faster than he had thought it would. "Of course, Sire. I'll just need some time once we stop tonight."

Tibalt scowled and said, "You'll have it. Just be ready to march before sunup." With one last uneasy glance at the sorcerer, Tibalt pulled on his horse's reins and rode back to the command group.

CHAPTER 30

Commander Toka took a long pull of water from his canteen, brought it down and recapped it. Glancing up, he saw Oman riding toward him. He offered the canteen to Oman and said, "I'm afraid today will be a very long one for those of us fortunate to stay alive."

Oman shook his head at the drink. "I sensed that, too. Even the horses feel on edge. Look how their heads are all turned to the east."

"I noticed that. They've been that way since the sergeant stumbled back into our lines." He took a long pause and then said, "You can stay back here with me in command. I could use you."

Oman laughed. "My wife would hug you for that, but you don't need me here. I'll find a spot in the centre of your troop. Where is your oversight position?"

"For now, just back from the centre of the line. The bugler will be just off to my right. Do you remember the calls?"

"Just the most important. The call to retire for the night and the call to eat." He grinned. "I'll be fine. I'll watch what the others are doing and follow them."

The commander nodded and said, "That will have to do for now." He watched as one of his officers joined them, listened to the man and sent him on his way. Turning to the bugler, he ordered, "Give the call to fall in line." As the bugle sounded, he shifted his attention back to Oman. "The time is almost upon us. I'm glad we had the chance to meet up again after all these years."

"Myself as well," Oman stated. "I only wish it could have been at a pub where the two of us could drink some beer in peace and reminisce about our younger years."

The commander grasped Oman's small hand firmly and said,

"Ride hard into these bastards. Don't get surrounded, and never stop your sword from moving."

"I shall," Oman replied, giving the commander a final nod before turning and riding into line with the others. He adjusted his chainmail, then looked hard through the tree line. The large field to his front rose slightly with intermittent copses of trees. He looked carefully but was unable to see any movement. The area was dead silent, and apprehension filled the men's minds. From the wind to their front came the odour of rotting meat hung too long in the summer sun. Then they came. Oman could see the enemy's first line cresting the top of the hill five hundred meters in front of them. Nothing deterred them: they flowed as steadily as a river over the top and oozed down the other side. They walked through and over anything in their way, never veering or faltering.

At three hundred meters out, the word was passed down the line to stand by. The horses could feel the anxiety of the men through their saddles and started to shuffle nervously. As the stench of the enemy grew stronger, permeating the air, the animals became agitated. Oman patted his mount and whispered, "We'll get through this, old friend. Stay calm." His eyes narrowed at the thought of the coming battle, and he could feel his body tense. Any doubts he had before were pushed away, and he focused on the daunting task at hand. He unsheathed his sword, feeling the familiar handle tight and secure in his hand. Its smooth, eighty-layer fine steel was honed to a razor-sharp edge on both sides that came to a perfect point. He rotated his wrist, feeling the sword's perfect balance and rested it lightly on his thigh, waiting for the command to attack.

The heat in the air was now unbearable and sweat ran freely into Oman's eyes. It would not be long now. Tersely, he muttered aloud, asking his father to protect him, and asking the gods to help those who would leave them today and take their turn in the afterlife. Finally, the men heard the booming cry, "Charge."

As one, all the men loosened the reins on their horses, pushing them into a full gallop. Fifty meters out from the wood line, Oman glanced to his left and right, ensuring he was in line with the rest of the company. Despite the heavy riders on their backs, the horses raced forward, struggling to keep their footing on the uneven ground. One hundred meters from the enemy, Oman tucked his head deep into the side of his horse's neck and brought his sword down and to his front. Seconds later, the animal smashed head-on into the undead army, scattering bodies left and right. Oman's sword slashed effortlessly through the first soldier he hit, slicing its arm entirely off. His horse blasted through the ranks, and Oman's blows never ceased. The first rush of a cavalry force was always intended to disrupt an infantry line. The animal's charge was like a battering ram.

Within minutes, he found himself on the backside of the dead army. He turned the horse sharply and looked back through the line. He was shocked to see the enemy slowly struggling back onto their feet. One of them bent over, picked up its severed arm and placed it back onto its shoulder, where it refastened itself. Within seconds, it had resumed its position with the rest of its comrades.

Looking up and down the line, Oman could see where the western troops had broken through. Some of them were knocked off their mounts and were now engaged in hand-to-hand combat. Their battle was one-sided, and they tried in vain to fight through, only to be cut down by the never-tiring foe. Oman once again went through the line, wielding his sword expertly and accurately. He moved quickly from one side of his mount to the other, striking the demons with every blow and finally rejoined his line. They pulled back fifty meters and turned abruptly for another charge. As they clashed again, Oman could feel his horse shutter and falter beneath him. The next second, the horse thundered hard into the ground, giving him mere moments to raise his feet so he wouldn't be pinned beneath the animal. The momentum threw Oman forward and off the dead horse. He had no time to grieve his loss. His first reaction was to bring his weapon into the high and back position. It was just in time to block a crushing blow coming in from behind him. He brought his sword forward, slicing into the enemy. Oman flowed with his weapon, continuing to the next monster beside him. Again and again, he attacked, striking blows and blocking, trying to slay everything in his path. Desolately, he realized the creatures would only reanimate and continue their relentless drive. From behind him, he could hear the faint sound of the bugle sounding a withdrawal. Oman glanced up and down the line and spotted a riderless horse. He jumped onto the animal, grabbed the saddle and hoisted himself up. Jerking the reins around in one motion, he kicked the horse hard and rode out of the battle. He pulled up after one hundred meters and turned the horse back to where they had been fighting. The dead army was slaughtering any of his comrades left behind remorselessly. Oman shuddered in horror, turned the horse and rode back to the assembly point.

Throughout the day, hour after hour, they attacked, to little or no effect. At midday, the company to the south joined them, bolstering their numbers. One company stood at the forefront fighting the enemy, and the other remained in a defensive position directly behind them. Once the lead company was exhausted, they would disengage and leapfrog behind the other to set up a defensive position. Time and again, they fell back, their numbers dwindling as the grey figures cut through their ranks with ruthless, never-ending efficiency. They tried to throw them off-balance using frontal attacks, left and right flanking and direct charges. The only cries they heard were from their own fallen men; the undead soldiers remained eerily silent. There was nothing they could do to stop the methodical, unrelenting advance of the undead; they could only slow it. The western army's initial confidence was now replaced by desperation, as fear and exhaustion set in. The long hours of fighting with little respite and no food or water were taking their toll. The horses were either wounded or killed in battle, and without them, they lost their mobility. Oman knew the early warning unit would be lost if nothing were to change.

Late in the day, he spotted the commander and galloped up to him. "We're down to twenty-five horses. Is there any chance we can bring up more?"

"I've already sent a runner back to the king, but to get them in, we'll need a pause in the battle."

Oman replied, "We'll need a break as well; the men are exhausted." They turned and watched as their soldiers cut into the line once again. This time, for some reason, the grey figures appeared to hesitate while attacking. They did not reanimate immediately when one was cut down but lay motionless for some time before rising.

"Something's changing," Toka exclaimed. "They're slowing down." Knowing he was ready to take any advantage, he declared, "It's a small chance, and I'll take it. It will be dark soon. I need to establish our lines before then, or we'll be stumbling around. I want to fall back to the bend in the river. We'll set up a defense and hopefully get some food, rest and new horses. The southern company that joined us earlier will be the right flank. We'll take the north."

Oman asked, "Who will take the rear?"

The commander lifted his eyes to the battlefield and turned back to Oman. He said, "It should have been our company to the north, but we've lost them."

"I can ride out and try to find them. If I do, what are your orders?"

"If you find them, they need to take the rear position. Tell the officer his lead man is to have a red lantern to signal to us that they're friendly troops coming in, not the enemy."

Oman replied, "I will."

"Good luck," the commander said before moving to rejoin his front line.

Oman kicked his horse sharply and rode back from the line three hundred meters, then headed straight north. He had a general idea of where the third company had been at the beginning of the day but knew their position would have changed after a full day of fighting. Riding hard, he stayed hidden in the trees and low ground, using small animal tracks as paths to get through some of the thickets. Breaking cover and moving into an open area, he caught sight of the dead army three hundred meters to his right. Instinctively, he wheeled back and rode into the trees. He was now two kilometers from where he had started and was ready to give up his search when a flock of buzzards circling in the east drew his attention. His stomach rose up in his throat as he knew the position was too far forward for the lost company to still be there. Thinking the worst, he crested another small hill and was surprised to see what looked like a hundred men tactically moving back to the rear. Pointing his horse toward them, he rode into their lines and found the company officer. The man's exhausted face was marred with mud, and he had bloody, ugly gashes on his shoulder and arm. Oman could see that the man had been fighting for his life since early that morning. He told the officer of their plan, knowing they needed to start their shift south immediately.

The man listened with bleak, tired eyes and said, "We'll try our best to make it. Tell them I've lost over half my people since first contact this morning. We've tried to shift our line to the south but couldn't make it. They've kept us separated here and know it's just a matter of time before we give in; these things are unholy."

Oman shook his head and replied, "Understood, sir. The other companies are in the same shape as you, but at least they're together." His mission completed; he was about to return when he caught a glimpse of a man going down. Without thinking, he turned back into the skirmish, drawing his sword and racing to the downed man. His blade was a blur as his horse barreled through, and he cut into the line toward him. Toka was correct; the enemy was not reanimating as quickly now, and their reactions were stilted. A final strike with his blade decapitated a demon reaching for the helpless man. The creature dropped without a sound, and Oman was relieved to see that the man could now get up and race back. He turned his horse, planning to ram straight through the enemy and back to safety. As he did, the creatures encircled him, blocking his return. There were at least fifty who were closing in. In desperation, he rode hard around them, trying to push his way out, to no avail.

He could hear shouts of alarm as the officer and his men tried to push forward to help him but were repelled. The circle grew tighter, and before he could react, he felt a hand reach up to his chest, grab his armour and pull him off his horse. Still gripping his sword, he slashed at the creature, cutting off an arm. He tore himself free of the grisly hand and held his weapon high, facing all of them. *I've fought giants before, and today will be no different*, he thought grimly. Oman sliced his blade through the stomach of one, and it fell. The next few moments were a blur. His small size allowed him to move quickly and smoothly between the now decidedly sluggish enemy. He slashed and struck at them with relentless fury, knowing that this would be a fight to the death. He saw a blade coming down on his head, but he blocked it with his sword. Then, from behind, he felt a stunning blow to his back that knocked the wind from his lungs and threw him hard onto the ground. Gasping for breath, he realized that his chainmail had stopped the blade from cutting through. He stared up past the dead, grey faces that studied him without expression. His eyes saw the sky as the sun continued its journey into the night. *The sun will be down soon*, he thought. *I guess this is a good time to pass to the next world. But not without a fight.* His hand clenched his sword tightly, and he tried one last time to bring it up, but he found that he couldn't move. The monstrous face of an undead soldier stood overtop him, his weapon raised up high, pointing toward Oman's chest. As he brought it down, Oman whispered, "Jossa, I will always love you." At that moment, the sun touched the horizon.

••••••

Jossa reached for a dishrag when a jolt of dread seared through her body. Esma, beside her, stiffened and gasped loudly. Within the sorcerer's hold, Anong jolted upright in her bed, a cold chill filling her.

CHAPTER 31

The blade above him froze in mid-strike, the tip of it just touching his chainmail. Without a sound, the creatures all turned as one and walked back to re-form their lines. They now stood frozen in place, at attention, with swords by their sides. Stunned, Oman looked around in confusion but quickly gathered himself together and ran for his horse. As he mounted, he was thinking furiously. The creatures were being controlled, and he knew that without a doubt. He surmised it could only be Zakalis. The man had to be close by, and now would be the time to stop him. He screamed back to the company officer, "Return to the river now, while they're frozen. I'm going back to try and find the sorcerer!" The officer gave Oman a quick salute of understanding and gave rushed orders, gathering up his wounded and retreating.

Oman raced straight through the path of destruction left behind by the fighting. Five minutes later, he reached the rise of a hill. Using it as a vantage point, Oman saw the eastern army moving up toward him. He quickly identified the command group, set slightly apart from the troops. His eyes caught sight of a fading red light surrounding a figure off to the side. Recognizing Zakalis, he swore softly to himself. He knew he was not close enough to the sorcerer to kill him, and it would be suicide to try. He would instead return to the river and report what he had seen to the commander. Riding back to the company, he recalled what he'd said to the Jogahoh council about how he would rather die with his sword in his hand. *Well,* he thought wryly, *I almost did.*

Oman arrived at the river bend and met up with Toka. The northern company had joined them only an hour before. They took stock of their situation and determined that they were now left with approximately three hundred men still able to fight.

They had lost over half of the advance group, and there were injured and dead men scattered all over a five-kilometre gap.

The officers were grim as they spoke with the commander and Oman. "I wanted to send out a patrol tonight and hit them behind their lines," the commander started, "but as we got our count, I realized we don't have the men. We can only make the withdrawal tomorrow. It's three kilometers to the gap in the hills, and that's where the king is set up."

"You know the enemy will be expecting us to make a stand there," said one of the officers.

Toka was grim but resolved. He replied, "You're right, and after today, they'll probably think they can roll right over us."

Oman spoke up. "If we move quickly after each contact and keep on moving, they will follow us into the gap. Let them get momentum on their side, and they won't want to slow down. Once they're deep into the gap, the king can spring the trap and surround all of them."

"If it works, and the undead are destroyed, our army can push through and attack King Tibalt's troops," the commander said.

"So, we have a plan," the northern company officer said. "I need to tell you what happened when Oman found us. He passed on your orders and was about to return when he saw one of my men in trouble. Instead of abandoning him, Oman rode straight into that god-forsaken army and saved him from certain death. If anything happens to me, make sure the king knows what he has done."

"I'll do that," Toka replied, then looked down at Oman with respect. "Thank you." Oman simply nodded, and the soldiers turned to prepare for the next day's fight.

• • • • • •

King Tibalt was barely able to contain his anger and irritation at Zakalis' troops. The sun had only touched the horizon, and they became useless, despite having another hour of light in which to push forward.

"Why have you stopped?" he demanded. "What is wrong with them?"

"Your highness, there is nothing wrong with them," Zakalis insisted firmly, knowing he could show no sign of weakness. "Your rear army has fallen behind. Stopping now will allow them to catch up."

King Tibalt's face flushed with anger, and he grabbed the sorcerer, pulling the man in tightly. "I command this army, not you." He grasped Zakalis' shoulder and turned him toward the mountains. "Do you see that passage cutting into the long line of hills?"

"Yes, Sire," Zakalis muttered.

"Do you see another passage?"

The sorcerer hesitated and replied, "No, Sire."

"That's right," Tibalt said, clenching his teeth and spitting as he talked. "Because there isn't one. What do you think lies in store for us when we get there?"

The sorcerer searched his mind for an answer but couldn't come up with one. He used magic for a living, and he wasn't a military tactician. "I don't know, Sire."

"The entire western army will be there, shoulder to shoulder, in and around that gap. We needed that time. Now there will be an entire blocking force there, all of them ready to die. Do you understand, Sorcerer?" Tibalt pushed away from him in frustration.

"Yes, Sire," Zakalis replied, his face revealing no emotion.

"We attack again at sunup. Have that army ready. Do you understand?"

"As you wish, Sire."

King Tibalt mounted his horse and rode back to his tent in the rear. The sorcerer watched the horse disappear and turned back to the pass, thinking about what he had to do tomorrow. He knew he could make no mistakes from this point on, but he also knew he had reached the end of his strength for the day. He was dead-tired and needed to see the girl again tonight. Zakalis recalled the sheer exaltation he experienced when her powers entered him and shuddered with need. When this battle was done, he would first dispose of King Tibalt. After that, he would get rid of the girl but not before finding a way to possess her magic.

······

The guards outside Anong's prison rotated their shift every day before sundown. Anong had known of them but never heard them before. Today, she was surprised to hear voices from outside her room, and she listened carefully as they talked.

Anong was sure that the sorcerer's grip on her must be weakening. The green mist that always surrounded her was now only oozing around her ankles. She wondered what was happening as she listened to the voices.

The men had just arrived for their next shift and began a walk around the perimetre of the building. The younger soldier asked the older one, "Do you wish you were at the front with the others?"

"Me?" the older man retorted sharply. "No, not at all. I've already gone through that and don't want to do it again."

"Why not?"

"Everyone thinks it's about glory and becoming a man. That ideal wears off fast after the first few seconds when the front lines meet. After that, it's just hoping you don't get run through, or if you're wounded, it's just enough to take you out of the battle and not kill you."

"I never thought of it that way," the younger man said soberly.

"You never think of those things until you're in it. When the first day is done, and you find your friends and foe together in death or ready to die, you think you've survived the worst of it. But the next day, you line up, march forward into the cauldron and do it over and over again. No, my days for that are long gone."

"I still want to go," the youth said stubbornly.

The older soldier's eyes fell on the younger man. "Learn how to shave first without cutting yourself. Besides, with everyone gone, the pubs have more women available."

"Yes, they do," the younger man laughed. "A lot more."

They both heard a man approaching, and the older soldier motioned for the young man to stop talking. Gripping the hilt of his weapon and peering into the dwindling daylight, the man ordered, "Show yourself, or I'll cut you in half."

There was a short pause, and the sorcerer stepped forward. "It's good to see you doing your job."

The soldier released his grip on the hilt of his sword and said, "You should have announced yourself, Sorcerer. You could have been mistaken for someone else."

Anong pushed her ear closer to the door, listening hard and trying to pick out every word. She didn't know the other voices, but she knew this one. The sorcerer was back for something.

"The battle has kept me busy until now."

"How goes the fight at the front?" the older man asked as the young soldier crowded in to listen.

"It has gone very well. We are less than a day's march from the pass in the hills."

The older soldier looked surprised and said, "It would have taken us weeks to move forward that far. You've done it in less than a day?"

"Yes. I believe we will be very successful in this fight," the sorcerer announced.

Anong could hardly hear the conversation but had heard enough to put it all together. The kingdom had started their war, and the sorcerer was using her magic to influence the outcome. Thousands of innocent people would be killed and any survivors driven into slavery. She wondered if the cold chill she had felt that day told her that someone she loved had died, and her thoughts immediately went to her father. He would surely be in this fight. Her thoughts ran clearly now. She was being used by this evil man, and it had to stop.

Anong was abruptly aware of footsteps approaching the door. She quickly returned to her bed and closed her eyes, pretending to be asleep. The sorcerer unlocked the door, entered the room and made his way over to her. He sat down on the bed and reached his hand out, running his palm up her leg. When his hand reached her thigh, Anong's hand shot out and grasped his wrist. She wrenched his thin, twig-like arm, turned it backward and applied a firm pressure on it. Zakalis shrieked in pain and fell to his knees, but Anong maintained a firm grip on the man's arm.

"You're a snivelling excuse for a man," Anong spat out. Her anger grew, and her grip on his wrist tightened.

"Oh, that's so much better," he murmured. Anong ignored him and applied more pressure against the wrist. "Yes, yes, that's it, my girl, just a little bit more," he said softly.

With a curse at her stupidity, Anong abruptly realized that her anger was once again fuelling him. She dropped his arm and backed away as far as she could, but it was too late. She could already see the green mist surrounding her again, and the voices from outside stopped.

Zakalis got to his feet, cocked his head and said smoothly, "You know, the two of us could be a real team if you would only work with me. With all your skills and with my direction, we could be unbeatable." He paused, chuckling to himself, and then said, "It's getting a bit old, isn't it? Me showing up, and the two of us playing this game?"

Anong forced herself to calm down, taking deep breaths, trying to gain control. She knew that if she were to attack, the mist would stop her. As she calmed herself, she sensed something dark emanating from him and, in an accusing tone, asked, "What have you done, Sorcerer? What evil have you created?"

Anong's power had once again transformed Zakalis. His stooped, tired body lifted, and the exhaustion slipped away from his face. "I have created nothing that was not already here," he said with an ugly smile.

"Was my father killed today?" she demanded.

"The Jogahoh? I haven't seen him," he replied, his face uncaring. He continued, trying once more to bait her on. "I've walked through hundreds of the dead today. He could have been one of them."

Among knew with certainty that Zakalis was lying. Within her, a strength was growing, and she felt her birthmark begin to pulse. She was somehow able to read him, see his intent and see through his lies. Her stomach untied itself from the knots that had clenched it. Her father was still alive. She also knew, however, that Zakalis' words held truth. He and his army had indeed killed hundreds.

His eyes lingered on her, a smile appearing on his face. "Anong," he said, using her name for the first time, "it's time for me to go now. I will have to rest before my army marches again. Think about what I said to you. If we work together, you can have everything you ever wanted." He turned, his robes swirling around him, and walked out the door.

Anong moved quickly over to the window and tried to look outside, but the green mist allowed her to see and hear nothing. She was frustrated that he was able to draw power she did not even know she had. Why was she unable to use her own magic, and why could she not perform the simplest of spells? The first step, she was certain, was to control her anger and rage. It seemed her emotions opened a door that would gain him access. She would find a way to keep that door firmly closed and to build a wall between them. Anong also knew that although unable to physically leave, she might be able to free her spirit. *He would be back*. The burden lay with her because she was the source of his power. If she did not regain control, thousands more would die.

CHAPTER 32

After Oman's shift on sentry, he walked back to where his horse was tethered and laid out his bedroll. He tucked himself under the thick hide, making sure every part of him was protected from the night air. Exhausted, he fell into a deep sleep as soon as he closed his eyes. He dreamed he was back in the land of the Jibay. The day was beautiful; the birds sang their songs, and the sky was a cloudless blue. The three of them, Jossa, Anong and himself, returned from a day by the river with a string of freshly caught trout. He and Anong cleaned the fish while Jossa went inside to stoke the fire. He watched as Anong expertly cut the fillets from the backbone. His pride in her overflowed. She had learned so much and had done so well. Turning, he saw Jossa at the doorway waving to him, and he motioned for Anong to bring the fish into the house. They walked together to the small cabin, Anong automatically shorting her stride so he could keep up with her.

From out of nowhere, he heard a gruff voice say, "Oman! It's time." Oman felt a hand shaking his foot. Confused, he looked around to see Jossa and Anong watching him without expression.

"Oman! Wake up," the voice said again, insistently.

The dream evaporated, fading from view, and the house and farm disappeared. He was torn away from everything he loved and thrust back into reality. With a jolt, he pulled himself up and drew his sword out from under the hide. Oman looked about in the darkness, breathing raggedly, not knowing for an instant where he was.

The voice spoke again, "Oman, are you awake?"

Oman gathered his wits and was now fully alert. "Yes, I'm awake," he said to the soldier standing by his feet.

"Good. The commander asked me to wake you. Sunrise is just

an hour away. He wants you to meet him over at his tent."

"I'll be there in ten minutes. Is the coffee on?"

"Ready and waiting for you."

Minutes later, Oman's belongings were packed, the horse was saddled, and he was ready for another day of fighting. The man who had woken him handed him a cup of coffee as he walked into the ring of people. Toka nodded to Oman at his approach and said, "I hope you got enough rest. We may not get much after today."

Oman chuckled softly and replied, "The bones are getting older, and they don't like the cold, hard ground."

The two men walked over to a log and sat down to enjoy their coffee. The commander turned to Oman and said, "I want you to ride back to the gap with the re-supply group. They're leaving in a few minutes."

Oman stared into his coffee mug and said, "I'll stay here with you."

"Oman, this is not your fight. The Jogahoh are not involved. Go and find your daughter. Take her and your wife far away from this place. Live on your own in peace."

"I can't," he said. "If they get through us, do you really think they'll stop at our border? The magic that protects us is no match for someone that can raise an army of the dead." He paused and then declared, "Besides, I made a promise to myself. I swore that if Tibalt ever raised an army again, I'd take up arms against him. He took my father. I'll stay here with you, pushing these bastards back as hard as we can."

Toka stood without replying to Oman. He called to one of his men and said, "Tell the re-supply team they are free to return now." Glancing at Oman with a sad, reluctant smile on his face, he said, "Good luck, my friend."

······

King Tibalt walked over to where he thought the sorcerer was sleeping and kicked the dark lump of blankets. There was no one there. To his side and from behind a boulder, he heard, "Sire, were you looking for me?"

Tibalt was surprised but recovered quickly and sauntered over to the voice. He stopped in shock the moment he saw him. Zakalis was surrounded by a brilliant red aura of energy and power. His face reflected an unearthly glow of strength and intensity, and Tibalt felt a shiver of fear run through his body. This man was dangerous, he knew. He would have to get rid of him as soon as this battle was won. "I thought you were still asleep," he said finally, trying to regain his composure.

"I've been awake for some time, preparing for today."

"Good. Once you see the sun clear the horizon, I want the army to march. The rising sun will be in their faces, and we can drive straight into them."

"Of course, Sire. I'll be ready."

Tibalt eyed the sorcerer suspiciously before departing without saying another word. Zakalis smiled to himself as the king walked away. He could hear the man's thinking and said to himself, *Getting rid of me won't be as easy as you think it will be.* He drank the last of his morning brew and walked out to where the dead army stood. They were as he had left them the day before; not a muscle moved, and no sound was heard. The sun was now halfway above the horizon, and he closed his eyes, holding his arms out. Zakalis called out a hoarse, ugly cry, and power rushed from him, rippling out and over the silent statues to his front. For a moment, the soldiers did not stir. As one, they came to attention, lifting their swords in a salute. Soulless eyes opened, and from their depths came a deep, low growl heard throughout the hills. Their blades began a steady rhythmic beat across their breastplate, the sound reverberating around them. As swiftly as it began, everything stopped, and they stood silent once more, waiting for the sorcerer to give the order. Zakalis opened his eyes, looking at the vast army in front of him and could see the sun now just clearing the horizon. A command screamed from his body and, as one, the army stepped off, swords at the ready. Zakalis mounted his horse and followed close behind.

••••••

Anong was still asleep when she felt the sorcerer's hold on her weaken. She sat up with a start and thought, *He must be using the magic now.* Knowing this was her one chance, she lay back onto the bed and put herself into a trance. The green mist that surrounded her stirred, swirling around her, sensing something amiss. Her spirit lifted from her body, and as it did, the mist tried to envelop it and capture her. Its tendrils reached up, but she slipped away. She continued, the mist always just beside her, trying to pull her down. She sensed the sorcerer's location and knew she had to confront him. Anong began to move away from the house, but a rope of energy tightened around her waist, stopping her. Roughly, it tried to pull her back to her prison, to her bed and body. Instead of fighting the pressure, she moved around it, dancing left, then right and back again, always moving and twisting. She could feel its grip loosen as she turned and spun. Anong turned to face the sun and immediately felt its morning rays fill her with strength. Adding its energy to her own, she wrenched herself upward, breaking the bonds that were holding her. Finally free, she continued her journey toward Zakalis and the eastern army. Within moments, she was above them, their attack already in motion. She recoiled in horror at the malevolent magic swirling around the undead forces in contact with the western front. Deep within her, she acknowledged that this evil magic was a part of her, and she felt ashamed. Reluctantly, she drew closer to the carnage and found the sorcerer behind their line, guiding them.

Anong watched in shock as the grey figures were cut down, only to rise again. The western army was fighting hard, but she knew they were no match, and the fight was hopeless. They were slowly being slaughtered by this evil, merciless man. She was crushed for not being strong enough to foresee this happening.

It's up to me now. I must try to do my best to stop this from getting any further. Anong was lost. She had only just discovered her powers. How would she end all of this?

The western army called their archers to the front and let go a flurry of arrows. They flew through the air and into the dead army's lines, momentarily stopping them. They then immediately used the opportunity to fall back.

The sorcerer was devoting most of his power to ensuring his army regenerated and regrouped for the next attack. A sudden awareness ran through him, and he felt he was being watched. He looked up to see Anong's spirit not far from him.

"I see you've found a way to escape," he laughed. Zakalis raised his hand up, palm open, and clenched it tightly into a fist.

Anong, above him, could feel Zakalis grip her tightly and try to drag her toward him. At first, his grip was iron, and as much as she fought, she felt herself being pulled closer to him. His army, however, needed more of his power to heal itself, and she could feel his grip weaken. She knew that her anger would only provide him with fuel. Anong drew a deep breath and calmly, without emotion, began peeling off his bonds until she was finally free. The undead army continued to demand his energy, and Anong could see the power draining from his body. Finally exhausted by trying to maintain his hold on both Anong and his army, the sorcerer loosened his grip on her. Her physical body was still under his control. She focused on his thoughts and asked, "Why?"

The sorcerer, his face pale and covered in a sheen of sweat, breathed in deeply, panting. Ignoring her, he tried to concentrate once more on the troops before him. Nudging his horse forward, he followed them. Glancing up at her, he said, "Why, you ask? For power. What are a few thousand lives in exchange for all this power?" He lifted his hand up, pushing it toward Anong, and she felt a blast of energy that took her away from him, leaving her just over the front line of the western army.

Looking ahead, she could see large hills five hundred meters to her front and in a direct line to the pass. The western army was defending the pass, and the eastern army was trying to get through it. The route was about two hundred meters wide and one kilometre long, twisting and turning in what was possibly the remains of an ancient riverbed. A flicker of movement caught her eye, and she watched with some trepidation how the western army was planning their ambush. She searched for Oman within the ranks but could not catch sight of him. *Where are you?* she wondered. *I hope you're safe.*

· · · · · ·

Esma and Jossa had settled into an uneasy routine, both worried and concerned for Oman and Anong. Esma still could not feel Anong's presence, and they had heard nothing from Oman. She felt fluctuations in the sorcerer's power but knew that Anong was still trapped in the house. Getting up just before sunrise, she set about her chores. Esma was carrying a basket of eggs back into the cottage when she jolted to a stop. She realized she could once more feel Anong's presence. Not in totality, she amended, but her spirit form was free. *Her body is still back in the house,* she thought. *But I can speak with her.* Calling excitedly to Jossa, she said, "I can feel Anong. I'm going to her."

Jossa looked up from the fireplace, where she was preparing their breakfast, and asked, "Is she all right? What do you need me to do?"

"Nothing, for now. Just stay here while I try to find her. She's in spirit form. I'll have to find her in the same way." Esma lay down on her bed and closed her eyes as Jossa hurried to her side. "I won't be long, Jossa. Don't worry. I'll find her."

With little effort, Esma lifted from her body and flew toward the shining light of energy that was Anong. She found her in minutes, searching for her father within the ranks of the western army. "Anong, why are you here? Why didn't you come to me first?"

Anong threw her arms around Esma and said, "I'm so glad to see you. I tried to get out before, but his magic was too strong for me."

Esma drew her back and asked again, "I understand that you were being held, but why did you come here and not to me?"

Anong sighed and dipped her head down. "All of this is my doing. I had to see what I caused."

"You didn't cause anything. It was Zakalis that caused all of this."

"But his power comes from me. I wanted to see if there was a way I could stop it. The sorcerer has done something to channel everything I have to him. He would come in and make me angry. Every time I fought him, he was able to pull my magic from me."

"It's because you're young and have so much potential. Your every thought and feeling is made from pure emotion. That emotion has tremendous power. So, it seems to me you've found a way to control your anger?"

"I think I have."

Esma looked down at the battle below her. "This will take up all his energy today, and he'll be looking for more. You need to be ready. Does he know your spirit is free?"

"He does. He's too strong for me to try and stop him in this form," Anong replied.

"You'll need to be careful and never believe a word he says. You must find him at his weakest. If not, he will find a way to take your power from you forever."

Esma looked down at the fighting going on below them and said, "Your father is down there somewhere. We can look for him together if you like."

Anong thought for a moment and realized a dreadful truth. "I can't. If I see my father hurt in any way, I know I won't be able to control my feelings. And that's what the sorcerer wants."

"Then you must return to your body."

"You must promise to help me get out of that prison, Esma."

"Of course," she said with a comforting smile. With that assurance, Anong reluctantly turned to the east and disappeared back to the house and her body.

Esma searched for the sorcerer and had little difficulty finding him, as he was surrounded by a dark, malevolent red glow of light. He rode confidently just behind his gruesome troops, concentrating on the battle. As she came nearer, he felt her presence and looked up at her, his face annoyed.

"Another visitor? What are you doing here?"

Esma knew she had no power or control over Zakalis while he was filled with Anong's magic. "You have no idea what you have created, Zakalis," she replied quietly. "You can stop all this now if you choose. I can help you."

Zakalis laughed sharply and dismissed her, saying, "Go back to your cabin, witch. This is far beyond what you know. I may call you if I need someone to wash my robes."

Esma pursed her lips and shook her head sadly. "This will not go well for you, that I can promise. I have given you fair warning. Beware, Zakalis. Hell holds a special place for people like you." Not bothering to wait for his response, she turned and left him, heading to the pass between the hills.

Zakalis' lip curled in anger, but he had little time to think about Esma's words. His army needed a constant supply of energy from him, and they were getting closer to the mouth of the pass. He turned back to the battle, his encounter with the witch forgotten.

• • • • • •

Oman could finally see the pass they'd all so desperately been looking for since sunup. They moved into the gap, spotting the line and hasty defenses put in place by the first company. Dismounting what horses they had left, they set them free. If the horses were needed after the battle, they would take the time to look for them, for it meant they were still alive. They could no longer use a fighting withdrawal; their numbers were too small.

Dirt and blood clung tightly to their clothing. Their throats dry and their bellies empty, they stood defiantly against the overwhelming odds. They knew there were only a few moments before engaging with the enemy again. Oman tiredly wiped his brow, glanced to his side and spotted Toka coming up to him.

The man looked down at him, smiled grimly, and said, "I'm happy you made it."

Oman raised an eyebrow and said, "I'm hoping they will follow us deep into the gap where we may have a chance."

"I'm sure they will. Their movement has been a steady forward advance from the beginning. Nothing has stopped them in two days." Before they could speak more, a clash of swords was heard, and they began the battle once more.

••••••

King Tibalt fully anticipated that the western army would lure their forces into the pass and conduct an ambush. He split his army into two halves, sending one to the left and one to the right of the pass to secure the high ground. They pushed upward in a steady stream and finally reached the crest of the hill, assuming little resistance. To their surprise, King Merck had anticipated the move and was prepared to defend the hilltop. The eastern army felt a chill run through them when they saw a flight of arrows heading toward their lines and heard the bugle call echoing.

The sorcerer was unaware of anything else going on around him. He could feel only an exuberant victory ahead of him as he pushed his undead army deeper and deeper into the tight pass. It was what he had been waiting for all these years. *I will rule this land.*

The battle moved deeper into the pass, which narrowed abruptly to only fifty meters. King Merck watched from the cliffs well above the two battles being fought, one in the pass and the other on both sides of the high ground. The undead army continued their relentless push deep into the gap, and the king could now make out the sorcerer bringing up the rear, chanting words of power.

He watched with satisfaction as his troops continued their retreat through the pass. When they had almost cleared it, and when the undead army was in the narrowest portion, King Merck gave the command, and a bugle call sounded. Ropes that secured stones, logs and debris to both sides of the valley walls were immediately hacked through. It set off an avalanche that sealed the entrance and stopped any chance of escape.

King Merck's men heard the bugle above them and immediately began a retreat to safety. As they fled, a loud roar of falling debris came from behind them as it crashed down the sides of the canyon walls. The dead army continued their steady march forward and was closing quickly. They were perhaps one hundred meters behind Oman, who was running as fast as he could when he heard another loud crack and roar. Looking up the side of the canyon, he could see where more rock and debris had been cut loose and was coming down fast. Oman re-doubled his efforts to escape the avalanche but could feel his strength rapidly coming to an end. Gasping for breath, he tried to continue, but his legs collapsed under him. At the very last moment, he felt a hand grasp the back of his shirt, and he was lifted into the air. The commander had watched the small man falter and, without hesitation, picked him up and carried him to safety just as the boulders and debris crashed and sealed the other end.

Toka and Oman fell to the ground in a heap, both breathing hard and covered in sweat and dirt. Oman recovered first and, without a word, held his hand out, helping Toka up. They looked behind them and saw that the valley floor had been transformed into a high wall of rock, dirt and trunks of enormous pine trees. Oman looked up and could make out figures along the pass walls, pushing heavy barrels filled with oil over the rim of the high cliffs. The barrels came crashing down and broke open onto the dead army trapped between the two sealed walls. There was a moment of silence before he saw hundreds of flaming arrows soar into the air and then arch downward. When they hit, Oman heard a loud whoosh and felt the heat and fire scorch his face. He turned his head aside to escape the intense blaze and waited until the searing heat waned. Finally, sword in hand, he climbed the steep side of the rubble barrier and cleared its top. The scene before him was one of apocalyptic bedlam. The dead army had been trapped in the cramped space and was now entirely engulfed in a roaring blaze. The demons howled in agony as the flames grew, but their demands for Zakalis' magic went unheeded. He had nothing left for them. There would be no regeneration from the fire, Oman knew. Esma had been correct.

• • • • • •

Zakalis, revelling within the deep thrall of magic that swirled in dark circles around him, did not hear the thunderous crash of the avalanche until it was too late. He watched in stunned disbelief as barrels were pitched over the cliff sides, smashing into the debris below and sending hundreds of gallons of oil everywhere. Seconds later, he saw flaming arrows arching high across the sky and coming down into the canyon. His horse panicked and reared, throwing him clumsily out of the saddle, and he landed in an undignified heap. As his troops were engulfed in flames, he felt his powers draining from him faster than he could ever have imagined. He reeled in shock and gasped as the entities once under his control relentlessly tried to extract more than he could give. Realizing that he would be drained if he did nothing, he managed to cut the bond and looked around in bewilderment. *What are they doing?* he thought, enraged as he helplessly watched his army flounder and fall. With a sudden start, he knew that this battle had been utterly lost. He did not have enough magic left in him to rejuvenate his troops and knew that the fire would destroy them.

Frantically, he scrambled clumsily up and over the rocks that blocked his exit. He had almost reached the top when the entire area exploded into a fiercely burning cauldron, a furnace that singed his hair and seared his skin. He staggered and rolled over the embankment into the dirt, trying to extinguish the flames licking his robes. In shock, he could only gasp for breath, his lungs scorched by the heat. The smell of his burned hair and the roasting bodies of his army made him nauseous, and he screamed at the pain from his blistered hands and face. Shocked and dismayed by the suddenness of the attack, he wanted nothing more than to hide and heal but was acutely aware that King Merck would be hunting him. He needed to escape, and he needed more power to heal himself. He needed Anong.

Using some of the precious tendrils of stolen magic he had left, Zakalis transported himself back to Anong's prison.

CHAPTER 33

King Merck's troops had decimated the entirety of King Tibalt's men on the high ground. On his bugle call, they pushed down and prepared for battle at the mouth of the canyon. Another bugle call signaled for his cavalry to attack the remainder of the eastern army, now advancing toward them.

King Tibalt was unaware that the troops he had ordered to the high ground had been defeated and anticipated little resistance. The sorcerer's army had been doing their work for them, and the king had let down his guard. He was about to order his remaining troops to attack when he was startled by the roar of the avalanche. "Where is the sorcerer?" he screamed at his lieutenant, who stood there mutely, unable to reply. Furious at everyone and everything around him, he ordered a small group of officers forward to find out what was happening. A minute later, the sky erupted into a brilliant cloud of flame, followed by an intense blast of heat and smoke.

King Tibalt tried to maintain his composure as he watched the group who had gone forward return. They were waving and shouting frantically but were too far from the command group to be understood. Suddenly, behind the riders, they could see the cause of their panic. Chasing them, spread out six hundred meters on either side, was a cavalry charge in full pursuit. They hit the unprepared main force like a battering ram, scattering the men, equipment and horses in all directions. The cavalry sliced through the ranks while panicked soldiers ran about, trying to form battle formations and drawing their weapons. King Merck's cavalry continued to push straight through the eastern army, then stopped, reformed and charged back into the confused and totally unprepared ranks. Again and again, they charged, slicing through everything and everyone that was standing ready to fight. King Merck watched the mayhem with his infantry just to the rear. Once their mission was complete, he ordered them into battle. His soldiers stepped off in formation, taking on those who still wanted to fight and imprison others. The battle was over with little resistance, and, two hours later, the prisoners were gathered up and the dead laid out. King Merck walked the long lines of the dead, looking for his brother. "He's not here," he said to his deputy.

"Sire, he may be with the prisoners," the deputy replied, "or perhaps among the injured."

"We have to find him," the king replied, determined. The two men began a long walk through the lines of injured men but found nothing. They had only started their inspection of the prisoners when King Merck stopped and returned to look more closely at one of the men. He was dressed as a common soldier, covered with dirt and grime. His head was down, and the king was unable to make out his features. "That one," he said harshly. Two guards grabbed the man roughly and dragged him in front of the king. "Strip his headgear," the king commanded. One of the guards ripped off the man's helmet and tossed it to the side.

Merck drew his sword and placed it under the man's chin. "Look at me, Brother," he said calmly, pressing the blade up and forcing the man to meet his eyes. "Many years have passed between us, but the eyes never change. It appears you have abandoned your king's robes for the dress of a common soldier." He paused, waiting for his brother to reply.

King Tibalt stared straight ahead, humiliated and seething in rage, looking for a way to exploit this opportunity to his advantage. Thinking quickly, he finally said, "Brother, could I have a word with you in private?"

"If you have something to say to me, say it now."

"This has all been a huge mistake. We were trying to go after those beasts. We were trying to stop them when your forces attacked us. The sorcerer, Zakalis, conjured up his unholy force without my knowledge and used his magic to trick us." He stopped for a moment, his mind scrambling.

King Merck ignored him and simply waved his hand. The guards quickly gagged him and tied his hands behind his back. Walking to the bound man, whose eyes were now wide with fear, King Merck studied his brother's face silently. With steel in his voice, he said, "I am going to ride now with my army as far west as I can. I will take everything that you own. What was once yours will now become mine. Every man, every palace, every animal, every sheath of wheat will be mine. You had enough, and yet you wanted more. I have a castle in the far north that sees only snow. You will be jailed there, deep within its dungeon. You will have enough to eat and drink. You will have a blanket for warmth, and when you become ill, my best physician will be dispatched to ensure you get well again. I want you to live a long life, remembering every day how good your life was before this. I want you to reflect on the people you have hurt and how greed overcame you. One day, when you are very old, and as you beg to die, perhaps I will let you." He turned to his guard and said, "Take him away."

Tibalt's words were garbled as the guards dragged him off. "I swear it was not of my doing, Brother! You are making a grave mistake!" King Merck had no pity left and ignored his wails. Their father had given them everything they could want, yet Tibalt always demanded more. He could no longer forgive him for what he had done to his people and the needless deaths he had caused.

His deputy joined him and said, "We've gone over all the bodies in the pass and haven't been able to find the sorcerer."

The king, confident, mulled over the deputy's words and then said, "That's fine. We'll find him another day."

••••••

Esma had watched the battle with horror and was now actively searching for Oman. She found him with Toka, standing on the rise of the debris that had almost buried them, surveying the gruesome, smouldering ruins. She drifted down and made herself visible to him. Oman looked up and, seeing her, his tired face filled with relief. He automatically thought of his daughter and, filled with anxiety, asked, "Esma! Can you feel Anong?"

"I'm relieved to see you again, Oman. I was able to speak with her for only a short while in spirit form. The sorcerer, though weak, still holds her in his grasp."

"Have you seen him?"

"I watched him when he went into the pass, but he abandoned the battle when the flames began. I know he is returning to Anong for more magic."

"Can you take me to her?"

"I can transport you, but I need to return to my body first. I will bring you to my cottage and send you to Anong."

"I must tell the king of my plans."

The commander had watched the interaction with some trepidation. He had never seen an apparition before but knew Esma was there to help Oman. "I'll let the king know what you are doing. Your concerns are with your family now. If you find and kill the sorcerer, the king will welcome it."

Esma disappeared without another word, her spirit returning to her body within seconds. Rising swiftly from her bed, she startled Jossa, who had never left her side the entire time.

"You've returned!" Jossa said. "Have you found them?"

"I have. I'm bringing Oman back now." Esma gathered herself together and, within minutes, had conjured a portal in which Oman could return.

Oman and the commander did not have long to wait. Within minutes of Esma's disappearance, a bright, shining portal appeared before them. "Till we meet again," Oman said, stepping through. "Thank you, my friend."

Oman passed through and found himself instantaneously transported into Esma's small cottage. Jossa cried out in relief at the sight of her husband and threw her arms around the exhausted man. "Are you all right?"

"I'm fine. It's good to be back," he said. He wrapped his arms around her before looking up at Esma and said, "Can you feel Anong?"

"Strangely enough, I do but not as strong as before. There is still a power that has its hold on her. We need to wait a bit longer and let her find her strength. Until then, you look exhausted and hungry."

······

The door opened, and the sorcerer staggered into Anong's room without saying a word. He sat down at the table, poured himself a cup of water, drank it down and poured himself another. After a moment, he wiped his mouth and looked over to Anong, his face reflecting pure venom. She was shocked by his appearance. His robes were almost completely burned off, and red, oozing blisters covered his body and face. Half of the hair on his head was burned away, and she could smell its acid stench.

"This is all your doing," he spat out. "If you'd just given me all your magic, this never would have happened. Instead, I had to squeeze it out of you in tiny bits, making me beg for more." His voice began to rise as the pain of his injuries overwhelmed him. Anong stepped back, frightened, and thought, *He sounds half-mad.* "All my plans, all my work, have been for nothing," he screamed and slammed his mug onto the table.

Anong's eyes narrowed slightly as she looked at the man appraisingly. Spittle was running from the side of his mouth, and he winced in pain as he glared at her. "Me?" she asked with surprise. "You blame me for this? You've kidnapped me, stolen my powers, yet still lose the fight, and this is my fault?"

With a crazed roar, Zakalis leaped up, grasped the table and overturned it with a pain-filled heave, advancing menacingly toward her. As he came closer, the last remaining bits of his stolen magic began to dissipate, leaving only a tendril behind. Through gritted teeth, he said, "I was so good to you. You wanted for nothing and had everything. You never knew what your powers could be used for. You could have given it all to me at the very beginning. I'm tired of bits and pieces, and now I want it all. If you don't give it to me, I'll beat it out of you."

Anong moved to the other side of the bed, keeping some distance between the two of them. She became aware of a pulsating strength from her birthmark. She realized that Zakalis' anger was allowing the magic to return to her. *If I can keep my anger in check*, she thought as she felt him weakening, *he won't get anything from me.*

••••••

Esma lifted her head, a look of relief on her face. She sighed and said to Oman, "I can feel her. His power is almost gone now, and she is coming through unheeded. We can't lose this opportunity. You must move now."

Oman did not hesitate. He hastily grabbed his sword, leaving his chainmail behind, and asked, "Where are we going?"

Esma shook her head and said, "You must do this yourself. Zakalis will feel my presence immediately, and I don't want him to have time to react. We need to catch him totally unaware." Oman grabbed a ladle of water from the bucket, drank it down, kissed Jossa on the cheek and said, "I'm ready."

Esma replied, "I'm placing you by the front door of the cottage. It will open easily now."

"And the guards?"

"Word of the defeat has already arrived, and they've abandoned their posts."

Moments later, he stood on the outside of Anong's prison door. Grasping the door handle, he moved it slowly and felt the latch unlock from its recess. He pushed lightly and felt it move under his weight. As it opened, Oman moved his head into the room, trying to see into it, but all he could see was a wall of darkness. He placed his hand on the hilt of his sword and pushed the door fully open. He heard movement and two people's voices, one he immediately recognized as belonging to Anong. Drawing his sword, he stepped into the dimly lit room. Spotting the sorcerer, Oman ordered, "Step away from her."

Both heads spun toward him, and Anong's eyes widened in joy and relief. "Father," she cried, "I knew you'd find me."

"I did," he replied, striding closer to them, sword at the ready. "You are the sorcerer who tricked my brother, kidnapped my daughter and is responsible for the deaths of so many."

Zakalis had never felt so exhausted. His burns were screaming, and all his plans had gone up in smoke, but he would not give way to a lowly Jogahoh. Gritting his teeth in pain, Zakalis bowed mockingly to Oman and said, "At your service. Anong and I were just discussing the business of magic, and I was trying to persuade her to give it to me. She has no use for it."

"And what did she say?" Oman asked calmly, tilting his sword back onto his shoulder.

"She doesn't seem to agree with me for the moment. But it's no concern of yours. Leave now before it's too late."

Oman knew that he had to bring this to an end quickly. "I don't think so. And not without my daughter."

"It will all be for the best, can't you see?" the sorcerer said, his voice rising hysterically.

"All for the best? And once you have all her magic, what will you do? Raise another army of the dead just for us to burn them again?" Oman took a step closer and pointed his sword at the sorcerer.

Zakalis knew that this would be his last opportunity to take Anong's magic. If he could bring her anger to a boiling point by killing her father, he would use the last of the mist to take everything from her. His harsh, almost maniacal laughter filled the room. Sarcastically, he said, "Oh, I don't know. Find a nice farm, a girl and settle down in the sun. You did outthink me in the pass. I never thought anyone would find that one weakness."

His voice became hard and filled with menace as he glared at Oman. "You do not understand," he said fiercely. "I was so very close to having it all, to having everything! And you took that from me!"

A sword appeared in Zakalis' hand. He looked at the Jogahoh with contempt, sure the small man would present no challenge, even without his magic. "I've warned you to leave, but it's too late now. This shouldn't take long."

"Then I guess today will be a good day to die," Oman replied, his sword steady. He called out to his daughter, "Anong, leave now. The sorcerer no longer holds you." Anong cautiously moved to the doorway, fearful for her father.

CHAPTER 34

The sorcerer looked at the small, fierce man in front of him and laughed dismissively. "How you managed to stay alive these past few days is beyond my understanding. You are nothing. Do you really think you are any match for me?"

Oman did not reply and would only concentrate on the job at hand. He needed to get close enough to strike, as was always the case when fighting larger opponents. The sorcerer attacked first, swinging down hard with his blade, hoping to crush Oman's skull. Oman easily parried the blow, and the sword harmlessly slid past him. He stepped in quickly, swinging his weapon low across the man's midsection, but the sorcerer stepped away just in time. Oman followed through in one smooth motion and came in hard from the other direction. Again, the sorcerer stepped back, letting the blade cut the air in front of him.

He laughed at Oman, twirling his sword smoothly before stepping forward and bringing down the weapon, slashing at him without pause. Oman met each blow squarely, the clash of the blades ringing through the air, but found himself being pushed back against a table. As Zakalis lifted his sword for another blow, the little Jogahoh ducked under the table and came up on the other side. The sorcerer's strike came down, and his blade became wedged in the wooden surface. Oman rushed around while the sorcerer tried to pull the weapon free. He could tell that Zakalis had once been a proficient swordsman, but those days were long in the past. He had replaced his weapons training with magic, assuming sorcery would do all his work for him. Oman could now see the sweat gathering on the sorcerer's brow and the deep heaving of his chest. The confidence that had been there minutes before was now replaced by a glimmer of doubt. Zakalis was wondering if he could win this fight.

"Sorcerer," Oman said, "perhaps this is not quite as easy as you thought it would be." It was his turn to go on the offensive. He began to rain down blows on the now visibly tiring man. Oman, relentless, saw an opening and, with a turn, slashed his blade across Zakalis' leg. The sorcerer felt a burning sting slip across his upper thigh, and he dropped his weapon with a cry, clenching his leg.

Oman swept his leg under Zakalis, kicking him to the ground. Moving swiftly, he thrust his sword into Zakalis' chest, just piercing the skin and then stopped. "Make your peace," he commanded.

Zakalis felt the tip of the blade as it cut into his chest and cried out once more. Panic was rampant across his face as he grasped the blade in a vain attempt to hold it back. Sputtering in fear, he said, "This was not my doing. It was the king and your brother who conspired together. They forced me to raise the army."

Anong stepped into the room and looked down at the pathetic man who had taken such great pleasure in tormenting her only a few days ago. "Father, let him be. It's over. Let's go home."

"No. I must finish this, or he will return." Oman forced the blade deeper into Zakalis' chest, stopping as the man's eyes bulged in pain and his agonized scream filled the room.

"He will never return, Father. Trust me."

Oman glanced at his daughter with a questioning look. "Is this what you want?"

"Yes."

Oman, stone-faced, turned back to Zakalis. "You're fortunate she has forgiveness in her heart," he said coldly. "The outcome would have been different if it had only been you and I."

Oman roughly pulled his sword up from the man's chest, keeping it close. "You're right. Let's go home," he said to Anong, and they walked out into the sunlight.

••••••

Esma could feel the exact moment that Anong was fully in

control of her magic once more. Not hesitating, she spun a spell to bring them back. Within moments, a bright portal materialized, and Esma and Jossa waited in anticipation. From behind Oman and Anong, Esma unexpectantly saw the sorcerer appear, arch his arm back and throw a dagger toward Anong. They had just entered the portal when Oman saw the blade. Instinctively, he jumped in front of his daughter, taking the full brunt of it. Seconds later, they reappeared in front of the two women, and the portal closed. Oman collapsed onto the ground, the weapon buried in his chest and blood spurting from the wound. With an agonized cry, Jossa ran to him, falling onto her knees beside him. Anong dropped down and cradled his head in her arms, sobbing, tears streaming down her face. Oman's chest heaved with exertion as he tried to bring in oxygen, but the knife had penetrated deeply. His eyes began to roll back, and his arms dropped in exhaustion. He had reached his end.

In that instant, Esma knew what had to be done and said, "Anong, this task will be yours to learn. We will be doing this together." Anong froze and lifted her tear-filled eyes to the woman. Seeing the look of resolve on Esma's face, she was filled with hope. Esma came to her and said, "Give me your hand." Anong put her hand into Esma's, and the older woman guided it to her father's chest. "When I take out the dagger, press your hand firmly over the wound. Feel what must be done and join the skin and tissue together as it was meant to be. Now come with me as we heal him."

Anong took a deep breath and let herself flow into Esma. The woman drew her quickly into Oman's failing body. With Esma's guidance, Anong began the healing process. She watched with amazement as the muscles and nerves re-attached and healed. "Healing the body is not difficult," Esma said after a moment. "It is convincing the spirit to return that will be challenging."

"What must I do?"

"I will show you. Your father's spirit has left, and we must convince him to return. Come with me." The two women closed their eyes and moved into their spirit forms.

"There are countless planes of existence in this spirit world," Esma explained. "You must first find where he is. Use your senses to search for him and tell me when you've found him."

Anong extended herself into the vastness that surrounded her. She silently sought the man who had saved her, who had been her teacher, guide and loving father. Their love was the key to finding him. "He's not far," she said tentatively. Finally, she whispered, "There he is. I can feel him."

"You are the only one that can take us to him and bring him home. Focus only on Oman, visualize his essence, and you can bring us to him."

Anong unconsciously filled herself with everything she loved about her father. Around her, the air began to glow. In an instant, they were transported through time and space to another field of existence, a place of dreams filled with quiet streams, green woods and a small, cozy cottage tucked into a clearing. Oman was sitting on a rocking chair on the front porch, a look of wonder on his face. He spotted the two of them as soon as they appeared and asked, "Who are you? Can you help me? I don't really know how I got here."

"Father," Anong said, "I'm your daughter. We've come to take you home."

"It's strange, but I feel like this place is my home," Oman argued. "Why should I leave?"

Anong reached to him and took his hand. Oman felt a flow of energy from her, filling him with memories of his life. "Where am I? How did I get here?"

Esma interrupted. "There will be time for explanations later, Oman. This place is not for you at this moment in time, and you must return with us now. We can't linger here."

"Why? This place makes me happy."

Anong now understood why bringing back the spirits of the

departed was so difficult. The longer they stayed, the harder it was for them to leave. Here there was no hunger, no anger, no fear. Her father was content, but their need for him was overwhelming. *Am I selfish?* "Mother misses you, Father," Anong replied softly. "I miss you. Please come home to us." She filled him with their memories of happier times, just the three of them. The laughter, their picnics by the stream, the frigid winters spent by a cozy fireplace, their adventures in the woods.

He turned to her with wide eyes. "Anong?"

"Yes, Father," she nodded. "Please come home with us."

"Can you take me back to Jossa?"

"She's waiting for both of us now, Father. We must go immediately, before it's too late."

Her father wavered for only a second. Then said, "I'm ready."

Anong swept all of them back into their bodies. She opened her eyes to see Jossa looking at her with concern.

"What happened?" Jossa asked. "The two of you were so still! What did you do?"

"We had to find Father and bring him back," Anong explained. "He's here with us now."

Jossa said disbelievingly, "He's alive?"

Esma smiled at Jossa's shocked expression and said quietly, "Your daughter is very powerful, but it is his love for the two of you that allowed her to bring him back."

Oman opened his eyes to find himself lying in his wife's lap, her tear-filled face looking at him with love and concern. He turned his head to see Anong and Esma beside her, smiling down at him. Disoriented and confused, he asked them, "What's going on? What happened?"

"What do you remember?" Esma asked.

He thought for a moment and said, "I was walking toward a portal with Anong, bringing her home. I remember seeing the sorcerer throw a dagger just as we stepped through and knew I had to try to stop it." His eyes widened in realization, and he said,

"The dagger. The dagger struck me." He looked down at himself, puzzled by the sight of only a faint scar on his chest before another memory came to him. "I was living in a small cabin, I'm not sure where I was, and you two appeared. After that, I remember nothing and woke up here."

"I'm sorry, Father. You were dying, and we weren't ready to have you leave us," Anong said. Oman looked at her curiously, not understanding what she was saying.

"Anong brought you back," Esma explained.

Oman stared at his daughter and asked, "How?"

"Did I do the wrong thing?" she replied, worry in her eyes. "Did you want to stay?"

He pondered the questions and honestly replied, "I don't think I was completely ready to leave this world."

"And I, for one, am glad that you weren't," Jossa interrupted, kissing him lightly on his lips.

"You need rest," Esma said. "Come inside."

Oman nodded wearily. "It's been a long week. We'll rest up tonight and leave tomorrow to speak with King Merck." They helped him to his feet, and the four of them made their way back to the cottage.

They said their farewells to Esma the next day, packed their horses and rode to the eastern palace to meet with King Merck, who had established his new headquarters there. Oman told the king that Zakalis had escaped, but he considered the sorcerer no longer a threat. He would never again be able to raise another army of the dead.

King Merck was pleased but said, "I am certain he will surface one day: if not now, soon. I will find him, and his punishment will be severe."

"What will happen now?" Oman asked.

"We will push my army as far east as we can, taking all of the eastern kingdom. I anticipate our task will be long and arduous, as there will always be resistance to new laws. However, once the people realize that they are free from my brother's harsh rule, I am certain they will join us willingly. I'll take their army, integrate the men that want to stay and dismiss the others."

They stayed with the king for two days to rest and recuperate. After that, Oman, Jossa and Anong would be ready to leave and confront Salem.

The day before their departure, King Merck spoke with Oman. "I could use you here, Oman. I trust you to act as my regent and rule in my stead. Your lives would be good."

Oman stared at the king in shock. The offer to act as the king's regent was generous, and he had not expected it. Finally, he said, "My thanks to you, Sire, but the business I have has not been completed yet. I must first return to Alfheim and confront my brother."

"Finish your business in your own time, and should you decide to accept the position, let me know. It will be yours when you are ready."

CHAPTER 35

Oman, Jossa and Anong set off early the following day, glad to return to the peace and quiet of their family routine, with just the three of them. After four days of riding, the small family stopped for the night and set up camp. Once supper was finished and the dishes cleaned, the three settled down around the fire. Jossa poured each of them another cup of tea and sat down beside Oman and Anong. She was concerned about what would happen the next day and asked, "Tomorrow we will be in Alfheim. Do you have a plan?"

Oman did not reply immediately. He stared deeply into the fire, watching the coals dance around the logs until, to his horror, it reminded him of the corpses they had burned a few days earlier. He shuddered and took a deep breath before he replied to his wife, "I don't know. I honestly don't know. Perhaps King Merck's offer is the better choice for us."

"You've never been one to sit back once you feel you've been wronged," Jossa observed.

"Salem must be held accountable for what he has done. If the council does not agree, they will reap the consequences of their decision."

"And what of Anong?"

Oman locked eyes with his daughter, her serious face watching him with concern. "Anong is part of us, and it's time they realize and accept that. We will not stay otherwise. Tomorrow, we ride to my mother's. We can stay there for the night, and I'll go to town and address the council the next morning."

Anong asked, "What do you want me to do?"

Oman put his arm around her and said, "I suggest you get to know your grandmother. She'll be very happy to meet you."

The next morning, the three broke camp and rode toward Alfheim. By late afternoon, they arrived at his mother's home. As they were dismounting, the front door opened, and Tana stepped out. Seeing the three of them, she let out a small cry of joy and ran to them, wrapping her arms first around Oman and then Jossa. She turned to Anong and said, beaming, "And who might this lovely woman be?"

"This is Anong, our daughter and your granddaughter," Oman said proudly.

Anong smiled at the small, vivacious woman and said, "It's so wonderful to finally meet you, Grandmother."

Tana walked up to Anong with her arms outstretched, her head reaching only as high as Anong's chest. The young woman dipped down and gave Tana a hug. Tana pulled back after a moment and placed her hands on Anong's face, searching deeply into her eyes. She accepted Anong without question, without reserve and without surprise. "I feel as if I've always known you. I'm so happy we've finally gotten to meet." She turned to Oman and Jossa and said briskly, "Come inside now. We'll prepare ourselves something to eat, and you'll tell me everything."

"Go on ahead," Oman replied. "I'll take care of the animals and be in as soon as I can."

They spent the evening talking with Tana, first telling her the tale of how Anong came to be with them and how they had raised her. Next, they told her how Salem kidnapped Anong and how the sorcerer used her magic. They spoke of how they found Anong again and how the western army finally conquered the eastern kingdom. Tana was both furious and disappointed at her older son's actions. "Your father knew that Salem would be angry at not receiving the leadership role. However, I never suspected he would have gone so far as to kidnap your daughter."

The next day, Oman woke early, put the kettle on and fetched more firewood. The morning dew was heavy, and the grass was still wet, as was the wood at the top of the pile. Digging down a few layers, he found the dry wood, picked up an armload and brought it into the house. He poured himself a coffee and walked back outside, sitting down under an old oak tree in the morning sun. It was the same spot his father had used when making hard decisions. As a boy, he'd woken many times to see him sitting there, drinking coffee and thinking. A hard decision was to be made, and he knew what had to be done. The answers could only come from himself, so he stood and returned to the house to prepare to confront the council.

An hour later, Oman left for the council hall. As he walked down the streets of Alfheim, he was met with shocked expressions and puzzled looks. He greeted all of them regardless, ignoring their whispers. Arriving at the council hall, he walked through the long hallway leading to the chamber's main entrance.

Oman pushed the door open and stepped through the doorway. Gathered inside were the leaders from all the tribes of the Jogahoh. At his entrance, the entire room went silent, all eyes upon him. He strode confidently to the head of the table, as he'd done so many times in the past. It wasn't until now that he realized exactly how tired he was. The time spent trying to find Anong and the vicious battle had taken their toll. He saw Salem, looking at him in astonishment, his mouth agape. Behind Salem sat his old deputy, Calam, who, upon seeing him, began to rise. He raised his hand to the man and said, "No need, my friend. I will not be staying long." He turned to his brother and said, "You look very comfortable in my chair."

Salem's eyes narrowed, and he replied sarcastically, "You abandoned your people and have broken our laws. I had no choice but to take up the reins."

"Is that what you want them to believe?" Oman asked quietly.

"You took in an outsider! You know that is against our laws!" Salem replied angrily. The tribal leaders began muttering among themselves, anger on their faces.

Oman turned to the group, his voice barely concealing his fury. "It's obvious the rest of you do not understand what has been happening. I'm hearing from you that I have been relieved of my position and banished for breaking the law. The law of not allowing a non-Jogahoh to live within our country. Hear me now. Obeying that law would have meant that the child would have frozen. You would be content with her death because the law is the law." Oman was beyond anger as he let his words sink in. "If I had ever heard that one of you allowed someone to die because of an antiquated law, I would have banished you for not showing compassion. For not being able to see the difference between right and wrong and not choosing kindness over blind obedience." Oman stopped again, his face reflecting his fatigue. "I never wanted to lead sheep. If I wanted to lead sheep, I'd have become a shepherd. I wanted to lead people that could think for themselves. Sadly, it is obvious that none of you can do that."

Oman continued, knowing that the council had to hear his words. "I must now tell you what has happened. Zakalis, the eastern king's sorcerer, wanted my daughter for the magic she possesses. Salem made a bargain with him to kidnap her in exchange for the leadership of the Jogahoh."

Salem erupted at Oman's words, leaping from his chair in outrage. "Your words are a lie! I've never heard of this sorcerer you speak of and have made no such bargain."

"So, tell me, Brother, what story did you tell them of how you lost your ear?" Oman said smoothly. Salem's face blanched as Oman turned away from him and back to the council members. "Anong was delivered to Zakalis by Salem and Bargun. He held her captive and exploited her powers to bring up an army of the dead for King Tibalt." Oman described the bloody battle that ensued and how they had finally defeated the dead army.

By the time Oman finished speaking, the entire council sat in silence. He knew that half of them did not believe his words, and he could only feel disappointed. Oman leaned forward, placed his hands on the table and looked at the council members, pity on his face. "King Merck has offered me the position of regent within his newly acquired eastern kingdom. I wanted to give this one last chance." There was a murmur throughout the crowd, but none of the men were able to look squarely into Oman's eyes.

Salem laughed scornfully and, with words laced with hate, spat out, "Oman, you have been banished, and I have replaced you. You have no say in these chambers. Remove yourself." He turned to the council and said fiercely, "You should not listen to this fairy tale. He has no regard for our customs and traditions."

Oman coolly turned to his brother and said, "Salem, sit down before you embarrass yourself further. I was given the leadership of the Jogahoh because our father thought I was worthy. If Father thought you were worthy, he'd have chosen you." He addressed the now-uneasy faces around the table. "It appears you have chosen to believe Salem's words. You must live with the consequences of your decision." He turned his back on the council and walked over to his old deputy. Oman held out his hand to Calam, who shook it firmly. "Calam, it was a pleasure to serve with you."

The old man's eyes filled with tears as he stood up and said, "Oman, the honour has been all mine."

Oman had said everything he wanted to say. He turned without another word and walked out the door, the silent, sullen faces of the others watching him.

Jossa was working in the garden when Oman came into the yard. He made his way over to her, and she asked, "How did it go?"

He replied in resignation, "I said what had to be said, and it went as I expected. They've sided with tradition, not reason. We'll go back to our home one last time, pack what we need and head back to the eastern palace."

"Are you sure that's what you want to do?"

"Yes, I'm sure. We can ask Mother if she wants to come with us."

"That's a good idea. Anong and your mother have already formed a strong bond."

Oman sent a message to King Merck saying he would be returning within two weeks and then spoke with his mother. Tana decided that she would join them once they reached the eastern palace. Oman, Jossa and Anong packed early the next day and then returned to the land of the Jibay and their home for one last week. Their journey was uneventful and quiet, each of them wrapped up in their private thoughts. Oman was apprehensive about the life changes they would be facing. Jossa was concerned about those changes as well but was also worried about Oman and Anong's happiness. Anong had been in constant communication with Esma, receiving instruction and guidance every evening and growing stronger in her powers. Finally, they reached the small homestead and quickly began their preparations for the next journey.

Anong sat on the front porch the first night after their arrival, tired but content with what the future held for her. She had learned much from Esma and could now easily control her emotions, allowing the magic to flow. In front of her, Anong suddenly saw the ghostly figure of John, the young boy she had befriended years before.

"You came back," John said, sitting beside her. "The green mist that took you pushed us away, and we could not help. I am glad you have returned." He stared at her for a moment and said, "You look different. Your light shines so brightly I can barely see you."

Anong smiled at him. "I have learned much these past weeks. I can take you where you need to go now."

"You mean I don't have to stay here any longer?"

"Yes. There is no need to be afraid. I will be with you, holding your hand until we arrive at the next world."

"I would like that very much," John said, his young face breaking into a wide grin.

Anong sent her spirit out, and, joining hands with the young boy, they flew into the spirit world. Anong knew instinctively where John had to go. They travelled for what seemed like hours and finally arrived in a small village filled with colourful homes, fresh gardens and bright blue skies.

"I know this place!" John exclaimed happily.

"You do. Look, someone is coming to meet us," Anong said quietly.

They watched as a woman in a brightly coloured skirt and blouse approached them with outstretched arms and a smile on her face. "Grandmother!" the boy cried out in astonishment.

"This is your home now," Anong said. "It's time for me to go now. We must say goodbye."

John turned to her and said, "Thank you for showing me the way home. I will never forget."

"I can never forget you, either. We had many adventures together, you and I," Anong replied.

With that, the boy gave a final wave and ran into his grandmother's arms. Anong nodded in satisfaction and returned.

A week later, their belongings were packed, and the household was completely closed. The small family walked around the homestead one last time. "I'm going to miss this place," Jossa observed.

"We all will," replied Oman as he mounted his horse. "But just think of all the new adventures that await."

EPILOGUE

In the following year, Oman settled into his new position as regent. There were adjustments to be made; he had always been a warrior first and a politician second. He could never hold this new position from long-range, as he had done with the Jogahoh. But he was content with that. He had grown older. The king warned him that his subjects would require daily guidance and leadership. Much remained to be done, but most of the kingdom welcomed King Merck's benevolent rule.

......

It did not take long for the Jogahoh to see Salem's true colours and realize that he was not suited to leadership. Bargun regained his memories and produced the preserved cardinal as proof of Salem's deceit. Soon after, Salem was unceremoniously stripped of his position. They had, at first, sent a request for Oman to return, but he refused and recommended that Calam take over. The experienced older man established strong trade agreements between the Jogahoh and the surrounding countries. The barrier that separated the Jogahoh from the outside world was taken down with Anong's assistance.

......

Anong continued her instruction in magic with Esma. Her search for the sorcerer did not take long. She found him, leagues away from the kingdom, existing on bare essentials in a small, worn hovel. He dared not use what little magic he had left, as he feared he would be discovered. Anong, however, did not need the scent of his magic to find him. Finally, when she was ready, she transported herself to the tiny hut. She spotted the silver-haired man immediately, crouched over a fire, his disheveled robes wrapped tightly around him. When she strode up to him from behind, he stiffened but did not turn to her.

"You've finally found me," he said simply.

"I never lost you," she said.

· · · · · ·

Anong and Esma's friendship and bond as teacher/student evolved into a mentorship as Anong's magic grew. She came to visit with Esma one day, and the two sat down for a cup of tea on the front porch.

Anong sipped her tea and then turned to Esma, a worried look on her face. "How will I know if my magic is good or evil?"

Esma thought back to her mother's words years before, when she was questioning her own powers. "Good and evil are in all people. You will never only be one or the other, and the choice will always be yours, Anong. You are the one who decides."

Anong nodded quietly but continued her questioning. "Esma, is it wrong to hate someone who has hurt you?"

"Such strange questions this morning," Esma observed hesitantly as she felt Anong blocking her. "Not necessarily, I suppose." Esma tried once more to see what Anong's purpose was when asking the question. But again, she was rebuffed, and a twinge of alarm ran through her as she caught sight of Anong's birthmark, the five-sided star, pulsating with a red glow.

"My thoughts are my own, Esma. Please understand and don't worry," Anong said, knowing that Esma was concerned and *perhaps,* she thought, *frightened.* "Would seeking revenge on someone who has hurt you make you evil?" Anong persisted.

"I have done that in the past," Esma admitted. "But as the years have flown, I realized that revenge is only momentarily exhilarating. It is the ability to forgive that makes you powerful."

Anong was quiet as she pondered Esma's words. Then, after a long silence, she said, "At that moment, however, it may be worthwhile."

Esma shook her head sadly and said, "It's never worthwhile. Going down to their level makes you like them and takes away your soul piece by piece."

She was still worried about Anong's words later that afternoon. Esma knew that Anong harboured resentment toward Zakalis. It occurred to her that she should try to locate him before Anong did. She hurried to the trunk in her bedroom, lifted the lid and pulled out the pouch that held a strand of Zakalis' hair. Opening it carefully, she peered inside. The pouch was empty.

······

Anong rode alone to the small cottage where she had been held captive, reflecting on Esma's words. Although she agreed that forgiveness was all-powerful, she felt that crimes must be punished. Within her, she felt the magic pulsing and building. There were times she could barely control it, and she shook with nervous excitement and anticipation. Anong knew there was more she could do to control her world and the world around her. There was evil there, but to vanquish evil, you needed complete domination. Complete authority over the people. *Perhaps*, she thought, *that was what she needed. Absolute power*. The idea moved dizzily through her mind.

Anong dismounted her horse and entered the cottage through the front door, locking it behind her. She walked over to the fireplace and slid out a single stone from the mantle. Behind the small opening was a tiny figure of a man no more than six inches tall.

"Why did you do this to me?" the sorcerer asked pitifully, the same question he asked every time she came to see him.

She smiled, unfamiliar red swirls of colour spinning in her eyes, and replied, "Because I can!"

Title *The Future The Past*
- Author: Gilbert Parrell
- Publisher: TotalRecall Publications
- Paperback ISBN: 9781648830280
- eBook ISBN: 9781648830297

Steve Johnson, a forty-year-old Special Operations Sergeant Major, is badly wounded while on Operations. He leans back against the stone wall, knowing that this time out will probably be his last. Just as he begins to feel himself slipping away, he is astonished to see a brilliant light opening and hands reaching out, dragging him into the light itself. Only snippets of memory remain, pain, of course, and the sound of people talking. He vaguely hears, "he's going to make it" before he falls into a deep sleep, full of odd learning sessions and confusing dreams. Two years later, Steve is brought out of his sleep, completely healed, and his body regenerated into that of his twenty-year-old self. Most shocking, however, is that he finds himself in an alternate universe, on a planet called Midgard.

Title *The Girl*
- Author: Gilbert Parrell
- Publisher: TotalRecall Publications
- Paperback ISBN: 9781648830648
- eBook ISBN: 9781648830297

This is a tale that tells two stories. It is first a tale about the struggle between two sets of brothers and how their lives intersect. The second is a tale of a girl born with immeasurable magic to fulfill a prophecy that will affect these brothers in a way they never imagined. In a world where magic is real and power absolute, can this young girl make the right choice between evil and good?

www.ingramcontent.com/pod-product-compliance
Lightning Source LLC
Chambersburg PA
CBHW021505110726
47899CB00001BA/299